W9-BLU-978

J AMBAU
Ambau, Getty T.
Desta and the winds of Washaa
Umera

WITHDRAWN

"In Desta's continuing epic adventure, Ambau paints awe-inspiring images of mountain, sky, and the cultural iconography that infuses the Ethiopian way of life. The engaging story is moved along lovingly with the author's painterly writing style. As a reader, I felt a canvas, less so a page, was set before me."
      –Merrill Gallispie, writer

 "The second novel in the Desta series expands the young man's search for himself and his understanding of the world around him. Desta is filled with wonder and curiosity, a brave soul who seems much older than his years, envisioning dream images and spiritual entities that challenge and encourage him as life unfolds. This is a real coming of age story of a distant land and its fascinating people."
      –Phil Howe, Author of *The Rune Master* Trilogy

"Excellent read! Live Desta's fantastic adventure, dream his dreams, listen to his wise ancestor The Cloud Man, or his ethereal guardian, Eleni, for they will guide you through his world, his adventure to find the second Coin of Magic and Fortune."
      –Ron Repp, Author of *Wooden Warriors*

"Oh my goodness, this book is so amazing. I wish I could put it in words how much I loved it! It was one of the best books I have ever read and I would recommend it to anyone. . . ."
      –Matty W., student

"Desta has won my heart and soul. I've read it slowly cherishing every word and thought in the book. I didn't want to miss a thing. I'm wondering about Desta 3 already." –Julie Koogler, reader

Desta

and the Winds of
Washaa Umera

Desta flying in his self-built aircraft

Getty Ambau

Book two of the epic adventure series of an Ethiopian Shepherd boy in
search of his ancestral family's twin sister Coin of Magic and Fortune

Copyright © 2013 by Getty Ambau

All rights reserved. This book, or parts thereof, may not be reproduced in any form without permission. The scanning, uploading, and distribution of this book via the Internet or via any other means without the permission of the publisher is illegal, and punishable by law. Please purchase only authorized electronic editions, and do not participate in or encourage electronic piracy of copyrighted materials.
Your support of this author's rights is appreciated.

Published by Falcon Press International
P. O. Box 8671
San Jose, CA 95155

Cover Art and design by Philip Howe of Philip Howe Studios
Cover arrangement by Getty Ambau
Flying Craft illustration by Baron Engel
Flying craft design by Getty Ambau
Coin Illustration by Jin Chenault
Coin Design by Getty Ambau

Library of Congress Cat. No. 2010927259

Desta & The Winds of Washaa Umea: a novel/Getty Ambau—1st ed.
Volume 2
p. cm.

ISBN: 978-884459-03-0

1. The settings – actual 2. School scenes – actual. 3. Desta and Abraham's trip to Kuakura and events that happen at the Batha Mariam church – fiction. 4. Abraham and Desta's trip to the old homestead – fiction 5. The scenes at the missionary clinic and the yellow hair woman story – fiction. 6. A lot of the events that happen in Dangila – fiction. 7. Desta's trips to Bahir Dar, Burie and Finote Selam – fiction. 8. The expedition to Mount Adama and events that take place there – fiction. 10. The flight craft building, the Peace Corps teacher, the President Kennedy story – fiction

This is a work of fiction. Names, characters, places and incidents are either the products of the author's imagination or used fictitiously. The author's use of the names of actual persons, places and characters are incidental to the plot and are not intended to change the entire fictional nature of the work.

The cover illustration is solely a product of the artist's imagination. The reader may have a completely different perception of the boy after reading the story.

Manufactured in the United States of America

Dedicated to:

Rosario

PREFACE

Although this book is a sequel to the first volume, *Desta and King Solomon's Coin of Magic and Fortune*, every effort has been made to make the two volumes independent of each other. Still, to get the most out of the story of Desta and the Ethiopian culture, the first volume should be read ahead of the second.

This ambitious book series is a narrative about Desta, the character, told in the context of his environment and his adventures, but this series is also intended to serve as a document about the Ethiopian people and their culture. The story explores certain traditional details and historical events. Historical descriptions are provided where practical, and translations from the Amharic are given to lend as rich a cultural experience as possible.

Certain ethnic references, which today are perceived as derogatory, have been retained to be true to the time and place. For example, the term Gala is considered offensive, having now been replaced with Oromo. A complete list of characters and cultural terms and their definitions are provided at the end of the book for the reader's convenience. Westerner readers should take particular note of the Ethiopian geography and calendar.

Although Ethiopia is located north of the equator, the seasons are the reverse of the seasons in most Western countries; hence, it is not unusual in Desta's world to find a carpet of wild flowers adorning a mountainside in September and October.

The Ethiopian calendar has twelve months of thirty days each and one mini month of five or six days (depending on whether there's a leap year). The Ethiopian New Year customarily occurs on September 11 and on September 12 during a leap year. The calendar lags behind the Gregorian (Western) calendar by seven years (from September to December) and eight years (from January to August). This difference stems from the perceived date of Jesus's annunciation, about which the Ethiopian Orthodox Church and the Roman Catholic Church cannot agree.

Being near the equator, most of Ethiopia receives nearly equal hours of sunlight and darkness. However, this does not always hold true for the more isolated, mountainous areas, such as where the story of Desta takes place. In such locations, the sun often rises and sets half an hour later or earlier..

Although the story is fiction, the setting, natural features, and events, culture, and customs presented are true to life.

This tale is probably unlike any you have read before. I hope you have a fun ride to Desta's far-off world!   –GTA

"The need to make my world believable to people who have never experienced it is part of why I write fiction."—Dorothy Allison

Maps of Africa and Ethiopia

Getty Ambau

ONE

Sometime between the watershed hour and the first cock's crow Desta woke. His head felt dull and bruised as if someone had poked it inside with a sharp object. His throat was chilled and raw as if he had been feeding on cold air all night long. He listened. Absent were the stomping of hoofs, his father's nasal rattles, and his mother's soft, deep breathing. He opened his eyes and the pitch-black face of the night gazed at him. The boy cringed. Where was he?

Once Desta reclaimed some of his senses, he remembered. He was in the town of Yeedib. He had come the day before to attend modern school and to begin to search for the second Coin of Magic and Fortune, the identical twin to the one his family owned. He was in the home of his uncle, Mekuria, and Mekuria's wife, Tru, who were little more than complete strangers to Desta. The uncle he had met only twice before, the new wife never.

They lived in a circular grass-roof house, much smaller than his parents'. The grounds were covered with tall eucalyptus trees that cut out much of the sunlight, the sky, and the fresh highland air. Bound by a man's height wooden fence, the property was accessed only through a shrouded, tunnel-like path that dead-ended at the half-moon bare earth courtyard in front of the home. Desta had winced when he first saw the ominous-looking walkway.

The house had a large circular living room with a rickety table and two chairs in the middle, a small bedroom on one side of this space, and a larder on the other. There were two built-in high earthen bank seats, one near the door, the second by the bedroom. His hosts had assigned Desta the seat by the bedroom as his sleeping quarters. The fireplace and kitchen were adjacent to the larder's doorway.

Desta turned over and lay on his back. He still stared at the night but he was not seeing it anymore. His mind had gone out of the room, to his mountain-bound country home, to the mysterious chain of events that had brought him to this dark, cold room. Like a pioneer traveling an unchartered course through strange lands, looking back to find his bearings, Desta looked back at the events, circumstances, and fate that brought him here so he would know where he was going.

When he was a toddler, one evening his mother had stood outside, leaning against the fence with him in her arms, watching a gargantuan moon rise over the eastern mountains. Desta wanted to be taken up there so he could touch the silver orb with his hands. As he grew up, this dream had transmuted into touching the sky and clouds.

Then later, while Desta was tending the animals, his grandfather's spirit, the Cloud Man, revealed himself and over the course of their few meetings told him of many incredible things, one of which was the ancient Coin of Magic and Fortune the family owned. It went back to the Bible's King Solomon, nearly 3000 years, and was one of two identical coins the wise ruler of Israel had fashioned for his two daughters, to be passed down through their descendants.

The Cloud Man had further revealed that the famous king had encoded on both sides of the coins important legends in each of the twenty-one visible channels. It had been predicted long ago, the grandfather's spirit explained, that a boy would be born to one of the family lines who was destined to unite the two coins, and for very important reasons. The boy was none other than Desta, his own grandson. The Cloud Man invisibly tattooed the coin image on Desta's chest above his heart, so that its powers would be readily accessible to him.

Then, as if to set the ancient divination in motion, Desta's dream of climbing one of the mountains that circled his valley in the hopes of touching the sky was finally fulfilled with the assistance of his half-sister, Saba. The boy didn't reach the sky but discovered a land so much bigger and more enchanting than his valley. This was followed by a trip to town on market day where Desta saw modern-school students marching through the crowd, one boy displaying a green, yellow, and red cloth at the end of a stick. This sight rekindled Desta's dream of learning how to read and write.

After pleading with his father and recruiting others to do the same on his behalf, here he was, finally, to pursue his modern school education. He got registered the day before and even had a taste of the classroom experience afterward. Desta held his breath for some time, thinking about all that had happened to him on his journey here. He let his breath out slowly with a hiss. Subsequently, he wondered what had caused the soreness in his head. He recalled the mental and emotional upheaval he had undergone at bedtime the night before.

In this cold, dark room, resting on the unpadded skin mat and rutted pillow, under this plaid blanket and wrapped in his small *gabi*—a thick cotton blanket, Desta had examined the life he had lived at home. Many painful memories— the beatings, neglect, mistreatment—had surfaced from deep within, giving rise to tears. To purge these memories Desta had cried and cried until his eyes stung and his brain was raw and dull. The emotional exertion was great. It had provided relief and allowed him to fall deeply asleep.

How Desta wished the night had instead been a celebration of his victory! He had won his father's heart to put him in a modern school and broken free of his isolated mountain home. How he would have loved to go with a big horn to the outskirts of town, stand on the edge of the plateau, and blow that horn three times at the top of his lungs, the way those at home announced a death, and declare to the world that Desta Abraham Beshaw was now a free boy! Free to learn his alphabet without fear or reproach from anyone! And then to come to his new home and celebrate his triumph all night long to his heart's content.

Desta shook his head. What good was celebrating his success alone, without his beloved sister, Hibist; his equally beloved half-sister, Saba; his devoted but now dead dog, Kooli; or the vervets, his monkey friends who had vanished when their trees around Desta's home were cut down? Here he had no one with whom to share his happiness and sorrows. He pressed his lips together and stared blankly, fighting to control the emotions that surged through him anew. He shook his head to chase the feelings away, and let out a long, deep sigh.

There would be a lot of things to get used to in this new place, and one of them was that tunnel-like path and the shrouded compound of his hosts. He would have to learn to live with the hum and noise of the crowd. Step by step, this ten-year-old boy would learn everything he needed to know about this new life.

The first thing Desta felt he must do was to find the strength within to endure, no matter his situation. He must keep firmly in mind his missions of becoming educated and finding the ancient coin. He couldn't afford to be emotional about this place or any of the people who were close to him at home. He couldn't allow himself to collapse under the weight of any hardship or dire circumstance he might face. For his own good and the purpose of his missions, he must sever his emotional ties to his birthplace and to everyone at home—to anyone or anything in his life that could interfere with his efforts.

A rooster's crowing interrupted Desta's thoughts and took him home for a few seconds. The animal sounded just like the one his parents had. He chided himself: he shouldn't be thinking of home at this moment of separation.

He placed his fingers on his forehead and cheek, and directed his thoughts to his present concerns: to adapt to this new world he must study peoples' eyes, faces, and mouths, and relate to them accordingly. Desta realized that these ideas, if put to work properly, could make his life easier. After all, the only people he knew well were his family and the animals he used to tend. He had not had any experience of living with complete strangers, other than his sisters-in-law, who later became like family to him.

The rooster crowed again, and again Desta was pulled away from his thoughts. Strangely, at that moment he felt closer to the rooster than to the people he had come to live with. "Why do all roosters sound alike?" he asked aloud, surprised by this sudden feeling of kinship to an animal he had not even seen. He didn't know the answer.

His thoughts of home suddenly filled him with fear. For the opportunity to read and write, he had sacrificed his career as a shepherd and future farmer. Now he was on an educational journey that none of his relatives or, for that matter, any of the valley folk had made. He had no idea how long this journey would take or what he might find at the end of it. Then there was the gold shekel, the sister coin to the one his family owned, that Desta had been chosen to look for.

He tried to visualize the size of his new world. *How do I possibly go about finding that coin?* As if by a swift gust of wind, Desta was shaken by his fears. His heart raced. His temples throbbed. He gasped for breath as if he were being chased. He wanted to scream but his vocal cords failed him. He listened hard, hoping that what he might hear could save him from collapsing beneath his fears.

All he heard was the wind and his pounding heart.

Desta slipped his arm under the blanket and pressed it to his chest, trying to steady the pounding organ beneath his ribs. Unconsciously, Desta firmly pressed his thumb against the spot where his grandfather's spirit had invisibly tattooed the image of that ancient magical coin. Instantly his heart tamed and his nerves eased. The air now felt warm and soothing.

Whew! He was relieved and surprised. *What was all that about?* The unexpected emotional turbulence and his sudden recovery from it bewildered him.

"This is to remind you that you're not as alone as you think," said a voice from behind.

Desta turned his head to look for the speaker. There was no one.

"That hidden image of the coin you just touched is your protector and companion for life. Trust it!

"What is more," the voice continued, "the Coin of Magic and Fortune was tattooed on your chest to give you access to the vast resources deep within your brain. These resources are unavailable to most humans because ordinarily it takes long and dedicated training, like that undertaken by magicians, to tap into and use them. Common folk are incapable of tapping into the magical powers they have within.

"As you were told before you came to live in this town, the first step to achieving any success is to clear out the clutter of your past. With the assistance of the magical channel of the coin, you will achieve an ordered mind and therefore accomplish deeds that far exceed those of professional magicians. Think of the coin image on your chest as a tool that connects your conscious self to your inner magical powers.

"It will take disciplined concentration and meditation to perfect the connection. Unlike most who try to do so, you will achieve the outcome you seek in a short time. Here is what you do: press on the coin image and concentrate on the result you desire, involving as many of your senses as you can. You will realize the outcome you seek immediately, or within a few days.

"Remember that, in many respects, you're no different from other people; you just have been given an extra privilege for reasons I have mentioned. Be humble. Respect the honor you've been given. Don't let anyone know about the coin or what you're capable of doing. Lastly, be watchful of false friends with wicked motives."

"Pardon?" Desta asked. "False friends?"

"Yes, there are those who roam the earth under the guise of doing good for people, but their intention is anything but good. And there are those who will seek your friendship solely for their own gain."

"How am I to know who is who?"
"Pay attention," said the voice.
"Who are you that gives me all this advice?"
"It matters not who I am. Good luck and good-bye."
Desta heard the voice no more.
Desta kept his hand over his chest and a moment later he fell asleep.

TWO

A razor-sharp sound pierced Desta's consciousness. He awakened and opened his eyes, feeling as if his head were splitting open. He listened, wondering whether the disturbing sound would return, but heard nothing. He pulled the blanket from over his face and looked at his surroundings. All he saw was the shadow of night, enveloping him like a fog.

A cold draft on his bare feet caused Desta to fold his legs and wrap the blanket around his toes. He was heavy-eyed and too confused to think clearly. He covered his face and rolled onto his side.

"I hope the sound of the door didn't wake you, Desta," said a woman's quiet voice, startling the boy.

Desta peeled the blanket from his face again and looked toward the source of the voice.

Tru was a mere silhouette as she sat near the open door, her head bent in prayer. Beyond the doorway, the dark gray morning looked placid.

"Oh, that's what it was," Desta muttered. His assailant had been nothing but the creaking door. He realized that it was one more thing to get used to: the creaking corrugated tin door, which was so flimsy that one could bust a hole through it with a fist. He would have to get used to the fact that hyenas didn't actually come into town at night, or any other nocturnal monsters, to roam the neighborhood, looking for people to eat, as he used to imagine they did when he lived at home. If they did, his hosts would never have fitted their entrance with such a pathetic door.

Tru cleared her throat, again taking Desta away from his thoughts. He raised his head to look at her. She wriggled a foot into one of her green plastic shoes then felt for the other, but the shoe slid away. She bent down to steady the heel with her hand and forced her foot into the shoe. She rose, tugged down the hem of her *netela*—shawl—over her forehead to protect her from the morning chill, and went out without closing the door.

The dark gray light of morning had transmuted into what Desta's mother, Ayénat, often referred to as the belly of the donkey, the light hoary time just before dawn. Desta now could see clearly the leaf-strewn courtyard and the tunnel-like footpath through the eucalyptus grove.

He rose to go to the outskirts of town to meet his morning needs and hopefully see his first real sunrise. He quickly put on his jacket and shorts, wrapped himself in his gabi and dashed out of the house and into the foreboding path. He ran through it and emerged into the open grounds. Wishing not to concern Mekuria and Tru, he wanted to return promptly after he watched the sunrise.

He turned left to find a side street that went to the outer reaches of town. He relieved himself in the trees then continued running. Five minutes later he was standing on rock-strewn ground at the edge of the plateau, behind a stone wall and a row of thorn bushes.

He gazed at the heavy, somber clouds above the eastern mountains and realized it was going to be some time before the clouds lifted and the sun brightened the horizon with light. He perched on the nearest rock he could find, and waited.

In the bushes, birds chattered noisily, anticipating the arrival of dawn. A brisk gust of wind whistled through quivering leaves and branches, and flapped the loose end of the boy's gabi against his back. Desta wrapped himself completely in the gabi, tucking its hem under the pads of his feet, and his hands in its folds, to protect them from the raw wind. His mind and eyes were now cued, anticipating the colors he would see around the rising sun. . . .

Where Desta was born and raised, sunrise consisted of, first, a glow of feeble golden light near the summit above his home. Then there was the birthing of the sun itself, seen indirectly by the activities that took place along the full length of the western mountains. Over the course of the cool morning hours, that dim light up on top came tumbling downhill, chasing the shadows of the eastern peaks, getting brighter and warmer, measuring time and distance. Then the sun finally appeared, like a weary traveler, having climbed high in the sky, above the eastern peaks.

Sunset was the same, only in reverse. The shadows of the western peaks crawled up the flanks of the eastern mountains, trailing the sunlight, which sputtered at the pinnacles, and eventually faded to give way to darkness. Seven months before, after Desta had climbed one of the peaks for the first time, he had observed a setting sun paint the sky with spectacular hues. This scene had moved his spirit and stirred his heart with joy so much that he had wondered since whether the ancient star tinted the edge of heaven with the same brilliant colors when it rose as when it set. He finally would be able to see what the sun did to the sky as it first rose above the distant horizon.

He looked down at the panorama of farmlands, the scattered cluster of villages, and the trio of churches that formed a triangle on the near-flat terrain beyond the foot of the plateau. As his eyes scanned the terrain, Desta considered the prophecy he was destined to fulfill: finding the second Coin of Magic and Fortune. It seemed utterly ridiculous that a boy of his age and size would be chosen for this grand adventure. Where would he start and which way would he go?

His eyes moved eastward, into the distance, to the series of sharp ridges that bound his birth valley, and farther, into the remote charcoal-gray haze. Desta couldn't imagine taking an expedition through a jungle of peaks like that, whose extent he did not know.

He shifted his bearing to the south. Here the land looked more forgiving. The plain below him became a low-lying massif, beyond which spread a broad, shallow valley edged by gently sloping hills. In this direction, too, the boy had no knowledge of how far the land went or where it ended. He sighed.

On the other hand, the terrain to the north was easy to look at, even exciting. Desta thought he would enjoy going in this direction to look for the owner of the coin. A trip that way would also give him an opportunity to see Kuakura, his father's birthplace, and the famed town of Dangila, where the woman with the yellow hair and milk-white skin lived.

Desta remembered what his grandpa's spirit had told him. To look for the person who owned the second coin, he must follow the sun, the Fourth Way. He couldn't see the Fourth Way from where he sat. The stone wall and tall eucalyptus trees blocked his view to the west, but Desta vaguely remembered from the day before what the land was like. It was nearly flat except for a craggy outcropping beyond the Gish Abayi Church. If most of the western lands were like this, Desta thought, he could probably handle a trek in that direction.

Additionally, the Cloud Man had said that the person who possessed the second Coin of Magic and Fortune lived near a large body of water. This further narrowed his search area, but even so, he would probably need a donkey or mule or horse to ride when he got tired of walking.

He had another thought, fleeting and wishful, of outfitting himself with a pair of wings, like the picture of that man he had seen on the wall of his parents' church. *That would be great*, the boy reasoned, *to fly like a bird and let the drift of the wind carry me smoothly and effortlessly, however far I need to go.* In his mind's eye he saw himself airborne, gliding across the blue firmament.

His mind returned to what had brought him to this place. Once again, Desta let his eyes soar east and climb up the inky mountains to settle on the dark clouds above those riotous peaks.

A long, feeble ray of red light pierced through a crack in the somber gray clouds. Desta perceived it as a sister light to the many thousands he used to watch drive the shadows down from the mountaintops behind his home in the morning. It was the red light that came from the sun. Desta nearly jumped with excitement. He was watching his first real daybreak. His open hands covered his mouth, the tips of his fingers pressing his nose. Lost in concentration, he gazed at the red sliver above the distant mountain. He didn't want to miss a moment.

The orb inched above the horizon. The clouds were thickest here, and most of the sun's rays emerged through a thinner layer of gauze farther up. The dark shades gave way to tints of pink and purple as the initial red light intensified. New colors burst forth near the sun: saffron and purple and rose pink. Farther afield, the milieu took on dark-brown shades of earth, rippled with skidding rouges and amethyst and scarlet red.

The sun rose past the heavy lower clouds and peeked through more translucent windows, a conflagration of bright red first, then cadmium orange, and, finally, gold.

Desta's hands fell from his mouth and he slowly breathed. *Wow. This is what I have missed seeing all my life!* His throat prickled with emotion. In his new world he no longer had to be content to watch only crawling shadows of the mountains as the sun rose and set.

The golden orb emerged from the layers of clouds, and many of the colors died off with that upward advance. When it fully appeared, its face looked bathed in a tincture of blood, but quickly the blood faded, leaving a brilliant, shimmering white light.

Unthinking, Desta whispered to the sun, "Welcome to my new world!"

A MAMMOTH GOLD-INLAYED alabaster door slowly opened in the sky. Through the portal emerged a figure that had a vaguely human aspect, shrouded in mist from head to toe. It leaned against a dense cloud and looked down on the ascending sun. The creature then extended a hand as if trying to pluck the sun out of the sky, but quickly snapped it back, as if singed by fire. It stood straight up and turned west to look at Desta. It had deep-set black eyes, each the size of a human skull. The colossal figure dropped into a horizontal position, pushed itself off the cloud ledge, and extended its puffy arms as if they were wings. It flew toward the boy, leaving a trail of white clouds.

Partly scared and partly thrilled, the boy slid down from his perch, all the while keeping an eye on the strange creature and preparing to flee if necessary.

To Desta's amazement, the cloak of cloud around the figure dissipated by degrees and the giant eyes disappeared as it came nearer and nearer. By the time it reached the airspace just above him, the flier had an unequivocally human aspect. It was draped in a long white voluminous garment, the loose fabric streaming all around in the wind.

Desta's mind and body were set to flee. He turned away and tried to walk back home, but his knees buckled. He tried again and again, but now his feet felt glued to the ground and he gave up the effort. He watched nervously as the visitor swiftly but gracefully landed on its feet a few yards away from him.

Arms firmly bracing his chest, Desta surveyed the stranger with a pensive and circumspect gaze. He could now tell it was a woman. Her dainty face was partially veiled, with just the cheeks, nose, and eyes exposed. Slender and delicate forearms extended from the sheer garment.

She cast a soft, pained look at the boy. "Good morning, young man! Welcome to your new world!" She took a few paces toward him. "Did you enjoy those colors of the sun?"

"Who are you?" Desta asked guardedly.

"I am Eleni, originally from the land of Nogero, and a member of the International Order of Zarrhs and Winds. For many, many years, I have been a near-permanent resident of the valley where you were born and raised, but I normally live far from here. . . . Although we have never previously met, I've known about you since before you were born."

Desta winced. "Before I was born?"

"Indeed! I know all about your ancestors, and more. I can share with you all these things, if you accept me as a friend."

Desta, transfixed by the woman's looks and her thin, soft voice, contemplated her words.

"What do you say?" She extended her hand in greeting.

"Nothing," Desta said, uncrossing his arms and crossing them again. "I am sorry, but I don't shake hands with strangers who drop out of the sky."

Eleni smiled, radiant and sweet. "I think you should. And you should be willing to get to know me. I've a lot of information about the second coin, and the person who possesses it. You will find it interesting."

Desta perked up, surprised, but he still didn't feel comfortable enough to engage in conversation.

"All right, then. It is good to have met you in person. I have faith we'll get to know each other and become friends over time. . . . I hope so, anyway," she said, grinning. "Good-bye for now."

She took little hopping steps, extended her draped arms, and became airborne. With her baggy clothes billowing out and the long material from her arms flowing on the air, she soared above the eucalyptus trees and vanished into the western sky.

Desta stared after her for a long time, baffled and afraid.

He heard a voice, thin and reedy, that said,

"The only friend you have is the coin and the invisible image of it that your grandfather's spirit tattooed on your chest. Don't let the aliens trick you. Unfortunately, they are part of your story. Remember to follow the sun. There's a reason you used to lie on your back as a little boy and watch it travel across the sky. It was to acquaint you with the true path of your life. You will ultimately get to where you are destined to go if you keep this advice in mind."

Desta covered his face with his hands, confused and scared by the appearance of Eleni and now by this voice. He took to his feet. When he reached the tunnel-like path to Uncle Mekuria's home, he stopped to catch his breath. Then he briskly walked through it. The courtyard was still shadowed, almost as if the sun had to climb over the trees before it was fully illuminated. Mekuria was still asleep and Tru was not at the house. Desta sighed with relief. To warm himself, he threw the blanket over his shoulders and lay down on his mat. He wondered where Tru had gone.

THREE

Tru returned holding dry eucalyptus twigs with leaves on them. She walked to the open fireplace at the other end of the living room, near the wall. She raked and pushed aside the old ashes with a stick, piling them against the three nearest *gulichas*—cooking stones. She snapped the twigs into pieces and placed them in the cavity she had created. From a pile of firewood nearby, she picked out a few slender sticks, arranged them into a cone shape over the cavity, and stuffed other leaves and twigs through the gaps between the sticks. She lit a match, held it until it fully flamed, and gingerly inserted it into the kindling. The dried leaves caught the golden flame first, followed by the twigs and the sticks. The emitted light obliterated the remains of the night, revealing everything in the room.

Tru's fire grew as she added more sticks, and Desta was about to go warm his feet and hands beside it, but the fire maker stood and came to him.

"Good morning! Did you sleep well?" she asked after noticing the boy was wide awake. "Sorry to have been gone for long. I had to wait for the old man to open his Kiosk so I could buy a box of matches."

"It's fine. . . . Slept very well," Desta said.

"Good. . . . Sleeping in a new bed can be hard sometimes."

"The bedding was very comfortable," Desta said, trying to please his hostess.

"Let me know when you are ready to go out so I can show you the *shint bet*—toilet," Tru said.

Desta was puzzled. *Is there a special place where people in town go to pee?*

He rose from the high earthen seat that was also his bed, and wrapped his gabi around his shoulders. Then simply he sat and waited for Tru, curious to see what the shint bet was like. Although he had already taken care of his morning needs, he moreover felt he could go again.

He watched as she washed a round-bellied, wide-mouthed clay pot and set it aside. Then she fidgeted with the three tapered gulichas in the fire pit, pushing them one way and then the other, until they rested at equal distance, so the clay pot would sit in perfect balance on the stones.

She fed more sticks into the fire between the stones to ensure even heating of the pot when she was ready to add the ingredients for her sauce. She peeled two red onions and placed them on a wooden cutting board, slicing them first into halves and then working them into a fine dice, which, magically, or so it seemed to Desta, formed a pile to rival an anthill. She threw in a spoonful of spiced butter and then collected the minced onions on the flat of her knife and transferred them to the pot. The butter-onion mixture sizzled. With a long wooden spoon she pulled from a nearby clay canister, Tru stirred the pot's contents and continued to swirl her spoon for a long while, as if the aroused blistery hisses gave pleasure to her ears.

Next she scooped out *awazay*—red-pepper paste—adding it to the stewing butter-onion blend, and worked the mixture for a few more minutes. This completed, she covered the pot with its cone-shaped clay lid, and the cooking sauce hummed like a migrating swarm of bees as it simmered.

Tru went to the backroom and returned with four eggs and a platter of *injera*—spongy flat bread. She placed the platter on the floor, squatted on her heels, and busied her hands with the injera, breaking it into crumbs and gathering them into a mound. This done, she removed the lid from the cooking pot and threw in two handfuls of the breadcrumbs. After she cracked and added the eggs, she used the wooden spoon to turn the mixture over and over, until all the contents were uniformly mixed.

She covered the pot once again then rose and walked over to Desta. A dew of perspiration veiled her brow, and her eyes glistened with onion-induced tears.

"Sorry for the delay," she said, wiping her brow with the back of her hand. "Let's go." Desta followed her. Out the door and around the house they went, to a closed room attached to the exterior wall of the home. "Here is the shint bet," Tru said, pushing open the door. "Close it after you're done." She turned to go but lingered when she noticed Desta's grimace.

Desta had realized the source of the penetrating odor that first hit him when they came around the house. He held his breath as he studied the dark enclosure.

In the bare earth was a hole, spanned by two planks of wood to support one's feet. The periphery of the opening was wet; no doubt the result of a series of misfires. Tru pointed to the randomly cut pieces of paper under the weight of a palm-sized stone and told him they were used to clean himself with. These pieces looked like they came from a whole paper that must have once carried stories.

"I know," Tru said with a smile. "You probably are used to doing it in the woods.

Some people in town do that, too, but we do it in this shed. You'll get used to it."

Desta let out the air from his chest, drew in and held a fresh breath, and walked into the odorous room. He tugged the door closed and carefully placed his feet on the planks. He felt like he was about to die of asphyxiation. His body ached for fresh air. He exhaled, relieving his lungs, and took in the smell in exchange. *Yes, I will get used to this, too*, he said. How he would miss the open space and clean fresh air of the country at such moments!

Returning from the shint bet, Desta stopped to study the tunnel-like path through the trees, trying to determine why it looked so foreboding. Finding no answer or reason, he turned to go inside. Tru came to the door with a tin can of warm water in her hand.

"Here wash your hands and face," she said, handing him the can. "You need to be ready to go to school. Sayfu and Fenta, the boys you met at school yesterday, will come for you soon. Sayfu and Fenta are also former shepherd boys who live with our good friends, *Ato*—Mr. Bizuneh and Senayit. Tru studied Desta's face. "Are you missing your family already?" she finally asked.

"No. . . . Why?"

"I see all those tear tracks," she said, running her fingers along his cheeks. "You must have been crying last night."

Embarrassed, Desta rubbed his cheeks. "Oh, I sometimes cry in my dreams when I am happy. That must be why," he said, covering up what had actually happened.

He took the can from Tru and carried it to the side of the house.

"You will get used to living in town," Tru said, as Desta ambled away. "But don't just cry when you feel homesick. Come talk to us."

Desta was thankful for Tru's thoughtfulness.

For breakfast, she gave him a portion of the steaming *firfir*—minced injera, onion, butter, and egg mixture—a dish he never had at home. Uncle Mekuria, who had gone outside while Desta was washing his face, returned and sat on the high earthen seat behind him.

Halfway through breakfast, Tru brought a hot brown liquid in a glass cup. He could not tell whether it was coffee or something else. He noticed at the bottom of the cup what appeared to be three large crystals of salt, like pebbles in a murky river. Knowing his mother always added small fragments of salt to the pot when she made coffee, Desta couldn't imagine drinking the brown liquid with that much salt.

He took the cup and set it down on the table.

A little later Tru returned. "Aren't you going to drink your *shahee*—tea?"
Desta knotted his face and picked up the cup.

"You have never drunk shahee before? Try it," she urged. "Most students drink shahee with their loaf or injera. Let me mix the sugar for you."

Desta watched Tru stir the russet drink with a spoon until the white cubes completely disappeared. Reluctantly, he brought the cup to his lips and drew a tiny sip.

His face relaxed as he smacked his lips, savoring the taste. "It tastes like honey," he said with a grin. He took a more substantial sip.

"It's sugar—sweet like honey." Tru smiled, and Mekuria chuckled under his breath.

Sayfu and Fenta appeared at the open door.

"C'mon in, boys," Mekuria said. "Desta will be ready in a few minutes."

"Thank you," Fenta said quietly. "We must run to school. I heard the bell ring."

Sayfu appeared anxious; his eyes probed Desta.

"Okay, Desta," Mekuria said. "Finish your shahee and go with them."

Desta drank the last drop of his tea, set the cup on the tray, and dashed to his sleeping area. He quickly folded the blanket and placed it on top of the pillow. He fixed to go to the door but lingered to hear Tru whisper to his uncle.

"I don't think he is going to make it till the end of the school year."

"Why do you say that?" Mekuria asked, louder than his wife.

"He looked unhappy this morning, and I think he was crying last night."

Mekuria pressed his lips, crinkled his brow, and glanced at Desta. "That was not the impression I got when we registered him yesterday. Abraham said it was Desta who pushed them to put him through modern school."

"Time will tell."

Desta wished he could tell Tru how happy he was. The warm food, hot tea, and her caring ways had already made him feel welcome and happy in their home.

Desta joined his friends at the door and they walked quietly through the wide tree-shaded path. Dappled with the morning light, the path was not as threatening as Desta had earlier seen it to be.

He glanced back and forth at Sayfu and Fenta, nervously wondering what they were thinking. Sayfu, his long, narrow face to the ground, darting twinkling eyes on the path, lips parted in a smile—he appeared eager to say something. Fenta was the opposite. His lips were clamped and his soft eyes steady;

his face conveyed nothing of what might be on his mind.

After they cleared the trees, Sayfu asked, "How old are you, Desta?"

"A little over ten," Desta replied, remembering what his father had told the registrar.

Sayfu shot a glance at Fenta. Seeing nothing on his cousin's face, he continued. "Fenta and I were wondering how is it possible that you have never seen a sunset," he said, recalling Desta's comments the day before.

Desta was wondering how to answer this blunt question when Fenta said, "What Sayfu means is, did you live in a *washaa*—cave?"

Sayfu apparently believed that Desta must have lived in a washaa if he had never seen a sunset all his life. When the three of them were coming home from school the night before, he had asked to be left behind so he could watch the sunset. Now he decided he would play up his companions' hasty conclusion.

"Actually, worse than a washaa," he said, looking at one boy and then the other. "We lived in a *gedel*—a hole."

"What?!" cried Sayfu.

"You're trying to be funny with us. Tell the truth," Fenta said gently.

"I am saying the truth. That's what people sometimes call the valley we live in," Desta said in a serious tone.

Sayfu's small eyes became mere slits. "Yesterday is the only time you've seen a sunset?"

Sayfu seemed to have forgotten what Desta had told them, that he had seen two sunsets before.

"No, that was the third time. The first was when I went with my sister to the top of the mountain, hoping to touch the sky. The second was when we were returning home from visiting this town on a market day." Desta remembered the sad but thrilling mountaintop experience he shared with Saba. Fenta and Sayfu stared at him in awe. "You climbed a mountain to touch the sky?" Sayfu asked.

"Yes, that was my dream since I was little."

"Who told you you could really touch the sky?" Fenta wondered.

"Nobody. My half-sister Saba thinks there may be a place in the world where a mountain is tall enough that you could stand on it and reach the sky."

"Your sister must not be much older or more intelligent than you for her to think like that," Sayfu sneered.

The boys had gone past the open market plaza on their left and a row of grass-roofed homes and corrugated tin-roofed shops on their right when a man came from a side street and stopped them.

"Good morning, boys!" the man said in a booming voice. "Is your uncle home?"

"Yes," said Fenta and Sayfu in unison.

"I have some court matters to discuss with him. I need to catch him before he leaves for the office." The man hurried past.

The man's mention of court matters reminded Desta of his father's trips to the *firdbet*—courthouse—with the papers he gathered from the straw box so that someone outside the courthouse would read or transcribe them for him. For a moment Desta was lost with these thoughts, dreaming about doing those same tasks for his father after he learned to read and write well enough.

Sayfu cleared his throat as if he was about to ask something, bringing Desta back to the present. To head off another barrage of questions, Desta asked, "What is it you have in your hand?"

"My *debters*—notebooks. You've probably never seen one," mocked Sayfu.

Fenta said, "They're specially bound papers we write in for our lessons the teachers give us. I'll show you one of mine."

The boy unlocked his pouch's three horn buttons, took out a notebook, and gave it to Desta to inspect.

Printed on the light blue cover were four postage stamp–sized photos, three men and a woman. They looked straight at Desta except for one, an older mustachioed man whose face was turned to the right and gazing into space. From the front of this man's neatly pressed jacket dangled four small, round gold objects, and a woven chord of the same color looped across his chest. With his clean fair skin, sharp pointing nose, and halo of groomed black hair, the man looked like he had nothing to do but take care of himself all day.

The woman had silky hair. It was wrapped above her head and secured with a glittering half-moon crown. She had dreamy eyes, as if she had just awakened from a long sleep. She had pendant earrings and a large silver cross on her plump chest. She also looked unlike any woman Desta had ever seen. He stared at her, wondering whether she would open her eyes wider and look deeply into his. When she didn't, he shifted his eyes to the cover's other figures. The two young men had chubby cheeks and big brilliant eyes. They, too, wore neatly pressed jackets with looping chords and small, round gold pieces.

Desta was curious about who these people were, but he was more anxious to see what was inside the notebook, which consisted of several folded sheets held together in the center by a pair of wire staples.

The first three or four pages contained text written mostly in pencil. Desta skipped these pages and went to those with no writing. He studied the lines printed on the pages. . . . They were narrower than those on the pages in his father's court papers. He ran his fingers over the paper in slow circular motions. It felt smoother and glossier than his father's.

The pages smelled different, too. His father's were musty, while these sheets had an unfamiliar but pleasant scent. Desta brought the open notebook to his nose, closed his eyes, and took three quick sniffs. He exhaled and lowered his nose to the page again to draw in the exotic odor until his lungs ran out of space. He held his breath for as long as he could and then slowly let it out. He raised his head to find Fenta and Sayfu gazing at him, seemingly amazed by his actions.

"Is what I just did strange?" he asked.

"Never seen anyone who likes to smell plain paper," Fenta replied. "Now we have no doubt about your past."

"Where do you get these notebooks?"

"Your teacher will give you one, once you can recite the alphabet without making a single mistake," Fenta said.

Desta could hardly wait till he relearned all his letters and got a notebook he could feel and touch and write in every day.

A bell rang in the school building. "That is the last bell," Sayfu said. "Let's go."

"If you want to see my notebooks after school or on a weekend," Fenta said, "I'll loan them to you. We need to run now. If we don't get there by nine o'clock, one of the teachers will beat our hands with a *masmeria*—ruler, or whip our legs with a *changer*—stripped twig."

They scampered to the school and arrived to find most of the students congregated outside. Students who had just arrived ran inside with their writing things, put them at their respective benches, and came back out.

Fenta told Desta, "Once all the students arrive, we'll line up by our class before that flagpole, say the Lord's Prayer, and sing the national anthem while the *bandira*—flag—is hoisted." Observing Desta's puzzled look, Fenta looked around and then pointed. "That boy is holding the folded flag. He will unfold it and attach it to the chord on the flagpole and wait until we take our positions in front of it."

The cloth with green, yellow, and red stripes had captivated Desta since the first time he saw it at the market with Saba. It was one of the things that had brought him to the school. How much he had yearned to touch it then; how much he had wanted to inspect the image of the cat at the center, holding a pole between its legs, with the flag flying at the pole's tip. That he might one day see it up close and touch it excited him. He was envious of the boy who cradled the flag in his arms like something precious that might break. Desta watched with unwavering eyes as the boy tied the flag to the long chord that looped down from the top of the pole.

Fenta tapped him on the shoulder. "I am going to line up with the third graders. You go do the same with the beginners. Come, I will show you who they are."

They walked to the first row. "Stand here until the prayers are said, the anthem is sung, and the flag is raised to the top." Desta stood last in line with his arms crossed, embracing his chest. A large boy from one of the upper classes stepped out and walked across to stand in front of the assembled students, waving a whip before him.

He turned his head one way then the other as he checked to see whether the students were standing in a straight line. "Quiet!" he commanded. When he noticed one of the rows was crooked, he ordered "You all get in line." Hushed, the offending pupils promptly aligned themselves. The school's only two teachers watched nearby, whips in their hands.

The flag-raising ceremony opened with a prayer, the students reciting in unison, *"Abatachin hoy besmay yemitnor. . . ."* Desta was mystified. *Who is the man in heaven that is a father to all these students?* He looked around. Some had their heads bowed down. Others looked up to the sky. Others still looked straight at the flagpole or at the backs of the students in front of them. Desta just listened and observed.

The flag bearer stood erect, eyes on the colored cloth, waiting for his cue. The student with the whip raised his hand and counted to three. All at once the assembly began to sing, *"Ethiopia hoy. . . "* The commanding boy turned to the flag, stood up straight, and harmonized with the rest. The flag bearer's hands sprang into action. Slowly, in time with the cadence of the singers, he pulled hand over hand on the cord. *How marvelous!* Desta thought.

The ceremonies ended. The students dispersed and headed into the building. Desta stood for a bit, thinking about what he had observed: the crowd and the noise, the orderly assembly, the praying, the singing, and the flag raising. These were the things he must do every day before his lessons, just as, at home, he had to release the animals from their pens and help milk the cows before driving them all to the fields and looking after them all day. *More things I have to get used to.*

Fenta tapped Desta on his shoulder, startling him. "You need to follow your classmates and go sit at a bench."

Desta walked tentatively toward the door, face down and mind chaotic. He wished he could have walked with Fenta away from the crowd instead. Many questions swirled in his head.

Indoors, Desta walked to the same rickety bench in the back of his classroom where he had sat the day before. Finding it occupied by three other students, he looked around for another place to sit.

"Desta," said Brook, the teacher, "would you like to come and sit in the front where there is more room?"

Desta hesitated. He didn't feel safe or comfortable with other students sitting behind him. One of the kids from the back bench noticed Desta's reluctance to sit in front and said, "I'll go."

Desta took the boy's seat in back and scanned the room, counting the students in his class. There were thirteen others. Upon the bamboo partition in front of the class hung a cream-colored, dusty cloth upon which was written the Amharic alphabet and numbers, accompanied by their English equivalents. On the left, near the doorway to the adjoining room, was Brook's chair. Between the studs in the bamboo partition, Desta could see the feet of students in the next room.

Brook picked up a slender reed pointer and indicated the alphabet. "Here," he said, handing the pointer to the first student in the first row, "get up and lead the recital."

The boy rose, took the reed from Brook's hand, and began pointing and calling out the letters on the hanging cloth:

ሀ ሁ ሂ ሃ ሄ ህ ሆ

("Hä…Hoo…Hē…Hä…Hã…Hĭ…Hō.")

The class repeated the sounds in loud, mechanical voices. Some of the students watched the letters as they recited. Others looked elsewhere as they repeated after the boy, looking restless and bored by the redundancy and familiarity of the lesson.

The boy finished the Amharic alphabet and numbers and then began the English: "A . . . B . . . C . . . D . . ." Once he was done he handed the stick to the next boy in his row and sat down. This student rose and took the class through the same exercise.

These activities went on till the ten-thirty break, which was announced by the ringing of a bell. The students spilled out of the room and ran to the field in front of the building.

The day was warm, but there was a brisk breeze unlike any Desta had felt before. He stood with his back against the school wall and watched all around. Some of the students gathered to talk in clusters of four or five. Others ran in the field, kicking a cloth ball. The wind seemed determined not to be left out of the game; from somewhere at the side of the building came a ball of dried grass, driven by the invisible "feet" of the air. Nobody kicked back this ball, however, and it rolled down the hill to smack against a barrier of thorn shrubs that bordered the field.

Desta was happy to be left alone so that he could watch undistracted. These people were still foreign to him, and so was the land. His eyes floated past the playground to the rolling terrain and hazy horizon beyond. He wished he had wings so he could fly like a bird, as far and wide as he could. This new world had whetted his appetite for travel and adventure. His dream was suddenly interrupted by the bell, which reminded the students the break was over.

Once the students again sat on their benches, Brook said, "All those who have notebooks, copy the letters from the alphabet cloth and then bring them to me. The rest of you, follow the lead boy as he recites the alphabet."

Half a dozen students placed notebooks on their folded knees and began to copy the letters. The newer students continued with their alphabet recitals. Occasionally, Desta looked at the writing students, their heads bent over busy hands at work in their blue notebooks. Desta wished he, too, were practicing writing in one of those books. But the recitals continued, and he committed to memory all the letters he had once learned on his own and then forgotten until now.

The bell rang. "Stop for now, children. It's lunch time," Brook said, rising from his chair. In all the rooms feet shuffled and mouths erupted with excited chatter. Smiling and orderly, all the students headed to the front door.

When Desta looked down outside, he saw the wobbly circle of his shadow beneath his feet, indicating it was noon. He was pleased not only by another break but by the idea that he could go home for lunch, a rare event when he was tending the animals at home.

When he arrived at his uncle's home, Tru greeted him with a smile. She had a freshly baked injera with warm *shiro wat*—pea sauce—and a glass of water waiting for him. He washed his hands outside and sat down to eat his lunch. As he ate, Tru came and sat next to him. "How do you like school on your second day?" she asked guardedly.

"I like it," Desta chirped excitedly.

Tru's voice took a happier tone. "That's good to hear. Mekuria and I want you to know we are happy you have come to live with us."

"Thank you. I'm happy, too."

"Just remember, if anything bothers you at school or here with us, tell us."

Desta was thrilled. His long-held dream of learning to read and write was coming true, and he had found caring and supportive people to live with. He stepped outside with a pitcher of water and returned after washing his hands.

The school bell rang. Desta dashed across the threshold and flew along the tree-lined path.

His afternoon lessons ran from two o'clock to five o'clock, with a fifteen-minute break at three thirty. The lessons, like those in the morning, involved reciting the Amharic and English alphabets and numbers for the new students and writing exercises for those that already knew their letters.

"When do you get a notebook to write in?" he whispered to the boy next to him, who was copying letters from the cloth.

"When you can recite the letters before the class while the teacher is watching," the boy replied.

"When can I do that?"

"You have to study the alphabet for a week or two. Get your father to buy you a *fidel*—a booklet or a parchment containing the Amharic and the English alphabets, numbers and some biblical verses—so that you can memorize at home. Then you ask the teacher to lead a recital," the boy advised without looking up.

"Do I have to wait that long?" Desta whispered back.

"Yes, it takes at least that long to learn and memorize the alphabet. You just started. . . . That is how I did it."

Desta looked at the boy's writing. Chaotic, squiggly letters marched in skewed formation, reminding Desta of his own letters when he used to copy them from his cousin Awoke's fidel—first on his bare thigh with a straw and then with a pencil on his father's papers. Suddenly, he was blanketed with mixed emotions from the past. He was once beaten by his brother for practicing his writing skills instead of watching the animals he was tending. He remembered his excitement whenever he wrote the letters correctly and cleanly. Strangely, he feared someone would whip him again for practicing to read and write. He shook his head, trying to chase away the irrational, intrusive thoughts.

When he came to his senses, he tried to visualize what he could do with sixteen pristine white pages. He could fill them with everything he could write and draw.

The bell rang once more. "Time to go home!" said the boy next to him as he quickly folded his notebook. There ensued a commotion as the students filed out of the building. Thoughtful after the day's events, Desta trailed out of the building following his classmates and headed home.

As he walked he realized that he had completed his first full day of an academic journey whose destination was as dark to him as the tunnel-like footpath through his uncle's eucalyptus grove. No matter where his journey led, he must not forget two things: as soon as he could, he must learn to read and write, and he must begin to look for the person who holds the second Coin of Magic and Fortune.

FOUR

When he finally fell asleep that night, Desta was thinking about the blue notebook he had dreamed of receiving. When he woke the next day, the image of the book was still in his head. As he walked to school, he thought about raising his hand to ask Brook, his teacher, to lead the class through the alphabet recitals so he could receive his blue notebook. During the session, he thought about lifting his hand each time Brook asked which student would like to come up next to lead the class. Each time he decided against it, afraid that the other students might laugh and ridicule him if he made a mistake.

Although he knew his Amharic alphabet and could recite it with his eyes closed, he was not entirely sure he could do the same in English. He remembered seeing those strange letters at the bottom of Awoke's fidel. But Awoke didn't know them and couldn't teach him. Desta finally decided it was better if he got up when he was completely confident that he could recite them well. He didn't want to delay getting a blue notebook by making a mistake.

He should study the letters at home on the weekend. Like the boy who sat next to him had said, he needed a fidel of his own to practice with. But where could he find one? He didn't want to ask Uncle Mekuria or Tru to buy one for him. He didn't want to bother them with his needs so soon—he had barely started living with them. He thought about asking Fenta to loan him his old one, but he didn't see him after school and didn't know where he lived.

THIS WAS SATURDAY, Desta's fourth day since arriving in town. It was a market day, and he hoped he would see some of his family so he could ask one of them to buy the fifty-cent fidel for him. If others didn't come, his brother, Teferra, the tailor, surely would. Teferra made clothes he sold at the market.

It was a warm brilliant morning and there was a palpable excitement in the outdoor air. The same energy seemed to have come indoors, too. Tru had risen early, swept the living room, and put away everything that had no purpose out in the open. She had made a fire and baked injera and cooked shiro wat for breakfast later in the morning. She had washed the small white coffee cups, the *gibena*—clay kettle—and the *genda*—the wooden serving tray—and placed them on the corner table to drip-dry.

Next, Tru spread three animal skins atop the high bank seats that spanned part of the living room wall. "We have neighbors coming for coffee," she said when she noticed Desta eyeing her curiously.

"Here!" she said, handing him a stick with a bundle of straws fitted to one end. "Sweep the leaves from the courtyard."

When Desta returned after fulfilling her request, he found Tru washing coffee beans in a wrought iron pan. She scooped the beans out of the water with both hands and kneaded them between her palms with a gyrating, opposing motion. The beans' dry filmy skin sloughed off and settled in the water. She threw away the murky liquid and rinsed the beans with clean water. After draining the rinse water, she placed the pan with the beans on the grill over glowing charcoal. The beans sizzled, popped, and crackled, emitting white tendrils of smoke and an exhilarating aroma.

Completing her preparations, Tru placed a few handfuls of a roasted mixture of chickpeas and wheat berries in a straw basket.

Mekuria washed his hands and face outside then came inside to sit on the high earthen bench.

A woman arrived at the door, her head partially veiled by her netela. She pulled her covering back and away from her head and entered, saying "Good morning" with a bow. Her voice sounded familiar to Desta.

She turned to Tru and said, "Is this the boy you told me about?" Tru was pounding the roasted coffee with a wooden mortar and pestle while the kettle with the coffee water heated on the charcoal fire.

"Yes, that's Desta, Mekuria's nephew," Tru replied, looking up.

"*Selam*—Hello, Desta!" the visitor said.

"Selam," Desta whispered, lowering his head briefly.

Desta scratched his head, trying to remember where he had seen the woman but couldn't place her. Then came an older couple and a single woman. The last to arrive was a man in a green woolen uniform. He looked familiar, too, but Desta was still left scratching his head. The man said something to Mekuria.

That rough, guttural voice—how could he have forgotten? He was the policeman who had short-changed his sister Saba by two silver dollars, when she and Desta brought her sack of *teff*—a fine brown or white grain—to the market several months before. Desta turned and looked at the first woman . . . of course that was the policeman's wife. Desta and Saba had gone with the wife to their home to deliver their teff purchase.

Tru passed around the basket of chickpeas and wheat berries, and everyone took a handful. She then brought the genda, laden with eight small coffee cups teeming with *abol*—first brewing of the coffee—and held it before each guest. "Thank you," each said, picking up a cup. The vertical blue, red, and green stripes on the surface of each cup seemed to float on the air like leaves of grass.

The policeman left right after the first serving of coffee. The other guests stayed for the *bereka*—residue from each of the previous two brews diluted with water. Each serving of the coffee was weaker than the last, but the added sugar or salt made up for the thinner flavor. No matter, the three-part ritual of coffee making was never compromised.

Shortly after the bereka was served, the guests left. The remaining members of the household ate their breakfast and Mekuria left for the police station, where he worked as a clerk. Tru got busy with her domestic chores and Desta decided to go to the market, hoping to find a relative who would buy him a fidel.

It was nearly ten o'clock when Desta set out for the market. Out in the open, the day was in full swing. People bustled in and out of the homes and shops along the way to the market. The air was thick with noise and it seemed to the boy that the fragrance of roasting coffee beans came from just about every other house that lined the market grounds.

Desta walked past a row of quiet homes and the fenced warehouse. At the gate of this enclosure, a man in a greased coat and long trousers stood as if he were waiting for someone. This was the same fellow who had bought his father's sacks of honey and cotton when Desta first came to town, for the purpose of registering at the school. Desta passed the man and arrived at the northern edge of the market grounds when a light turned on in his head—something he had wondered about the town of Yeedib was now clear.

The town looked like a balding man's head. Perched atop a curving plateau, a copse of dense trees hugged it all around like a shock of hair. A series of trails fed the spacious bare summit like tendrils from a long mane—the wide caravan road to the south striking the face and chin. Taken together, the scene resembled, uncannily, the pate of a balding man. Desta smiled at the thought.

Before him, women sat on stones, on folded skins or clothes, or directly on the bare ground. Each displayed her few bottles of *areqey*—home-distilled whiskey. These were mostly farmer women, dressed in voluminous gowns secured at the waist with several turns of a multicolored girdle. Occasionally, with hopeful faces, they squinted at the sun, an important but not always cooperative business partner.

On Desta's left, near the fence, sheep and goat breeders had tied their animals to the fence posts and rails. Easter was only a week away and these animals, particularly the lambs, were desired sacrifices for the holiday. There were a lot of them that morning. The sellers were mostly men, dressed in jacket and shorts, their shoulders draped with gabis.

Straight ahead, at various locations, people had begun to array their merchandise upon cloths or skin mats. Everywhere legs scurried, hands swung, and mouths chattered. While the fevered activities were engaging enough, the evolving milieu was far more interesting to the boy. But like the distant mountains, farms, and villages Desta used to stare at and study when he lived in the country, this scene, too, needed the leverage of space for him to observe and study what was developing before his eyes.

He retreated to the fence and stood leaning against a post. For a boy who grew up beholding tints of blue, red, yellow, green, brown, and gold in one or another of the seasons, this nearly white tableau, and its variances of cream, saffron, and gray, was as interesting to him as to someone looking at the moon for the first time. The lack of definite variations in color, however, caused him to lose interest very quickly. Desta's eye was drawn to the few bright hues of blue, green, and red the town's women wore, but they were mere specks of paint on an artist's palette. He shifted his attention from the colors to the people and their activities.

Out of nowhere appeared a woman who looked as if her nose had been hacked off by a butcher's knife. Her pastel-colored dress swooshed and twirled around her as she walked. She had draped her shoulders with a skimpy white netela with large purple borders, and her head with a bright red scarf. She strode on long legs around the areqey sellers with an attitude and disposition Desta had never before seen a woman display.

Each gesture, attempt at eye contact, or nod of greeting the woman offered the whiskey sellers said, "I know you have a better nose, bigger eyes, and softer hair than I do, but look what I got on you: pristine clothes, a pair of plastic shoes, a neat head covering, and my face is washed and oiled with a special cream, not the butter or cooking oil you dab yourself with."

There was a farmer woman, her soiled gown frayed at the hem. Her shoulders were draped with a netela that had not seen soap and water for many months. Her dusty bare feet were tucked under the ample dress. Rivulets of sweat glistened on her temples. She had just arrived after a long trek up the steep mountain with her four bottles of whiskey, which she carried in a leather sack on her back. Desta thought that for all that the farmer woman was, the snooty town woman appeared justified in her superiority.

The town woman crouched before an areqey seller. She picked up one of the bottles and raised it high in the sunlight. She briefly studied the alcohol's clarity then put the bottle down. "*Sint new?*—how much?" she asked in an indifferent tone.

The seller replied, "Six *birr*—the Ethiopian currency." The town woman countered, "How about four?" She explained her reasoning, citing imagined and real flaws in the beverage. She picked up the bottle and again raised it against the sun. She shook her head, put down the bottle, and walked off. The seller pursed her lips, picked up the bottle, and viewed it against the bright light. She had already done this several times, after first filling the bottle the day she distilled its contents and again that morning before coming to the market. She was proud of her work and happy with the purity. She didn't see anything wrong with it. Now—though mystified—she, too, shook her head as she placed the bottle back on the mat.

As Desta watched the town women haggle over the price of the areqey, he wondered whether they had any idea how tedious and complicated it was to make the powerful drink. He remembered the many days and steps in the process, not to mention the sweat and tears, it had taken his mother, Ayénat, to make the three twenty-four-ounce bottles for his siblings' weddings.

First, she fermented for three days a few handfuls of pulverized hops with three gallons of water in a six-gallon jar. Then she added chunks of barley bread and several scoops of pounded *bikil*—germinated and dried barley. She sealed the jar and let it ferment for three more days, and then she added several handfuls of roasted barley and a gallon of water. The resulting mixture was left to ferment for another three days. She mixed in four more handfuls of roasted barley and similar amounts of bikil and hops. After another two or three days, the mixture was ready for distillation.

Distilling the areqey was equally involved but more interesting to watch than the previous steps. First, the paraphernalia. From the *guada*—larder—Ayénat brought out a round-bellied, long-necked five-gallon clay pot called *gembo*—specially made for distilling areqey or as a vessel for holding *tella*—homemade beer—a pint-sized jar with a hole in its side the circumference of a silver dollar. She also brought out a three-foot-long bamboo pipe with a hole near one end; a slender reed the length of a woman's open hand; an aluminum flask; and a deep, circular wooden vat.

Then, the setup. Early in the morning she kneaded a mixture of earth, water, and fine straw, setting that aside. Next, on three fireplace stones, she balanced the jug with its neck tipped down at an angle slightly greater than a bow. She transferred about two gallons of the concentered *difdif*—the fermented mixture—to the gembo to distill it with a gallon of water. She topped the jug's opening with the little jar, its neck inserted into the gembo. She introduced one end of the bamboo tube into the hole in the side of the jar and into the bored opening in the other end she fitted the reed.

His mother placed the aluminum flask in the middle of the vat and secured it in place with granite slabs. She moved the vat under the end of the bamboo pipe and jiggled it until the attached reed lined up and dropped into the mouth of the flask. She sealed all the jug-jar and bamboo-reed-flask joints with the plaster of earth and straw mixture, smoothing it with her wet hands and turning the jug-jar fixture on top so as to resemble a freshly shaved woman's head. She then filled the vat with cold water.

Finally, she stoked the hearth under the jug by placing twigs and sticks through the gaps in the stones, and lit the fire with a torch from the kitchen fireplace. The areqey took all day to distill, and it was Desta's job to keep the fire going under the jug.

Desta happily obliged. He was as fascinated by the setup as by the miraculous production of the areqey, which percolated down the bamboo pipe and collected in the aluminum flask.

About an hour after distillation began, Ayénat brought out a bowl of water and some rags. She dipped the rags in the water and wrapped the bamboo with them to keep it cool. And that is what Desta had to do, too, all day long, as soon as he noticed the rags were getting hot. He couldn't see what was happening inside the bamboo and his mother's explanation was truncated and vague, but he didn't want to ask questions. By the time Desta began to help her make areqey, he was mature enough not to bother adults with his questions anymore.

So all day long Desta tended the fire and wetted the rags. Once in a while Ayénat came and patched any fissures in the mud covering, sometimes burning her fingers and causing her eyes to tear from the escaped steam. She changed the water in the vat whenever it got warm. After all this work, Ayénat produced three bottles of the powerful clear liquor.

All that effort, and the town woman had bargained to pay two dollars less than what seemed already a hugely discounted price. Desta shook his head in dismay.

MORE TOWN WOMEN CAME, some accompanied by their *ashekers*—houseboys—or *bet serategna*—women servants. Some dressed in their *harr*—silk dresses, others in traditional, casual white skirts with netelas thrown around their shoulders.

They buzzed from one whiskey seller to the other, like bees hunting for nectar in a flower garden. They buzzed back to the last and again to the first, checking and rechecking the clarity of the alcohol and the competitiveness of the prices. In the end the selling women yielded and sold their bottles of whiskey for one or two birr less than they had asked at the beginning.

Those who came to the market with their bet serategnas or ashekers handed them the bottles they had purchased to carry in their bags. The women who came alone tucked their bottles under an arm and walked off.

Desta woke from his daydream: he saw before him the amazing behavior of the town folk, the strange ways people buy and sell things. He navigated through the crowd and the din, people pouring from all directions, carrying things in their hands—on their backs, shoulders, and heads: sacks of grain, rolled raw hides, chickens hanging upside down from sticks, their feet fettered.

Desta kept looking down at his shadow to see if it had pooled into a circle beneath him, indicating noon. That was about the time his family would arrive. He saw only a slanted silhouette of himself. He walked some more, until, finally, his shadow had shrunk into a puddle beneath his feet. He didn't know for sure which of his relatives would come, except for tailor brother Teferra. He always brought the clothes he made to sell in the market. Desta wished Saba would also come.

Desta arrived at the tailor's row and found his brother at his stand surrounded by farmers who were keenly examining the clothing. Desta's eyes met Teferra's but the man was too preoccupied to fully acknowledge his presence.

The brother's coat pocket was bulging with coins and birr, money from the sale of his clothes. Desta eyed it hopefully and enviously. Two men bought a trouser and jacket set and left. The others passed on without buying.

During this intervening moment, Desta asked Teferra for one *shilling*—a half birr—so he could buy his own fidel.

"I made you shorts and a jacket, now you came to ask for money!?" barked his brother. "Doesn't the school provide that? You pestered and bugged us so you could come here, now we have to pay for you to be here, too?" He gazed at Desta, waiting for an answer.

Desta was not prepared for this. He said nothing, surprised by his brother's harsh response.

"For your information," Teferra said, his face severe, "mother is still reeling from your decision to come here, abandoning her and father and your responsibility as keeper of the animals. The best way for you is to return home, to realize that living in town and going to school here is not for a farm boy like you." He stared at Desta, waiting again for a reply that did not come. "You better make up your mind to come home. Now is better than later."

A couple approached the stand, and the husband bent over to pick up a green jacket.

Dazed, Desta walked off. For a long time it seemed to him he didn't hear the noise of the market or see the crowd around him. He blundered along, not knowing where he was going.

He had cleared the market and was standing outside when he finally became aware of his whereabouts. *If mother is holding a grudge,* he thought, *that means I can't go home.* His mother never forgot things like that, and she probably would never forgive him for coming to town to go to school. He was struck by a sudden sense of loss. He felt completely alone.

No matter, I am not going to give up my dream of learning to read and write. At that moment, the little fidel he wanted to purchase seemed as far away as the sky he dreamed of touching but couldn't. This meant his hope of receiving a blue notebook once he could recite the whole alphabet would have to be put on hold indefinitely.

Then he remembered his father—who had given in to the pressure that Teferra's wife and Saba had put him under and decided to bring him to school. If he had come to court today and if Desta could find him, perhaps he could get the fifty cents he needed. Knowing how stingy his father was, however, Desta couldn't count on it. Then he thought of his half-sister. Had Saba come to the market to sell something?

Tentatively, thoughtfully, Desta waded through the crowd. He passed the rows of spices and peas, finally arriving at the grain. Nervously, he stumbled and bumped around the buyers who were bending, standing, and squatting on the ground, talking and haggling with the sellers.

He looked as far as he could through the crowd but didn't see Saba. Desta's hope of finding her had faded by the time he was halfway down the aisle. But just a few feet from the end of the lane he found her, head covered with her nete-la, looking tired and talking with a woman who had just bought some of her teff.

"Desta!" she shouted, smiling broadly. "Excuse me, that's my little brother. He started modern school a few days ago and I had hoped to see him before I went home," she said to the woman. A pair of deep-set eyes in a weathered face glanced at Desta. The face turned down. "I need to go myself," the woman said. "I hope to see you again. I like the quality of your teff."

"Come sit. I don't know where Mekuria and his wife live, so I was going to finish here and then go see Teferra to tell me how to locate the house. I wanted to see how you like your school and living in town. . . . How did you know I was coming?"

Desta winced at the mention of Teferra. The hurt was still fresh in his mind. "I just guessed and hoped."

"Is everything okay? Are you not happy here?" Saba asked, seeing his disconsolate look.

"No, no, I am. I was just worried I might not see you. Do I still look it?" Desta threw a half smile at his sister.

"I do hope you're okay. We worked so hard to convince Baba to help you fulfill your dreams. You can't disappoint him, like the others did," Saba said gravely.

The severity of Saba's voice reminded Desta of the responsibility he was shouldering, *to not disappoint his father like the other children had.*

"You didn't sell the whole sack of teff?" he asked, trying to change the subject.

Saba smiled. "I was trying to be smart this time. I decided to retail it, selling it by the basket. It's more money for me. I'll never let these townspeople cheat me again."

Desta thought of telling her that the policeman and his wife had come for coffee that morning, but not wishing to upset her again, he nipped that thought.

A young woman with a cloth sack stopped to ask Saba her price for a basket-ful of teff. "Three shillings."

"Do you have enough for two baskets?"

"I think so," Saba said, pressing on the remaining teff in her leather sack. She lifted and transferred the brown grain into her measuring basket until it overflowed. The woman held her sack open and Saba poured the teff into it. She measured another and transferred that, too.

Noticing almost all of it was gone, the woman asked, "Can you sell me the rest for a shilling?"

Saba measured the remaining teff; the basket was three-quarters full. "How about two shillings?"

"A shilling!"

"Okay, give me the money."

The woman counted seven shillings and handed the coins to Saba.

Saba turned to Desta. "Your lucky number."

Desta grinned from ear to ear. "It might indeed be! I believe that seventh shilling is meant for me."

"Do you need money?"

"I don't need money, except to purchase a fidel. It costs one shilling."

"Oh. Here, take it."

"Are you sure?"

"Of course! For you, this is nothing."

"Thank you. . . . How is Destaye?"

"He is already over a year now. Did you know that?"

"Yihoon and I have not stopped thanking you."

"Don't thank me. Thank grandpa."

"You were the chosen person."

Saba always had a way of making Desta feel good about himself. "Are you going home now?" he asked. He got up, happy and eager to go purchase his fidel.

"Yes, I am. I need to give you something before I leave, though."

Desta looked at Saba with curiosity.

"And by the way, thank you for saving me from having to beg Teferra to show me where your uncle and his wife live." Saba handed him a puffy round thing wrapped in a cloth. "I made this *dabo*—loaf—for you, fearing that you might be going hungry. Teferra keeps telling us how food is scarce in town and that you might soon come home after the hunger became unbearable."

"He seems to agree with mother that I don't belong in school, but about this dabo, Saba . . ."

"It's not much, but hide it some place and have it as a snack whenever you feel really, really hungry."

Desta's eyes brimmed. "Saba, I've been eating three meals a day, to my heart's content. Don't worry about me. But thank you for your kind and sweet thoughts."

"Glad to hear it. You go now. Buy your fidel. Hide the bread under your gabi when you take it inside the house, and keep it in a safe place." Saba kissed and hugged him and then they parted.

Desta skipped and snaked through the crowd, thrilled by the prospect of having his own fidel, finally. He purchased the book and went straight home. He handed the cloth-wrapped dabo to Tru and told her who had given it to him.

"Does she think we might be starving you here?" Tru asked as she unwrapped it. "It's a beautiful rye bread. The spicing smells wonderful, too." She broke off two nice chunks, giving one to Desta and keeping the other for herself.

"Wonderful, authentic country bread," Tru said, as she munched.

"Saba always bakes great bread," Desta said, puffing with pride for his sister.

He finished his bread and went outside with his fidel. He sat on a stump in the eucalyptus grove and recited the Amharic alphabet and numbers and all the English letters and numbers a dozen times.

Half an hour later, Tru showed up with a folded cloth under her arm. "Desta, I want to give you a bath," she said, interrupting his studies. "Your hair is dusty, your skin is dry and ashen, and your feet are not clean."

Desta folded his fidel and looked down at his feet. Embarrassed, he drew his feet underneath him, covering them with the hem of his gabi.

Tru pulled the folded netela from under her arm, holding it out in front of her. "Get up," she ordered gently. "Go inside the house, remove your clothes and wrap yourself with this netela, then come back out."

Desta rose reluctantly. He put his fidel in his jacket pocket, taking the folded fabric from Tru. "I'll wait for you in the back of the house," she said.

Desta draped himself with the netela and walked around the house to find Tru standing near the entrance of the small room that protruded from the exterior wall.

"Go in there," she said, pointing to the door. Desta saw a large aluminum vat filled with steamy warm water. A tin can floated in it. In the corner was a bench with a towel and white fragrant bar of soap. A round stool was the room's only other furnishing.

"Take off the netela and sit down on the bench," Tru said.

Desta's feet were suddenly immobile, his mind engulfed with a memory of the horrid water treatment his mother and the head priest from his parents' church had subjected him to, trying to exorcise a *Saytan*—Satan—they thought had possessed him.

"What's wrong? The water is not cold."

"It's not that." Desta shook his head as if waking from a dream.

Realizing that what had happened to him was long ago and there was no obvious threat, he stepped inside. He pushed the towel aside, peeled the netela up from his torso, and sat on the bench on his bare bottom. The bench felt cold and rough but Desta didn't mind.

Tru helped him remove the rest of the netela and tossed it onto a log near the entrance of the room. She scooped water into the tin can—after telling Desta to close his eyes—and poured it over his head; the water cascaded down, spilling over his chest, shoulders, back and legs. She applied the soap and lathered him nearly all over and began scrubbing him with her free hand.

"When was the last time you took a bath?" Tru asked, surprised by the dark brown bubbles in the lathered soap on his head.

"Nearly three years ago."

"How many?" Tru couldn't believe her ears.

"After my sister, Hibist, got married, nobody gave me a bath or told me I should."

Tru shook her head. "What about your mother?"

"She was always too busy."

"Your father?"

"He was always gone and never cared for me."

Shocked, surprised, and thoughtful, Tru didn't know what to say for a few minutes. She kept lathering the boy's head, torso, and legs, staring at the brown soap bubbles as if her conversation was with them.

The warm liquid, and Tru's gentle hands and voice, were to Desta like rainfall upon dry, parched earth. He felt a sensation he had not had for a long time.

She rinsed him with more cans full of the warm water.

After she wiped the last drops of water from his body, Desta wrapped himself in the towel.

Tru pulled the round stool from the corner and sat on it. She grasped Desta's ankle. "Lift your foot."

Reluctantly, Desta let Tru have his foot. The cracked and disfigured nails were bad enough, especially after having seen all the students at school who had nice feet and toenails. He had been ashamed of his own every time a schoolmate looked down at them. Somehow he felt it was his fault that his nails were disfigured and his heels dry and cracked, as if it were his fault he had a mother who didn't want him, a father who never cared for him, and brothers who hated his guts.

A wave of emotion surged through him—to have discovered a complete stranger who seemed to love him so much. *Why didn't I have Tru for a mother?*

He watched as she turned his foot one way and the other, studying the sole and the sides. "What are all these wood splinters doing in here?"

"Those are bits of thorns that pierced my feet when I walked in the field to look after the animals. I never took them out because the only safety pin I had I gave to my father to give as a gift to grandpa when father was preparing to go look for him."

"And these?" asked Tru, pointing to the horrific-looking nails.

"Some of them were damaged by chiggers, others by rocks."

Tru shook her head, saddened by what she was hearing and seeing. "We need to take these thorns out." She removed from the shoulder of her dress a safety pin, which she used to fasten her sleeve to the neck of her dress to avoid getting it wet.

Tru pierced the skin around the splinters and pried them out one after another. Some were deeply embedded and hard to get to, while others, having decayed, crumbled away with a mere wriggling of the pin. A few splinters required cutting deeply into the skin, causing blood to ooze and Desta to flinch and grit his teeth from the pain. In the end Tru removed fourteen thorn tips from both feet, and still there were quite a few left.

"At least you don't have to worry about walking on thorn-infested grounds here in town," she said, putting Desta's foot down. "I'm sorry your family hasn't taken care of you better, a handsome boy like you."

Desta did not know what "taken care of you better" meant. The only life he knew was how he was brought up. That afternoon, Tru's compassion made him realize what he had missed when he lived at home.

Tru got up. "I need to go inside to prepare dinner before your uncle Mekuria comes home."

DESTA WENT TO BED THAT NIGHT still feeling wonderfully clean and happy. He had found someone in this strange new world who genuinely loved and cared for him. Once again, though, his thoughts settled on the blue notebook he hoped to receive from the teacher on Monday. That blue notebook reminded him of the blue sky he had attempted to reach but couldn't. But this blue object was achievable; everything was within his reach.

Twice he recited the Amharic and English alphabets and numbers. Then he covered his face and went to sleep.

FIVE

Desta studied his alphabets some more on Sunday. When he woke on Monday morning all he could think of was the blue notebook he hoped to receive from the teacher. He took his little fidel and sat on the stump in the eucalyptus grove to quietly recite the English letters three times. The Amharic alphabet he now knew by heart.

He ate his breakfast and left for school, focused and determined to do well in his recital and receive his blue notebook. After the flag ceremony, he filed behind his classmates and went to sit on his bench in the back. All the boys who had blue notebooks placed them on their folded knees, pencils in hand, and waited for instructions. There was a long wait, giving the students an excuse to whisper to one another. When the teacher finally emerged through the door, the class stood. "Sit down, class," he said, patting the air down with his hand. He had three crisp new blue notebooks in hand, which drew Desta's eyes like a bee to nectar.

"I have three exercise books left to give out today to those students who recite both the Amharic and English letters and numbers without a *single* mistake. We ran out of pencils, so those who receive these notebooks will have to buy their own pencils. I know we have at least six new students who have been reciting the alphabets for two weeks, and I hope that there are at least three of you who can recite for me today. Do you understand?" He scanned the room from one side to the other.

The students nodded.

"Okay, who wants to go first?" Seven students, including Desta, raised their hands.

The boy to Desta's left pulled on his sleeve. "No, not you! Didn't you hear him? He is calling for all those who have been here for two weeks. You have not even been here a full week."

"I know," Desta said, jerking his arm free.

"That means you should have memorized all two-hundred fifty-six letters of the Amharic alphabet and twenty-six of the English along with the numbers," whispered the boy to the right. "Don't make a fool of yourself."

Desta ignored him.

The teacher called on a boy in the front row. The numbers were easy for him. He then recited the Amharic letters without an error but skipped *m* from the English letters.

The second student got all of them right. The third mispronounced two of the Amharic letters and one of the English. The fourth changed his mind about getting up. The fifth got all of them correct. The sixth recited half of the Amharic alphabet then got nervous and sat down.

The boy on Desta's left leaned over and whispered, "See? It's not easy. All those students have been reciting the letters for a long time."

Now Desta was having second thoughts about getting up. The teacher looked at Desta and asked, "Anybody else?" Desta's hand sprang up again, almost mechanically. He imagined himself holding that beautiful blue notebook. He couldn't let this chance slip away.

He rose and strode to the front. He picked up the stick and began to recite the letters. The room was so hushed that he had to turn around twice to see whether his classmates were paying attention. He finished all his letters and numbers flawlessly.

"Bravo!" the teacher said as he handed him his notebook.

Desta held the spotless blue notebook to his chest with both hands, as if afraid he might lose it or someone might steal it from him. He went back to his seat.

The boy on his left stared sheepishly. "Did you study at church school before you came here?"

"No," Desta said, still holding his notebook to his chest.

"But the church schools don't teach the English letters," the boy on Desta's right said, with a glance at the other boy.

"Quiet, children," Brook said. "Now all of you who have notebooks and pencils, copy the letters and bring them to me when you are done. Those who don't have pencils, bring them whenever you're able to copy the letters."

At the morning break, Desta took his notebook outside and was leafing through it when three of his classmates approached.

"Did you study at church school before you came here?" one of the boys asked.

"No," Desta said, almost in a whisper. He closed his notebook and braced it to his chest.

"Did you live in a hole or a cave before you came here?" another said.

Desta pursed his lips in disbelief and looked away.

"Obviously," the third boy said, glancing at the first, "he wouldn't have lived in either of those places if you think he went to church school."

The bell rang and Desta returned to the classroom without saying anything.

As he was walking home during the lunch break, Fenta trotted up and said, "I heard you got your first blue notebook. Did you know your letters before you came here?"

"Not really. I had studied them on my own two years ago, but then I forgot them. Over the weekend I recited and studied on my own, and that helped me remember. Do you know where I can get a pencil?"

"Why? The teacher didn't give you one?"

"He said they are out of pencils."

"I'll see what I can do. Talk to me after class this evening," Fenta said, as he turned onto the path to his home. Desta was glad Sayfu was not with them. He suspected it was he who had given the boys the ridiculous idea that Desta had lived underground.

After class that day, Fenta gave him what looked like a chopped pencil. "I thought I had extra but I couldn't find any, so I broke the one I have into two. You can have the half with the eraser."

Desta tapped the soft ruddy material. "You call this end 'eraser'? What is that for?"

"To erase your mistakes."

"Is that what it's for? My cousin Awoke and I thought it was for decoration, especially with the brass ring around it."

Fenta smiled. "No, it's to remove the writing when you make a mistake."

IN THE ENSUING DAYS AND WEEKS, Desta accurately copied the simple words and sentences that Brook wrote on the blackboard. He also started teaching basic addition and subtraction, and Desta did well with these number exercises, too.

At home in the evenings, Desta perched on the tree stump with his notebook and practiced his writing and addition and subtraction. A favorite exercise was to take a string of numbers, like 1949—his birth year—and add the digits together. He learned to do this from his grandfather's spirit, which had shown him how the different combinations of the coin box measurements corresponded to the day and year of his birth and his ranking in the family constellation. That a big number like 1,949, when combined this way, could shrink to twenty-three and finally to just five, fascinated the boy.

Desta would arise before dawn and watch Tru as she prayed with her face in her hands, seated on the high earthen bench by the open front door. After she went out, clearing his view, Desta would gaze along the dark, tunnel-like path.

The passage's mysterious and foreboding quality had become a metaphor for his future, as were the mountain he had climbed before he could discover his new world and the sun that went home after splashing the sky with red, purple, orange, and gold. Desta shuddered. What will become of me? How will I ever find the owner of the second coin?

SIX

It was Sunday. Tru and Mekuria had risen early and gone to church. Desta too was up early and now was sitting at the small dining table in the middle of the living room, thinking about the things he and Fenta had discussed the day before. Since he had come to town, the purpose of his modern education and the places where he would look for the person with the other magical coin, had been mysterious.

In an attempt to solve the mysteries, the boys had gone and sat behind the old Italian fortress, on the north side of town, to discuss the different levels of education Desta could achieve, assuming he got past the fourth grade, the highest level of learning offered in their town. And they talked about what he could potentially become after he finished.

To get a job that would pay a substantial *demoz*—salary—first he must finish fourth grade, then go to Finote Selam or Burie to complete grades five through eight; after which, he would go to Debre Marcos, the provincial capital, for grades nine through twelve.

Desta had learned that unlike boys who studied at the church schools, where the main goal was to become a priest, those who studied in modern schools were presented with nearly unlimited possibilities. And what was equally important, when those boys became adults and decided to marry, they didn't have to worry about wives who refused to take the communion ruin their careers, as had happened to his older brother, Tamirat. Tamirat gave up his priesthood because his wife declined to take the flesh and blood of Christ with him, and he in turn refused to remain celibate afterward, which their orthodox church required of priests who divorced and wished to remain in the profession.

But Desta didn't like any of the careers Fenta had proposed: teacher, judge, policeman, court clerk, or governor. The teaching work he dismissed, saying that he didn't want to whip students when they come late to school. Judges took bribes and made decisions in favor of the people who gave them money and valuables;

he didn't want work that would tempt him to do the same. He didn't want to be a policeman because they jailed people and cheated farmer women like Saba. He didn't know much about the other two options but in the end decided he could make up his mind later.

Then there was the matter of the coin he must search for. His grandfather's spirit had indicated that the owner of the ancient relic lived in an area with a lot of water. Desta had no idea what that really meant and discussed this with Fenta during their meeting.

To his surprise, he learned that there indeed existed such water. It was called a *bahar*—lake—and there was one not far from their town. This was incredible to a boy who grew up believing that all water sank into the earth after rain fell or got carried away by creeks and rivers. Water sitting on the ground like rocks or houses was quite inconceivable.

Desta was now just as anxious and excited to see this water as to search for the person who held the Coin of Magic and Fortune.

What Fenta didn't say and Desta forgot to ask was how students who had no family to support them could continue their education. Desta had no kinfolk in either of the school towns Fenta mentioned.

Abraham, Desta's father, was considered one of the richest men in the valley, not only because of his large land holdings but also because of the great number of cattle he owned and the several jars of Maria Theresa silver thaler he supposedly had hoarded over the years. Thaler, although no longer in circulation, was still a highly prized underground currency among country people. One silver thaler could garner as much as three or four paper birr.

Yet Desta knew his father would never part with his money or an animal to pay for his son's education, when he would rather Desta forsake his schooling and return home. Abraham's sense of woe over Tamirat's abandonment of the priesthood after twelve years of training was still heavy in his heart. There were several reasons for his unwillingness to pay for Desta's schooling besides plain tightfistedness. He had once told Desta that, as the purity of gold is tested with fire, the strength and character of a boy was measured by the hardships he endured.

"Look at all those who study at church schools. They fend for themselves. They get their daily rations by going around the neighborhood before sunset and asking people to give them food. They cloak themselves with pieced sheepskin, which lasts them for many years. And they live in one-room huts near their *mergetas'*—teacher's residences."

From such accounts Desta had realized that he couldn't depend on his father for support while he pursued his education and traveled far distances to look for the owner of the coin. Even if someone put a gun to his father's head and made him sell a heifer or one of his mookit goats or change a dozen of his silver thaler to the legal currency, which might pay for one or two semesters of Desta's living expenses but not for the full twenty-four semesters through grade twelve. And Desta's mother and brothers didn't care how he ended up. They wouldn't chip in to help. He would have to figure out a solution on his own.

He felt confident that Mekuria and Tru would support him through fourth grade. It was the lack of relatives in the other school towns that worried him. Everything past the fourth grade was dark. At that point his education and his search for the coin, if he couldn't find it nearby around the bahar, could come to an end. These possibilities frightened him, like the shadowed pathway from Tru and Mekuria's home.

Looking out the door at the tunneled path, Desta became aware of the physical manifestations of his emotional exertions: the tenseness in his nerves, the sweating of his palms, his fevered brow, and the knot in his stomach. He chewed on the interior of his lower lip as he thought about this—the palpable reality of his fears.

Granted, Mekuria and Tru's home was shrouded by the tall eucalyptus trees, and for a boy who grew up gazing at the sky and distant mountains, this was bound to create a sense of isolation and confinement. The only open space he could see from the threshold was the twenty-five-foot radius of the half-moon courtyard. There was nothing else around the house that inspired fear like that tunnel of a pathway. Was there anything in it that could objectively be the cause of his fears?

Desta rose and strode to the door. He crossed the threshold and looked around. The morning sunlight had penetrated through much of the eastern grove where the trees were sparse, making everything around the house bright and the air warm and pleasant. The long passageway was still shadowed but visible enough that he could see things inside.

His head bent down with his thoughts. Desta took measured, meditative steps toward the opening of the path and stopped. He gazed at the cool, eclipsed walkway, studying the tangled branches that grew from each side of the path, creating the effect of an arched roof. Unlike elsewhere in the compound, the trees here were so closely grown that that their bows and branches intertwined, their luxuriant leaves filling the spaces, keeping out sunlight and giving the path its dark, somber appearance.

Yet nothing he saw was personally meaningful. He dropped his gaze to the lane, seeing as if for the first time the thick layers of dry, decaying, and packed leaves where Tru and Uncle Mekuria had stepped when they went to church. Desta found no clues to his fear here, either.

Disappointed and disillusioned, Desta was about to go back inside the house when he lifted his face and noticed something surprising: the path looked much longer than he remembered, and it was not exactly straight but curved to the left farther along.

Curious now, he decided to find out exactly how long it was. He used his strides to measure the path the same way his father took the dimensions of a plot of land. Beginning from the shadowed line of the path's entrance, he strode in an even gait, counting his steps. By the time he reached the other end, he had logged 147 steps. To make sure he had counted correctly, he counted again going back and tallied exactly the same number. He paced the width of the path: four steps. Neither number seemed significant. They were neither seven nor twelve, the two important numbers connected to the coin and to him.

Thinking further about the number 147, Desta realized that it was, indeed, meaningful. It contained the magical number seven and its multiple, fourteen. To fully interpret these numbers, Desta needed to work them out on paper. He dashed to the house and returned with his notebook and pencil. He sat on his stump in the grove and wrote down the individual digits: 1, 4, and 7. He added these together and smiled at the result. Twelve: the cycle in a year, round as the coin and the sun . . . the symbol of wholeness. Desta was excited. Were there any sevens in the total figure? He quickly saw that 10 sevens were seventy, and twice that amount plus seven equaled 147. Looking at it differently, the length of the path could also be represented by 21 sevens.

This discovery thrilled the boy. Twenty-one was another important number in his life. There were twenty-one legends encoded in the coin. His grandfather's spirit had told him about the cup-shaped pass in one of the mountains that circled his home, represented by *Ha*, the first letter of the Amharic alphabet, or *U*, the twenty-first letter of the English alphabet. Both of these were connected to Desta. Doubling twenty-one yielded forty-two, his birth year in his native calendar. And seven added to forty-two was forty-nine, his foreign calendar birth year. Desta rested his elbow on his knee and his chin in his hand and gazed down at the strewn leaves for a long time.

He shook his head and then returned to his notebook, looking at the original numbers again: how was the width of four related to the length? He multiplied the length by the width, as Tadeg, Mekuria's contractor friend, had done with the dimensions of a plot of land he planned to build on. The resulting total of 588 didn't seem significant at first, but when Desta added the individual digits again, the result was twenty-one. Astounding!

The hair on the back of his neck bristled. This can't be mere coincidence. The path that he had come to dislike so much contained all this information about him, just like the coin and the coin box and the cup-shaped mountain pass back home did. Desta stared at all the numbers again, thrilled.

Another question crept into his head. Were there any sevens in 588? He was still raking his head with his fingers and playing with different combinations of seven and other numbers when Fenta showed up.

"Good morning," he said. "What are you doing?"

"Good morning," Desta replied. "Come, come. I need your help."

Fenta handed him a folded paper. "Here is a map I drew for you to get to the lake."

"I'm not going to go today as I had hoped. But thank you." Desta inserted the paper in the back pages of his notebook.

Fenta gazed down at the notebook. "What do you need help with?"

"Look here," Desta said, pointing to the five and the 2 eights. "Do you know whether there are any sevens in this number?"

"What do you mean?"

"What number when multiplied by seven gives 588?"

"All you need to do is divide 588 by seven."

"We haven't learned how to do that yet. Here, show me how." Desta rose to his feet and handed the notebook and pencil to his friend.

Fenta sat on the stump and went to work. He swiftly drew two perpendicular crossing lines. He wrote 588 on the left side of the vertical line and tucked the number seven on the right side. He looked up at his friend and said, "This is how you set up your divisions." He carefully went through each step and concluded, "There are 84 sevens."

Desta quickly added the four and eight together in his head. "The cycle in a year, round as the coin and the sun!" he shouted in excitement.

Fenta looked up quizzically then studied his numbers again, wondering if he had made a mistake.

"And there are 12 sevens in eighty-four," cried Desta in a ringing voice, after quickly churning the numbers in his head. He jumped to his feet. "My beautiful number seven, the symbol of perfection, light, and music, and so many other things, joins with the equally beautiful number twelve, the representative of the sun, my family's ancient treasure, and my life . . . to describe the dark mysterious path . . . the interpreter of my future!"

Fenta wondered if Desta had been possessed by spirits. "What's all this about? Are you all right?"

"I'm . . . I'm . . . I'm . . ." Desta restrained himself. "I'm just happy with those numbers because they have a personal meaning."

"I am glad to see you this happy." Fenta got up and handed back the notebook and pencil. "I have things to do and need to go now. Good luck with your trip to the lake."

Desta felt like a big cloud had lifted. He walked to the courtyard and stared into the tunnel. He wasn't afraid of it anymore. He also felt confident about his future, that he would find the coin and that things somehow would work out for him. But now doubts crept into his head. How could he be that confident? Were these numbers really his oracles or mere coincidences? How else could he explain the identical mental and bodily reactions when he thought of his future as when he stared at the deep, dark footway?

What had his father once said about coincidences? "Predetermined events are what people call coincidences when they happen." Desta thought that he shouldn't doubt his fortune–tellers: seven and twelve, and their derivatives. Desta jumped to his feet again. He was giddy with enthusiasm. He felt as if he was levitating. When he realized his feet were still on the ground, he sighed, long and slow, feeling each molecule of air exit his nostrils. He kept saying, "This is incredible, incredible . . ."

SEVEN

That evening, Desta decided he would go to Lake Gudera to look for the bearer of the second coin. He had only two weekends left until the end of June, when school closed and his family expected him to help out on the farm during the two-and-a-half-months break. The lucky numbers he and Fenta had unraveled earlier in the day were somehow associated with his future, both his educational goals and the search for the coin; his spirit was emboldened and his heart filled with courage. He was anxious to go.

Desta was no longer worried about the lack of support from his family, or the absence of relatives in the towns where he could receive advanced schooling. He now felt that his educational future was bright and assured. *I have the blessings of the numbers seven and twelve, and everything will work out to my advantage.*

"What are you so excited about?" Tru asked when she saw Desta in the court-yard, twirling a twig in his hand, his face beaming.

"Fenta told me all the things I have to do for my schooling and about the Lake Gudera that I want to go see."

"I'm glad you're excited about your education, but what's so thrilling about the bahir?"

"I never thought so much water could sit on land. I want to see that for myself. And there's a relative I want to meet who is supposed to live near there."

"Oh, I can take you there if you're really interested, but I don't know when."

"I was planning to go next Sunday."

"By yourself?"

"Yes. Fenta said it's not far and it's easy to get to."

"I know, but don't you want company? You may run into kids who would harass you."

"I have no fear of them. I have protection."

Tru tugged at her chin in surprise. "Do you have an amulet?"

"Something like that."

"We'll talk about this next weekend," Tru said.

Desta was relieved he hadn't had to explain too much. This was a personal matter. *The less others know about my trip, the better.*

EIGHT

The night before his trip to Lake Gudera, Desta tossed and turned. He was excited, anxious, and apprehensive all at the same time. This was going to be his first journey out to a strange land trying to locate the person who owned the other Coin of Magic and Fortune. And he had no idea what or whom he would meet on his way. Realizing he would be soliciting information from many people who might know this individual, he wanted to have a clear idea of what he would say to them.

About the person's identity, should he say it's a man or a woman? His grandfather's spirit had referred to "sweet and sour" as the meaning of the moniker given the coin bearer. From this, Desta thought the person was probably a woman. About his relationship to the woman, should he just say that she was his cousin and not say anything about the coin? If the generations of people in her family line were like Desta's, they probably had tried to keep everything about the ancient treasure secret. And what kinds of things should he bring with him? A notebook and a pencil to record what he observed, a loaf of bread for a snack when he got hungry, and, merely as backup, a big stick to protect himself from dogs; the tattooed image on his chest was his primary defense against any threat.

With these plans in order, Desta laid on his back and stared at the enveloping darkness, trying to see in his mind's eye the bahir and the various places Fenta had described: the green, nearly flat land that extended from the outskirts of town to the edge of the plateau, below which was a valley containing a large amount of water surrounded by villages, farms, and cattle fields. This geographical detail seemed to describe the same area his grandfather's spirit had recounted; the area where the owner of the coin lived. He closed his eyes and hoped that sleep would come soon to take him quickly across the night into tomorrow.

When he woke, Tru and Mekuria had already risen, washed their faces, and dressed to go to church. "This is Sunday! You can sleep in as long as you want,

Desta," Tru said after seeing the boy stretch his arms and rub his eyes. "I have prepared shahee and left you injera and dabo on the table. You can have that with the leftover dinner sauce when you get up," she added, as she and Mekuria headed to the door.

Desta had a long day ahead of him. He put on his jacket and shorts, wrapped himself with his gabi, and spilled onto the floor. He attended to his personal morning needs at the shint bet and then sat at the small table to eat the injera with the previous night's sauce. The dabo he saved for his trip. After eating, he remained seated, thinking about his journey. *What name means 'sweet and sour'?*

His grandfather's spirit had given him many other hints, but this one stuck in his brain more than the others. *And why this name, which gives rise to such a variety of meanings?* He sighed and absentmindedly caressed the rough tabletop as he contemplated his impending journey to the valley with the lake.

Having brought his thoughts to completion, he rose, put away the food tray, and dashed to his bedding area. He emptied his *bursa*—bag except for his pencil and the notebook with Fenta's map, and he then returned to the table with the bag. He wrapped the dabo in a cloth and placed it inside the bursa, slipped the hanger up his arm and over his shoulder, and headed to the door.

The ground outside was damp under his soles from the rain that fell overnight. He scampered into the trees and returned with a straight, sturdy walking stick. Nervous and anxious, he walked the precious path through the grove and out to the open corridor. Passing by the closed warehouse compound on his left and the row of tree-lined homes across the big open space on his right, he pressed forth to the now-empty and desolate market grounds. The strip of shops and tea and tella houses that bustled with activity on market days was that morning shut and lifeless.

After traversing the full length of the market, he reached the southern end of the town and the beginning of the caravan road Fenta had told him about. Thoughtful and meditative, he walked this road a couple of hundred yards to its intersection with another caravan route. Here he stopped and took the map from his bursa. A right-pointing arrow showed that he must turn west. The new path was rain-washed and pitted, making his walk down to a sleepy creek uneasy. Past the stream the land leveled into a sweeping green field, extending several miles away to the famed Gish Abayi Church on the right. Cattle, sheep, and horses grazed leisurely, but Desta didn't see any herder boys.

After traveling for half an hour, he saw ahead the top of a spreading *warka*—wild fig tree—near the edge of the plateau and a glimpse of a pale, glass-smooth surface farther away. Desta wondered if this might be the bahir. He quickened his pace, looking up occasionally to the unfolding scenery ahead.

He marveled at the genius that made it possible for that much water to sit above ground without seeping through. And where did it come from?

He slowed his stride as he neared the fringe of the plateau, his eyes fixed on the placid, metallic-looking water down in the valley. When he could see a bigger section of it, he stopped to gaze, shaking his head at the thought of all the marvelous new things his world was presenting to him.

He continued walking. The road passed under the warka tree and Desta was pleased when he finally reached it. It was under a similar tree where he first met his grandfather's spirit, which led to the solving of Saba's problem with her miscarriages and the discovery of his grandpa's remains, along with the family's ancient coin.

Flat-topped stone seats dotted the ground beneath the tree—indicating a popular resting spot for travelers. A few feet away, a narrow, less traveled trail crossed the main road, coursing through the shadow of the giant tree and curving along the periphery of the plateau. He looked to his left and then to his right to see whether there was anyone traveling that scant path, or whether he might notice people in the villages or farms served by it. There were none. Even on the main thoroughfare, he seemed to be the only journeyer. He didn't see anyone coming up the hill in front of him or following behind him.

This was Sunday, though, so roads big and small were more likely to be free of travelers. Most people were probably at church or at home in observance of the day. Much of nature appeared to be doing the same. No birds rustled or tweeted in the tree branches above him. No bees or flies buzzed in the air or insects chirped in the grass or the bushes below. The sun couldn't have been any gentler nor the air calmer.

Desta's eyes descended once again to the expanse of water, to the clustered villages around it and among the foothills, and to the green cattle fields and brown, freshly tilled farms in between. He sat on one of the rock seats near where the two roads intersected. He wanted to study the tableau a little more from this vantage point and record in his notebook what he was seeing before he walked down to it. He propped open his notebook on his knee and quickly sketched the lake, the villages, and the conspicuous things around them. His head bobbed up and down as he captured the images with his eyes then recorded them on the pages.

He finished drawing and returned his notebook and pencil to his bursa. Again he gazed dreamily at the panorama, wondering what impermeable material kept all that water from percolating underground. Where had the water come from and how long had it been sitting there? Was this the only lake in the whole world? He had forgotten to ask Fenta about this. Now with no one to give him answers, he turned his mind to the main purpose of his journey.

On which side of the lake should he start looking for his cousin? The Cloud Man had said that the coin bearer lived on the east side of the water. So Desta would go left once he got to the bottom of the hill. He had already figured out what to ask people he met about the mysterious individual but realized his limitations: "sweet and sour" were the only direct references he had as to the identity of the coin bearer. How can he possibly find this person with such meager reference at hand?

No matter, he needed to go. He was just about to rise and walk down the hill when out of the corner of his eye he saw what appeared to be a bird touching down. He turned to look. It was not a bird but a human-like figure. Maybe it hadn't descended from the sky, the boy considered; it might have simply walked into his field of vision. He stared at it. The figure had the gait and physical appearance of a woman, and it was covered head to toe in a loose, lustrous fabric. "She" walked toward him along the narrow, intersecting path. Slightly alarmed he tilted his head one way and then the other to get a better look at the stranger through all the flowing fabric but without success. He bit his nails and watched intently as she neared.

"Good morning, young man!" the woman said in a detached but lilting voice.

Desta tipped his head down in greeting. Much of her face was veiled. Just her nose, eyes, and a part of her cheeks and chin were visible. She held on to the hem of her garment. Her winter–gray eyes looked sad and pained. Her narrow straight nose rose out of pasty, light brown skin. She looked as if she had not slept all night or eaten a meal for days.

"I am glad I found you here before you left," the stranger said.

Desta flinched. "Who are you?"

"My name is Eleni. You probably don't remember. We met three and a half months ago after you finished watching your first sunrise. You and I have been associated since before you were born. I was sent from a far-off land to monitor your conception and birth. After you were born, I stayed in your valley—up in the sky, that is—for a week or two at a time, creating all those animals and other things in the clouds that entertained you and kept you company; they were badly needed diversions from your problems." The stranger smiled knowingly.

"Who are the good people that show so much interest in me when my own family doesn't even care about me?"

"The International Order of Zarrhs and Winds," Eleni said, in a serious, almost whispered voice. "Your birth was foretold in many documents of antiquity, inscribed on ancient monuments and on monastery portals, and encoded inside mountains. I was sent by the Order to influence your conception and be helpful to you when necessary."

Desta was mystified and baffled. "So what exactly do you want from me?" He studied her features and eyes, trying to access her feelings and thoughts.

"Well, let's see . . ." Eleni paused to gather her thoughts. "First, now that you're on your own, I wanted to reacquaint myself so hopefully we become friends. In this big wide world where you hardly know anyone, you need someone like me to guide you and keep you company. I can be your stand-in mother —the loving mother you never had, although that was not entirely her fault." Eleni tightened her lips and looked away ruefully.

"I don't need anybody," the boy said, pointing to his chest, near his heart. "I have all the friend and mother I need in here."

Eleni quailed. Something in what Desta was pointing to, which she couldn't see, caused her to wither. She quickly regained her confidence and said, "Second, I think you will come to appreciate me when you realize that I can be more than a friend or a mother. I've a lot of information about the coin and the *individuals* who own it."

Desta stared at her, trying to discern the veracity of her claim. "Individuals?"

"Yes, individuals. And you will be surprised to know who they are and why they were called 'sweet and sour.'"

"*You* know the meaning of sweet and sour?" he asked, astonished.

"Not conclusively. A team of my friends of the Order are researching ancient records to ascertain the reported facts. I shall let you know once we find out, which brings me to my third point. I know you plan to spend the day looking down in the valley for the bearer of the coin. Don't waste your time. You don't have adequate information. The spirit of your grandfather didn't have sufficient knowledge about the other coin or its owners, only vague references, such as those two words and the water. But we do. For now, go home. Concentrate your efforts on your studies. I shall share the information as soon as I find out. And now I need to go. I'm needed elsewhere."

Desta didn't know what to think. "You still have not told me who you really are—a spirit or a human being. You show up out of nowhere, give me fragments of information, and now you're going? It's not fair. Honestly, I don't need your information. What I've got in here"—Desta again indicated his chest—"is all I need."

The corners of Eleni's lips twitched. She said, "I'm sorry. That's how things are with me. I'm always in a hurry as I travel the world. But you're important enough for me to come and share what I have."

"Won't you at least tell me the name associated with 'sweet and sour'?"

"I'll let you know when I know more." Eleni turned away from Desta. She extended her arms and waited several seconds until the fabric under her arms went taut as her voluminous garment billowed in a sudden wind.

Desta noticed an object the size of a man's fist under her veil, right above her neckline. He stared at it for as long as the woman was there, wondering what it might be.

Eleni spoke over her shoulder, "See you next time." An instant later she was airborne and then just a point that vanished in the ether.

Baffled and envious, Desta dropped his gaze toward the lake but for a long time saw nothing. When he came to his full senses, he realized that his mouth was dry and his body stone cold, as if somebody had dowsed him with ice water. He couldn't allow a complete stranger's advice to influence his plan for the day, but there was something in what she had said that caused him fear and wonder.

He moistened his mouth with a piece of the dabo. He held it firmly between his forefinger and thumb, gnawing at it like a dog with a bone. His mind was elsewhere but his jaw and teeth went at the loaf, mechanically, as if of their own accord. Soon after he began eating, his saliva started to flow steadily. The chewing and mincing became easier and his mouth felt normal again. With the sound of chewing in his ears and the reflexive act of swallowing—the flavors and aromas liberated from the bread—his fears subsided and Desta again felt at ease.

He slung his pouch over his shoulder, picked up his stick, and began walking down the steep mountainside. He moved carefully and deliberately, trying to avoid the sharp rocks and the craggy outcroppings along the path. Now and then he lifted his face to glance at the lake and valley, but his mind was occupied with the things he must do and what he must say to the people he would meet in the villages below.

At the bottom of the slope, the road split into three. One went straight ahead, to the open flat land in the direction of the lake. The other two branched left and right, skirting the foothills around the valley. Desta took the left because, according to his grandpa's spirit, the person who held the coin lived on the east side of a valley.

The boy heard the sibilating sound of a stream farther ahead. He felt a sudden and urgent desire for water. When he got near the stream, he snipped the largest leaf he could find from an *abo* plant—a luxuriant plant with large shinny leaves—and fashioned it into a cone. He pinched and folded the tip and held it between thumb and index finger; he then walked a short distance along the bank of the stream until he found an access point to pooled water. He crouched to clear away the floating debris and scooped up water with the cone. He tipped his head back like a chicken and drank with one continuous chug. After three rounds, he was satisfied. He thanked the creek and then rose and crossed it, continuing on his journey.

A few minutes later he found the fenced homes, farms, and fallow fields of a village before him. Beyond, more villages looped along the eastern foothills around Lake Gudera. That the path continued past the first set of hamlets both daunted and excited Desta. On his right, outside a fence in a grassy area, he saw a boy loading a rock into a sling. He stepped closer and said, "Excuse me, do you mind if I ask you a question?"

The boy looked up and Desta was surprised to see the eyes of this stranger focused on different places, one on him, the other somewhere behind in the infinite distance.

The boy suspended his activity. "What's the question?"

"I am trying to find a long lost cousin who is supposed to be living near water like that," said Desta, pointing to the lake.

"What's your cousin's name?"

"Nobody knows her exact name, but it means 'sweet and sour'."

The boy jerked his chin and squinted in confusion.

"No, really!" Desta said, holding the boy's one eye. "That's the translation of her name. I don't understand it myself, but I'm dying to find out."

The boy looked down at his sling as if to ensure the rock was still in its pouch. Near the sling-shooter's feet were about a dozen fist-sized rocks. "I think that's going to be very hard," he said, finally looking up. "I have never heard of a person with such a strange name."

"Since you are the first person I've run into, I thought I'd ask. Thank you, just the same."

"Maybe some of the people in the other villages would know her. I know for certain there is no one around here who is called anything like that." The boy turned and looked toward what appeared to be a fat wooden post about one hundred feet away.

"What are you looking at?" Desta asked, glancing at the boy's sling.

The boy wheeled around to face Desta. "What do you mean?"

"Where I come from, we use slings to drive out monkeys or baboons from grain fields."

"Oh," the boy said, clipping his breath. He pointed to the post. "My father thinks practicing on that target with a sling could help correct my eyes over time."

"Have you been able to hit it?"

"Not yet." He pulled on the strings and lifted the pouch, holding the rock in place with one hand and pulling taut the strings with the other. The boy measured, with both eyes this time, the distance he would need to spin the loaded sling freely overhead, and warned, "Step back." He raised the assembly and sent it whizzing in circles above his head, fixing both eyes on the target. A few seconds later he released the cord and the rock flew like a bullet to land several yards from the target.

"You see that?" the boy said, eyes sore with disappointment. "I have been doing this once a week, twelve rocks at a time, for six months. Yet I have not hit that post even once." His cocked eyes brimmed.

"I am sorry," Desta said, shaking his head. "What keeps you going?"

"Hope," the boy replied with a faint smile. "My father says all I need is persistence and patience and I will hit it one day."

Desta clamped his lips and nodded his head. "That's good advice," he said, realizing this was what he needed to do in his search for the gold coin. If he couldn't find his cousin that day, he must never give up, no matter what others, including that strange woman, said to him.

"At this point I don't care about my eyes. I just would love to hit it even once," the boy said, wiping his tears.

"I need to move on . . . but I wish you good luck," Desta said.

"Good luck to you, too."

As he strode along Desta noticed that all the houses, clustered into groups of three or four, were on the right side of the road. Their spiraling circular walls and conical grass roofs reminded him of home. The luxuriant ornamental banana plants behind the houses, the smell of dung from the barns, the roaming chickens in the front yard under the watchful eyes of the rooster, and the swarm of mayflies all took Desta back to his birthplace for a brief moment. He felt at ease here.

Tall bamboo fences circled the next set of villages. Within the complex, pathways led to individual homes like termite tracks. Desta couldn't see anyone outside and all the homes looked shut and quiet. "Is anybody around?!" he shouted from the main gate.

Two girls about eight years old came out of the first house. They cupped their faces with small saucer-like hands and stared at him.

"Are your parents home?" the trespasser asked, coming closer.

The girls stepped forward in unison. "Who are you?" one asked.

"My name is Desta. I am looking for a cousin who is supposed to be living in this area. I'm here to ask people if they know her."

"Our parents are at church," the second girl said.

They asked him for his cousin's name and giggled when he told them. They promised to ask their parents when they came home. He could check back with the girls later.

Desta walked on. The midday sun beat down on him, wilting him like a parched leaf. He crossed another creek and climbed an uneven hill toward what appeared to be a burned field. He came to charred fences and realized that he was looking at a village that had been gutted by fire. It gave him the chills to think that the coin bearer might have lived here and was now burned and buried in the ashes.

He knew it was far-fetched, but Desta gave in to the urge to search the charred earth for the ancient treasure. Recent rains had packed the ashes and soil; the ground was dust-free and easy to walk on. As he strolled along looking for the coin, he would now and then spy a shiny object and bend down to inspect it, moving the dirt with the end of his stick. After working at this for a period of time, he found nothing of interest and returned to the road.

He crossed other creeks, climbed other hills, and passed through an ever-growing set of villages. What he could see of the lake continued to grow, too, and now its farthest extent vanished into a distant haze.

It was already mid-afternoon and Desta's search would have to end soon. He had to return home before darkness fell, so he decided that the next cluster of homes would be his last for the day. Here he battled two dogs, one that nearly took a chunk of meat out of his leg, had the coin image on his chest not saved him.

The dogs' owner came out to see what the commotion was about, and Desta told his story. "Somebody is playing games with you, boy," the man said. "We have no person here whose name means 'sweet and sour'." But the man laughed uncertainly, as if the odd name had touched a nerve.

Desta's stomach lurched. He felt like he had come to the end of his journey before it even properly began. He looked away, wondering what other question he could ask to give him hope and encouragement.

The man interrupted Desta's thoughts. "What's your name? I didn't mean to call you just a boy. I apologize."

"Desta."

"If it makes you feel better, Desta, there used to be lots of people in this valley, an entire community of several thousand, until one night a small fountain in the middle of the valley grew into the lake you see around us. It swallowed everything—people, animals, homes, trees. They say most of the people and animals—their descendants, anyway—are still alive beneath the water. In the morning we sometimes hear the rooster's crow from under the earth."

Desta was astonished. "How long ago was that?" he asked, his hope revived. "Is there an entrance to where these people live?"

"This happened before my grandfather was born, over a hundred years ago. As for an entrance, I don't know that one exists. People have long tried to find it, but a way in has yet to be found."

Desta's hope was not dashed entirely. The woman with the 'sweet and sour' name could still be alive—her ancient coin tucked under her bosom—in a chamber beneath the bahir. He took a step toward the road, intending to move on. "Thank you for the information."

"Okay," the man said, tightening his lips. "Next time, don't go looking for your cousin by yourself. There are a lot of dogs out here more vicious than mine."

"Thank you for the reminder."

As he walked home, Desta realized that his method of searching was impossible. He certainly could not walk all along the lake asking people about the woman he was looking for. He had to find other, more efficient methods. He could ask his father to loan him his horse so that he could ride to the various churches and ask the priests whether they would share his information with their congregations. Or as a last resort, he could make a sign and stand with it near the caravan route on market days.

Desta thought further and became depressed. These ideas were unlikely to succeed. His father wouldn't loan his favorite animal even to one of his stronger and older children, and certainly not to Desta. Without a horse, he would have to walk long distances to contact the priests, and the priests might not be there when he arrived. Standing by the market entrance on Saturday would be easy, but a sign would be meaningless to country people who didn't know how to read, and he would have to endure countless questions about the strange name and why he was looking for the woman. Desta shook his head in dismay.

Glancing sideways, he noticed the boy with the sling he had met earlier by the first set of houses. He stopped and they exchanged stories for a bit. Desta gave the boy a summary of what had happened to him. The boy told him that he had gone home for lunch, napped afterward, and was now back to finish slinging his rocks. "Don't worry," Desta said, "that your eyes are not even now. All you need to do is imagine hitting that post over and over again, at every opportunity you have, then come here and try to hit it. That's what my grandpa once told me, to see whatever you wish to achieve in your mind's eye first, then go for it."

"How?"

"I will help you." Desta stepped close to the boy. "Close your eyes and imagine hitting the post. Really, really imagine hitting it."

The boy did as instructed.

"Now pick up the sling and load it."

The boy obeyed.

Desta took several steps back to avoid being hit by the spinning sling. He placed his right hand over the image of the coin on his chest and imagined the boy hitting the post.

"Now lift the sling and twirl it," Desta commanded.

The boy implemented his practiced motions and this time the rock crashed into the post and crumbled into a hundred fragments. He couldn't believe his eyes. He stood in shock, tears streaming down his cheeks.

Seeing the boy overtaken with emotion made Desta want to cry, too. At that moment, he had forgotten his own disappointments. "I am glad to see you happy. What's your name?"

"Yewegey," the boy replied, wiping his eyes.

"Yewegey, from now on practice seeing yourself hitting the post in your mind, and you will consistently hit it. Do the same thing for your eyes. Imagine having a perfectly even set of eyes. I will help you do that."

"How?"

"I will imagine seeing your perfect eyes every time I go to sleep. Once they are corrected, come to town and show me. My name is Desta. You can find me at the school."

"I can't wait to tell my dad what just happened. This is like magic." Yewegey gathered his sling, and poised to fly home.

"I want to try to do something before I go," Desta said. He reached for the area on his chest where the coin image was hidden and rubbed the skin with his fingers.

"What are you doing?"

"Close your eyes. I want to see if this works."

The boy closed his eyes and waited.

With the fingers he had just touched to his chest, Desta reached for the lid of the boy's crossed eye, lightly caressing and massaging it. He whispered, "Correct this eye, correct this eye."

"Are you like a *deb'tera*—shaman—or something? Mother has taken me to all kinds of deb'teras, given me medicines, and had me baptized in holy water but nothing worked. Then someone gave my father this crazy idea of doing target practice."

Desta smiled. "No, I am not a deb'tera, but I believe in the power of magic."

"If my eyes are corrected, I will definitely ask my father to bring me to town so you can see them. Thank you so much."

"Take care, and good luck."

"What did you say is your name again?"

"Desta. It means happiness."

The traveler quenched his thirst with two double-handed scoops of water from the first creek. He then sat on a rock to eat the rest of the dabo and with renewed energy returned to the road to clamber up the steep slope. The failure of his trip seeped into his mind, dragging him down, but the glow he had seen in the cross-eyed boy's face kept his spirits up. *For now, that was worthwhile enough*, Desta said to himself, contentedly.

NINE

Desta was not only disappointed by his trip to the lake but also overwhelmed. Trying to locate the person with the coin was like looking for a tiny bead in a sea of sand. He didn't know where or how to continue his search. He decided that until he had another opportunity to go on a similar adventure, he needed to focus on his schoolwork.

After he came from school each day, he studied his assignments and did his homework. The large tree stump in Mekuria and Tru's eucalyptus grove was a perfect place to study undistracted. Knowing how dedicated Desta was to his education, his hosts left him alone.

From the beginning of March to the time he took the year-end tests in the last week of June, Desta learned how to read and write very well in his Amharic language. He knew over a hundred English names of animals and other things, and memorized the multiplication tables up to the number nine. He could add, subtract, and multiply simple numbers with great ease. Brook was pleased with his new student and often asked Desta to stand before the class to read from a book or write on the blackboard the answers to questions.

One of the final exams consisted of reading a page from a storybook, copying three paragraphs from the blackboard, and giving the English names for the animals and objects listed on a large roll of parchment paper. On another exam, he and his classmates had to write the Amharic translation of a list of words the teacher wrote on the blackboard. They were also tested on their math skills in addition, subtraction, and multiplication. Finally, each student had to recite the Lord's Prayer and the national anthem.

When the teacher reported the grades afterward, Desta had earned perfect scores in all the subjects except handwriting, for which he received 90 percent. Brook said his letters were tentative and halting, like a priest's hand. "You need to work on your scripts," he wrote on the exam. "The letters in modern writing should be smooth and flowing."

On the day the school closed, Desta was declared the top student in the first grade and awarded an English book. The second student received a similar book, but it was written in Amharic. The third got two notebooks and a pencil. His class ranking had no meaning to Desta, yet he was thrilled to receive the book.

"See, I told you he studied at church school before he came here," one of the boys said to another.

"How else can he be first?" the second boy whispered. "He has been with us less than four months."

"I think he is on an *este-faris*—the hashish plant—," a third boy chirped, who had overheard the conversation.

"What do you mean?"

"His parents must have given him hashish leaves to make him smart."

"I don't know about that. Maybe he studied harder than we did. It will be interesting to see if he is first again next year," the first boy mused, pursing his lips with envy.

As Desta walked home, excited and anxious to share the good news with Tru, Fenta ran up and said, "I heard you stood first in your class!"

"Yes, I got this book!" Desta said, running his fingers over the book's cover.

"You're a smart boy!"

"Not as smart as my brothers. They finished their lessons in half the time it took the average church school students, and they both started from scratch. I knew my Amharic alphabet before I came here."

"No matter, you still did very well. . . . Can I see your book?" Fenta leafed through the pages. "Did you know how to read and write in English before you came here?"

"English was all new to me. I didn't even know the alphabet."

"Give credit to yourself. You won this book because you did better than all your classmates, and you even started your English from scratch."

"Well, I don't think winning this book will cause my father's head to inflate like a *duba*—a pumpkin."

"Huh?"

Desta's face twitched. "My father often told the story of how proud and happy he felt when the teachers at the church school told him about my brothers' excellent performance and how they finished their studies in much less time than it took the average student. Because of this news, he said his head grew like a duba."

"I think he should be happy at what you have done in just four months, too."

This response made Desta want to fly home. More than any of his family, he knew Tru would be very happy to hear this. "See you later," he said, taking to his feet.

Fenta just shook his head as he watched his friend dash off.

"Tru! Tru!" Desta called breathlessly when he saw her. "Look what the teacher gave me for doing good on my tests." He handed her the book.

Tru flipped through the hardbound book. "How wonderful!" she said with a broad smile. "It's all in English. You must have done well in the subject."

"I must have done well in the other subjects, too," Desta mumbled in a low voice. "The teacher said I received the book for being first in my class."

"You stood first in your class?!" Tru bellowed, her eyelids flaring.

"Why, is it that good?" Desta finally realized what it means to be first: important and impressive.

"Now this is cause for celebration and another gift from you-know-who," Tru said with a broad grin.

"All for being first in my class?"

"Yes, not everybody can achieve what you have. How would you like to celebrate your success?"

"I don't want a celebration, but can we do something together that would be like a big celebration for me?"

"What?"

"Go on a walk with me. I have not had a long walk with someone since I came here."

"You would prefer to do that instead of inviting your classmates and our neighbors to have a loaf and tea and coffee?"

"Yes. Why should I invite my classmates so they would know I did better than they did? I would rather take a quiet walk with you when you can."

Tru didn't have much to say in response to Desta's unexpected, thoughtful, and deliberate statements. She agreed to go on an excursion with him some weekend soon.

That evening, Tru reported the news to Mekuria.

"I knew there was something unusual about that boy. I am not surprised," Desta's uncle said with pride.

TEN

Desta's four-month introduction to modern education ended with school letting out for the rainy season, which had begun a month ago. This meant his wonderfully comfortable and carefree life in town was about to end, at least for now. It had been arranged before he started school that he would go home during breaks to help out on the farm. Desta didn't want to go back, dreading not only the work but also his situation with his family.

He tried to think of ways to get out of his commitment. He could claim he was sick or intent on remaining in town to continue his education on his own. Or he could say he needed the time to go back to Lake Gudera to talk to people who might know the coin bearer and to look for the underground portal to the people who lived under the lake.

Noticing his sad and distraught look, Tru invited Desta to go on the walk she had promised they would take; she wanted to find out what was troubling him. It was a glorious morning after a night of heavy rain and gusting winds. The courtyard and the path through the grove were wet and covered by a thick layer of fallen twigs and leaves. In the morning sunlight, raindrops still clinging to the leaves appeared as glass ear ornaments. Walking on the cold wet ground wasn't exactly easy on the soles of Desta's feet, but finally going on his walk with Tru brought happy memories of the walks he used to take with his sister Hibist when he was little.

The long, wide, graveled market plaza was deserted except for a few stray dogs that romped and snarled and chased a bitch in heat. The usually bustling row of tella and teahouses along the sides of the marketplace were closed and hushed. Steam rose from the ground of the tepid graveled surface, a pleasant change to Desta's feet.

After they crossed the desolate grounds, Tru suggested they sit on one of the benches. There were rows of them facing the expansive terrain to the west, where market-goers sat while selling their merchandise. Desta liked the idea because whenever he and Hibist went on a walk, they would always stop for a while at a spot with a view. They would sit side by side and talk about anything that interested or bothered them. This was one of Desta's most precious memories of home.

Tru had her own reasons for choosing that spot, but not for anything happy. She had come here in the past, she said, to stare at the place of her childhood and find relief from a migraine, a chest pain, or stomach cramp she might be experiencing at the time. She also had come here when she felt depressed, or after a nightmare. That distant lot across the Abayi River, near a copse of eucalyptus trees, held the memories of her tender years and many of her dead relatives, who were buried beneath the lot's weed-covered ashes. For twenty years this land had been a source of anguish and pain, as well as relief, when she came here to gaze upon it.

That was how she had dealt with her problems in the past. Then the head priest at her church recommended regular prayer as a possible permanent solution to her problems, and that's what she had done for the past year. She prayed early in the morning and again in the evening before her head touched the pillow.

Since Desta had come to live with them, Tru had been happier: she was better able to feel her emotions and she laughed more easily. It was as if she had needed the boy to find her soul and connect with her spirits.

Desta's recent sad and thoughtful face had reminded Tru of what hers looked like before she began praying.

"That empty land across the Abayi River near the grove of trees, is my parents' *badima*—old homestead. That is where my sister, brother, and I were born," Tru said, choking with emotion.

Desta was surprised and saddened by Tru's sudden succumbing to these raw feelings. He was afraid to ask her about it. He rested his chin on his open palm and looked down thoughtfully. He noticed a handful of wheat berries tucked under a rock, as if somebody had purposely hidden them there.

Tru shifted in her seat and cleared her throat. Desta lifted his head and saw her eyes deeply probing the distant badima, as if she had asked it a question and were waiting for an answer.

"Oh, my goodness, I am going to cry," she said apologetically. She blinked and jerked her head, trying to chase the tears away.

"So what happened on that land?" Desta asked nervously.

"That is the place where I lost my childhood, my mother and brother, an entire community of relatives, thanks to the Italians." The tears she had tried to stem were welling up in her eyes, waiting, Desta thought, for another wave of emotion before they swelled and overflowed.

Tru clamped her mouth with her hand, trying not to let out what she had bottled up over the years.

"Go ahead," Desta said.

"All my life I have not been able to weep in connection with these memories. I thought I was made of the desert, devoid of even a tiny oasis . . . of tears." Tru smiled awkwardly.

"Allowing yourself to cry is probably the best thing you can do. . . . That's how my sister Saba dealt with her sorrows. So what, exactly, did the Italians do to your mother and brother and the rest of the people?

"They bombed the whole village, killing my mother and my little brother and all those who had not gone to fight in the war, mostly women and children and the elderly."

Desta touched his brow and slowly shook his head, sorry for the people who had died and for Tru, who had suffered for so many years from these losses.

"I apologize for this," Tru said, now openly crying. "I didn't mean to burden you with my heartrending past."

"Believe me, it's not a burden." Desta fixed his eyes on Tru, hoping she would turn to look at him. "I have been through a lot myself. In fact, my whole family has been through a lot."

Tru wiped her eyes. "What happened to you and your family?"

"It's a long, involved story. I will tell you sometime if you really want to know. For now I'd like to hear your story. Not that I need to know, but if it helps relieve the sadness in your eyes and face. . . ."

"You're so sweet and thoughtful, Desta," Tru said, finally turning toward him. "Thank you for your concern."

"What about your father? And where were you when the bombs fell?"

"My father went to the war and never returned. We believe he was killed on the battlefield," she said, pausing.

"I was eight years old when they bombed our village. I had gone to visit my grandmother in Lichma. My sister and uncle, who also were absent when the bombs were dropped, visited the burned remains of our village and described some ghastly scenes of charred and dismembered human and animal remains.

I was lucky to live and to be spared these gruesome sights."

Desta just covered his mouth with his hand and stared down at a rock near his feet, trying to visualize the place Tru described. "What happened to you afterward?"

Tru paused for a few seconds as if waiting for her sad memories to run their course. "When my aunt heard about the horrible event, she came from her home in Addis Ababa and took me. My sister, Banchi, stayed in Yeedib with our uncle. My aunt put me in school, where I finished up to the tenth grade. Then I worked at my aunt's *buna bet*—a bar and restaurant—for a couple of years, serving food and drinks. It was there where I met my first husband, a teacher. We got married shortly after my eighteenth birthday.

"Our marriage lasted two years and then we divorced, mostly because I was so unhappy and depressed, haunted by the events that cost me my relatives. After I divorced, I came to Yeedib in the hope of leading a quiet existence with my sister. I desperately needed to get away from the noise and crowds of the big city. It's here where I met Mekuria, and we fell in love and married. My life has been happy since then, happier still since I met you. You are so much like the brother I lost when the Italians bombed our village."

"I feel the same way about you," Desta said with a warm but heavy heart. "I too had a sister whom I dearly loved. She got married and moved away. Of course, my loss is nothing like yours. The kind way you have treated me these past four months has brought back the memories of my Hibist. I know I am supposed to spend the rainy season with my family. But I have nobody left that I'm really close to, and I would rather stay here with you and Uncle Mekuria."

"I am sorry to hear there is a hole in your life, too, and I would love for you to stay with us. In late August, Mekuria and I are going to Addis Ababa to visit my aunt for two weeks and to celebrate the new year, but you can stay with us until then."

"No, my father will come to get me this weekend because my family needs me to tend the animals. That is the promise I made to them before they brought me here to school."

"It will be only two and half months. The time will go very fast, and you'll have something to look forward to in September," Tru said in a happier tone. She placed her arm around Desta's shoulders. "I'm planning to bring you very special things from Addis Ababa, including a nice pair of shoes."

Desta's face lit up, as if Tru had thrown a switch in his brain. For a while he just stared at her, not knowing what to say. All his sad feelings and thoughts lifted like a morning fog in bright sunlight.

"Shoes?" he asked excitedly.

"Yes, *shera chamma*—tennis shoes. They are a lot cheaper in Addis than in Burie or Finote Selam."

Desta tried to imagine what it would be like to wear such shoes. "Are they easy to walk in?"

"Yes, they're very easy and comfortable, so long as you get the right size. They can protect your feet from the cold and dirt."

Desta was thrilled by the thought of wearing shoes like some of the other students. The comfort they would provide, though, was a secondary consideration. A thousand times more meaningful was having found someone who thought him special enough to deserve a pair of shoes.

"Thank you so much for thinking of me." Desta wished he could hug and kiss Tru right there and then, but he reined in his impulses, saving them until she actually gave him the gifts. "I can't wait to wear a pair and see how it feels to walk in them," he said instead.

"Good. I look forward to watching you saunter to school in them every day. So in September, not only do you have school to look forward to but a pair of shoes—and many other things."

The two sat quietly on the bench, content with their thoughts. Finally, Tru said, "Let's go back. Mekuria will be coming home for lunch. Thanks for letting me share with you the sad events in my family. Just from doing this I feel a sense of relief and inner peace. I hope you will allow me the privilege of hearing your personal story when we see each other in September."

"We can come here to the same spot and I can walk in my new shoes."

"I'm looking forward to it."

Tru placed her arm around Desta's shoulders and the pair walked home, happy and hopeful.

ELEVEN

When Abraham arrived to collect Desta, Tru and Mekuria were readying to go to a funeral service. Abraham and Mekuria greeted each other with a handshake and three kisses on the cheeks. Desta kissed his father's knee, followed by Abraham kissing him on his cheeks. Tru explained that she and her husband were going to bury a neighbor's child and that she was sorry she could not stay to make coffee and visit. Abraham, in turn, said that was really okay, as he needed to get back home for personal matters. Abraham, Tru and Mekuria chatted in the courtyard while Desta packed his clothes and school things. The boy tried hard not to show his sadness when he joined the trio outside.

"Ready to go home?" Abraham asked his son.

Desta slowly moved his head up and down.

Tru turned to Mekuria. "I will escort them out of the grove. Finish getting ready, and we'll be on our way when I come back."

"Give our greetings to my sister," Mekuria said. "Tell her we hope to see her at the end of the rainy season. . . . She must be busy with work, and that is why she has not come to visit us."

Abraham acknowledged that indeed was why Ayénat had not come to see them.

Through the cool path they went, Tru with her arm around Desta. "You will be happy to know that your son did very well in school," she said to Abraham.

"Is that so?"

"Ask him. He can tell you everything on your journey."

"I am curious to hear it," Abraham said, flashing his chipped canine tooth.

Once they cleared the grove, Tru hugged and kissed Desta. "Be good. We'll see you in September," she said, tears trailing down her cheeks. She hugged and kissed him again.

Abraham was touched by Tru's display of emotion.

"The two and a half months will go by in no time. If he is not needed, he can come on a market day to see you a few times. Otherwise, we'll bring him shortly after the *Maskal*—the finding of the True Cross—celebration in September."

"I look forward to seeing you both at any time."

"Thank you. May your *Kiremt*—rainy season—be a time of health and peace," Abraham said. He tapped Desta's shoulder, urging him to move on.

Tru wiped her tears. "May it be the same for you and your family and the animals."

Shortly after they parted, Tru ran back up to them. "Sorry. I had meant to take the measurement of Desta's feet. Come stand next to me." She slid off one of her green plastic shoes.

Desta and Tru stood side by side and brought their opposing feet together. "Aha! That will be easy. Your feet are the same size as mine, except yours are wider and a bit more arched." Noticing Abraham's quizzical look, Tru said, "I promised to buy him a pair of shoes when Mekuria and I go to Addis Ababa to see my aunt for New Year's."

"I appreciate your good thoughts, *Weizero*—Mrs. Tru but I don't think it's a good idea to indulge the boy with such convenience and comfort. He is only a student."

"Students cannot wear shoes?" Tru asked, raising her brows.

"One, I don't want him spoiled with things we cannot afford, much less sustain for the long term. Two, if he is too comfortable, he may not pursue his studies diligently. Think of our church school students, who wear one *debelo*—pieced sheepskin—and one gabi year round. They live in a hut. They go around the neighborhood to solicit for their daily rations. By the time they finish their studies, they are usually well-disciplined and well-adjusted priests. This boy has none of those hardships and that worries me—the end he will come to, I mean."

"I don't think you need to worry about this boy and his commitment to his education. He has already proven it. Besides, just because of what you think, he should not be denied the comfort and conveniences available to modern school students."

She slid her shoe back on and left, her face composed and thoughtful.

THE ROAD OUTSIDE of town descended sharply. As father and son walked side by side, negotiating their way down the rocky, potholed road, Abraham asked, "So you did well in your lessons, Desta?"

"Better than all my classmates," replied the boy matter-of-factly. He glanced briefly at his father, trying to gauge how he would react to this news.

Abraham gunned his big eyes on the boy. "But did the teacher say you finished your lessons in half the time it took other students?"

Desta tightened his lips, puzzled by this response. "I started at the beginning of March. By the end of June, I did better than all the students in my level."

"Yes, but did the teacher say you did it in half the time it took your classmates? You don't know when those students started school. They might have started a week or two or even a month before you did."

Desta was at a loss. "That I don't know, but what difference does it make? If you knew that was so, would your head grow like a pumpkin with pride?" He asked, forcing a smile.

"Who knows? It might," Abraham replied, cracking a grin. "I just wondered if you did as well as your brothers. Tamirat and Asse'ged both finished their lessons faster than anyone else. But they, unfortunately, never took their educations to completion. . . ."

Desta kept quiet, thinking about his father's loaded comments.

"If you don't plan to finish your education, you better quit now. It would be a great waste of your time—and your life—to abandon it after many years of learning. Think of Tamirat!"

"I have no desire to quit, Baba. I am not studying to become a priest, and no wife will disrupt my studies or career. Don't worry about me becoming like Tamirat. We have none of the church school restrictions in modern school."

"That's easy to say now. Don't say later I didn't tell you."

Desta trundled down the path, pondering what his father had said. Not only did he have to fulfill his commitment to his grandfather's spirit to find the other coin, he also had to shoulder his brothers' failures.

They reached the bottom of the mountain and crossed the Goder River, traveling over springy, flat turf to another river and the hilly terrain beyond. They climbed the Wondegez Mountain, traversed a rocky ridge, and finally descended the mountain toward home.

Desta walked behind Abraham, quiet and contemplative, occasionally looking to the bottom of the shadowed valley, his old stomping grounds. Although it had been only four months, he felt as though he had been absent from home for a year. It wasn't because he missed it but because so much had happened to him in those four months.

Abraham finally found his tongue. "What is the name of your teacher?"

"His name is Brook. Why do you want to know?"

"I'd like to talk to him about your lessons. And I'll let you know afterward if my head grew like a pumpkin or not," Abraham said, his face beaming.

Holding back tears, Desta said, "You know, it's not that important, Baba. I just wondered if what I had done in school was good enough for you to be proud of me. . . . Ask Uncle Mekuria, he will show you where Brook lives."

Abraham's voice softened. "I'm not trying to lessen your accomplishments. I just want to hear what the teacher has to say about your overall learning."

Desta tried to change the subject. "Saba told me that you have a new shepherd boy."

"Yes, we do—a good one," Abraham replied, himself happy to talk about something other than personal stuff. He proceeded to tell Desta that the new helper was called Mekibeb and that he was fifteen years old. He had no father and had lived with his mother and one sister in a corner of the valley before coming to live with Desta's parents. He had been hired at the end of the year in exchange for a she-goat and two sacks of teff for his mother to make use of. Desta would now mostly take care of the animals at night and in the morning, and otherwise help with the farm as needed. "As you must have already heard," his father said, "Your brother Damtew has now built a beautiful home on Saba's old property. He and his wife moved there a month ago."

"No, I didn't hear, but that's good," chirped Desta. *One less person I have to deal with this rainy season.*

They walked quietly again, Abraham balancing his weight on his walking stick when he lost his footing or when he felt an invisible force was about to bring him crashing down.

Although he wouldn't admit it to Desta, Abraham didn't quite know how to handle the eddies of excitement he was feeling about the boy's academic achievements. He didn't want to share his feelings with his son just yet, wishing not to set himself up for another disappointment. He thought he'd been a fool to be elated with the school performance of his two older children before they had properly settled with their lessons. This time he felt he needed to defer his elation to a later date, until Desta finished his studies and graduated from school.

Desta had no walking stick. He hopped sure-footed from one craggy spot on the road to the other, defying whatever force kept tugging at his father's body. Although disappointed that his father's head had not inflated, he was buoyed by the thought of the shoes Tru would give him when he returned to school in September.

The more he thought about the shoes, the more sensitive his feet seemed as he landed each step on rough rocks and hardened earth. He imagined walking the same path in his new shoes and couldn't wait to see his family's faces when they saw him romping in them. He even managed a smile as he wondered what Kooli, his dog, or the vervets, his monkey friends, would think had they been around to see him in his new footwear.

When Abraham and Desta finally reached the outskirts of the homestead, the evening had begun to ink. The west side of the valley darkened by degrees, as if someone was progressively smudging it with charcoal. The sunlight had nearly vanished, except for sputtered, fading rays on the eastern peaks. Dark winter clouds hung over the eastern mountains but no rain was falling.

Desta stopped in his tracks, struck by an overwhelming odor of dung. He felt as though he had come to a different place than home: was the smell of manure always this vile? He placed his hand over his mouth and nose and stared toward the barn.

"What is wrong?" Abraham asked.

"The cow dung—it smells so bad."

"You were raised smelling this, son. How can it smell bad now? I think *ye kettema nooro*—town life—has spoiled you already."

Desta tried to make light of his reaction to the offensive odor. "I think the problem is my nose, not my living in town."

They walked to the house, and as Desta crossed the threshold, again he was hit with the scent of dung, this time from the horse stalls inside. It was as if he had never smelled this odor before, either. Now he was convinced that there really might be something wrong with his nose. He held his breath and entered the house.

"Oh, there is our town boy," Ayénat said the moment she saw Desta. She was sitting on her stool, baking injera in the main fireplace in the living room. Desta flinched at her cold, detached tone and scornful, loaded words.

He had not seen his mother since he started school four months earlier. He didn't know whether she had come to the market during that time. He went to her and bent over to kiss her knees, but she grabbed his chin and kissed him on his cheeks three times. Ayénat rarely allowed him to kiss her knees. He felt her cold lips but not her feelings. He crossed over to the other side of the fireplace and sat on the skin mat next to his father, where he always used to sit.

The house felt eerie to Desta. Yes, there were fewer bodies now.
Damtew and Melkam had moved out and were living in their own home. But it
was not simply their absence that made the difference. It was something else.

It was the absence of the dark, gloomy countenance that was Damtew,
perched on a stool across from Desta, arms intertwined over folded knees, the
turns of his gabi concealing his mouth and nose, almost up to the hacked black
mole on the bridge of his nose, his dingy eyes fixing him with a cold, hard stare.

That Desta would not have to endure his brother's grim gaze again was
a great relief. Yet he felt no animosity toward Damtew. He had forgiven his
brother shortly after leaving for school, one evening in Mekuria and Tru's dusky,
chilly living room. In doing so, he had found his own freedom and happiness.
Desta was grateful for the courage he had found to part ways with his cruel
brother and in the process find inner peace.

Mekibeb the shepherd boy came in and sat next to Desta. There was not sufficient space on the goatskin mat to seat them both. Part of the mat was pinned
under Abraham's four-legged stool. The father rose and lifted the clumsy bench
so Desta could release enough goatskin for the two boys to share it comfortably.

"Sorry you have to sit sticking out from the fireplace, Mekibeb," Ayénat said.
"That place used to be Desta's."

"We're okay," Mekibeb mumbled.

Desta was puzzled: why didn't Ayénat invite Mekibeb to sit in Damtew's
former place, right next to her, but it was not hard to figure out. She probably
didn't want anybody else to occupy the space formerly held by her favorite son.
She probably worshipped and blessed the spot every night before she went to bed.

Shortly after dinner, Abraham rose and clambered onto the high earthen
bed. Mekibeb climbed up to the loft where Damtew and Melkam used to sleep.
Ayénat remained behind. She had questions to ask Desta about her brother and
his wife and about Desta's schooling.

"How are Mekuria and Tru?" she asked casually. She picked up a partially
burning stick and began poking at the fire, containing a smoking ember that had
rolled out to the center of the pit.

"They are well," Desta said. "They send you their good wishes and hope to
see you once the rainy season is over."

Ayénat pretended she didn't hear and kept poking the ashes. With her eyes on
the stick, she said, "Are you still interested in pursuing that Saytan's education?"

Desta gave her a hard look. "Without a doubt!"

"Just about everybody at church says we are making a big mistake by allowing you to earn that kind of education."

"It's not a Saytan's education, Ma, and everybody that tells you so is wrong."

"Our head priest, Aba Yacob, can give you all the reasons why that kind of education won't be good for you."

"You know what, Ma? I think you and your friends and Aba Yacob are absolutely right. It's the Saytan who made me pursue this education. . . . Don't dare to invite that horrible priest again and have him treat me with his holy water and cross, trying to part me from my Saytan possessor."

Ayénat reduced her beady eyes into slits and gazed at the boy. "You still think you're clever to talk to me like that."

Desta returned the look with equal severity. "No, Ma, you've always asserted that I'm possessed by the Saytan, so it is *he* who talks to you this way." He felt a slight sense of victory as Ayénat looked away.

Turning back to him, she said, "I know. It was not your fault but your father's weakness to yield to the pressure that you and your sister and Teferra's wife put him under." She rose and strode across the living room and crawled into her bed.

Desta stared into the fire pit, thinking about his mother's renewed reference to the Saytan and her attempts to stop his modern education. He rose and gathered several logs from the mill room and then stoked the hearth with more firewood. He brought a rolled up goatskin from the closet and spread it by the fire.

I'll show you what my Saytan's education means to me, Ma. I will practice it not only under your roof but also beneath your nose.

He sat on the skin mat and folded and crossed his legs. He pulled out the English book he had been awarded and placed it in the space between his folded limbs. Hunching over, he began to read.

The first several pages contained names and illustrations of animals, objects, and land features. Desta quietly vocalized the names next to the illustrations, remembering how to combine the letters to form words and pronounce them: däg, kat, kaŭ, gōt, lam, hôrs, tā-ble, cher, be-d, mir-er. Some of the words he could say easily and naturally, while others got stuck on his tongue as if coated with glue. He struggled to get them out of his mouth. Even those words he could say easily sounded strange to his ears, making him unsure of the pronunciation.

And yet the idea of learning a language so unlike his own and his voice sounding so dramatically different excited him.

He wondered whether his father would wake any time soon and watch what his son was doing. He knew Abraham would rise at least by daybreak. Desta decided he would stay up as long as it took for his father to find him studying. He hoped Abraham would be so proud that his head would swell like a pumpkin.

For that opportunity not to pass, he had to make sure that he didn't fall asleep and that he kept a vigilant eye on the back of Abraham's head. For a better viewing angle, he moved his sleeping mat from one side of the fire to the other. Now when he looked up, he could see his parents' heads over their leather pillow on the earthen platform bed.

To keep himself awake he engaged in a variety of activities. He read from his book and then copied words and sentences from it. He drew the animals and objects he saw in the book. He flipped over his notebook and tried to memorize the multiplication table on the back of it, from the numbers nine to twelve.

Seated on his mat, Desta arranged and rearranged himself throughout the night, crossing, folding, or stretching his legs in front of him. When these fatigued him, he would lie on his belly and then his back, to stare at the smoke-stained bamboo ceiling and think about the daunting problem of finding the gold coin. When this thought overwhelmed him, he brought his mind close to home: he imagined Damtew sitting on his venerated goatskin mat across the fireplace, watching his kid brother with burning envy as Desta read, wrote, and drew—frustrated that he could no longer stop Desta from studying.

In the intervening moments, Desta glanced to see whether his father had awakened and was looking at him. But Abraham was fast asleep. He seemed to have gone to another world, ratifying his unconscious presence with strident nasal rattles and the occasional smacking of his tongue and lips as if he were chewing cud.

When his snoring became unbearable and awakened Ayénat, she would elbow him. Abraham's nasal fury would transmute into a guttural purr and then fizzle into regular deep breathing. But several minutes later, he would resume his sonorous roars, until Ayénat again nudged him. Each time Abraham quieted down, Desta looked up to see whether his father was looking in his direction. Abraham never noticed Desta's activities by the fireside, but whenever Ayénat awoke to nudge her husband, she turned her head and said, "Aren't you going to sleep?" Desta would reply, "I will in a while."

The only eyes on Desta were those of the horses, who occasionally pressed their curious faces between the gaps in the partition's wooden planks as if asking Desta to explain this night-long vigil. The tied-down mookit goats were completely indifferent to their returning caretaker. They dreamily lay on folded legs, chewing cud.

Despite his father's oblivion and his mother's defensive slumber, Desta was fully realizing what books and learning meant to him. Just as he was once enthralled by the world outside him—the mountains, the sky, the sun, and the clouds—he was now thrilled by what he was discovering inside himself. To learn and think about new things and travel far and wide, both in his new world and his imagination meant the possibilities were now limitless.

That night he also understood that through his thoughts and imaginings—his reading and writing—he could keep himself good company. Reading and writing would now be his best friends, just like his sister Hibist, his dog, Kooli, and the vervet monkeys had been when he lived in the country. Unlike his previous friends, these new ones would be with him anywhere and at any time. He would never have to worry about losing them.

A couple of hours before dawn, the rooster crowed, startling Desta and reminding him that much of the night had already passed into obscurity. Desta glanced at his parents' bed, tilting his head one way and then the other, but he couldn't quite see his father's face. Had he secretly stirred to spy at Desta from under the covers?

Moments before the first tearing, guttural calls of the colobus monkeys from the nearby forest and after the rooster's several dawn-delivering crows, Abraham finally woke. He peeled down the edge of the gabi from his head and face, and with a rustle and a thud arose from the high earthen bed.

Desta quickly sat up straight and folded and crossed his legs. He pretended to read his book, but all his senses were cued to his father's movements and any observable inflation of his head.

"Were you that cold to have slept here by the fire?" Abraham asked as he hurried past.

"No, not really." Desta bit his lip. His eyes, tense and hard, followed Abraham as he headed to the door. He noticed no increase in the size of his father's head, no smile on his back, and not even a slight swagger to his walk. Desta couldn't believe it. A wave of emotion surged through him, constricting his throat and bringing tears to his eyes. He placed an open hand over his mouth and pressed it firmly, staring into the fire that now was invisible to him. He shook his head. *How can I expect recognition from a man who has never had any feelings for me?*

He removed his hand from his mouth and sighed. Cold air from the open door rushed through his nose and throat to fill his lungs, comforting him. Disillusioned and confused, Desta gathered his books and placed them in his cloth pouch. He rolled the goatskin and raised himself on languid limbs to return the mat to its place in the closet. Then he clambered to his own high earthen bed. He lay his head on the grass-filled leather pillow and vanished into himself, hugging the sadness and disappointment to his bosom.

TWELVE

Desta slept for four hours, awaking in the mid-morning light. His eyes felt sore and his brain dull and raw, as if he had taken a remedy that deadened it. He pressed a thumb and index finger over his eyes and held them there. The pressure was soothing, and he lay peacefully for some time. When he finally removed his fingers, the warm, relaxed sensation in his eyes had returned and the blur in his head had faded. He squinted at the metallic gray sunlight that was streaming through the chinks in the walls and the open front door and settling into the rooms like an uninvited guest. Everything around him was eerily quiet. For a brief moment, Desta couldn't remember the day, why he had slept in so late, or where his family had gone.

The aroma of freshly baked *mekleft*—bread made from unfermented teff dough—reminded him that it was Sunday, when his mother made the special injera to take to church. So his parents were probably at church and Mekibeb gone to the field with the animals. The smell of the injera was overwhelming. Desta's stomach churned and his mouth watered.

Yet he was emotionally spent, and his eyes still bothered him too much to get up and get something to eat. He rolled to his side and rested his head over his folded arms, hoping he would fall asleep again. Instead, he became more awake. A solitary tear seeped from a corner of his eye and nestled in the crook of his arm. *This must be one of the tears I stopped in its track earlier today.* He recalled the struggle with his feelings after his father said nothing when he found Desta bent over his book by the fire.

His efforts had been futile, he realized, and anger and resentment flooded his head once again. He had grown up being told he didn't amount to anything; he was not a good enough shepherd, not big or athletic enough to ride horses, and according to Damtew not even a full human being because he had been born two months premature.

Desta squelched his tears. He uncovered his head and sat up. A thread of pale blue smoke rose from the smoldering remains of the fire. It swayed like a willowy tree in a gentle wind. Desta was enchanted by its color, grace, singularity, and animation as he watched it fade into invisibility. For a moment he forgot the discomfort in his eyes and the sadness in his heart.

A few feet from the fireplace stood the multicolored *mosseb*—table-like bread basket—resembling a billowy woman's skirt. Its circular lip met nearly seamlessly with its conical cover. Then there were the enduring gulichas, the trio of stones in the fire pit.

Desta stared at the gulichas for a long time and then shook his head to chase away the intruding emotions. He wrapped himself in his gabi, hopped down onto the floor, and went outside for his morning ritual. When he returned, Desta sat on his father's wooden bench, gazing down at the fire pit. The smoke from the stubby log was now strewn into mere wisps, the lazy tendrils spreading out in all directions before dissipating into the air.

You and I have a lot in common, don't we? Desta thought, addressing the stones. *We are both unappreciated and unacknowledged.*

Desta paused for a few seconds, as if waiting for them to answer. Then he told them about their tireless service to the family, every day withstanding the licks of fire and the weight of the cookware, enduring his mother's neglect and abuse the way he had endured his family's neglect and abuse. He told them that they must feel trapped—eternal prisoners of the fire pit—the way he used to feel when he lived in this valley. "Do you know that if you were picked up and thrown by someone with a hefty arm, you could maim flesh and shatter bones? Even more, if you were rolled down a steep mountain, you could crash into and bust everything in your way, even people?"

Desta smiled as he gazed down at his companions. He was used to talking to unspeaking animals like the vervet monkeys and his long-dead dog, Kooli. So in his mind he didn't feel entirely strange addressing the dumb stones. "I don't have a hefty arm, but I'm sure I could push you down a steep mountain. I'd watch you knock, crash, and pound the earth, trees, animals, and maybe even humans in your way. We all would feel good then!" Desta smiled as he imagined the three runaway stones in his mind.

Maybe that's what I should do; I should climb one of the mountains and push stones down its steep side all day long, he thought, looking out the front door. *At least the effort and activity would help me release what's been pent up inside for so long.*

Desta needed to kill his hunger before he could make the arduous journey to a mountaintop. He rose and opened the mosseb, the source of the wonderful smell he'd been inhaling since he woke, and found a freshly baked mekleft. He dragged the mosseb to his father's bench and sat down. He tore off a piece of the injera and placed it in his mouth. He sank his teeth into the spongy flat bread and began to chew. The soft and sweet flavor sent waves of pleasure to his brain and stomach. Desta took his time eating, savoring the moment, the activities of his jaw and mouth. *I needed something like this to take away my anger and frustration.*

He felt better after eating the bread and was having second thoughts about going to the mountaintop. *I would rather spend my time with someone who can talk back to me—someone who can understand how I feel—than spend it with rocks,* Desta reasoned. *And it would be better if I planned and prepared for a journey up into the mountains.*

Desta decided instead to visit his sister Saba, assuming she had not gone to church. He figured that, even if she wasn't there, his niece, Zena, would likely be.

He closed up and put away the mosseb, put on his shorts and jacket, and left for Saba's house. Above him, patches of dark clouds, a hoary tint at the edges, hung across the dome of blue. The sun, masked by gauzy clouds, slid upward like a crowned spirit. The rains of the previous weeks had revived the months-dormant life. The landscapes around the valley were cloaked with freshly sprouted grass and leaves.

"Guess who is here!" Zena shouted when she saw Desta from afar. For a moment Desta saw only Zena. When he got nearer, he noticed Saba sitting behind her, bent over something in her hands.

"*Era,* Desta?!" echoed Saba when she saw her brother. "What a vision!" She dropped what was in her hands and rose. Her son, Destaye, stopped riding his stick horse and stared at the guest.

Desta grinned widely, delighted to see his sister and happy that she made him feel welcome. She kissed him three times on his cheeks. Zena followed suit.

"Sit here," Saba said, pushing away a burned mosseb cover from a skin mat next to the one she was sitting on. She looked at him endearingly. "Is school out?"

"We got out for the season a couple of days ago. Father came to get me yesterday."

"Wonderful! Then we'll get to see you all through the rainy season?"

"I'm afraid so. I hope all the problems we had in this place are behind us now," Desta replied, feigning a smile.

"Everything is just fine, thank God. Damtew and Melkam now live on their own."

"I know. I hope Damtew is happy."

"Oh, he is. You should see him. He smiles often and he is no longer unfriendly toward us. I'm just glad it all ended the way it did." She looked at her son, who was now sitting next to his mother, studying his uncle.

"Destaye has grown a lot since the last time I saw him," Desta said.

"He's been well-fed and cared for. He is so precious to Yihoon and me," Saba said and turned to her brother. "Yihoon will be pleased to see you. It was he who kept reminding me to bring you a loaf or two every time I came to the market. He's gone to church now but will be back later. So tell me, do you like living in town? Do you enjoy your learning? Those few times I saw you at the market, I didn't get a chance to ask you."

"Yes, I do like living in town and going to school. Tru is just like a sister to me. She feeds me well, washes my clothes, and gives me a bath once a week. I couldn't have asked for a better person to live with."

"That's wonderful! Don't think I didn't notice. Each time I saw you, I told Yihoon how well and how much happier you looked. I think the good Lord has chosen the town life for you, not the country shepherding and farming life."

"I think, like grandpa's spirit said, there is a greater purpose to my leaving the life I had here and fulfilling the ancient prophecy encoded in the coin." Desta's voice trailed off. His eyes drifted toward the eastern mountains as he thought about the coin he had to find.

"Well, maybe that, too. . . . Baba once mentioned that much of your life is connected to that precious piece."

"That seems to be so, but I wish I knew why."

Desta looked at the things his sister had before her. Cold water in a clay bowl. Two bunches of *grammitas*—long, ridged straws. One bunch was made up of plain strands, and the other *alelas*—colored strands. Additionally, she had a bundle of *sendedos*—long, golden straws around which the grammitas or alelas are wrapped and woven into the basket. Saba's alelas were dyed red, blue, and green.

A tapered five-inch metal awl stood welded onto the already woven top ring of the mosseb lid over which the new one was being added.

"Don't stop what you're doing. We can still talk while you're weaving your basket."

"Thank you. This is the only day I can work on this thing. That's why I declined Yihoon's invitation to go to church with him." Saba picked up the basket. She pulled the awl out, inserted the diagonally snipped end of an alela into the hole and pulled it tightly while holding the edge of the basket securely with the other hand. She arranged and smoothed the flared coiling sendedo straws, and then once more pierced a hole in the bottom ring, inserted the colored straw, and pulled it. The border of the stitched strips touched together, completely covering the bundled straw. She stopped and studied the patterns she was creating.

"I managed to burn this mosseb top," Saba said, pointing to the charred basket next to her.

"What a beautiful choice of colors!" Desta remarked, glancing at the array of colored strands Saba had split, wetted, and spread out on the grass next to the skin mat.

"I am trying to duplicate the design of the original basket." Saba fingered the wet strands of blood red straw. "Do you know where the color I used for these straws came from? From the dye you wanted to use to paint your name on the sky."

"Really? When did you get it from mother?"

"The day after we returned from our trip to the mountaintop, I asked her if I could keep it. She gave it to me gladly, saying that she didn't have any straws to color and didn't want to see it wasted. Immediately after I came home, I soaked the straws in it overnight. After they dried, I stowed 'em away."

Desta shook his head, remembering his disappointment at not being close enough to touch the sky, much less write his name on it with the red ink.

Saba picked up the basket she was weaving. She removed the awl and inserted a red-colored strand through the hole, pulled the end tightly, and rubbed out a slight wrinkle. "This dye is one of the best I have ever seen," she said.

"It would have made a wonderful display of my name in the sky," Desta said regretfully.

"If I knew how to write, I could weave your name on this basket."

"It's not that important anymore, but if you want to do it, I can write out the letters for you. There are only three of them in our language."

"I'd love to do it."

"I will draw them in big letters and bring the paper to you tomorrow to copy from."

"Great. It would be fun for me to learn how to write, too," Saba said, flashing her beautiful teeth.

"I'd love to teach you how, if you're serious."

"I am too old for that, really. Besides, it would be of no use to me, but I would be happy to write your name on this basket as a memento of our trip to the mountaintop."

Desta grinned. "I think it would be nice indeed to have a record of it some-where."

"How are Mekuria and Tru doing?"

"They are doing great. They are staying in Yeedib for most of the rainy season. At the end of August they plan to go to Addis Ababa to celebrate the new year with Tru's aunt. Tru promised to bring me a pair of shoes and a bunch of clothes. I cannot wait till I see them again in September and to put on my first pair of shoes."

Saba's eyes flared. "You're going to wear shoes?"

"Yes, why not?"

"Why would you want to ruin your feet?"

Desta laughed. "Shoes won't make my feet go bad; it's just the opposite." Desta studied his sister's face to see whether she was serious. For the first time he noticed how beautiful her eyes were: deep brown pupils in a pure white fields, fanned by long, elegant lashes.

Saba was serious. "Once you start wearing shoes your feet will become soft like a baby's and you'll no longer be able to walk barefoot. Then God forbid, if you had no shoes and had to run away from danger, you couldn't flee fast enough because your feet couldn't run on rough surfaces anymore. That is one thing. The other is, once you wear them out, who is going to buy you a new pair? Father for sure won't. For him such things are frivolous. And I doubt Mekuria and Tru will buy you a new pair of shoes every year."

Saba's points all seemed valid. Should he decline the shoes Tru was going to give him? He was no longer sure. He looked at Saba's feet, which were barely sticking out from under the hem of her gown. "Look at yours," he said. "I bet they would be even more beautiful if you had worn shoes like those town women." He stared at her, waiting for her reaction.

She stared back, not knowing how to respond to such a ludicrous sugges-tion. "First," she said, "I would be a double-dealer to wear shoes, even if I could afford them. Second, I was not born with them, so why would I bother to wear them now? If God had wanted me to have something strong and lasting, he would have given me a hoof like a horse or a cow. Third, just for the sake of conversation, if I put a pair on and went to church on a Sunday, imagine the laughter and snickering I would get from the women and men. I would be the talk of the valley for weeks on end. Would I want that? Of course not!"

She looked away thoughtfully, but after reflection she laughed. "You know, I don't think I could get used to walking in them even if I had a pair. How did you get me into this silly conversation?" She laughed again. "I am a farmer's wife. I am happy with what I wear on my feet—nothing," she said with finality.

After a moment, Desta said, "You know what else? I often wonder how elegant your hair would look if you let it grow out and cascade down your back like some of those town women do."

"Compliment my mother. She had the silky luxuriant hair. I just inherited it," Saba said with a touch of pride. She looked up at the sky. "We're already into mid-afternoon and I have yet to prepare Yihoon's lunch. Would you like to come with me and continue our conversation? That way you can have lunch with us later, too."

"Actually, I ate before I came, and I won't be ready to eat probably until evening. I need to go home, but would you mind coming along for a short distance?" Desta rose from the mat. "I have something personal to share with you."

"Sure," Saba said thoughtfully. She turned to Zena. "Look after your brother. I will be back shortly."

After they walked several feet, Desta stopped and turned to his sister. "I want to talk to you about something that has bothered me since father picked me up from Tru and Uncle Mekuria's house yesterday. You know that father used to tell people how his head grew like a pumpkin when Tamirat's and Asse'ged's teachers told him how well they did in their studies, right?"

Saba nodded.

"Well, I told him I did better than all the students in the class, but his head didn't grow and he didn't say anything nice to me. Last night, I stayed up all night reading and writing, trying to show him my dedication to my education, yet when he found me by the fire hunched over my books in the morning, he said nothing. I went to sleep only after he went out. And before Ma went to bed she was telling me that my going to modern school is no good because it's Saytan's work. We had a big argument about that. When I got up a short while ago I was depressed thinking about these things. I'm afraid I'm going to have a problem with mother this rainy season. Is there something terribly wrong with me?"

"Let's sit here for a moment," Saba said, motioning Desta to a large log. She sat but Desta remained standing. "To answer your question, no, there is nothing wrong with you, at least as far as I know. You're just different. I told you that a long time ago. Regarding Baba, I don't think he meant his head physically grew when he heard those stories from Asse'ged's and Tamirat's teachers. He just meant that he was so happy and proud that he felt as if his brain were increasing in size. It's a manner of speaking. Concerning your mother, as you know, she is so much into God and the church that, to her, any other thing is ungodly or satanic."

"I know what you mean about mother," Desta said, "but Baba's indifference surprised me. Here he has been looking for a son who would make him proud. I thought I came close to fulfilling his wishes, yet he didn't even offer me a nod of approval."

"I know. You're looking for acceptance and recognition from Baba because you never had these from many of our family members. If you'll allow me to share with you a little wisdom, you need to accept yourself first. Believe in yourself and in what you do. The rest of us don't matter. This is not my original thinking. My mother, bless her soul, gave me the same advice when I was about your age." Saba rose and placed her hand on Desta's shoulder. Desta brimmed with emotion.

This was exactly what he wished his father had done the day before: he had wanted him to rest his big hand on his shoulder and tell him, "You've done a great job, son! I am so proud of you!" Desta held his breath and stilled himself. He pressed his hand against his tattooed chest. His emotions subsided. He sighed deeply.

"Are you all right?" Saba asked.

"Sorry. Yes, I am."

"You know, that advice has saved me many a heartache and disappointment. It is particularly apt for you now that you live where so many people are complete strangers. Come, let me give you a hug before we part."

Saba held the boy's small frame tightly, caressing his newly grown crop of hair. "Everything will be all right. Come and share it with me if you have something else to talk about. Remember what I told you. . . . I must go now."

Desta smiled. He thanked her and went home.

THIRTEEN

"This is how my first vacation home from school will start?" Desta asked under his breath, shaking his head. He was leaning on a wooden shovel in the middle of the horse stall, surrounded by piles of manure. The familiar smell was overpowering. He placed his hand over his mouth and pinched his nose. It was futile. He could hold his breath for only so long. He dropped his hand from his face and gasped for air, taking in a generous quantity of the putrid air. He coughed, managing ultimately to get an even greater whiff of the awful smell. He gave up, held his chest, and began to breathe normally. Gradually, as he continued his work, the odor bothered him less and less until he barely noticed it.

What bothered him now was being in the middle of that pile of horse droppings. He shuddered in revulsion. He felt as if the muck was getting all over him. He looked down at his feet and wished he had the shoes Tru had promised. His impulse to run out of the stall was checked when he noticed Ayénat watching him through a gap in the partition that separated the horse stall from the living room.

"What are you waiting for?!" she barked, coming around to the horses' entrance. "This is the same work that Hibist, Melkam, and I used to do until my back went out. We have nobody else but you. It is your job to clean this stall every three days," Ayénat commanded.

"Why do you let it go for so long?"

"We have had nobody to clean it for the past few days. Melkam has her own house to care for. Even so, she has been coming to clean the stall once a week. Do I have to remind you that horses produce a great quantity of dung every night? This is only four days' worth."

Desta looked around. There were a pile of dried dark gray clumps in one corner of the stall, glistening wet ones in another, and loose and fractured balls in the third corner. But the majority of the manure was where he was standing, trampled and strewn around.

"Do you know how to use the shovel?" Ayénat asked.

Desta indicated he didn't. He had seen Hibist and Melkam clean the horse stall but had never done it himself.

"I'll show you how," Ayénat said, stepping into the stall. She took the shovel from Desta, scooped the manure in front of her, and tossed it toward a small opening in the exterior wall. Then she walked to the opening, Desta in tow. "Once you have enough piled here, push a scoop or two at a time with the shovel and shove it through the hole, like this," she said, stuffing the partially dry muck through the opening. "If the shovel doesn't work, as it often doesn't, use your hands."

Desta grimaced. "My hands?"

"Of course! How else are you going to pass all this manure out of the stall? Whatever you can't push with the shovel, you thrust with your hands." Ayénat seemed to derive pleasure from Desta's protestation.

The boy looked over the amount of horse dung and then studied his hand. Not only did he not want to touch that filth with his bare hands, he was troubled by the incongruity of his small hands and the amount of manure he had to remove. He gazed at the dust particles that swirled and floated peacefully in the shaft of sunlight that had come through the cracked mud plaster in the wall and flooded the top edge of the wooden plank next to the partition wall. Watching these specks dance lazily helped soften the edges of his anxiety.

Ayénat tapped Desta on the shoulder. "Do you now understand what to do?"

"I guess so," Desta replied, trying hard not to show the stress he was feeling.

"Get to work then. You can't just stand and watch the air," Ayénat snapped, handing him the shovel.

Desta sighed. He scooped up and tossed the manure toward the hole in the wall. After what he had thrown grew into a heap, he sat on his heels and pushed it through the opening. What he was passing through quickly built up on the other side of the wall, blocking the hole.

"You have to go outside and clear what you've pushed through before you can push any more of it," Ayénat directed.

Desta trundled out of doors with his shovel and scooped and tossed several batches of manure toward Ayénat's spices patch. By the time he finished the work he was sweating profusely. He stopped and looked at the luxuriant verdure covering the lot beyond the spice plants. This was Ayénat and Abraham's potato garden. Desta stared at this sea of forest green as memories of his past life filtered through his head. He remembered the times he and Hibist had come to dig potatoes here, and their finding some of the biggest tubers where the concentration of manure was the greatest.

Desta smiled absently as the image floated back to him of their excitement whenever they found those potatoes. At that point, the modern school student felt as if he had found a gem that had been buried in manure years ago, a high point of his childhood. That sweet recollection was what he needed to feel good about himself once again.

"What are you staring at?" Ayénat asked, leaning over the fence. "There is more work you need to do. Finish that job quickly!" Desta slowly and thoughtfully walked back indoors. After four more rounds of the same activity, he was done.

The sweat had evaporated from his face and the muscles in his legs and arms had become stiff and sore, but his brain had awakened to something he had never thought about before: how hard life was for the country woman.

Ayénat brought him a bowl of warm water and soap to wash his hands and feet. As he scrubbed and cleaned himself, he remembered the many different things Hibist or Melkam had done every day. After cleaning the horse stall, she would go to the creek to fetch water in a big round earthen jar she attached to her back with a cord. After she fetched two jars of water, she would grind teff or wheat. In the evening, she would milk the cows. Then before the rest of the family members came home, she would prepare dinner. After dinner, she would wash their parents' feet and those of any guests who might have joined them. She rose the next day to do the same thing all over again.

Desta thought if there was anything he could do to make their lives easier, he would go to any length to do it.

FOURTEEN

Desta had never seen Abraham so mournful. Even after they buried Abraham's father over a year ago, he had not been this sad. The three of them—Abraham, Mekibeb, and Desta—were sitting around the fireplace, their hands intertwined on their folded knees, faces somber, and eyes staring into the fire they were not seeing. Ayénat puttered in the kitchen behind the parapet, also thoughtful and sad.

This was the rainy season. It was the end of July, and Desta had worked his first day with Damtew, Melkam, and Abraham, in the farm field up on the mountainside. Part of the forest had been cut down during the dry season—December through March—and the fallen trees and cut branches had been burned. Damtew, with the help of friends from across the Davila River, had cleaned up the charred debris and readied the steep land for tilling.

Since the rainy season arrived at the end of May, Damtew had plowed the virgin, loamy soil twice and was now plowing again for the third and last time. Abraham was there because he was good at removing tree stumps and also good at sowing seeds—two things the father was known for. Melkam and Desta were there to help clean up the dead weeds, grass, and twigs in preparation for sowing.

Melkam, who was three months pregnant, was staying only until noontime. All morning, Desta and Melkam gathered extraneous things and piled them into discrete *gulels*—mounds. They used their hands to pick and sort through the tilled soil, knocking apart and pulverizing the big clumps to make the soil consistent and level. At midday they went home, Desta to get lunch, Melkam to rest.

At mid-afternoon, Desta returned with a freshly baked round of rye bread and spices and a gallon jug of tella in a round-bellied calabash. Abraham, having sown most of the field, was resting with Damtew under the shade of a gottem tree, facing the panoramic valley below.

Desta handed the basket of dabo to Abraham, who first blessed the dabo by

making the sign of the cross over it. He then broke off big chunks for Damtew and Desta and himself. Desta took a bite from his bread then set it aside.
He poured tella into horn cups for his father and brother, filling a third cup for himself.

As they ate, Desta's eyes fell on his outstretched feet. He had never seen them that dirty before as this was the first time he had worked on a plowed farm.

Dried mud was caked around his toes and the pads of his feet. His arches were pale, scratched, and smudged with dirt. Damtew's and his father's feet were worse. Desta was thankful his feet would be like that only for another two months. They would be liberated from dirt when he went back to school in September and could wear the shoes Tru had promised him. These thoughts caused the boy's feet to tingle with excitement.

He looked up and noticed that dark rain clouds had gathered over the eastern peaks. Desta knew this didn't bode well. They would soon grow massive. Indeed, by the time they finished eating, it had begun to rain on the slopes of the eastern mountains.

"We'd better be prepared to take shelter," Desta said to Abraham. "That rain is going to come across the Davola River very soon. Desta had watched and studied the same event every winter season since he was a toddler and he knew exactly what he was talking about.

"Desta is right, Damtew. You should make two canals going in opposite directions, to divert any flood that might come down the farmed lot."

"I only have three or four rounds of the tilling left. I will make 'em once I'm done plowing," Damtew said.

Abraham went to finish his sowing. Desta got back to work breaking up lumpy soil and shaking and gathering the wilted weeds, piling them into mounds. Occasionally, he stopped and turned and looked at the rain and the charcoal black clouds in the eastern sky, which seemed to grow by the minute. Lightning flashed. Thunder cracked in the sky and temporarily deafened their ears. It didn't look good. Desta ran toward Abraham, who was hurrying to finish his seeding.

"Baba, it's best you stop now!" Desta shouted, waving his arms wildly. "We need to find shelter or we'll be finished."

"*Era!*" cried Abraham when he noticed what was happening on the east side of the valley. He gave the leather sack of seeds to Desta and scuttled toward Damtew.

Abraham clapped his hands at the older son. "Undo the yoke from the oxen," he ordered, "and drive them to a place of protection right now!"

Damtew had so far made only one of the canals but now the rain began to tumble from the sky, first in large drops and then as hailstones. Damtew, Abraham, and Desta ran to the gottem tree. The oxen stood in place, unfazed by the storm.

The hail shredded the leaves of the gottem tree and pelted the people below. It assaulted the plowed earth with a vengeance and soaked the soil, turning it into slush. A mere nudge would send the liquid earth cascading downhill.

Abraham placed his head in his hands and prayed to the God of Israel. Desta clung to the tree trunk with one hand and with the other pressed his chest, praying that God let him live so he could go back to school and wear his first pair of shoes.

The storm was unrelenting. Just as it seemed to be abating, a new cloudburst came from behind the first. The tilled soil began to break, first into rivulets, then into streams, and then with more rainwater coming from higher ground, into a full-blown flood. The three watched in horror as the topsoil, Damtew's month long work, Melkam's efforts, and Abraham's seeds were washed down to the creeks below. When the rain finally subsided, nearly all the topsoil had been washed away and all that remained were mere islands and patches.

Damtew interlocked his fingers behind his head and surveyed the aftermath of the erosion—what was left of his sweat and hard work. He felt sick inside and didn't know what to say. He had never been a man of words, but as usual his eyes and face spoke volumes. His skin became darker and darker; his small eyes sunk deeper and deeper into their sockets. He dropped his hands and shook his head. He spat. "What's left of my months of toil is a washed, useless, bald earth," he said, finally.

He had expected the newly cleared land to produce good harvests for the next three or four years. Now it was not going to give even one year's harvest.

Abraham walked from one side of the lot to the other, saying "era, era, era," as he inspected what remained of the soil and the barley seeds. Those meaningless sounds came nowhere near to expressing the gravity of his sadness, but that was all he could muster at the moment. For him it was the loss of the potential harvest; for Damtew it was the meaninglessness of all his effort, cutting down the trees, clearing the land, and tilling it three times—three months of effort washed away.

That evening, Abraham wanted to say something to someone who would listen. What had happened was too painful to simply forget. "It's a crying shame that we lost our months of sweat in one afternoon's rain," he said.

From behind the parapet, Ayénat said, "It was a rain unlike any we have had before. Even so, I had hoped that much of the tilled soil would be spared."

"Nope. All the soil and seeds are gone with the flood," piped Desta. "I have never seen rain and hail like that, except perhaps that time when Damtew's goat got killed."

Mekibeb looked questioningly at Desta.

"I wonder if it's a punishment from God," Ayénat said, "for our continuing to cut the trees and chase the animals that used to live in them."

"I tell Damtew to stop cutting down the trees but he doesn't listen," Abraham said. "I am not afraid of God in this matter; I am just afraid we are going to lose our future and our children's future." He stared into the darkness.

"How do you mean?" Ayénat asked.

"If we continue to destroy the forest and chase the animals away, we'll soon have nothing left but the barn and desolated land. This worries me a great deal."

"Yeah," Desta said, "like what happened to the vervet monkeys and all the birds after Saba and Yihoon moved to their new land."

Ayénat said, "I just worry about the now, like Damtew and Melkam, who will have less grain this coming year. We at least have our leased lands from which we should get enough to last us through the year."

Abraham unwound his arms from his knees. "There is nothing we can do at the moment. Do you have dinner? I'm hungry."

After dinner Abraham quickly climbed to bed. Mekibeb headed for his loft. Ayénat stayed in the kitchen to finish up. Desta remained by the fire, thinking about the rain and the flood and the lost soil and what Abraham had said about the future. He was sad for the animals and the trees, knowing that once they were gone, they would never come back. He shuddered. He then got up and crawled into bed.

THE THOUGHT OF THE RAIN and flood haunted Desta. He wondered where the water with all the soil and the seed went after it left the valley. He wondered whether it might collect in one big bahir and, if so, where that might be and whether people lived there.

If it wasn't far, he thought he might go there to look for the bearer of the coin. He would ask his father about such a place when he got up in the morning. With that promise to himself, he fell asleep.

DESTA WOKE EARLY. After returning from his morning outing, he sat by the fire Ayénat had made and waited for his father to get out of bed. The sun had risen, light was filtering through the cracks in the walls, yet Abraham still had not gotten up. Desta looked over at his parents' bed and saw neither his mother nor his father. A mystery. Soon after, Ayénat walked in with an empty bathing pot in hand, having just washed up.

"Where is father?" Desta asked.

"I don't know. He left pretty early."

Another mystery.

Sometime later, Abraham walked in looking tattered, his legs wet up to his calves. The hem of his gabi was soaked and dragging.

Where did you go?" Desta asked.

"Oh! I had a horrific dream last night. I saw in my dream that all the remaining soil of the farm we were working on yesterday had been washed off, so I went to confirm what I had dreamed. It rained last night and the possibility was there."

"And?" Desta asked, holding his breath.

"What was left was still there."

"I am glad. . . . I have a question."

"Yeah?"

"Where does all the water and soil that leaves the valley go?"

"As you know, all the water produced in this valley flows into the Davola River, which in turn brings it to the *Abayi*—the Blue Nile. Many other rivers join the Abayi, and all combined flow into the *Tana Hyke*—Lake Tana."

"Is Lake Tana big?"

"The largest in the whole country, I believe."

"Do people live near there?"

"That is where the town of Bahir Dar is."

Desta's heart leaped. "That's it!"

"What is?"

"Grandpa's spirit told me that the person who holds the coin lives near big water. I bet that is where this person lives," Desta said with a smile.

"Oh!"

"Is it far?"

"Two long days' journey on foot."

"I hope to go there someday."

"It's always possible. Just don't forget to pursue your studies, too."

"No worries. As you know, I love learning."

"By the way . . ." Abraham said.

Desta looked up at his father, wondering what had suddenly changed his thought.

"I talked to Brook, your teacher."

Desta was all eyes and ears.

"He said you're a good student and did better than your classmates."

"Wasn't that what I told you when you came to collect me?"

"I know. I just needed to find it out from the source. It's always better that way." Abraham grinned, barely showing his chipped tooth.

"And?"

"And what?"

"Did your head grow like a pumpkin?"

Abraham laughed. "Just a little." He laughed again. "I am proud of you!"

Desta clamped his mouth to stop from crying. He had waited so long for a moment like this.

Abraham ate his breakfast, changed into his better clothes, and left.

Desta skipped and jumped out the door.

FIFTEEN

In Desta's world, September was the beginning of spring. Bright sunny days fostered abundant growth of weeds in the vegetable garden and the farm fields. This was a time when every available hand was needed, and for Desta also the time for school to reopen.

With Damtew and Melkam gone and with no other help in the house, Desta knew that his family would need him to help weed the garden and the farm fields. Already Ayénat depended on the boy to do many of the chores her daughter-in-law used to. Ayénat's physical limitations, problems with her back and knees, meant she was less able to grind grains, milk the cows, fetch water, and cook. All these facts don't bode well for Desta when the time to go back to school arrives. His mother could demand that he stay at home and continue to be of service to her.

He thought about these potential problems at night while lying in bed and staring at the reflection of the fire pit's light on the beetle-black ceiling rafters. He thought about them while he walked by himself and as he knocked apart the clumps of soil on the freshly plowed farm fields.

He also thought about what would await him when he went back to town: new lessons, the gifts Tru and Uncle Mekuria promised to bring him from Addis Ababa—shoes, pants, shirts, and writing things. The closer he got to September, the more anxious and excited he became.

"What are you thinking about so much?" Ayénat asked one time after studying his eyes and face for a while.

"Oh, nothing much, just about things," he replied casually. Knowing how his mother distorted things, he didn't want to say what really was going on in his head.

Desta needed to somehow resolve the quandary he was in. One bright Sunday afternoon, he took a walk across his parents' property. He wanted to really think through his options in the event his parents decided he should stay at home when school reopened. He wished he could meet his grandfather's spirit again so he could ask him the solution to his problems.

He walked the south side of the cattle field toward the ravine where the family treasure and his grandfather's remains had been found. At the bottom of the field he stopped and stared at the handsomely grown trees Abraham planted in memory of his father and as reminders of what had been excavated there. Thoughts came rushing back to Desta of his different journeys to this place—the first one with just Desta and the Cloud Man and the second with his whole family to ascertain the identity of the remains and the coin.

He kept his eyes fixed on the place, waiting to feel something that would indicate he must go to the old gulch. No such feelings came, and he realized there was nothing he could gain or find by going there. He instead went to the sholla tree, his place of comfort and of shelter from the rain and the sun—the spot where he and his grandfather's spirit spent pleasant times.

Once he reached the shielding canopy, he looked around. Nothing had changed except that the tree's talon-like roots and his old stone seat were covered with bird droppings. He wiped off the seat with freshly fallen leaves, and sat down.

He propped his back with both hands, stretched out his legs, fixed his eyes on his toes, and wistfully dreamed about seeing his grandfather's spirit once again. When this seemed too improbable, he thought about his circumstances. When he realized he could be made to stay at home when school opens after the Maskal celebration, he became scared.

It was then that he noticed a figure descending from the sky in the far corner of the southern field, which then came walking toward him. At first, Desta thought he was hallucinating, given the warm, shimmering afternoon sun. The closer the figure came, however, the more familiar it looked. . . . the white shroud . . . the rocking gait . . . the hooded face. *It's that strange woman. What's she want from me now?*

He rose and was about to flee but then had second thoughts. He had his protection over his heart. What could she possibly do to him? Who knows, he thought, considering she had come down from the sky; she might even have a message from his grandpa. He'd better stay put. He sat back down.

"Good afternoon, young man," Eleni said with a nod.

"Good afternoon," Desta said indifferently. He cast his chin down in greeting.

"I was passing through and noticed that you were out alone, so I thought I'd stop and talk with you for a bit," Eleni said, her winter-gray eyes holding his gaze.

"I'm not in need of any company and I wish you would stay away from me," Desta said sharply.

"I shouldn't think that's the kind of thing you would want to say to me, considering what you're going through. Do you mind if I sit down? I've important matters to discuss with you."

Desta stared, wondering whether to grant her wish. "Important matters?"

"Indeed."

After Desta gave her permission, Eleni sat on a stone seat next to him. "I know you are unsettled at seeing me. I believe this is because, first of all, you don't know me well enough. Our previous meetings didn't give us enough time to talk about anything personal. Also, I believe you see me as a threat to your well-being. Why this is, I do not know, but again perhaps because you don't know me well enough.

"Like I mentioned before, I knew about you before you were conceived. Everybody in the Order of Zarrhs and Winds knew. We didn't know exactly what you would look like, but we knew your birth had been prophesized and where you would be born, just as we knew about the birth of the coin bearer you seek.

"In a similar way, I and another person were sent to the birthplaces of the two coin bearers to monitor their conception, birth, and life paths. I'm in no way here to harm you or interfere with your plans. Apart from my assigned mission, though, I could be of help to you in many ways because I once was a mother of five children." Eleni suddenly looked forlorn, her eyes far away. She shook her head a little and continued. "I cannot predict or influence the things that happen to you, but if by chance I learn or sense something that is coming your way, I will try to forewarn you so that when it happens you'll be better prepared to deal with it. Any questions?"

Desta, who had been poking the dirt with a stick while listening to Eleni, lifted his head and studied her face. He said, "You didn't answer my question from last time. Are you a spirit or a human being?"

"I'm a spirit who has assumed a human form," Eleni said quickly, pleased that Desta had asked something about her. "To come back to what I was saying, if I do something that upsets your plans or seems hurtful to you, I want you to know that it is not done out of malice. I'm only doing what I've been assigned to do. In fact, the physical abuse by your father and Damtew, and the neglect and hatred you experienced from your mother and your other brothers, wasn't perpetrated out of any malice they had toward you."

"Then what have I done to deserve the mistreatment?"

"You've not done anything wrong. It's not your fault. In the story of the coin and you, that's how things were predicted to happen. I came here today to tell you that the days and months ahead don't bode well for you. Brace yourself. I know you're strong enough to withstand what's coming. I'll see you next time." Eleni stood up and opened her arms until the fabric of her garment was tautly stretched. A strong breeze began to blow, causing the fabric to balloon. She lifted into the air and floated away. Desta rose, capped his brow, and watched her with envy until she vanished into the sky.

He sat back, closed his eyes, and stilled himself. *That's how things were predicted to happen?* He could see her individual words and the letters that made them, right before his eyes. He could taste them on his tongue. He could hear Eleni's sibilant voice as she said them. And he could see her entire being, including that round, fist-size object behind her neck under her costume.

Whatever the days and months ahead would bring, he'd just have to bear it because he was powerless to change the outcome.

SIXTEEN

Submerged in thought, Desta sat on the fence outside the front door, waiting for the golden band of morning light to descend from the mountain above his home and warm his chilled body. This was the third day since his family welcomed the new year. The valley was still in a nothing-to-do, tranquil holiday mood. Desta liked it like that because he could look inward and connect to his feelings and thoughts without external distractions.

That morning, amid his uncertainty about returning to school and the foreboding, "brace yourself" advice from the Wind Woman, he decided to go to town in his imagination. He saw himself in Yeedib, in Tru and Mekuria's home, surrounded by their gifts from Addis Ababa: a sweater, a jacket and shorts, a pair of canvas shoes, and writing implements—a fountain pen, an inkwell, and a notebook. He strutted in his new shoes while Tru and Mekuria gleefully watched. He walked across town in his new shoes and clothes, books tucked under his arm, looking very much like the other students as he made his way to school. People watched him, but they didn't laugh like Saba had said would happen if she wore shoes to church. On the school grounds, his classmates ogled his new clothes and shoes with envy.

Suddenly, Desta's daydream was shattered by the sound of throat clearing. Abraham had just come out of the house with rolled skin mats under his arm. He took note of Desta on the fence, dangling shoeless, chilled feet. Ayénat, thoughtful and apprehensive, followed Abraham. Desta's eyes were on his parents, but he had not fully awakened from his reverie. He hated his father for disrupting this blissful moment.

Abraham unrolled the skin mats and randomly placed them on the grassy part of the yard. He told Ayénat to sit down.

"Tell me nothing's happened to my mother," she said.

"No, your mother is fine."

"Then who died?"

Abraham didn't reply as he sat down next to Ayénat. Yihoon and Saba emerged from behind the home, cheerless and meditative. They said good morning and sat down, sharing a skin mat. Shortly after, Teferra and Laqechi arrived, followed by Damtew and Melkam. The last to arrive were Asse'ged and Mulu. They came from around the fence where Desta was sitting but didn't seem to notice him as they walked straight to the gathered relatives. The newly arrived took their seats on the outer skin, next to Damtew and Melkam.

Ayénat knitted her brow and dimmed and darted her eyes anxiously every time a couple arrived. She shifted in her seat and ran her fingers over her brow and gazed down thoughtfully, unable to imagine what news Abraham had for them. She seemed terrified of the gloomy air that was enveloping her.

Desta didn't like what he saw. Without knowing why, he felt sick to his stomach.

"Come join us, Desta!" Abraham called out.

Desta dismounted from his seat and walked over in halting steps, as if to the edge of a precipice.

"Come sit next to me," Saba said, extending her hand to the boy.

"What is going on?" he asked her.

"We don't know, but Baba invited us all here. We'll find out soon," she whispered.

Abraham cleared his throat. "Thank you for coming. . . ." Abraham began in a rugged voice. Everyone looked at him anxiously, hanging on his words. Ayénat clutched his arm.

"A week ago, I learned that Mekuria and Tru were killed in a bus crash while on their way to Addis Ababa. It happened on that unforgiving, perilous part of the road at Abayi Sheleqo. No one was spared, not even the driver or his helper."

Ayénat gasped and covered her mouth. Her eyes drilled holes into the ground near her feet. Saba embraced Desta and held him close. The rest of the women clamped their lips and gazed into space. The men wound their gabis up to their noses and stared like deer in the night stunned by torchlight.

Moments later, Ayénat raised the edge of her netela to her nose and began to yowl in a monotonic, skipping cadence. The women, and all of the men, except Damtew, harmonized with her. Desta had lost his voice, his emotions, his feelings and thoughts. He refused to accept the news. He stared blankly into space, listening to the mourners but not registering their emotions.

Saba, who had her arms around Desta's shoulders, tugged him and whispered, "Aren't you going to cry?"

"I will save my tears for the day when I feel the losses," Desta said without looking at her. His daydream was still fresh in his head, and in his mind he was still wearing new shoes and clothes and reveling in front of Tru and Mekuria, happy and excited.

Saba hugged him closer.

The vocalized mourning faded after a while, first the men, then the women. Ayénat was last to stop.

"How did you find out?" Teferra asked in a rough, somber voice.

"I ran into Ejigu, Tru's brother-in-law, when I went to court last week and he told me."

"For those who have never seen it," Teferra said, "the road across the Abayi gorge is like driving around a cliff. It's a miracle there aren't accidents every day."

Abraham cleared his throat. "I know about that road. It's one of the reasons I refuse to go to Addis Ababa."

"You know, Mekuria left the family to live in town at a young age," Ayénat said, wiping her cheeks with the hem of her netela. "We feared that he might get killed by someone during a fight because he had a hot temper, or that he might catch one of those town diseases, like *kitigne*—syphilis. After he married our beautiful Tru, his life changed. He started to live a stable and normal life. Now all that has ended in such a tragic way." She started to weep again.

"Tru was a very unusual young woman, a blessed spirit from head to toe," Saba said, knowing what Tru had meant to Desta.

Desta nodded, his face still a lifeless mask.

"It's unfortunate that such a person's life was cut short like this," Yihoon chimed in.

Desta sighed, trying to ease his mounting tension. Half of his brain still held to the image of Tru and Mekuria he saw earlier.

"Ejigu said there will be a memorial service for them in two weeks, on Sunday," Abraham said. "It will be in their church, outside of Yeedib."

A wave of chatter ensued and all finally agreed that they would attend, except Teferra and his wife, who were going to visit her dying mother.

The family rose, hugged Ayénat, and departed, saying, *Egziabhere Yatsenash*—may God give you strength during your grief.

Saba tapped Desta on the shoulder. "Why don't you come back with me."

"No, I will stay here. Thank you."

"If you suddenly become emotional, you will have somebody to talk to."

"I am fine, Saba, really. Right now I don't feel a thing."

"You heard that Tru and Mekuria are dead?"

"I had not plugged my ears. I heard everything and listened to your crying. Me, I'm not meant to cry now. When it happens, I'd rather be alone. This is how I handled all my previous losses."

"You're strange—different—like we have always known you to be."

"That is me, I guess. Go. Destaye is probably waiting for your return."

Saba embraced Desta and kissed him on the forehead. "I have woven your name on the basket top. You should come and see it. It looks beautiful."

"You have? I look forward to seeing it soon. Thank you!"

Abraham gathered and rolled the skin mats and brought them inside the house.

Desta leaned against the fence, staring at the eastern mountains, lost and confused. The boy knew about death. It's final. It's irreversible. It deprives the living of the joy, love, and friendship they had with the deceased. But this time he was unwilling to accept this fact.

He had been deprived of the love and friendship of his dog, Kooli, after the animal died. When the trees on the property that became Saba's were cut down and burned, the monkeys, birds, and other animals were deprived of their home, and Desta the enjoyment of their friendship. Desta experienced the meaning of death again when his grandfather's spirit left the area after his remains were buried. Those horrible times again tugged at his heartstrings.

Tru and Mekuria were gone forever. He would never see them again. They wouldn't be waiting in their home to receive him when he returned to school. He didn't have anybody else to live with while continuing his education. With nobody to entrust him to, Abraham more than likely would keep him at home to continue with his shepherding, and prepare him for farm work.

Desta felt a tightness in his head. He began to breathe rapidly. He passed his hand over his heart. The muscles in his neck twitched and he became light-headed.

"Come inside and lie down," Abraham said when he noticed Desta's consternation. "I, too, was shocked when I heard about it. What can we do, son? That is how life is." Abraham supported and guided Desta inside the house. He spread a goatskin by the fire and laid Desta down.

"He has not eaten his breakfast. He is probably hungry," Ayénat said. She brought him a platter of freshly baked injera and a tumbler of milk, but Desta refused to eat until his parents insisted. The food seemed unwilling to stay put in Desta's stomach. He braced his chest with his hand in preparation for what seemed to be coming. His stomach churned and his chest heaved. He leaned over the edge of the fire pit and let out onto the ashes a slippery gray liquid. Half an hour later, Ayénat fed him again, but it was as if she was giving him poison. He threw up once more, this time into a wooden bowl Ayénat placed by his side.

Desta's parents looked at each other, mystified. "I think he's just shocked by the news," Abraham said. "I know he and Tru were very close."

"No more food," they said almost in unison. "But give him an extra blanket," Abraham ordered.

Ayénat brought Abraham's old gabi and threw it over Desta's spare frame. His father added more logs to the fire to keep the boy warm. He shook violently for a bit but then calmed down. Abraham and Ayénat eyed each other. "He will be all right. Sleep will help calm him down," Abraham said.

Desta woke early in the evening, just before the animals came home. There was a dull sensation in his brain, like a wound or a bruise. He propped his body up with his arm and stared at the front door, thinking about the events earlier in the day. He remembered the profound jolt when Abraham shared the news of Tru and Mekuria's death, and then recounted the mounting tension within him while everyone was crying.

All the sad feelings that coursed through him had culminated in nausea and tremor. He felt his modern school education had ended before it barely started. A complete stranger who had shown him so much devotion and love was suddenly taken away. He felt alone and out in the cold, to face the world all by himself. He felt scared, sad, and betrayed. Now he might never leave his childhood hole. He might remain here forever, cleaning horse stalls for his mother, working as a shepherd and a farmer. Desta convulsed.

He got up and went outside, taking aimless, angry steps, frustrated by his misfortune. He had no power or control over events like this that had dogged his life. He wished tears would well up and wash away his fear, sorrow, and grief. But his tear-producing places seemed numb and frozen, the way his whole body had been feeling at times.

Night was rapidly falling. Desta returned home, fatigued, hungry, and cold. Mekibeb had already put away the animals. Ayénat had just returned from milking the cows. "Where did you go?" she asked, her brow creased.

"I just wanted to have some private moments. I went on a walk here on the grounds, hoping to ease the pain I have been feeling in my head."

"I know. We feel the same. *Yaltaseb Eta wotobachew new. Min enadergalen. Egziabhare bitcha yawkal.* They met unexpected misfortune. What can we do? Only God has the answer to their sad demise," she said as they entered the house. Desta said nothing.

Abraham was sitting on his stool, caressing his goatee, eyes on the fire. "Sit down, Desta," he said. Desta sat at his usual place beside Abraham, on the part of the floor that circled the fire pit. "I know you're distraught about the loss of Tru and Mekuria. Unfortunately, that is how life sometimes is. Death comes unexpectedly and unannounced, and in a flash we're gone. Sadly, the loss of your uncle and his wife means we have nobody you can live with when school opens.

"This was one of the fears I had from the beginning. Not that I expected they would die, but I worried that if they moved or divorced, you might be forced to stop your education. This, as you know, is the last thing I'd wish to happen, considering the educational tracks of your brothers. I am afraid, though, that may be the case with you as well. I have been racking my head over what we can do. We know nobody close enough in Yeedib to ask that they take you in, and we have no money to pay for your living expenses if you were to board someplace."

Abraham might as well have poured *mitmita*—the spicy hot pepper—over Desta's gaping wound. "I don't want to discuss any of that at the moment, Baba," he snapped. "That is my problem. Not yours anymore!"

"But he can go to our church school," Ayénat said, "if he wants to continue with his learning. "He could become a wonderful priest." She pressed her tongue hard on her palate with the word *wonderful*.

Desta had had enough. He rose, strode across the living room, and went straight to his bed.

"You're not going to eat dinner?" Ayénat asked.

"No. My hunger just went away."

Having discovered his new world, and that he could travel on his own, Desta felt independent and free. But first he wanted to make sure the world beyond the mountains, including the town of Yeedib, was still there. He would rise early in the morning and travel to the mountaintop to assure himself of their existence.

HE WOKE AT MIDNIGHT and found hunger gnawing at his stomach. He gnashed his teeth and stretched his arms. He then quietly rose and blundered his way into the kitchen. He located the mosseb where his mother kept the injera and next to it the pot with the leftover sauce. He lifted the conical lid from the mosseb, peeled the top layer of the bread, and placed it on the upturned lid.

He then removed the cover from the pot and scooped two ladles of sauce onto the injera in the lid. He placed the improvised platter in his lap and ate his dinner in the near darkness. Afterward, he fetched water from a jar in the larder, drank half of it, and washed his hands with the other half. He returned the covers to their containers and went back to his bed.

Desta slept peacefully through the rest of the night on his folded arm, waking with the first crow of the rooster. His head felt clear and tranquil but thoughts of Tru and Mekuria filtered back to his consciousness, and he rolled onto his back to consider them. He wove his fingers behind his head and stared up at the graying night. He wished he could cry and liberate himself from his grief and sadness, but no tears came. Feeling powerless over his emotions, he deeply sighed.

He decided to get up and go outside, where he had the power to do something: look at the eastern peaks, watch the sunrise, listen to the chirping of the birds in the nearby woods, or go to the mountaintop and push rocks downhill all day. Yes, push rocks all day as a tribute to Tru and Mekuria, That's what he must do!

He unwove his fingers, raised his head, and looked around. There was still time before the night faded and light from the rising sun filtered through cracks in the walls and brightened the house.

He placed his head back on his arm and dozed off but woke again shortly after the rooster's last call, announcing the night's passage and the imminence of dawn. Desta sat up, and with his arms bracing his folded knees, thought again about going to the mountaintop and pushing rocks downhill for as long as his body could endure it. He had to do something on behalf of Tru and Mekuria, to celebrate his friendship and their passing.

He quietly put on his shorts and jacket and wrapped his gabi around his shoulders. He hopped down and went to his parents' closet. He grabbed his old cloth pouch from where it hung on the wall. He moved to the larder, opened the mosseb, and pulled out two injeras, folding them into a compartment in his pouch. From the wall in the larder, he took down Abraham's old aluminum canteen, which his father had used when he fought in the Italo-Ethiopian War. Desta filled it with water, securely topped it, and dropped it in the pouch.

He slung the pouch on his left shoulder and walked across the living room to the tool loft above the horse stall. He drew a pick from the pile of axes, sickles, and hoes, and threw it over his shoulder.

Chilled morning air brushed against his cheeks like cold fingers when he stepped on the threshold. He hopped across the island of stones and into the wet grass, past the slush and mud by the entrance. It had rained the night before.

It would be quite a while before the sun rose, but it was light enough for Desta to begin his journey to the mountaintop. Listening to the birds singing in the bushes nearby, Desta walked the trail that went up the mountain above his home.

By the time he reached the mountain's wooded section, the sun had cleared the crest of the eastern peaks and washed the western half of the valley in gold. There was plenty of light now and he could walk through the woods without stumbling and falling over rocks.

Halfway up the mountain, he stopped, feeling tired and hungry. He sat on a stone by the side of the road and ate a breakfast of half an injera and water. As he ate, his eyes roamed over the season's verdure, which now blanketed the entire valley, while his mind roamed from Tru and Mekuria to the implications of their loss on his prospects. He thought of what his parents had said before he went to bed the previous night. *They couldn't have found a better excuse to keep me trapped in this hole the rest of my life.*

He traced a line with his index finger from the middle of his forehead to the tip of his nose, lost in thought. Then he shook his head, trying to chase away his fears and gloomy thoughts. He gathered his things and continued walking up the hill.

Desta smiled when he reached the first plateau and glimpsed the lands far away. At least the world beyond his mountain home was still there. After he climbed the second hill, he could see all the places he discovered when he first came there with Saba: the jagged terrain in the east, the table-like earth in the south, the flat country in the north, and the curving plateau in the west, atop of which sat the town of Yeedib like a roosting hen. *They were all there!* He exhaled happily.

He walked about until he found a spot where he could see both his valley and many of the land features outside it. Recalling that the rock he and Saba sat upon when they came here had views to either side of the peak divide, Desta scampered and perched on the same rock.

He stared at Yeedib's eucalyptus grove. Images of the town's landmarks swirled through his brain, one picture giving way to another, finally settling on Tru and Mekuria's home and with it the realization that they no longer lived in it, having gone to the sky for ever and ever. And he would never live in that house again and walk the shrouded pathway, the place where he had discovered information about the coin and his destiny.

It seemed terribly strange and unfair that what he had thought a beautiful arrangement with great promise, at least from what he had gleaned from the tunnel path measurements, would end up like this. He closed his eyes and tried to block out the images that streamed through his brain, wishing not to believe what had happened.

He thought about what Tru and Mekuria had meant to him. It was in their home that he found peace and security for the first time in his young life. It was with them that he discovered what it felt like to be accepted and appreciated, to realize that he was as good as anybody else, even though he was born two months premature. Tru and Mekuria were the first who promised to shower him with gifts. How much he had looked forward to the most thrilling moment of his life, the pleasure of wearing shoes, sweaters, shirts, and *bolalay*—wide-leg pants. He had imagined himself in these outfits over and over again throughout his long break. Now all those things would remain a dream.

He ate another half injera and chased it down with the water. Because he couldn't express his grief and sorrow with tears, as everyone else had done, he would remember Tru and his uncle Mekuria by pushing and throwing rocks down the mountainside.

A few paces from his perch were a great number of rocks, some small enough that he could lift and throw them with his slender arms. Others the size of a human head he could carry to the edge of the plateau. Even larger rocks he could push or roll to the edge. The mountain here was steep enough that any rock he pushed would fly from the outset, hurtling down to the flatter terrain of his parents' fields.

In the middle of the fallow land below, about a hundred paces from the edge of the mountain, stood the charred remains of a tree. Its two leafless branches point-ed to the sky like someone asking God for provisions or mercy. Desta decided to use this tree as his target, a representation of death—death that had robbed him of his grandfather, his beloved Kooli, and now two of his most favorite people. He would attack death with rocks and all the power he had in him.

He gathered seven of the smaller stones and lined them up near the ledge. He then carried medium-sized stones—one at a time, seven of them—creating a second row behind the first. Finally, making a third row, he rolled the same number of large stones into place behind the others.

He stood up, sighed deeply, and said, "Tru and Mekuria, these twenty-one stones before me serve as tokens of my salute to your passing, to your kindness and love, and the support you extended to me during the four months we knew each other. Although my heart aches from your loss, I have not been able to express my sorrow with tears. I'll throw and push these rocks down this mountain to honor and celebrate you and our friendship, as substitutes for the tears in me that refuse to flow."

He slipped his hand under his jacket and ran his fingers over the coin on his chest as he imagined hitting his target, the dead tree trunk. He picked up the first stone from the first row. He leaned back and extended his load-bearing arm as far as it could go, while his eyes traced a trajectory to the tree. He released the rock with as much force as he could muster, hitting the dead trunk and splintering it.

He picked up the second rock and shot again. He smacked his object, but this time the rock disintegrated on impact, with minimal damage to the trunk. To his amazement, Desta struck the object of his pain with the remaining five stones, riddling it with holes.

He could manage merely rolling the next series of stones. He ran his fingers over his chest again and went to work. He moved the first rock to the edge of the mountain, counted to three, and shoved it with all the power he had left in him. The rock tumbled, bounced, and rolled, gathering speed and power. To the boy's delight it, too, crashed into the dead tree trunk. By the time he delivered the twentieth rock, the battered tree appeared ready to fall, but it was going to take a much bigger rock to knock it down.

While picking his rocks, he had noticed a big boulder—as big as or even slightly bigger than himself. He liked that rock because it looked round, but it was partially buried. *It would be great to dig this rock out and watch it go, but how to dislodge it from the grips of the earth?*

He grabbed his pick and dug the soil from around the boulder. The dirt on one side was packed with stones, making the digging very difficult. Every time he swung the pick, sparks flew. Some of the stones loosened; others didn't budge. The other side was not as bad, and here Desta continued to dig. After much perspiration, huffing, and grunting, he cleared much of the soil.

There was still work to do on the other side. After much more struggle and perspiration, however, he managed to remove the smaller stones and free the big boulder. He sighed with relief and triumph.

Then with a combination of the pick handle as a lever and his own hands, Desta pushed and rolled the rock to the ledge. He looked over the precipice and aimed at the battered tree trunk. Before pushing the boulder, he ran his fingers over his chest once again and focused his mind on his target. He stepped behind the rock and inserted the pick handle underneath it. Holding the metal tip securely with both hands, he lowered himself, which raised the lever and tipped the rock over the edge.

He leaned on the pick and watched the rock as it pounded the earth. It decimated the bushes, flying higher and higher after each strike. The speeding rock struck its target, and Desta's symbol of death stood no more. It shattered into a million pieces, avenging the friends he had lost and his own grief and sorrow.

The rock itself remained whole no more. Upon impact, shards flew in many directions, into his parents' grain fields and into the trees at the bottom of the mountain. From the direction of his parents' grain field, a sharp pained cry pierced the air, but Desta couldn't tell whether it was human or animal.

The boy was happy to express the depth of his feelings through action instead of his tears. He was also exhausted, hungry, and thirsty. He ate the second injera and drank several swigs of the water from the canteen. He then spread his gabi and lay down on it, buttressing his head against the pick handle, and closed his eyes. He wanted to rest before he went home.

When he woke two hours later, he found the part of his gabi surrounding his head drenched in cool water. Desta knew it was neither perspiration nor rain nor spilled water from his canteen. *Finally!*

The sun had tilted down the western sky. He needed to get home before it got dark. He gathered his things and headed home, relieved of his sorrows and grief, at least for now.

SEVENTEEN

On Monday people had started to come to pay tribute to the deceased couple, and visitors would continue arriving over the ensuing weeks. These were mostly friends and relatives from across the Davola River who had heard in church on Sunday about the death of Ayénat's brother and his wife. They came alone or in groups of two and three and four. When Desta saw visitors from a distance, he would dash to the house and tell Ayénat to be ready to receive them. She would quickly throw her netela over her shoulders, wrap part of it around her, and step outside.

The moment she saw the visitors, she would tip her head forward and rub her brow with a section of her netela for a few seconds. Then she would stand erect, cover her mouth with a part of the fabric, and yowl, sometimes reciting mournful lyrics and sometimes simply intoning sad sounds. The guests hummed their own sad sounds and words or yowled with her. At other times Ayénat would say *wondemalem*—my brother, my world.

Desta thought his mother was being insincere by calling him her world, the half-brother who hardly ever came to visit her or she to see him. Mekuria to her was only a brother in name.

After the yowling and crying, which lasted five minutes or so, the guests and Ayénat greeted one another. Then she would invite them to sit down and visit, on a log or a skin mat she would have someone bring from the house. They talked mostly about Mekuria and Tru, how they died, where they lived, whether they had children. Once they finished talking about the departed, they talked about one another's well-being, their farms, and their animals. In the end, Ayénat invariably invited the visitors to come inside and get something to eat. If it was a weekday, the guests would just as invariably decline, saying they had work to get back to. If they came on the weekend, though, and were close relatives, they would come inside, get something to eat and drink, and visit some more.

In the first days of grieving, the novelty of the ritual was intriguing to Desta. He watched the guests and listened to their mournful singing and yowling. Later, he got tired of the visitors and even found their crying and talking about Tru and Mekuria depressing. As soon as he placed the mats for them, he would retreat to the back of the house. Then people just stopped coming—either all those who were considered relatives or friends had come, or there were no more who cared enough to come—ending Ayénat's two weeks-long public mourning.

ONE WEEKDAY EVENING, Desta and Abraham had a conversation about his returning to Yeedib when school opens later in September.

"I need to go back, even though I have no one to live with anymore," Desta said, struggling with his feelings.

"I want you to go back. I talked to your teacher the other day while I was in town. I told him what happened to your uncle and his wife, and he said we should do our best to find an alternative arrangement. Unfortunately, we know nobody that you can stay with. I have talked to friends and acquaintances and none are willing to have you in their home. They have their own children to look after," Abraham said grimly.

Ayénat butted in. "I say he should stay here until after January, when the harvest is over, if he continues to insist that he attend that kind of school. I'm trying to take custody of my niece's two daughters, and that won't happen until three or four months from now. I have told you about this," she said to Abraham.

"I cannot be missing school, Ma," Desta said. "I don't want to fall behind my classmates."

"Your father just told you that we have nobody you can live with. The only option you have, which will be good for all of us, is for you to return in January. I will have my helpers by then and the harvesting season will be over," Ayénat said. "By that time, we may even find someone you can live with," she added cheerily.

Abraham studied Desta. "What do you think?"

"I understand what you're saying, but I think this is also an easy excuse for mother to keep me here. I really think I should go back to school when it opens next week."

"If you could stay through January," Ayénat said, "I will sell one of my goats and buy you shoes. I know you've been dreaming about them for the past two months."

"You just found the solution, Ma. If you can afford to sell a goat, how about you sell one and hire a helper with the money. Shoes are not that important to me, Ma." Desta held his mother's eyes. "My education and finding the second coin are!"

"There is no point in discussing this anymore," Abraham said, tapping Desta on the shoulder. "Let me see what else I can do in Yeedib. I am going there this weekend." He rose to go to bed.

"I will come to Yeedib with you," Desta said, fixing to go to bed himself.

"What will you do there?"

"I will talk to some of Tru and Mekuria's friends and see if they will let me live with them."

"You're pretty determined about this, aren't you?" Ayénat barked.

"Yes, I am, Ma," Desta said, heading to bed.

Ayénat's lips quivered, but no word came from them.

ON THE APPOINTED SATURDAY MORNING, Abraham came to Desta's bed and shook him lightly until he woke. "We need to leave early. I have to be at the courthouse before my name is called."

They quickly ate breakfast and left while the sunlight was still up in the mountains. The thought that he wouldn't see Tru and Mekuria in Yeedib was heart–wrenching for the boy. *I have to be strong and bear this loss as I have all my other losses.* One of the things he had learned in his young life was to endure. He had gone through so much already that he knew he could handle this.

A medley of many aromas mingled with the fragrance of freshly roasted coffee and eucalyptus leaves greeted Abraham and Desta as they approached the market.

Bright morning sunlight shimmered off brand-new corrugated tin rooftops and scattered in dazzling colors as it shone on the bottles of homemade whis-key that the farmer women had brought to sell. The same light glowed from the pleated red, blue, and green dresses the women wore, and the purple- and pink-bordered netelas draped over their shoulders.

Abraham stopped when they reached the open grounds and turned to Desta. "Go talk to whomever you want to talk to. When you're done, come to the court-house and look for me."

Desta welcomed the suggestion. He visited six couples and a single woman. The couples gave him many different reasons they couldn't have him in their homes. One said their income was barely enough to support their own family, while another was nursing a mother with a broken foot and didn't have extra room. A retired couple, whom Desta thought would be the best candidate because they knew him well and could use an errand boy around the house, also said no. Their *yetureta genzeb*—retirement income—was barely enough for them. The fourth and fifth couples had other excuses, real and imagined. They all said they admired him for his dedication to his studies and for being a good student, but none of them had the heart or the wherewithal—or the space in their homes.

The single woman's name was Yengus. She was a personal friend of Teferra. She supported herself by selling tella and tea and only God knows what else. Yengus had always treated Desta like he was a close relative, giving him a loaf of bread with tea every time he went to see her. If Desta could have chosen whom to live with, it would definitely have been her. But the last time Desta visited Yengus, she had said she and Teferra were no longer on speaking terms.

When Desta arrived at Yengus's house, he found three women sitting on a skin mat on the floor, studying the bottoms of their fist-sized, multicolored coffee cups. There was coffee brewing in a clay kettle over glowing charcoal in a square-topped aluminum burner. A column of white smoke from incense burning in a piece of clay by the entrance swayed gently before it vanished into the air. The fragrance of the incense and aroma of the coffee were invigorating.

Yengus greeted Desta happily. She kissed him three times on the cheeks and led him inside, holding him by the hand. The other women set their cups on the floor beside the skin mats and looked absently at the visitor. After a brief chitchat about Desta's vacation and why Yengus had not seen Teferra for a long time, they turned to the main purpose of his visit. "I'd be delighted for you to live with me, so long as your father gives me money for part of my rent and brings us some teff for injera and peas and butter for our sauces."

"I don't know about the money part, but he will bring the teff and peas. My mother controls the butter, so I'm not sure about that."

"Ah-ha," Yengus puffed. "If he brings us enough teff each month, that will be okay. We can always sell a part of it and buy butter with the money."

The women picked up their empty cups, tipped them, and again peered inside to study what was on the bottom. One showed hers to another woman, pointing into the cup. She touched her head to the other's, whispered something, and they both burst out laughing.

"Thank you for your willingness to take me," Desta said. "I will tell my father what you said." He got up to go, but he was dying to find out what the women were seeing in their cups that they found amusing. "Do you mind if I ask you a question?" he said to Yengus.

"Sure," Yengus said with a nod.

"What is funny about those cups?"

"Ahh, they are just being silly. They are seeing things in the coffee grounds that they think will bring them good fortune today."

"Oh, that is exactly what I need. Can I take a look?"

Yengus picked up one of the cups. "I was studying this one before you came." She tilted the cup against the incoming sunlight and pointed inside. "You see, there is a gentleman riding a beautiful horse. He is followed by a group of young men, who my friend Asqual thinks are his *ashkers*—boy servants. From the way he is dressed, he looks very rich. Asqual thinks he might pay her a visit this evening."

Desta squinted at the black residue and saw nothing but trailing coffee granules arranged into a long, tapering V from the top to the bottom of the cup. He thought of what Hibist used to say after she failed to see the animals and objects he pointed at in the clouds: "Desta, you're just imagining things." He wondered whether the women were making up the people they claimed to be seeing or whether these people were simply not revealed to ordinary human beings like him.

" Interesting, and thank you—I need to go," was all Desta could manage to say.

"Give my s*elam* to your brother. I hope your living with me will give him an added reason to come and see us."

"I will," Desta said as he stepped out of the house. He was anxious and excited to see his father.

"ANY LUCK?" Abraham asked.

"I think so, but it all will depend on you. A woman named Yengus said she will be happy to take me if you bring her money, teff, peas, and butter every month."

"She said that?" Abraham asked, his voice tinged with surprise. "Who is she?"

"She used to be a friend of Teferra."

"I know about those types of women. It wouldn't work, son."

When Desta asked why, Abraham replied, "A woman like that will use the grains we give her to feed her friends, people like Teferra. She won't care for you."

When Desta pressed his father, Abraham answered in more vague and cryptic language. The topic sounded complicated and the boy stopped asking any more questions.

Abraham and Desta ate lunch at a small grass-roofed restaurant and left for home by mid-afternoon. Ayénat appeared to be on pins and needles when they arrived, and they had barely gotten into the house before she asked, "Did you find anyone for him?" Her small eyes darted from Abraham to Desta.

"No, I didn't," Abraham said. "Desta found a single woman who would take him in but she wanted grains and other things from us."

"Who is she?" Ayénat inquired warily.

"She is somebody I know and Teferra knows," Desta answered.

"Is she *shermuta*—prostitute?"

"I suspect so," Abraham said.

"Forget it, Desta!" Ayénat exclaimed, glaring at the boy. "You have no business living with a single woman like that." Desta kept quiet. Asking his mother to explain what was wrong with a woman like Yengus would only aggravate the situation and rile her even more. "Besides," she continued, "what's the hurry? He can go back to his schooling once we find a reputable family for him to live with. Like I said, we need him here for the next few months. When we're done with harvest and I have helpers here in the house, he can go."

"He can go now if he wants to," Abraham said, almost as if he were talking to himself. "We can always arrange for help. The problem is his dependence on others during the many years he will be going to school."

Desta was surprised at his father's response. "Are you saying I should stop my learning altogether?"

"I guess so. If you don't stop now, you will no doubt be forced to stop at some point later, when there is absolutely no one who can offer you a place to stay." Abraham fixed his big eyes on the boy. "Why postpone it? Why waste your time?"

Desta had a sick, twisted feeling in his stomach. He stared at the fire for a long time, debating in his mind if he should accept his father's pronouncement on the fate of his education. But Desta intended not only to earn a modern education but also to find the Coin of Magic and Fortune he was fated to.

"You don't have to stop learning if that is what you really want," Ayénat said.

"Go to the local schools where you don't have to worry about finding someone to live with and how you get your food."

Abraham said, "This modern education thing that our *negus*—king—brought into our country is partly the problem. Spoiling students, buying them this and that, providing them with a place to stay and food to eat. It's too expensive and too complicated."

"I know," Ayénat concurred. "You don't have to do any of that with our church school students. They fend for themselves. That's why I have been telling him to stay here." She was pleased by her husband's unexpected switch to her line of thinking.

Now that Abraham was in agreement with Ayénat, Desta felt like a door was rapidly closing on him. He'd had enough. He got up and went straight to bed.

THE FOLLOWING MORNING Desta said to his father, "Baba, I have a solution to my problem of finding someone to live with."

"Tell me."

"How about I live with my sisters Enat and Tenaw."

"You want to walk two hours each way, every day?"

"Why not? I am sure I can do it."

"Tell you what, if you are that driven about this modern school thing, I will go talk to them myself and see whether we can arrange that. I am sure they wouldn't mind."

Desta had to rein in his excitement. He saw a glimmer of hope to his ordeal.

The following day, Abraham went to talk to Enat and Tenaw. In the evening he returned to tell Desta, much to the chagrin of Ayénat, that his sister and husband would be happy to have him live with them while he goes to school. The only drawback they both said was the distance Desta had to travel every day to and from the school. To Desta this arrangement is next to none and he was willing to walk three hours each way so long as he can continue his education.

Nearly two weeks after the school opened, he began to live with Enat and Tenaw, and resume his pursuit of a modern education.

EIGHTEEN

For Desta, living in the country with Enat and Tenaw and walking two hours each way to and from school was a greater problem than just the sheer distance he had to travel every day. He rose before dawn, ate his breakfast, and left for school early because if he was even a few minutes late, he would get a whipping from one of the teachers. When school closed at five o'clock, he left quickly to arrive home while it was still light for fear of becoming a meal for the hyenas.

Enat and Tenaw had no kerosene lamp by which he could read or do his homework. With no light and forced to get up early to make the long trek to school, he went straight to bed after dinner. This pattern repeated five days a week for the entire first semester of Desta's second grade. He turned eleven on January seven, at the end of his first semester of second grade.

It was because of this impractical, unsustainable, and unproductive living arrangement that Abraham decided to take Desta to the town of Dangila, one and a half days journey on foot, and so he could go to a new school and live with Zewday, a distant relative, and his family. The rest of the family thought Abraham was out of his mind to leave an eleven-year-old boy with people who were little more than complete strangers. No one else had even heard of Zewday.

When Saba asked Abraham why he didn't find someone in their little town of Yeedib who could provide Desta a place to stay, the father replied, "A relative, however distant, will not let him go hungry. The common sacred blood that courses between them will oblige the relative to share even the very last bread they might have."

Desta was taken aback by Abraham's flawed logic, because he would never expect such goodwill from his own brother Damtew. His father's assertion also seemed to mean that people who were not blood relatives could never have it in them to extend the ultimate in kindness and devotion. Tru was not his relative and she had meant a lot more to Desta than his own mother.

To the boy, family relations had always been nominal. But he didn't argue with or challenge Abraham because any reason that took him farther from home, and into a greater part of the world, he welcomed with open arms. He was both anxious and excited to go to the famed town of Dangila.

I couldn't have asked for a better birthday gift, a birthday nobody in my family even acknowledges that I have. Desta realized that traveling to and living in Dangila had many advantages. Among other things, the trip would fulfill his dream of seeing Kuakura, the seven-hundred-acre farm estate his grandmother had abandoned that was his father's birthplace.

Desta's Aunt Zere had invited Abraham and the rest of the family to attend, at the end of January, the annual, Batha Mariam—Saint Mary's church holiday celebration in Kuakura, which was on their way to Dangila. This meant Desta would have a chance to watch the famed horse races that were part of this event—races his grandfather used to compete in.

The Dangila school ran through the eighth grade, so Desta could complete his primary education in one town, as opposed to finishing the fourth grade in Yeedib and then the fifth through eighth grades in Finote Selam or Burie, where his family had no relatives with whom Desta could live. Another advantage was that Dangila was closer to Bahir Dar, the town by Lake Tana where Desta might look for the person with the magic coin.

"I know we're taking a chance on this man Zewday," Abraham said to Desta one evening as they sat by the fire. "I have not seen him for over three years, and I don't know if he will be amenable to the idea of having you at his home. Do you still want to go?"

"The only risk is missing two weeks of classes at the Yeedib school. I think I can afford to do that."

"In that case, we'll go next Saturday, in time to arrive for the Batha Mariam festival."

On Thursday evening, while Abraham and Desta were feeding the mookit goats from separate baskets, Saba appeared. She greeted father and son, and then she sat down on the bench with Abraham. "Yihoon and I talked about your decision to take Desta to Dangila, and we think it's a mistake. God forbid if something bad happened to him; we wouldn't know soon enough to go see him."

"Saba, his current living arrangement with Enat and Tenaw has not worked out well for him. Zewday and his wife, Mebet, are good people. They will take good care of him."

"Yes, Baba, but he's only eleven years old. It worries us that a country boy who's barely been out of this valley will be left behind in a big town like Dangila."

"What do you think might happen to him?"

"I don't know. He might get lost, or someone might take advantage of him—anything."

Desta said, "Saba, I appreciate your concern, but I'm not a sheep or a goat to get lost. I've thought about this opportunity for some time, since Baba broached it with me a month back. I'm excited to go. I'm anxious to see that lady you saw, the one with milk-white skin and yellow hair, among other things." Desta smiled.

"Seeing that *Ferenge*—white—lady won't do you any good. But seriously, if you were fourteen years old, Yihoon and I wouldn't be so bothered. . . ."

"Saba, Saba," called out Abraham.

She turned to her father.

"You're fretting over imaginary things. The boy will be with a relative. My sister's children go to Dangila just about every Saturday, and I'll make sure they check on him. Okay?"

"*Indalh*—whatever you say. . .," Saba countered.

"Tell Yihoon not to worry," her father said.

"When are you going?" she asked.

"This coming Saturday," Desta and Abraham said in unison.

As Saba rose to go home, Ayénat came out with something in her hand. The two women greeted each other. Saba asked her stepmother, "What do you think of Desta going all the way to Dangila for his schooling?"

"I don't like it, but I've long given up on those two. The boy has his father wound around his little finger and makes him do whatever he pleases." Ayénat pursed her lips in disgust and spat.

"I just think . . ." Saba lost her train of thought. Ayénat's venomous air had caught her off guard. She began to walk home.

"Wait," Ayénat said. "Frankly, Saba, wasn't it you and Laqechi who pleaded with your father to put Desta into modern school, disrupting our lives and our futures? Why didn't you think about these problems before you decided to meddle? If you didn't care what would happen to him then, why are you so worried now?"

"I'm sorry, Ayénat. We were only trying to fulfill the boy's dream of getting a modern education."

"At our expense?"

"What do you mean? Are you saying he shouldn't have his own life and choices?"

"Farming is his life, like every boy born and raised in this valley. As for his choice of modern schooling, he could have tried to be a priest like Tamirat had wanted to be." Ayénat looked away dreamily.

Saba shook her head. She realized that nothing she could say was going to change Ayénat's mind. "Well, I need to go home now," she said. She shook her head, saddened by Ayénat's stubborn ways. She began to walk home but a few seconds later turned back. "Ayénat, I hope someday you'll have it in you to forgive Desta for trying to do something other than what you want him to do."

"Pfff," hissed Ayénat. "Be of service to your mother," she said to Desta, "and return this to Melkam." She handed a wide-mouthed, cylindrical aluminum pot to the boy.

For a brief moment Desta didn't see or hear his mother, although she was only a few feet away. What he had just heard had numbed all his senses.

"Desta, your mother wants you to take that pot to Melkam," Abraham said, waking the boy from his daze.

Desta rose and sauntered toward Damtew and Melkam's home, across the southern creek, where Saba and Yihoon had lived. Halfway en route he stopped, switched the pot to his left hand, opened his right, and stared absentmindedly at his fingers. Starting with his pinkie, he counted "one, two," pointing with the pad of his thumb. *That's how many days left before I leave home, before I feel free again.* In his imagination he was already falling in love with Zewday and his wife, Mebet. Tru and Mekuria had given him an idea of how loving and kind distant relatives and complete strangers could be. He could barely wait to meet them.

NOW THAT DESTA WOULD BE GOING to live and attend school in a completely new place, he had to do two things before he left. One, he needed to transfer onto skin parchment the images of the coin and coin box, as well as the coins' twenty-one legends, from the original goatskin illustration his grandfather's spirit had created. Two, he had to learn and practice how to smile.

For the first task, Desta rummaged through Abraham's storage chest one evening. He discovered the desired parchment, rolled and tied with string. He unrolled it and noticed that it had nothing written on it. It measured roughly seven by twelve inches. He smiled, pleased. Looking further in the box, he found a blue inkwell and split-tip reed pen, both of which must have belonged to his brother Tamirat when he was in church school. Desta went deeper still into the box; he found the original goatskin rolled tightly and covered with a cloth. He was ecstatic.

He spent half of the following day carefully copying the images of the coins and their legends. He also made an illustration of the coin box, which he positioned at the bottom of the parchment. Once done, he rolled the original goatskin, covered it with the cloth, and returned it along with the inkwell and the pen to Abraham's chest. Then he rolled up his new parchment, brought it home, and put it in his bursa with his notebooks.

For the second task, he had told himself he would practice how to smile a while back, when he started living in Yeedib. But he had never actually done anything about it. This time he must. It will make him happy when he is sad and encourage people to be more friendly toward him.

However, Desta didn't really know what he looked like when he smiled. He rarely saw himself in a mirror, and when he did, he had no reason to grin. He needed to find out about this important facial expression and practice smiling while he was still at home. That way he would be better prepared for the different people he was bound to see in the new town.

From his mother's clothes basket he fetched her little round mirror, in its silver case, and went to the back of the house with it. After he sat down on the grass, he pulled the mirror out of its case and held the piece in the palm of his hand. He stared at his own reflection. He was surprised to see that his excitement about his trip to Kuakura and Dangila was not just in his head. It had also splashed across his face. His dark olive skin glowed, while glints of light shot off the pupils of his eyes. He grinned. "So that's what I look like when I'm happy, huh?" he said under his breath. "Not too bad. If I were a stranger and met a boy with a kind face like this, I certainly wouldn't mind being friends with him." He smiled again, comforted by the thought that if he could show his smiling face at all times, he would have plenty of friends in school and in town.

Then he wanted to know how many different smiles he could register on his face. To find this out, he began by parting his lips and showing his teeth. Then he held his lips closed and pulled the corners of his mouth outward, into a grin. Next he held his lips firmly in place and beamed, without showing his teeth. Afterward he held his face steady and let his eyes do the smiling.

From these simple exercises, Desta discovered that there are many different ways to smile and that each smile conveys a different meaning: suspicion, doubt, surprise, sarcasm, and maybe even disdain, particularly in those grins in which the eyes were actively involved. All these were forced smiles of course, but the messages they contained were still the same. The best smile for him was the one that came from his heart; it was a smile that made him feel good when it showed up on his face and one that would cause people to smile back.

Then the boy conjured up different attitudes people might show toward him: coldness, distance, disdain, warmth, indifference. He thought about how people could also sometimes be rude or insulting. In all these circumstances his response would be kind words and a cheerful smile. He imagined himself smiling when someone greeted him for the first time. He saw his smiling face as he said good-bye to someone and laughed openly in situation in which he found amusing. After committing these scenarios to memory, he closed the mirror and came home. He returned it to its place in Ayénat's box.

ON THE DAY OF THEIR DEPARTURE to Kuakura, Abraham and Desta rose early, ate their breakfast, and prepared to go. Abraham harnessed their horse, Dama, threw grandpa's beautiful multicolored cover over the saddle seat, and festooned the harness and the cascading straps along the horse's flanks with strands of colorful yarn.

"Are you planning to showcase this horse?" asked Ayénat, surprised by the care Abraham took to decorate the stallion.

"God willing, I plan to take part in the races, even if I have to do it solo," he replied, his eyes on his busy hands.

"At your age . . . why now?"

"I know. Taking part in one of these races in honor of my father has always been my dream. I don't want to die without fulfilling it."

"Whatever you do, I hope you don't plan to engage in the mock battle scenes," Ayénat warned, and then went inside.

"Go get your things," Abraham said to Desta. He hitched the horse to a fence post and went inside. Desta followed right behind.

A little later Desta returned with his books in his cloth pouch. He threw the hanger onto the pommel and looped it a couple of times. He untied the horse's lead from the fence post and waited for his father.

Abraham came out with his walking stick, Ayénat trailing behind. Desta waved good-bye when he saw his mother, but when Abraham said, "Is that all?" he handed the lead to his father and toddled over to his mother.

Ayénat stood by the entrance, one hand holding the doorjamb, looking as dejected as someone who had lost a wrestling match. When Desta bent to kiss her knee, she let go the door, stooped and kissed him on the brow.

"Perhaps I should not be surprised that you seem so excited about this trip," Ayénat said bitterly. "I hope that Zewday and his wife are still in town and that they take you in happily." The hollowness of her words resonated deeply in her voice. Desta didn't feel they deserved a response. He simply walked off.

"We'll see," said Abraham to Ayénat. "Make sure the animals and our home are kept safe."

"We are all in the Lord's hands. I cannot keep us safe, but He will."

Father and son and horse had not come to the end of the fence when a frantic voice called after them. It was Saba. They stopped and waited for her.

"I made these *dabo kolo*—small rolled dried bread—you can snack on until you get to Kuakura. If you don't finish them, Desta can bring them to Dangila. They can keep his fingers and mouth busy while he is studying," said Saba, smiling at her brother.

"Saba," Abraham said, his eyes going wide. "That's way too much."

"I'm sure you'll regret having said that when you're hungry later and these rolls come in handy. . . . Look," she said, hanging the bag of dabo kolo over the pommel, "Dama will appreciate them too, as they counterbalance Desta's books from the other side. Right, good steed?" She patted and rubbed the horse's great neck.

Dama waggled his head and flapped his ears as if in agreement, and Desta smiled at the easy communication between Dama and his sister. Abraham just shook his head, watching Saba's swift, industrious motion.

"Don't worry. . . . Like I said, whatever is left, bring them to Dangila with you. They can be a helpful snack to Desta when he returns from school."

Desta's eyes brimmed, touched by Saba's thoughtfulness.

"Don't be emotional over nothing," Saba said, opening her arms. "Come! Let's hug and kiss before we part."

Desta was overwhelmed by a sudden surge of emotion that immobilized his limbs and deadened his senses. When his tears began to flow, his feelings returned. He handed the lead to Abraham and let Saba's wings enfold him. The boy cried more intensely, finding his sister's warm embrace a safe haven to let out all that had been pent up inside—his mother's cold, intense hatred never seemed to let up, and it had frozen his heart that morning once again.

Saba rested her chin on Desta's head and wept, too. When the tears finally gave way to relief and serenity, they let go of each other. She mopped her cheeks with the sleeve of her gown, swabbed her nose with her finger, and flung her sniffles to the side. Desta dabbed his face and eyes with the hem of his gabi and exhaled deeply.

"I know you were hurt by what your mother said the other day," Saba said, resting her arm over the boy's shoulder. "Don't think I wasn't, too. I saw the expression on your face and I was deeply bothered. But thank God we can have moments like these to find solace for anger and resentments. Tears are your best medicine. Don't be afraid to cry." Saba nudged Desta's shoulder to see if he was listening.

"I agree," Desta said, grasping her long fingers. "Thanks for the relief, and I'll remember your advice. I can walk happily now."

"You're welcome! Be strong. Everything will be all right. If we can manage it, Yihoon and I will come visit you."

"It will be a great joy."

Saba kissed him warmly three times on both cheeks. "One more thing," she said, pulling out something wrapped in a cloth and tied with string. "These are rosemary seeds. Whenever you feel sad or depressed, take out this little bundle and smell it. It can be a good remedy."

Desta took the gift, brought it to his nose, and sniffed. The aroma filled his entire being with a warm, mollifying sensation. He put it in his pocket.

"Go on," Saba said. She tapped his shoulders, and left.

Abraham wiped his eyes. "That's Saba for you. All heart . . . just all heart."

Desta could only nod. He had not fully recovered from the surge of emotion.

"Now we just need to pray that Zewday and his wife will be at home and be willing to have you in their home," Abraham said, handing the horse's lead to Desta.

"For now, I don't even want to think or worry about what may or may not happen," the boy said, poised to get back on the road. "This moment is too special to waste it on something we can deal with in the days ahead."

"Good thinking," his father replied. "Desta, sometimes you come up with ideas that are beyond your age. Thank you. I can use that philosophy myself."

They took their regular road to the Davola River. At the caravan route, they turned left to go north. As this was after harvest and the middle of the week, there were very few people traveling or working the fields along the river.

Desta walked in front, holding the horse's lead. Abraham followed behind the animal and sometimes walked alongside Dama or Desta. The first time Desta had walked that road was when he went to church with his mother to receive communion for the dog disease his parents thought he might have contracted. It was then that Desta discovered the existence of other lands outside of his valley; Ayénat had pointed and said, "That's Kuakura, your father's birthplace."

He was finally going to that mystical land with the strange name. From the fragments of stories his father had shared about his boyhood, Desta imagined Kuakura to be a beautiful place covered with lush pastures and dotted with rolling hills. *Green grass grew so abundantly that cows which fed on it came home spraying their path with milk*, Abraham said at the time.

Shortly after they emerged from the Timble forest, Desta saw something that stopped him in his tracks. "Walk around it, walk around it—wide!" shouted Abraham after noticing what Desta was gazing at nervously.

"Who left that food and dead chicken on those banana leaves?" Desta asked, covering his mouth with his hand. Flies swarmed over the meat and sauce-soaked injera.

Abraham studied the hideous victual from afar. "Probably someone whose family member was sick with a disease that wouldn't go away. They hoped whatever had ailed them would be left here with the food and then travel elsewhere. They normally do this on a weekend when there is more human traffic."

"This is very strange," Desta said, afraid.

Abraham looked up at the sun. "Don't worry, Desta. Other people have probably passed by here already. Whatever disease came with that food probably went with them."

Desta was still afraid and worried. He didn't want to get sick and end up abandoning his trip and returning home.

The farther they walked the flatter the terrain got, making Desta feel they were going into the bottom of the earth. There were no mountains or far horizons. The lower edge of the sky vanished in a blue-gray mist. He stopped and turned to his father. "Is Kuakura flat like here?"

"Most of it is."

"How about Dangila?"

"All of it."

Desta wondered whether he would be happy living in a place where the land was as flat as his mother's baking pan. But he quickly realized that *choice* was not an option in his current circumstances. So long as Zewday and his wife accepted him, he could live without the luxury of looking at mountains and distant horizons.

The sibilant sound of a river, faint and far away at first, became louder and closer. Desta was about to ask what the river was called when Abraham preemptively said, "We are about to cross the Abayi River. Grab the horse's lead."

Desta was surprised. "The same Abayi that starts near Yeedib?"

"Yes, Abayi is the mother into which nearly all other creeks and rivers flow."

Desta wrapped the lead around his folded hand twice.

They hopped from rock to rock in the first and last section of the river, where the water was shallow, and waded through the deeper portion, in the middle. Desta felt at ease once they had crossed, as if he had left all his grief and sorrow on the other side.

Abraham suggested they rest and eat some of Saba's dabo kolo before they continued. He took down the bag containing the dry rolls from the pummel and untied the string at its opening. They sat down on the river bank with the open bag between them and munched on the rolls, listening to Abayi and thinking of Saba and appreciating her provision. Once they had enough of the rolls, they cupped their hands and drank from the great river. Dama helped himself to the lush tufts from along the bank and drank to his heart's content. Then they rose. After Abraham closed and mounted the bag on to the pummel, they pressed on.

All around them flat-topped acacia trees arrayed the land over thorny shrubs and waist-high grass. Bird nests of twigs hung from the tree branches like ornaments. It was as if they had entered a church courtyard.

After walking for an hour among the acacias, they emerged onto an open, gently sloping panoramic terrain. Rectangular white, gray, and golden stubble punctuated the land like a checkered blanket. The surrounding environment was scorched and dreary—the grass and bushes appearing not to have had water for months. The only sign of life was a smudge of green under the creeping shadow of the eastern hills.

Desta looked up at the setting sun, hoping they still had some distance to go before they reached the beautiful and lush land of Kuakura—the birthplace of his father—where grass grew abundantly.

"How long before we get to Kuakura, Baba?"

"We are in Kuakura, a part of it. Those homes over there are Aunt Zere's and her children's." Abraham pointed to a cluster of circular, grass-roofed homes in the middle of a brown patch a couple of miles ahead.

Desta didn't know what to think, but he felt somehow cheated again, the way he felt when he first climbed the mountain above his home. The sky and clouds he imagined were there had vanished when he finally made it to the top. Kuakura, too, was not the green meadows full of cattle, horses, sheep, and goats he had imagined it to be.

Almaw, Aunt Zere's youngest son, was the first to greet Abraham and Desta. After the ritual of three kisses on the cheeks, Almaw took the horse's lead from Desta and hitched it to a fence post.

"I will remove the harness and saddle shortly and give him hay," Almaw said as he led them to the biggest of the three homes.

Flaming fires in the living room and kitchen brightened and warmed the home. A half-dozen men and three women rose when the guests and Almaw entered the house. Two other women, one with her head partially veiled and eyes closed, the other with a toddler nursing at her breast, remained seated. The veiled woman clutched a wooden-bead rosary in her lap with both hands. She moved her head one way then the other at the sound of the shuffling feet. The nursing woman rocked and tipped her head at the guests, causing the large silver cross on her chest to flash in the firelight.

"Sit down, sit down," Abraham said with a wave of his big hand.

Almaw bent before the woman with the rosary and spoke into her ear. "Ma, we have new guests."

"Who?" she asked, turning to the source of the voice.

"*Gashé*—honorific—Abraham and Desta."

"Good heavens! What a blessed surprise!" Aunt Zere cried as she brushed back the hem of her netela from her face.

"Bend down and kiss her knee," whispered Abraham to Desta.

Desta hesitated, but Abraham pushed on his back and he took a step toward the old woman.

"Ma, Desta wants to kiss your knee," Almaw said.

"Come, come, blessed child, I will kiss your knee instead," Zere said, fumbling her hand in the air to reach the boy. She touched Desta's hand as if by accident as the boy bent down to kiss her knee. She squinted her left eye and grabbed the boy's hand, pulling it toward her. She embraced him with both arms and then tipped her head and kissed the boy's knee.

"Era—unthinkable," Abraham gasped. "An old woman kissing the knee of a boy?"

Zere held Desta's hand and turned to the other guests. "This is the young man I was telling you about, the one to whom our father's spirit chose to communicate the location of our family treasure and his remains, ultimately bringing peace and freedom to our family."

All gazed at the boy with incredulity.

"Ma," Almaw said, "they are probably tired, thirsty, and hungry. Let them sit down first."

"Yes, of course. Abraham, I didn't mean to forget you. Come let me kiss you, too. Probably not your knee," she said, chuckling. "After all, I am six years older than you."

Aunt Zere let go of Desta. Abraham stooped and kissed his sister three times on alternate cheeks. He then greeted the rest of the people, kissing the cheeks of those he knew and shaking the hands of those he didn't.

"Sit down, sit down," Aunt Zere said, gesturing with her hand, her eyes barely open.

Two guests who had arrived earlier were sitting across from Zere, on the other side of the fireplace. These men rose and moved to the back, giving up their places to the newly arrived. "How are your eyes?" Abraham asked his sister.

"Not good, Abraham, not good," Zere replied. "Strong lights bother me a great deal. I barely open them when I go out of doors or when I am sitting near a fire. I stumble around like a bat, always shielding my eyes with my hand. If I keep them open for any period of time, they begin to tear profusely. I'm really in bad shape, my dear. . . . Never mind about my problem. Tell me about Ayénat, the rest of the children, and your animals."

Abraham explained that they were all fine, and that the children and Ayénat had sent their good wishes to her and were sorry they could not come.

A young woman brought tumblers of tella for Abraham and Desta. "Please bring water for their hands, shortly," Zere told her. "I bet they are very hungry. It's an all-day journey from where they have come."

All the guests washed their hands, and dinner was served. A beeswax candle affixed to the side of the roof-bearing post provided most of the lighting. Abraham and some of the other guests ate from one mosseb while another group ate from a second mosseb.

Aunt Zere and Desta ate together from a third. Zere felt special. She was sitting with the boy chosen by her father's spirit, who had freed her from the bondages of her past and brought her peace and happiness. This was the first time Desta had sat down to eat with a grown-up and he felt important.

"How old are you, son?" Zere asked, barely cracking her eyes. "You must be a shepherd by now."

"Turned eleven early this month. . . . No, I'm in school."

"Where, at your parents' church?"

"No, I am in *asquala temareebet*—modern school—in town."

"Ye Ferenge temareebet? What good will it do for you or your future? That is just like Abraham, he falls for novelty easily."

"No, it's my decision."

"No, son," Zere said. "That kind of education will do no good for you or your community because you can never become a priest. . . . But it's not my business."

Desta shrugged.

"Where are you learning that education?"

"In Yeedib, but I cannot go there anymore. Baba said I can learn it in Dangila with our relatives there."

"Maybe I'll convince Abraham to put you at our church school instead," Aunt Zere said. Desta couldn't tell whether she was grinning or frowning. Whatever she had meant to convey, it got lost in her wrinkles.

Desta raised his eyes and stared at the candle, hoping his aunt would drop the subject. He watched the wax liquefy below the advancing flame and turn into bumps and ridges, a paradox that always intrigued Desta. If the wax melts and runs away, what is the purpose of the wax? Was the fire's purpose just to melt the wax? If not, why didn't the wax burn like a piece of wood? No one could give him a clear answer, and he'd concluded the purpose of the wax was to give the wick form and rigidity.

Aunt Zere turned toward the kitchen and knocked on the parapet. Yeseru, Almaw's wife, appeared before them. "Please check that the guests have enough to drink. Desta and I need some, too," Zere said.

Yeseru replenished the guest's cups and, soon after, dinner was over. Abraham and two elderly men said their blessings of the food, the house, and the animals. Aunt Zere thanked the guests for coming to visit her and wished health and prosperity for all. Then everybody went to bed.

NINETEEN

The next day Desta stirred to life at a rooster's crow. Everything around him was pitch black and quiet, save for his father's soft, deep breathing next to him. He was happy about attending the Batha Mariam church celebration later that day, but his thoughts were preoccupied with the journey to Dangila the day after. He was hanging on to hope and remote possibilities, and his heart fluttered with excitement. But what if Zewday was not at home when he and Abraham arrived, or he refused to take him in? Desta shuddered.

He felt his father's legs move. Desta could barely see the profile of his face in the muted light. "Are you awake, Desta?" Abraham whispered. Desta whispered that he was.

"Let's get up," Abraham said quietly. "I want us to receive a holy water bath at the church grounds." He sat up, wrapped himself in his gabi, and then rose. He dropped his long legs to the floor and gingerly tiptoed around the sleeping people in the living room. The door creaked as he opened it, causing some of the sleepers to lift their heads and look, and others to suspend their nasal rattles for a few seconds.

Shortly after Abraham went out, Almaw descended from a loft in a corner of the house beyond the chicken coop, and he went outside, too.

Desta pulled the covers over his face and rolled to his side, trying to doze off, but he kept thinking about the holy water bath Abraham had mentioned. *What for, and why now? Does father think that I am possessed by Saytan, as mother has always believed? Why does he need to take this bath?*

He couldn't fall back asleep. He put on his shorts and jacket, wrapped himself in his gabi, and spilled onto the floor. He hopped across tangled feet, circumnavigated sleeping heads, and went out through the open door. Chilled air hit his face and bare feet like a splash of cold water.

He looked around for trees or bushes, but there were none. At the edge of a harvested cornfield, several yards from the fence, Abraham and Almaw stood leaning against the fence and talked. A thin gray mist enveloped the flat land to the east, while copper- and gold-tinted clouds cloaked the sky around the rising sun.

Desta wished to keep company with his thoughts and feelings instead of the men. He sauntered across the courtyard and through a passageway between two houses, finally emerging onto the open, arid brown land. He claimed for himself the western portion of Aunt Zere's farm and the view up the hill toward the Batha Mariam church. One bodily need was more urgent than the other and he let go while standing. He shook off the last golden drip and let his feet take him where they may.

His walk was a prop that nudged his thoughts to flow in tandem with the movement of his limbs, and he became absorbed in his reflections on the trip to Dangila. He was farther from home than he had ever been, in a land without perspective: the sky came down around him in seamless unification with the flat edges of the earth, like the domed cover to his mother's baking pan. Strangely, he had no fear—no desire for the people and places he had left behind. He was willing to sacrifice anything to earn his education and fulfill his grandfather's wishes.

He had walked nearly a hundred feet before he responded to his second bodily urge. After he took care of it, he journeyed back to his aunt's home. He found Abraham and Almaw leaning against the fence nearest to the house entrance and talking.

"Do you know if my sister still has my father's shield?" Abraham asked.

"She does," Almaw said. "You know, that shield means so much more to her now. After we came back from burying grandpa's remains, she made me take it out of storage and clean and oil it. She said since she couldn't have the coin, her father's shield would be a good substitute for one of her children to inherit."

"I am sorry about the coin. It was not my decision. And even we were not meant to have it. . . . Do you think your mother would let me borrow the shield just for today?"

Almaw's brow creased, his twinkling brown eyes narrowed, and his lips twitched as he searched for the proper reply. "What are you going to do with it?" he asked, finally.

"I plan to take part in the horse races at the festival and I need the shield for a performance in memory of my father—a reenactment of his brave deeds in these horse races."

Almaw blinked in surprise. "That's all right with me, but it's mother's decision."

Abraham pulled on his goatee. "Tell her that nothing will happen to the shield. I don't plan to engage in the mock battle scenes with other racers. It will be my own individual race to acknowledge father. Desta and I are going for the holy water bath, and I'd like you to harness Dama and bring him and the shield to the event. I would like to see the condition of the shield before we go."

"You're not coming back afterward?" Almaw asked, squinting at Abraham.

"Desta and I will go to my parents' badima and then directly to the church festivities."

Almaw opened his mouth to pose another question, but Abraham cut him off. "We need to go," he said, as he tapped on Desta's shoulder, urging him to move.

Almaw dashed into the house and reappeared with a cloth-wrapped object. He unwound the cover to reveal gilded, leather-bound armor, shaped like a cone, with an opening roughly twenty inches across. The oiled leather glinted and the gold strips flashed in the morning sunlight.

The intricate relief work on the cladding skin and the radiating metal strips—from the cone to the circular, solid base—held Desta's interest the moment Almaw removed its covering.

"I don't ever remember its being this beautiful," Abraham said, holding the relic before him with both hands.

"Like I mentioned, mother made me polish it after we returned from grand-pa's funeral," Almaw said thoughtfully. "It seems everything that belonged to him became very important to her all of a sudden. You should have seen its condition before I cleaned it up."

"I remember how it looked when we divided up our parents' belongings after mother died. It was caked with dust and streaked with chicken droppings—and God knows what else."

"Can I see, can I see?" asked Desta, tugging at his father's sleeve. He had his chin edging over Abraham's forearm the whole time.

Abraham handed the boy the shield.

Holding it with both hands in front of him, Desta scanned the surface, "Omigod!" he cried out.

Both Abraham and Almaw screwed their faces and fixed their eyes on the boy. "What are you seeing?" the father asked, setting his gaze on the shield.

"I see just about everything you find on the coin and its box."

"What!?" shouted both Abraham and Almaw at once.

"The seven channels in the form of the metal strips, the writings, and just about every image you see on the coin box is on the shield."

Abraham grabbed the shield from Desta and scanned it. Almaw examined the pattern, too. It didn't make any sense to either of them.

"You are right, Desta! I see a lot of the animals we have on the coin box. . . . This is strange!"

Desta stood on his toes, trying to have a good look at the surface again. "Do you see the image of the man on this side and horse on the exact opposite side, as they appear on the front and back of the coin?" Desta said, pointing to one side of the shield first and then the other.

Abraham nodded.

"Do you think, then, this shield is as old as the coin?" Almaw asked, his eyes fluttering with excitement.

"I doubt it. Leather doesn't last that long. However, I am curious about who had the coin and its legends copied onto this shield," Abraham said, without moving his eyes from the renewed object before him.

"Who knows!" Almaw replied, his eyes probing the surface of the shield. "I don't think mother was even aware of the existence of these things. Much of the surface, like I mentioned, used to be obscured with all kinds of dirt."

"This shield is probably not more than one hundred years old. So it's safe to assume that one of our great-grandparents had it made to take the place of the coin—something to placate a disgruntled heir."

"Maybe so," Almaw said, excited by the discovery. "Wait till I show mother the shield."

"I am sure she will be happy. . . . But we need to go now. As I requested, please bring the shield and the harnessed horse to church later. We'll meet you at the horse races. I am doing this more in honor of my father than for the purposes of any grand demonstration."

With these comments, Abraham handed Almaw the shield.

Almaw hesitated and then said, "Okay, I will do as you say, but I cannot guarantee that I will bring the shield."

"Tell your mother what I said and she should have no problem with it," said Abraham. He motioned to Desta. "We need to go now for the holy water blessings by the stream."

After leaving Aunt Zere's compound, Abraham and Desta took the path that went west toward the Batha Mariam church. Desta's fearful preoccupation with the holy water treatment was interrupted by what he saw before him. The earth along the path and under the sparse dry grass beside it was cracked like dried mud. He looked around and noticed the same brown land that had greeted him the day before. This was Kuakura, his father's birthplace, which in his imagination had been lush and green. Why were things not the way he had hoped they would be? Why did the things he desired to see, touch, and feel up close seem to recede from him like a mirage when he came near to them? The sky, the clouds, the horizon, and now the famed land of his father's birth all vanished the closer he got.

As Abraham and Desta neared the edge of the woods, the father said, "I hope there aren't too many people already. On Saint Mary's holiday, there generally are a great many people who come to take the holy bath."

"It makes no difference to me. I am not going to get one," Desta replied.

Abraham stopped and turned around. He fixed his big eyes on the boy. "Why not? This is Saint Mary's holiday. Bathing in water that flowed out of the church grounds will be a blessing to you."

"I am not possessed by Saytan. I am not sick. I don't need it."

"You can use baptism by holy water for many other reasons, including improving your chances of being accepted by Zewday and his family.

Desta thought about this for a bit. "Do I have to decide right now whether to take the holy water treatment?"

"No, just be prepared to take the treatment. The water can be very cold, but you will get used to it once you are under the cascade," Abraham said in a conciliatory tone. Then he turned in the direction of the church grounds and continued walking.

"I'll see how I feel once we get there," Desta said, hoping Abraham would drop the subject for now.

"It's for your own good, son. Baptism by holy water, just like a sincere prayer, can be good for you."

They continued walking. The cool, herbaceous aroma of the woods, the pulsating, sibilant sound of a distant stream, and the melody of chirping birds were pleasant and soothing company to father and son.

Deep in the woods, a hundred yards from the road, a few dozen men had congregated—some standing, others perching on stone seats. Many others were coming and going. Desta scanned the tree-covered grounds.

To one side of this group a turbaned priest stood against a moss-draped outcropping and read from a book. Several feet away from the priest, water flowed down a cantilevered bamboo conduit and fell over a naked man. He sat with his legs folded and crossed, his hands echoing on his chest the configuration of his lower limbs.

A slender young man came toward Abraham and Desta the moment they reached the crowd. "Please sit here," said the man, pointing to a granite slab, "and wait until your turn comes. I think you are either number six or seven."

They sat down and Abraham muttered a complaint about the long wait.

"You can take my turn if you like," said a man sitting beside them. "I have decided not to take the bath." They looked at him keenly, and the man added, "People say the water is very cold. I can't bring myself to go under it. So you're welcome to take my turn unless you, too, have a change of heart." The man smiled at Abraham.

"You know, people . . ." Abraham began to speak but suddenly thought better of it. "Thank you," he said instead and turned to Desta. "I will go first. Be ready to go right after me, assuming we don't get complaints from the guard for going out of turn."

"He can take my turn," chirped a boy next to the man who had offered his place to Abraham. "I am not sick or gone mad, and I don't need a cold *tebel*—holy water—like that."

"Neither am I," replied Desta, glaring at the boy.

"I need to tell the watchman that I have given up my turn to you," said the man, rising to tell the guard. He returned shortly after and sat back down.

Desta looked up at Abraham to see whether he was still interested in going under the freezing waterfall. "You know, people survive bombs and gunshots. What can a little cold water do to you?" said the old warrior, as if he read his son's mind, pleased to find a benign target for the completion of his earlier thought.

Desta kept quiet. He didn't want to argue with his father in front of other people.

The two men ahead of them went under the shower of water, one at a time, and came out shivering. Their teeth chattered and their shoulders shook. Desta gazed at them and winced as each walked past him.

Next was Abraham. He took off his clothes near the stream, covered his genitals, and stepped gingerly onto the slab beneath the cascading water. He perched on the stone bench and closed his eyes, his hands crossed over his chest.

The priest continued to read, glancing occasionally at Abraham, who sat like a statue, his long curving nose piercing the sheet of falling water. Although his clenched teeth, stiff shoulders, and tense facial muscles indicated that he was forcing himself to endure the cold water, his totally calm demeanor made Desta wonder whether his father might have been transported to another world by the priest's prayer and the holy water.

The boy's thoughts shifted from his father, the priest, and the falling water to the overwhelming serenity and quietude of their surroundings. Desta had encountered something similar when he'd gone to church with his mother a few years back: that feeling of comfort, the presence of something extraordinary in the air and in the woods, the hushed reverence that even the birds and insects and animals seemed to have for their surroundings.

The priest finished reading, and Abraham came out quickly, covering his groin with one hand and wiping the water from his body with the other. He dressed and walked back to the group.

Desta was nervous. "Is it very cold?" he asked.

"It is when the water first hits your body. Shortly after that, you won't feel it," Abraham replied through clenched teeth. His stiff lips and taut jaw said more than he was willing to verbalize.

"Thank you for offering us your turn," Abraham said to his neighbor.

"I'm glad a brave soul like you could take advantage of the opportunity," the man replied with a half-smile.

It was Desta's turn, but he didn't want to go.

"This tebel is for your overall good. It's a blessing. And considering the problem you're facing of finding someone to live with in town, you can use all the blessings you can get. Get up and go!" Abraham commanded.

Desta thought about this for a few seconds. He would endure anything, even another forced cold water dowsing by a priest while pinned down by his mother and brother, if it helped him win the hearts and minds of Zewday and his wife.

He quickly removed his jacket and shorts, wrapped himself in his gabi, and dashed to the freezing water.

The cold rough slabs of stone sent shivers throughout his body. He stared at the streaming water as it fell and spattered.

He counted to three, quickly removed his gabi, covered his front like Abraham had done, and stepped under the water.

The water stung like a wasp and Desta jerked his head out of the way. It stung his bare feet even more. Many of the onlookers chuckled, but Abraham was not amused. Desta wondered what he could do to redouble his courage. He suddenly thought of his tattoed-on coin above his heart. He slid his hand over his chest and pressed on the area above his nipple. He instantly felt calm and at ease.

He shoved his head under the water. It didn't feel cold at all. He gingerly stepped onto the platform directly below the stream. He closed his eyes and prayed, asking Saint Mary to bless him and Zewday and his family for their charity and kindness—that they might allow him to live with them so he could go to school.

Desta would not miss this critical opportunity—his second and simultaneous mission in life—finding the mate to the Coin of Magic and Fortune his family possesses. So he also petitioned the Mother of God to intercede on his behalf and ask her Son to put Desta on the path that would lead him to the coin bearer.

As he prayed, Desta had feelings unlike any he had felt before, and a warm sensation enveloped his body. He didn't quite know where he was or why everything around him seemed so tranquil and quiet. When his thoughts finally connected with his feelings, he slowly opened his eyes. He couldn't believe what he saw. His body was shrouded in a steaming mist and, like twinkles of starlight through clouds, sets of eyes peered at him from stunned faces.

Confused and mystified, Desta removed his hand from his chest. The hazy cloak of steam rapidly dissipated, revealing around him a ring of stupefied people, including Abraham, the priest, and the guard. The boy quickly stepped away from the tebel and wrapped himself in his gabi. Hesitant and nervous, he snaked through the crowd to collect his shorts and jacket. He used his gabi to dab dry the remaining droplets from his body. He put on his clothes, glancing occasionally at the people who were gawking at him in awe.

A man stuck his hand into the falling water but was disappointed to find the water was not warm anymore. Others placed their feet into the pooled water around the rocks and were equally disappointed.

"Have you seen anything like this before, Aba?" a bystander asked the priest.

"No, not the water suddenly turning warm and steaming."

"I think Jesus's Mother was performing a miracle on Her holiday right before our eyes," said another man to the group.

"How do we know it wasn't Aba's reciting of the Holy Scripture that caused this strange occurrence?" asked the first man.

The priest looked confused and lost. He stared at Desta and slowly nodded his head. He said, "I have seen cripples stand up and walk and blind people able to see after treatment with the holy water, but I have never seen anything like what we witnessed today." He approached Abraham. "Is there something special about your boy?"

"Strange things do happen with him sometimes and our family can't explain them."

"The good Lord chooses certain individuals like him to do his miracles," assured the priest. "This is the work of Jesus Almighty, fellows. We just witnessed a miracle right before our own eyes, on His Mother's holiday!"

All the men bobbed their heads in agreement.

Abraham turned to Desta. "Let's get going before people start asking too many questions," he whispered, his eyes darting about nervously.

They hurried to the priest and received their cross blessings—three times on the forehead and lip.

The priest said to Abraham, "Thank you for bringing that boy to serve as a channel for the Lord's work." Abraham acknowledged the priest's words with a bow and then father and son left the gathering.

They turned west onto the road and through the woods. The air was still cool, the ground damp, and the place tranquil. Morning rays filtered through the trees and mottled the ground with yellow light.

Desta was thrilled by what the magical coin on his chest had enabled him to do. Abraham kept shaking his head as if he had a bug in his ear. "That was a true miracle indeed, Desta," he said, finally finding his tongue. "You should be happy God chose you to perform one on this special day."

"No, that was just pure magic," Desta replied with a grin.

Abraham stopped and gazed quizzically at his son. "What are you talking about?"

"Magic. You know, the magical power of the coin."

"I don't get it."

"I'm sorry, I know this is hard to believe. One of the channels of the coin is dedicated to performing magical acts like what you saw happen with the stream."

"You have the coin with you?!" Abraham asked, surprised. He didn't think anyone else knew where he has hidden it—buried in the ground under his and Ayénat's bed in a new box he had built for it.

"No, I have it *on* me."

Abraham narrowed his big eyes and furrowed his brow. "Are you playing games with me?"

"No. I'm not."

"Where is it?

Desta unwound his gabi from his shoulders, pulled back the lapel of his jacket, and pointed. "In there!"

Abraham stooped and studied Desta's bare skin above his heart but saw nothing. "Now you're being really silly," he said, relaxing his brow.

Desta let go of his lapel and threw his gabi over his shoulders. "Let's go on, and I will tell you."

As they walked, he explained that his grandpa's spirit, the Cloud Man, had tattooed the coin image on his chest but had made it invisible to keep away the curious.

A mixture of disbelief, fear, happiness, and surprise seeped through Abraham's brain. That his son had the power of the coin permanently on his chest pleased him, whereas the supernatural nature of it concerned him. "Don't ever tell anybody else about this," he said. "Some jealous person might want to harm you."

"Grandpa's spirit told me that already. I told you because you are my father and I had to explain what happened."

"That was a very strange thing, indeed! I feel like I just came out of a dream, or as if I just witnessed a miracle." Abraham went quiet as he thought about his father, the coin, its power, and its future.

AFTER THEY CLEARED the woods, they crossed a saddle-shaped plateau with farm fields and a quintet of homes. The westward road, which must have gone straight through at one time, now skirted the fenced compounds on the south. Abraham explained that this road to his parents' old homestead also went to Dangila, but they would take a different road tomorrow when they went to the town.

As they began to descend from the plateau, a sea of green earth before them stopped Desta in his tracks. The tableau stood in such sharp contrast to its seared surroundings. They gazed at the verdant land for a long time, Abraham as if seeing it for the first time.

Desta spoke in a low, reflective voice. "What is the name of this valley?"

"That is Abo Gundree, part of my parents' old estate."

"What a beautiful place! Grandma abandoned such a country to go and live in that hole?"

"At the time, she thought it was a matter of life or death, and she chose life."

"Why is it so green, while most of the surrounding land is dry?"

"Much of what you see is grain fields. The land is irrigated during the dry season, which allows crops to grow year round. The neighboring cattle fields receive plenty of water from the irrigation runoff, keeping the grass green all the time, too," said Abraham, gazing into the distance. "You know, I haven't come here in a long while. We all avoided it like it was a community of lepers. We just didn't want to remember our past and what we had lost."

Desta's eyes went from his father to both of their shrinking shadows and back to his father.

"I'm anxious to see it up close," the boy said as he pressed forward. He didn't want his father to get too sentimental about his childhood and the land that was no longer his family's.

The father followed, his face downcast, eyes on the path, weighed down by the memories of many years ago. For some time neither of them spoke.

The morning sun on their backs felt sumptuous and soon they walked with pleasure, absorbed not by thoughts of the past but by what they would find when they arrived at Abraham's childhood stomping grounds.

This journey was one of the many ironies in Abraham's life. For years he had planned to come here for a single purpose: to kill. Two jealous men—they were brothers—had poisoned his father, making him go mad and abandon his family and estate, so he had thought. As a consequence, Abraham's mother, for fear of her life and the lives of her children, left the estate and went to settle in a remote valley.

The brothers died before Abraham was ready to come with a gun and kill them. As it turned out, they had nothing to do with the father's disappearance: the cousins of Abraham's mother were found to be the actual culprits.

Abraham shook his head in dismay for having wasted so much energy on grudges and anger for the wrong people. But he was happy now that he was going there not to hurt anyone but to visit the place with his son and share some of the precious memories of his childhood.

When they reached the bottom of the hill, Abraham said, "There is the syca-more tree!" He pointed to a giant mushroom-shaped tree a hundred yards away on the side of the road. Near the tree were four circular homes, each with tall eucalyptus trees and ringed with wattle fences. These were the only residences on the extensive estate.

Several dogs, sensing the presence of strangers, began to bark.

Desta studied the sycamore, its canopy and droopy branches, and enduring dignity. It reminded him of the warka tree where deb'tera Tayé's spirit work enabled Desta to meet the ghost of his grandfather for the first time. He felt he had come full circle, and for a moment he almost expected to see the Cloud Man under the tree.

Abraham motioned Desta to a heap of rocks on the side of the road. "Let's sit here for a moment and think through how we should go about this. Those dogs sound ferocious."

They perched side by side on the warm stone pile, at first apprehensive of the dogs but soon absorbed by the scenery before them.

"There is the timeless Abo Goondree Church," Abraham said, pointing to a wooded mound at the edge of a field. Cattle, horses, and sheep grazed peacefully in the green pastures between tilled lots. Men and women dressed in white holiday clothes scurried along the footpaths across the plain, heading to the Batha Mariam church.

As Desta and Abraham observed the landscape, the wavy eastern peaks drew their eyes and held their gazes. For the son, they were beacons of freedom, for the father, symbols of his hallowed childhood.

"It all makes sense now," Abraham whispered to himself. Desta turned to his father and found him gaping at the distant mountains, pulling on his salt-and-pepper goatee, twirling and pinching the strands as if pressing them into dust. It seemed Abraham needed these props to travel back to his childhood and bring forth something profound that had been stowed deep within his mind.

Desta was afraid to intrude but finally screwed up the courage to say, "What makes sense, Baba?"

"The evening of the day when my father left, never to return, I saw a man of extraordinary size swallow the sun while two similarly large men watched him, dismayed by the act. The red coloring in the sky, which I initially thought was formed by the setting sun, was actually human blood.

"For a long time afterward, I was not sure if I had hallucinated. Now, knowing what actually happened to my father on that cursed evening, it is obvious that I was witnessing his murder through the images I saw on the mountains." Abraham sucked air between his teeth and sadly shook his head.

He gazed at his feet for some time and then lifted his head, saying, "It looked strange to me then and still looks strange in my mind. How was it that I witnessed the murder of my own father from so far away?"

Desta said, "That's what grandpa's spirit told me, too. You saw his murder but you couldn't figure out what was going on, or how or why you saw that. There are a lot of things we don't know about the power of the coin."

"I guess so. We didn't know it then, but that night was the beginning of the end of our life here." Abraham coughed, feeling a lump in his throat.

"The day that changed your life and the lives of everybody else in your family forever," Desta said, looking at his father pensively.

"Sadder still is that my father lost his life on my behalf."

"On the coin's behalf," Desta corrected.

"No matter, it was very bad for all of us. We lost my father and the benefit of the coin and also all of this land." Abraham cleared his throat and stared once again at the distant horizon.

Desta followed his gaze to the eastern peaks. "That's true. How wonderful it would have been to live in a place where you don't have to climb or descend a mountain every time you want to go someplace, and where your eyes can travel far and wide."

Abraham didn't hear Desta. Sounds and images from his boyhood in this place—some vivid, others vague and blurred—trickled through him and crowded his head. He realized then that it was not just the old homestead he had come to revisit but the many other reminders of his short-lived childhood. This was the place where his fate as a person, husband, and father was shaped and sealed. Deep within him were things he had never fully understood as a boy—their meanings and consequences, the direct and subtle effects they had on him as he passed through life.

As he now surveyed the open green field, he recalled the weekend strolls, swimming practice in the Kilty River, and the nighttime stories parents told the children while sitting around the fire . . . and then that fateful night when his father left for town, ostensibly to buy Abraham a birthday gift, and never came back. He remembered how Abraham the boy had waited by the gate all that day and continued waiting, around the fire, in the evening. He recounted the desolate faces and tear-stained eyes of his mother and sisters in the days following, the search teams that combed all the nooks and crannies of the countryside looking for the remains of his father, or a murder weapon. Finally, he recalled that when

Abraham's father didn't return, how the family had abandoned the farmland estate and come to the isolated valley of his mother's relatives.

They couldn't officially bury a man or mourn his loss if they didn't have a body to entomb. So they lived most of their lives hoping father would come home one day and surprise them. The family kept their sorrows personal and private.

All this had made Abraham who he was as a man and a parent. To come here now and be faced with these reminders stirred up what had been buried in his mind. His past was a festering corpse he was never able to weep over or entomb. As he and his family had finally done with his father's remains, he had hoped by coming here he could, once and for all, do the same with his past.

The dogs were barking less and less, now yelping at random intervals. They seemed to have accepted the visitors as though they were fixtures, like trees or fence posts. A man emerged from the open, gateless entrance to one of the homes. He was draped in a gabi from head to knee; his shadowed face appeared a mere smudge from where father and son sat.

"Somebody is coming," piped up Desta, waking Abraham from his daydream.

The man walked toward them. "Good morning," he said, bowing a little and peeling away from his head the edge of his gabi.

"Good morning," Abraham said, tipping his head.

"I came to see what the dogs have been barking at. Are you *yegziabhare ingdawech*—guests of God?"

"No, I brought my son here to show him my birthplace. My parents used to own this land."

The man jerked his chin and crinkled his brow. "Your parents? How . . . when . . . I am afraid you have come to the wrong place."

"It was long ago, but I'm certain about the location." Abraham pointed. "That sycamore tree was about fifty feet from our fence when we lived here."

"Nobody but my parents has owned this property, sir," the man said firmly, "and before them, their parents and grandparents." The man coughed then turned his face to the side and spat.

Abraham realized the conversation was not going to go well. "No matter who owned it, it's no longer important to me or anybody in my family. Can we just walk around here for a bit?"

"What for?"

"Just, uh-hmm . . . just to walk about and admire your beautiful land, show the boy that sycamore tree because he has never seen one, and take him up close to those grain fields because where we come from crops don't grow in the dry season," Abraham said, fumbling with random thoughts.

The man looked away for a long time, his fine profile silhouetted against the distant peaks, his big eyes sinking deep in their cavities, his oily brown skin glistening in the morning sunlight. He turned and eyed Abraham. "Where do you come from?"

"It's very far from here, a full day's journey on horseback." Abraham fudged the truth, wishing to allay the man's concern. "We came to the area for a holy water treatment. We're staying with a relative and going back home in a couple of days."

"I see," the man said thoughtfully. The creased skin on his brow relaxed. He glanced at Desta and said, "Let me make sure the dogs are secured before I let you walk on the grounds."

"Okay, thank you. We won't stay long."

The man shuffled off to his home. A few minutes later he came to the gate and signaled to the visitors, indicating it was safe for them to walk around.

Abraham, thoughtful, and Desta, excited at the prospect of strolling on the old family property, headed in the direction of the sycamore tree. They walked through the wide corridor between the animal pen and the tenements. The air was warm and thick with the odor of dung. Flies swarmed around them as if pursuing delectable prey. The dogs continued to bark from their confines but powerless and less threatening now.

They stopped near the giant tree, and Abraham looked about to see what else he could remember from his boyhood. The low-hanging branch he used to climb and ride, pretending it was a horse, had been cut off, leaving just a stump near the trunk. The tree itself seemed to have aged: its roots were gnarled and protruded from the ground like the talons of a giant bird, and it seemed to have fewer leaves than he remembered.

There used to be a granite slab on which his father had carved out six pairs of pockets for *gebeta*—a board game. At first he thought somebody had removed it, but after pacing around for a few minutes, he found it on the south side of the tree, covered with leaves, the holes filled with dirt. He brushed off the leaves, dug out the dirt, and stared into the holes, which stared back at him like six sets of eyes. Memories of the many hours he spent with his sisters playing the game galloped back, and Abraham smiled. Then he remembered *liqmoshi*—a pebble game he used to play with his mother and sisters—and smiled again.

"You know," Abraham said, pivoting on his heels toward Desta, who was shadowing him quietly, "We used to bring out skin and palm leaf mats and sit and watch the pedestrians across the river, the cattle and grain fields—when we were not playing games. And then on Christmas Day some relatives and friends in the area would come to kill a bull or cow under this tree and share the meat. Afterward, vultures came from nowhere, looking for entrails and meat scraps, anything left by the dogs and cats, that is."

"It sounds like your family spent more time together than we ever did," Desta said wistfully.

"Unlike me, father had no court case or other business matters that took him away from us," Abraham replied remorsefully. "Sit here and wait for me. I am going to take a private walk."

Desta was puzzled by his father's sudden request for privacy but didn't ask him where he was going or why. He simply said okay and sat down to wait at the edge of the granite game slab.

Abraham strolled meditatively toward the fence line on the south side of the homes and then turned west and walked toward the Kilty River. Wherever he saw a group of stones, he crouched, lifted one or two of them, and dug for a bit with a stick. Then he put back the stones in their original positions and continued walking. After doing this a few times, he threw the stick away and just walked slowly along the river. Occasionally, he stopped and looked across to the grain fields.

Desta guessed that Abraham was talking to his long-dead mother, asking her questions about why she abandoned this beautiful land. Why didn't she have the foresight and courage to stay put until she knew who had actually killed her husband?

"Do you know," Desta imagined his father telling his mother, "that our newly cleared mountainous land can produce for only three years? Do you know that the land you once owned continues to grow abundant grains year after year because of the annual flooding of this might little river? Do you know that your grandchildren and great-grandchildren will barely eke out an existence if they continue to live in the mountainous valley to which you brought their forebears? That in years to come they'll either die of hunger or flee the area like the animals and birds did when we cut down their shelter?"

Abraham strode back to the sycamore tree, thinking about his own mistakes. Why had he not come back when he was old enough to handle legal matters and try to wrestle this land from the settlers by suing them? Why instead had he spent so much time focused on avenging his father without even investigating what had actually happened? Like his mother, he had lacked the foresight to salvage the land that his family had lost. Abraham was angry and disappointed with himself.

Desta, who was watching every movement and gesture of his father, was also eyeing the man with the dogs. He was sitting on a log outside his gate and observing the visitors' every move.

"What is it you have been bothered with?" Desta asked the moment his father returned.

"I just wish mother had stayed put," Abraham replied wearily. "All this beautiful land would still be ours."

"Things are not that simple," Desta said. "Without knowing it, you all complied with the ancient prophecy, the things encoded in the coin and in the mountains where we now live. Don't beat yourself up over this."

"That may be so," Abraham said, looking across the river. "It's still sad because the future doesn't bode well for our family. You're lucky in this regard. If you advance in your education, you will have a much better future than any of your brothers."

"What were you looking for in the ground?"

"Mother once told me that Baba buried silver coins in a jar somewhere around the sycamore tree. I knew it was a long shot, but since we're here I thought I'd poke at the places where I figure he might have buried them."

"If there was a jar, I'm sure someone found it already." Desta looked toward the tenements. "The man has been watching us the whole time. We better get out of here."

Desta and his father walked back toward the corridor.

The man hopped down from his perch when they were just about to pass the gate of his house. "Did you find what you were looking for?" he asked mockingly.

"No," Abraham said simply. "But I enjoyed the walk."

The man invited them to come eat something. Abraham declined, saying they wanted to watch the *genna*—hockey—game before the priests brought out the *Tabot*—a square holy plaque of wood on which the Ten Commandments are written.

When they were halfway up the hill, Abraham stopped and turned around. Desta followed his father's eyes and gazed at the beautiful green grass and waving crop fields. Abraham probed the verdant land as if searching for something he had forgotten to look for while they were down there. Tears welled from the corner of his eye.

Abraham stared gravely at the valley, while Desta kept his eye on his father's tears. The dammed liquid eventually broke loose and tumbled down the outer flank of his cheekbone, where it hung as if afraid to fall or as if waiting for Abraham's hand to wipe it away. But Abraham's mind had gone to another world. More tears followed after, and now they cascaded, plunging into the dust near Abraham's feet.

Desta realized that these were no ordinary tears. They emanated from deep within his father's heart; they had purpose and meaning. They allowed the usually private and unemotional man to openly mourn his many losses—the attentive father he would never have, the opportunities to benefit from the information contained in the family coin, and this picturesque land neither he nor his children would ever own.

In a sense, it appeared to Desta, those tears were his salvation, relieving and freeing him from his bondage and troubles. As the tears departed, he saw a change in his father's mood.

Abraham looked down where his tears had fallen and noticed a patch of wet dirt. He wiped his face with the back of his hand and dabbed at his cheek with the hem of his gabi.

"Do you feel better?" Desta asked.

"I do. The earth always has a way of relieving us of our burdens. I was lightened after we buried the remains of my father and felt redeemed when I saw the seven beautifully grown eucalyptus trees I planted on his behalf. Now, by burying my sorrows and losses with my tears in this earthly manner, I feel like I have now completely parted with things related to my parents, this land, and the anger and hurt that have been deep within me all these years. I hope to lead a happier life till the earth swallows me whole when my time finally comes."

Desta shuddered, saddened by the thought of the earth swallowing his father whole.

Seeing his son's mournful face, Abraham said, "Let's move on. We should arrive before the genna game starts." Within minutes, Abraham's eyes and face became peaceful, his jaw line eased, and the tautness around his mouth faded.

Father and son quickly got back on the road. Abraham's mention of the hockey game had lightened Desta's heart. He couldn't wait till they got there.

By the time they reached the church grounds, the sun had gone past the midpoint in the sky. Farther ahead in the woods, they could hear drum beats and muted noises. In the shade of the trees and in the open plaza, well-dressed people stood or sat on stones and wooden benches, bald men throwing a corner of their gabis across their shining pates as protection against the sun. A few women stood and chattered, their eyes on the path to the church compound, evidently waiting for something.

"It appears the priests and deacons are about to bring the Tabot out to the field. The will probably settle under the sholla tree," Abraham said, pointing to the west side of the field. "We need to go and watch the hockey game for a while first. It may be about to start."

They walked side by side to the northwest section of the grounds where there were groups of raucous young men and a good number of older men. Although he had often seen kids across the Davola River play hockey, Desta had never played the game nor did he really know why Jesus's birthday is also called genna.

Abraham explained that the game is still played on *Lidet*—Christmas Day— because when Jesus was born, the children in the neighborhood celebrated his birth by playing a hockey game but also now at many church holidays, including on ordinary days. Regarding the name, somehow over centuries Christmas had come to be known as Genna.

Traditionally on Christmas, after the families have killed a cow or lamb and eaten its meat and drunk tella, later in the afternoon someone will go around the neighborhood blowing a horn to announce a game of genna. The children and youths and older men gather in a field. Then two or three elderly men come to the center of the field and bless the players and the game.

"The children are assigned one portion of the field and the others a different portion. There is no specific number of players to play the game. Any reasonable number of people who have hockey sticks can participate. The goal lines can be landmarks such as trees or knolls or posts or rocks on opposite ends of the field. The ball is made from strips of leather woven tightly into a sphere that would fit in a man's fist. The play can go until dusk, marking the end of the day's festivities."

ABRAHAM AND DESTA STOOD at a corner of the field and watched, transfixed, as the ball got hit and passed, or as it sailed over the crowd. Desta wished he had a hockey stick so he could run and hit the ball like the others. He had experienced the thrill of the sheer act of running when he and Hibist used to race in the field below their home during the spring season, chasing butterflies and trying to catch the elusive golden creatures.

There seemed to be no order to the game, and the only rule was to always run toward the ball, try to take it away from the opposing team, and drive it toward the other team's goal line.

The crowd of players moved on the field like a tidal wave, shifting its movement from one side of the grounds to the other as one player, then another drove the ball along the turf, dodging his opponents.

A SLOW, PONDEROUS BEATING of a drum and muffled noises from the churchyard stole their attention. "The Tabot must be out. We need to go and watch the procession," Abraham said.

"These drumbeats sound different from the ones we heard at grandpa's funeral," Desta commented.

"You remember well, son," Abraham said, resting his hand on the boy's shoulder. "Those we heard at grandpa's funeral were for mourning. These are for the spirit of celebration, to express happiness. Let's go and watch the parade and listen to the drums closely."

They broke away from the crowd and a few others followed, as if they had been waiting for someone to lead. When they reached the open plaza, just outside of the wooded grove, they found two-dozen men mounted on horseback. They were dressed in their best holiday clothes: light jackets, breeches, and white gabis. Some had donned multicolored half-waist capes and tongue-like strips of cloth that cascaded over their broad chests. Some of the capes were embroidered with red, blue, and yellow yarn. These same men wore headgear with tufts of horsehair projecting from the center that curved up and down like raised eyebrows, making the men look ferocious. Other men wore white headbands of multiple rounds of cotton fabric. A half-dozen of the men had combed their hair out into a round, black halo.

Some of the participants wore capes of black-and-white colobus monkey skins. Others donned cloaks embroidered with red, blue, and yellow yarn.

There were men who carried spears with double-bladed tips; others carried pointed walking sticks. A third group had gleaming leather-clad shields hooked on their arms. The horses wore colorful adornments on their faces and flanks.

The horsemen kept glancing toward the footpath that trailed out from the church courtyard, anxiously waiting for something. The horses stamped their feet and whooshed their tails to chase away the aggressive flies. One horse lifted its front legs and tipped the rider backward as if trying to throw him off, but quickly landed back on its hooves.

"What are they going to do?" Desta asked.

"There will be a horse race later," Abraham said. "This is the event your grandfather used to ride in every year, but I never had a chance to watch him race. . . . You know, Almaw was supposed to be here with Dama. I wonder where he is."

Desta's eyes were on the man with the strange headdress. "The man with that wild hat looks scary."

"He is a showman," Abraham replied. "In the old days, men wore the mane of a lion or the skin of a leopard they had killed as a symbol of bravery. Now they try to imitate those past deeds by wearing stitched horsehair pieces." Abraham's eyes darted about as he looked for Almaw and Dama.

Along the wooded pathway from the church came a procession of priests, surrounding a man who carried on his head a square object covered with a pall of green, red, and gold colors. Some of the priests held umbrellas over their heads, and an umbrella was positioned over the man with the square object. He moved slowly and gracefully, watching every step, as if whatever was mounted on his head might slide off and break into pieces.

"What is he carrying?" whispered Desta.

"That is the Tabot—the representation of the saint or angel of a particular church," Abraham replied.

"Is that God?" Desta wondered aloud.

"No, this church belongs to Saint Mary. It has to be a representation of Her. The beautiful plaque of wood itself contains important documents from God."

Desta was confused, but he didn't have time to ask any more questions. The throng gathered around the priests and the awaiting cavalcade. The horsemen split into two equal groups and led the priests and the rest of the crowd to the west side of the field, near the big, spreading sholla tree.

The assembly began to chant and sing as it followed the drummers and the priests toward the tree. The adults walked a leisurely pace in tempo with the priests' steps. The younger members of the crowd were restless and erratic—less observant of the rituals. Once they reached the tree, the priests gathered under the outstretched branches and began to chant. The drummers continued to fill the air with their slow and melodious rhythms.

This was the first time Desta had been with his father at a large gathering. He was astounded by how many people came and greeted Abraham, and the great reverence they showed, bowing to him like he was a high-ranking government official. He realized that his father, with a commanding height of six feet three inches, broad shoulders, an erect posture, big brown eyes, a noble visage and a regal bearing, was unlike any other man Desta had ever seen. He hoped people would treat him like that when he grew up.

The horsemen veered off and gathered in the open field about fifty feet away. Some of the people followed them, while the rest stayed with the priests and continued to clap, chant, and sing.

It was then that Almaw—a glimmering shield held tightly to his chest—arrived riding Dama. "I am sorry," Almaw said as he dismounted. He wiped the perspiration from his brow. "We had a problem at home that delayed me."

"That's all right. We were wondering what happened to you," Abraham said, taking the lead from Almaw. He inspected Dama as if looking at him for the first time.

"By the way," Almaw said with a smile. "I took Dama to the river and gave him a bath. Mother said grandpa never took his horse to the races before he was soaped and washed to perfection."

"Thank you. Your mother remembers Baba's routine at these events better than I. She was the eldest."

Desta stepped close and ran his fingers over Dama's shoulder, feeling the lustrous hair and inhaling the waxy *Martello*—a brand of—soap. His eyes followed along the beast's curving, muscular neck and across his broad flank to the whooshing, luxuriant tail. He was at a loss for words.

Dama seemed to enjoy the attention and caresses. He nuzzled Abraham, who in turn rubbed the horse's face and spoke a few words of appreciation. For that brief moment neither Abraham nor Desta heard the activities around them. "Thank you again," Abraham said to Almaw. "I have never seen Dama look so beautiful."

"Yeah, he smells nice, too," Desta chirped.

"The only thing is. . ." Almaw said, his voice trailing. "Mother said that if you plan to engage in a mock battle with another racer, you can't carry the shield."

Abraham stared at the shield. "No, I wouldn't risk damaging it. I will just ride with it, at least one round by myself, presuming they give me a chance to do so. As you know, I'm not a member of this association, which father belonged to years ago."

"I'm sure they will let you race if you really want to. Just mention grandpa's name. Mother said there are many people, including younger ones, who still remember his name. In his time he was one of their star horsemen."

"I wonder if they know what happened to him . . . But that is irrelevant at this point." Abraham extended his hand. "Let me have the shield."

Almaw slid the cone-shaped armor down his right limb and out of his hand. Chinks of light flew off the golden strips.

Abraham grasped the shield gently and studied it for a few seconds, as if seeing it for the first time. He grasped the handle and brought it to his chest. Motioning to Almaw and Desta, he said, "Let's go talk to the association leader."

The association leader was pairing up the riders and arranging the order in which the men would race when the trio arrived with Dama in tow. The man's name was Teka. He was about five feet eight inches, and he wore knee breeches and a faded khaki coat over his gabi. With three of the four buttons of the coat tightly fastened, Teka looked like a barrel that would roll away if he were to fall on sloping terrain. He had just finished setting up the last riders.

Teka crinkled his brown face when Abraham excused himself upon approaching. The two greeted each other with bows. Teka listened intently as Abraham talked, but Teka's face displayed the impatience of a man unhappily distracted from what he was doing. "Beshaw Mekonnen?" Teka asked, swiveling on the balls of his feet. His eyes held Abraham's. "The name rings a bell, but I can't place it."

"You are too young to remember him. He used to be one of the best horse racers at this event," Abraham said, his eyes boring into Teka's.

"Era! If you mean the Beshaw Mekonnen my grandfather used to talk about, of course I know the name. The two used to be good friends. My grandfather used to wonder what had happened to him and his family."

"It's a long story. What I'm here for is to ask if you would permit me to participate in your event. I want to take part in honor of my Baba."

"It would be a pleasure to have you run a race or two. . . ." Teka became thoughtful. "But I don't have anybody to pair you with."

"That's not important. I just want to have one or two solo rides. At my age, I'm not a match for your young and experienced riders. I want to do this, in part, for my son," he said, patting Desta's shoulder. "I never had an opportunity to watch my father race when I was my son's age."

Teka walked over to the racers and talked with them for a few minutes. When he returned, he said that Abraham could ride at the end of the already-set racers. With that, Teka ordered the crowd away from the runway. The racers gathered behind the starting line, each holding a shield and a spear with one hand and their horse's lead with the other. The spectators gathered a fair distance behind them.

Teka signaled the first pair of racers and they quickly mounted their horses after handing their shields or spears to someone who was with them. One of the men, a hairy, dark-skinned fellow, wore a white band around his forehead to hold his mane of long hair. He wore just a light jacket and breeches. He held a spear with one hand and the reins of his horse with the other. His horse was dark brown and stocky.

The second racer, a tan-skinned man with a receding hairline and big serious eyes, wore a charcoal-gray jacket and breeches and held his skin-clad shield against his chest. His horse was dark gray with a white patch on his face. It looked well fed, and its coat glistened in the afternoon light.

At Teka's command, the men leaned forward. He gave them a hand signal and shouted, "Go!"

The men beat their legs repeatedly against their horses' flanks and shouted at them, causing the animals to fly down the runway. The long-haired man with the spear yelled, "*Yaz, yaz*—hold up, hold up—your shield!" and raised his spear high in the air. The tanned man lifted his shield and tried to protect himself. The long-haired man launched his spear at the shield but missed. The spear flew inches past the tanned man's head and landed in the earth with a shiver. Desta shuddered. That the spear could have entered the man's skull and trembled like that in his brain was a terrifying thought. He looked up at his father. "In the name of tradition and sport, that man could have easily died."

"I know. But fatal accidents rarely happen at these races." He turned and looked at the second paired races set to run. Teka gave them the command and they took off. The long-haired man with the spear hit his target, but the spear ricocheted away from the shield and fell horizontally onto the ground.

Desta's heart was in his throat. Why on earth these men would take such chances he couldn't understand.

On their second round, the roles of the racers were reversed. Those who threw their spears at the opponent in the first round now held their shields before them and became the recipients. The long-haired man now wore his shield on his arm and the tan-skinned man carried a spear. On the run, the spear split the shield and went whizzing past the long-haired man's head.

After the second and third set of racers ran twice in their reversed roles it was Abraham and Dama's turn to take the runway. Abraham was glad he didn't have to aim at anyone or have anyone aim at him. Before the guest had his solo performance, Teka stepped onto the runway and explained who the next and last racer was and why he was riding solo. Chatter ensued, with many of the people wondering who Beshaw Mekonnen was. Others who had heard of the famous racer waited eagerly to see if the son had the father's athletic prowess.

At Teka's signal, Abraham stepped forward, with Dama in tow and Desta beside him.

"Selam, the good people of Kuakura . . ." Abraham said, bowing a little. "First, I must thank the good Lord for giving my son and me an opportunity to be here with you on this great holiday and at these horse races. I had once dreamed of taking part in the races when I was a little boy, but, sadly, I never did.

"Second, I would like to thank *Ato*—Mr. Teka—for his graciousness in accommodating me today. We have never met before and I had not made prior arrangements to be here. Yet he still offered me a spot so I can run my horse a couple of rounds on behalf of a former member of this association.

"My name is Abraham Beshaw. I was born in Kuakura, and my family and I lived here until I was seven years old, when we moved to the highlands of Sekela, about one hundred miles south. I have been there for over forty years. . . . Many of you might wonder what a man of my age is trying to prove—why I'm intent on racing my horse in this field of brave young men, particularly after the great performances we've just seen. Believe me, I have no illusions about my athletic prowess and I am not trying to prove anything," Abraham said, chuckling a little. His eyes panned the crowd.

"I am here to remember and honor my father, Beshaw Mekonnen, who once was a proud member of this association and a widely-known horseman. Some of you may have heard his name or have elderly relatives who were friends of his." Abraham paused.

The crowd, hushed and motionless, listened, hanging on Abraham's every word. Desta was all ears, too, as his eyes went from the crowd to his father and

Dama, who stood with his handsome face touching Abraham's back.

"Abraham continued. "Then one day he vanished. He was supposed to have gone to Dangila. In the days and weeks following his disappearance, our relatives and friends combed the area and sent search parties to Dangila and other places, thinking that harm had come to him. They found no trace of him, and no one remembered seeing him.

"Then we suspected that jealous neighbors—we had a few of them—might have somehow slipped him a drug that caused him to lose his mind and flee his family and home. Fearing more bad things would befall us, mother decided we should move to our relatives' remote valley where we currently live, leaving our extensive farmland estate. To mother, the safety of her children—there were four of us, ranging in age from five to eleven—was the most important thing.

"Then two years ago we found my father's remains in a ravine a few hundred yards from our current Sekela home. That's forty-two years after he disappeared. Apparently, he had come to the valley the day he vanished and was murdered there. He had not gone to Dangila as we had thought. How it all happened is a bit complicated to explain, so I won't go into detail. We spent all those years not knowing whether our father was dead or alive. Ironically, he was there next door to us all those years; we had followed in his footsteps to live in the same general area. . . . We gathered his remains and buried him in the churchyard.

"During the funeral procession, knowing a dead horseman's casket is often accompanied by a procession of horse-mounted comrades, I had secretly wished a few of my father's remaining friends could have been there with their horses to give him a deserving send-off—however deferred by two scores and two years.

"Mother used to tell me that my father's friends from this association had continued to ask after him whenever she ran into them over the years. My appearing here today is in part to let any of my father's friends know what happened to him. I want them to have the chance to bury him in their thoughts as we all have done."

My father had been murdered by my mother's cousins—the same relatives we came to live with several months after he vanished that fateful day. You see, one of the cousins had stolen a very precious family treasure and father apparently had gone to Avinevera to retrieve it. He managed to obtain the treasure through a special arrangement he had struck with the man's daughter. However, shortly after father left with the treasure, the man discovered it missing. He recruited his own brother and they went in hot pursuit. Before they could wrestle the treasure from my father's grasp, out of desperation, he swiftly swallowed it. So they killed him. They had planned to return in the light of day to open his stomach and collect the treasure. As it turned out, when the two men came back the next day, they couldn't locate the body. My father's spirit made sure the place where he had lain was invisible to the men.

Some of the women gasped, putting their hands over their mouths, when Abraham revealed his father's murderers. The men just stared, doe-eyed, mesmerized by the speaker's story.

Abraham flourished his hand and paced a short distance—his big eyes engaging the crowd. His great face dimmed, lit up, twisted, or relaxed in accordance with the emotions he felt in the story he was sharing. His beautiful bass voice rose and fell in a measured and precise cadence. Unfazed by the crowd, Dama stood or took steps following his master.

The speaker was in complete control of his words and the manner in which he delivered them. He was also, as usual, in absolute command of the air—the halo-like aura that seemed to surround him.

"Thank you all for allowing me to share these memories," he said when he finished. Abraham cleared his throat again, this time almost as if he was about to cough. "Now I will race my Dama a couple of rounds in honor and remembrance of my father," he said. After telling Desta to go wait for him, he quickly led Dama to the starting line. He hooked his left foot in the stirrup, made a couple of hopping motions as he readied to mount, and finally, he shot up and swung his free leg over the horse. At Teka's count of three, Abraham and Dama took off, the rider spurring the animal on with legs and whip.

Desta watched with his hand over his lips first and then under his jacket, on his chest. "Dama—fly, fly, fly—Dama, fly," he began to say, remembering the picture of the flying horse and Saint George he saw on the wall of his parents' church. To the crowd's astonishment, Dama and Abraham appeared to levitate as they reached the final stretch of the course. When Desta let go of his chest, Abraham and Dama came down gracefully. People capped their faces, bent, and gawked at horseman and steed unsure whether what they were seeing was real, or just the afternoon sun playing tricks on them.

Many were convinced what they had seen was not real. Abraham turned his horse around for the return trip. Once the two were halfway back along the course, Desta again slipped his hand under his jacket and pressed the area over his heart, saying, "Dama—fly, fly, fly!" As the horse rose into the air, Abraham gripped tightly on the pummel. The crowd shouted and yelled and parted, clearing the ground should the horse decide to fly past the starting line. Desta removed his hand as before, and Dama landed just at the spot where he took off. Many gaped at horse and man, stupefied. Some appeared immobilized, seemingly afraid to come close to the horse and horseman.

Teka was the first to approach. "This was the best show we have ever had—a miracle really!" the short man said, his face more than his words articulating his thoughts. "And then that moving story you told: a fitting eulogy. We were all touched," Teka added.

"I wanted to formally acknowledge the passage of my father. I thank you again for allowing me to do so at this venue," Abraham said.

"And then your flying horse—" Teka said, his thoughts clipped.

"I don't know what happened," Abraham said. "As to the flying thing, I have no answers or explanations." He shook his head.

"We have never seen anything like this," many of the men said. They studied Abraham and Dama, and shook their heads.

"It's just Saint Mary performing a miracle on her holiday, right before our eyes. . . . Hallelujah!" a woman said.

"Can you do it again?" some of the boys asked, once they could navigate their way to where Abraham and Dama stood.

Desta just grinned contented and happy that he could help perform magic on behalf of his beloved grandpa. At that moment he felt like he was the most powerful person in the whole world.

"I don't know. . . . I have no idea what just happened to us," Abraham kept saying to just about everybody who approached and asked him to explain what they saw.

"Let's go home," Almaw said, once he managed to reach his uncle. "I had not expected you to put on such a show. The crowd was mesmerized."

"I had to get it out of my system once and for all . . . but that extra stuff, I am equally stunned," Abraham said, still catching his breath.

The priests concluded their Dance of David and headed back to the church.

Abraham agreed they should go home because he and Desta had to set off for Dangila early the next day. He felt overwhelmed by all the people who kept asking about his flying feat and his father.

Almaw tapped Abraham and said, "We'd better go quick. You may not realize it, but you've provided great fodder for the gossip mill. Your performance and the story you shared will be repeated over and over again; it will be exaggerated and distorted and embellished for months to come."

"That's how these sorts of stories often go," Abraham said in a rugged voice. "It'll keep the tongues occupied of churchgoers, market-goers, and men perched on the grass outside of their homes on weekends as they drink tella and snack on roasted barley and chickpeas."

"Yes," Almaw said with a smile. "You just resurrected grandpa's name and status, too, the way it used to be. We all should be pleased."

As they walked back to Aunt Zere's home, Desta piped up, "The name of the racing headman is intriguing."

"Why is that?" Abraham asked.

"Well, Teka means 'he who succeeded.' You now have succeeded your father as an accomplished racer," the boy replied, grinning.

"Oh, Desta, you're always clever at thinking of these things. I am too old to claim myself as a horseman, but I set an example for my son," Abraham said with a wink at the boy.

Desta thought about this comment for a moment.

"That is right, Desta," Almaw said. "You could carry grandpa's baton, which, regrettably, none of us older grandchildren have done."

"Me," Desta said. "I am a student. I am going to become . . ." But he had no idea what he would become once he finished school and found the second Coin of Magic and Fortune.

FOR BOTH ABRAHAM AND DESTA it had been a great day. Abraham had come full circle, reliving his childhood, connecting with his deep feelings, and purging himself of the past once and for all—first with his tears and then through the eulogy to his father. He felt he could live happily hereafter.

Desta had experienced the true power of the coin image on his chest. He had fulfilled his long dream of coming to Kuakura to visit his father's birthplace and walk on the grounds his grandparents had owned and his father roamed. He felt good to know that he came from somewhere bigger and wider than just that confined valley. He had added to his self-worth and pride in who he was and where he came from.

That night, before they fell asleep, father and son both prayed that their meeting with Zewday's family would be a success.

TWENTY

Desta spent much of the night tossing and turning and, occasionally, raising his head and looking toward the entrance for any hint of dawn along the edges of the door. He would then lay on his back and try to catnap or listen for a rooster's crow to announce the arrival of daybreak.

His hopeful future as a modern-school student and improved chances of locating the bearer of the coin hinged on the outcome of the trip to Dangila. It was a shot in the dark. None of the six families he personally knew in Yeedib had offered him their homes or their hearts, so why would Zewday and his wife, who were little more than complete strangers? Desta shuddered at the thought that the trip might be another dead end.

He rolled over and lay on his belly, thinking of the consequences if Zewday declined to accept him: two weeks' worth of lessons at his Yeedib school lost, a flogging by one of his teachers for returning late after the Christmas break, and possibly even a refusal to let him come back to school.

He was mortified at the thought of being a shepherd again and, ultimately, a farmer—forever. He would have to endure constant ridicule from his brothers for being fool enough to want a foreign education, a sacrilege to the family and community at large.

When he finally awoke from his restless slumber, he heard Abraham whispering a prayer, asking God to make their journey a success. This from a man who rarely prayed meant Abraham, too, was worried.

When it was light enough, Abraham rose and went out, and Desta followed. The dreary landscape, made worse by the charcoal-gray, melancholy clouds, mirrored what Desta had been feeling all night.

"Ah-ha, you remembered. Thank you," Abraham said to Almaw, finding his Dama harnessed and ready for the road when he returned from his outing. Almaw's wife, Yeseru, had also risen early; she had prepared the travelers' breakfast. Aunt Zere was sitting by the living room fire, her face partially covered, counting the beads of her tawny wood rosary.

Once father and son finished eating their breakfast, each gathered his belongings and prepared to go. "Go kiss your aunt's knee first," Abraham said to the boy. Desta promptly complied. Aunt Zere, in return, blessed him profusely and then added that her sons would visit him when they came to town on a market day.

"I will see you this evening," Abraham said, bending a little.

"May your journey be blessed and your meeting with Ato Zewday be a success."

"Thank you. Stay well."

When they stepped out of doors, Desta was pleased to see the eastern sky had brightened a little. Above the straight, pencil-line horizon, discrete clouds floated over a sprawling layer of sienna, with a golden tint near where the sun, a shrouded ball, was being delivered to the world. A blush of pink and amber rippled across the puffy, languid clouds, and the boy wished he were a painter so that he might capture this once-in-a-lifetime moment before the sun fully rose and whitened everything. Down on land, the view was dotted with a sparse cluster of sleepy villages, and shrubs and trees, all veiled in silver-gray mist.

They bore north on a dusty path, Desta leading Dama, and Abraham following behind. They crossed a creek and then hooked up with a larger road that went under the shadow of a bell-shaped mountain. Desta's anxieties returned to invade his consciousness, causing him to stumble, but he realized there was nothing he could do at that moment to influence the outcome of their mission and soon felt better. For the rest of the trip, he kept his head clear of worries, filling it instead with excitement about visiting the famed town and the people he hoped to meet there, including the lady with the yellow hair.

Abraham stepped a few yards off the road to pee. Desta wound Dama's lead around his wrist and waited. The day was hot and muggy, causing the boy to throw a section of his gabi across his head as protection against the strong sun. "Baba," he said when his father returned, "I have a question."

"What is it?" Abraham wiped his perspiration with the pads of his fingers and flung it.

"How close a relative is Zewday?"

Abraham thought for a few seconds. "Well," he said, closing his fist and springing his thumb as he began to count. "There is my mother, Simegne." He sprang his index finger and said, "There is my mother's father, Meshesha."

He popped a finger for each name he recited from the previous generation, finally ending with his pinkie finger and a woman named Amelework. Then he went through the same count on Zewday's side of the family, starting with Zewday's father and going back six generations until Abraham reached an ancestor who was a twin sister of Amelework's, Abraham's fifth great-grandmother.

Desta couldn't believe his ears. "You mean to say that a person who is so remotely related to us would care enough to give me accommodations?"

"Of course they will, both Zewday and his wife," replied Abraham confidently. "No matter how distant, the blood that courses through his veins is still identical in some ways to yours. Those identical things are enough for him and his wife to be sympathetic and kindly toward you."

"But whatever those things are, they are mere scraps in me if he is that distantly related," Desta said, disheartened. His stomach felt as if he had swallowed a bitter herb and his apprehension increased a notch.

"Not only are you and Zewday blood relatives," Abraham said excitedly, "you have our family's lucky number seven as a fortifying bond between you. Both you and Zewday are seventh generation from Amelework, your common ancestral mother."

Desta wanted to believe his father but it all seemed way too illusory. "When was the last time you saw these people?" he asked.

"About three years ago."

"Do you think they will still be around?"

"What do you think would happen to them? Let's keep going."

Desta unwound the horse's lead from his wrist. "They could be dead," he said. "Think of what happened to Tru and Mekuria. Or they could have moved."

"Nothing like that would happen to them because they don't travel much, and he is a clerk at the court, so it's unlikely he would have moved. C'mon. We want to arrive before Zewday returns to his job after lunch."

Desta was not convinced. While they walked, he turned around to Abraham and asked, "How is it that we don't have any closer relatives in Dangila or any of the other towns?"

"I'm sure we do. I just don't know who they are. It's the curse that's afflicted us for years, since we left this area and went to live in that remote valley. Over time, mother lost touch with many of her relatives and Baba's. She used to tell me that we were descended from a line of the Gonder kings, which means you're a *lule*—prince—Desta," Abraham said with a smile.

"Yeah, right, a shepherd lule," Desta said, even though he didn't exactly know what a lule was.

"Mother also said that Empress Taitu Bitul, who founded Addis Ababa, was her grandfather's cousin."

"All those people mean nothing to me, Baba. I just wish we had relatives close enough for me to live with, like Tru and Mekuria."

"If we are lucky, you will have Mekuria and Tru in Zewday and his wife, Mebet. Don't worry."

"What is Mebet like?"

"I don't know her that well. She's a beautiful young Agew girl."

Another mystery for Desta. "What's an Agew person like?"

"They are like everybody else, except that they say it's hard to find their heart."

"Hard to find their heart?! That's great!" Desta hissed in exasperation.

When they finally reached Dangila, Desta couldn't tell whether they were coming to a forest or a town—it was completely shrouded by pale-green eucalyptus trees. Even at a distance he could smell their herbal fragrance and see their pointing tops swaying in the wind.

A broad and level gravel road came sweeping around a grove of acacia trees and a cluster of newly built tin-roofed houses from somewhere on the south side of the town and traveled straight north, passing a copse of eucalyptus trees and grass-roofed tenements. The road was built in some places over a bed of rocks and otherwise over graded earth that crowned from ditches on either side. Desta stood with Dama in the middle of the road and looked one way first and then the other, marveling at its evenness. This was unlike any road he had ever seen.

Abraham noticed Desta's enthralled look. "This is *godana*—a road—for *mekeenas*— cars."

"What are cars like? Have they no feet like horses or donkeys that they would need a road like this?"

Abraham smiled. "If we are lucky, we might just see one before we leave the area. But we need to get out of the way in case one comes soon."

They crossed the ditch and began walking on a dusty footpath alongside the roadway. Desta tried to imagine what a car must look like. Just from the name itself, he could tell it was not like an animal. That he had figured out. The sewing machine his brother Teferra had at home was also a mekeena. But that mekeena didn't need a road to travel on, only his brother's feet for driving the wheel below the table, which in turn moved the parts of the machine above and enabled him to do his sewing.

Desta wanted to ask his father what a mekeena that travels on a road looked like but he stifled the thought, wishing to savor the moment when he finally saw one. He prayed a mekeena would come before they left the road, and then he heard a deafening, syncopated sound coming from far away. He turned in the direction of the sound and listened some more.

"Desta, you're lucky," Abraham said. "A lorry is on its way. It should be here shortly."

"Lorry? Not a mekeena?" The boy was confused. Whatever "lorry" was, the sound it made was like a monster that could annihilate anything in its path. It coughed, groaned, blared, and gasped as it came nearer and nearer. Desta could sense its speed, too, because just moments before, it had sounded like it was coming out of a cave. Now it was at full blast, splattering the air with its force. His heart raced and he was tempted to run for cover. Abraham, though, was unfazed by the sound of the oncoming beast and this comforted Desta, just a little.

"Be sure to cover your face when the lorry passes by," Abraham said. He wet his index finger and held it up in the air. "The wind is blowing in our direction. . . . We need to secure Dama, too." He grabbed the horse's lead from Desta and coiled it around his hand.

A horrendous object on four round black things, with a gray metal-and-glass box in front and a rectangular wooden frame filled to the brim with sacks in the back, sped toward them.

Desta stepped closer to his father and Dama. The lorry whizzed by, throwing a cloud of dust over their heads and shoulders, and assaulting their legs and feet with a shower of gravel. What was left in the air after the lorry had gone was noxious and caused Desta to gag and cough. "What is that horrid smell?" he asked between wheezes.

"Gasoline, the fuel that runs cars. That's probably what's causing your coughs, that plus the dust."

They continued walking and soon came near a woven wire fence that bounded a large rectangular compound. A white building stood at the center of the enclosure.

"That's the *mitsion*—mission," Abraham said, observing Desta's glances.

"The place Saba came to get treated for her miscarriages?" Desta asked, briskly. He was happy to finally see the place where his beloved sister had come as a last attempt to find a cure for her problems.

Abraham said it was.

"The place where a woman with milk-white skin and yellow hair lives?"

Abraham nodded.

Desta halted and gaped through the fence, hoping to see the woman.

She is probably busy treating patients inside the building," Abraham said, indifferently. "If Ato Zewday and his wife agree to have you, you will get a chance to see her some weekend. She walks around the grounds sometimes."

A little disappointed, Desta followed Abraham and Dama. After crossing a sleepy river and walking for a couple of miles along a car road that went north-south, they reached the center of town, a circular open space of bare dusty earth, roughly two hundred yards across. Shops of various sizes, coffeehouses and teahouses, and food-selling outlets arrayed its perimeter.

Abraham noticed Desta's glances at the food-selling places and said, "We are not far from Zewday's house. I am sure his wife will give us something to eat and drink."

They veered right, across the eastern portion of the plaza, and walked toward a passageway where two rows of shops converged at a right angle. Men and women outside the big open windows bargained with merchants behind long counters. Desta lingered and studied the shopkeepers. They were all men. Some wore light-colored skullcaps, and each had a bulging cheek, as if having stuffed it with something—leaves, Desta thought: he could see a dry, green residue at the corners of their mouths. In between their chatter they chewed on the stuff.

"Wait for me at the end of the passageway. I will be there in a moment," Abraham said and walked to one of the windows that was clear of people.

Desta was happy to have a few moments to look around without being rushed. He and Dama cleared the walkway and came to a narrow alley that ran along the back of the shops on the left. On the other side stood a row of old, corrugated metal-roofed houses with ribbed doors closed or partially opened.

A few yards away on the right, the alleyway joined with a bigger dusty street that went north. On the outside corner stood a small lone building with its door partially closed. Through its only window Desta could see a middle-aged man, his head wrapped with a multicolored cloth, hunched over a counter. A brown hook-like object stuck out from the corner of his mouth, reminding Desta of a goat with a twig it had snatched from a bush or a tree. But the man was not chewing his twig like a goat, at least not from what Desta could tell.

The man was so concentrated on what was before him that Desta thought he probably had forgotten to chomp on his twig. This odd person was unlike any man Desta had ever seen before: his too-fair skin, his lush salt-and-pepper beard, his detached persona, his uncommon head wrapping.

Dama snorted loudly as if he found the air on this side of the shops disagreeable. The man lifted his eyes from the counter and stared at them. He removed the brown twig from his mouth. The man then reached and pinched something from a box and transferred it into the hooked, cup-like receptacle of the twig and replaced it in his mouth.

He struck a match, shielded the flame with curved hands, and lit the thing he had stuffed into the vessel. A cloud of smoke billowed forth, as did tendrils from his mouth and nostrils. He leaned back in his high chair, contented. With one hand holding the hooked end of the brown object, he continued to exhale the white stuff and momentarily cloud his sallow face with it. The man seemed as intrigued by the boy as Desta was with him. He absentmindedly pulled on his twig and puffed out the smoke. The man's thoughtful manner and retiring disposition were a mystery to Desta, and he wondered who the man really was.

A boy about twelve years old barged onto the scene astride a metallic-blue horse which came rolling on two thin round black things, disrupting Desta's concentration on the man and vice versa. The intruder, fair-skinned with luxurious, curly jet-black hair, hopped down from his horse, leaned it against the wall of the little building where the smoking man was, and vanished through the partially opened door.

"Go on," Abraham said, startling Desta. "To the right."

"What do you call that?" Desta asked, pointing to the blue horse the boy had left outside.

"I don't know what they call it. Move on," Abraham urged, after a long side–glance at the object.

"And that man?"

"What about him?"

"He looks different."

"He is an Arab."

"Is that like a Ferenge?"

"No. They are different."

"Where does he come from?"

"From his country."

"Where is that?"

"I don't know. Some place far away. Stop asking so many questions."

Desta hesitated at the corner of the street, wondering which way to go.

"Turn left," Abraham said.

It was a dusty road bordered by a row of tin-roofed buildings and grass-roofed homes. Desta led the horse, glancing from side to side as he went along. Long, narrow tables arrayed with drinking glasses stood in the center of the home's living rooms, indicating these were probably tella or *tej*—honey wine—houses.

Zewday's home was set back from the street, behind a grove of coffee plants. Twin circular houses squatted inside the fence line, facing the street.

A footpath to the left of the houses and through the plantation led them to Zewday's residence. This was another pair of circular houses, one older and squat to the right of a circular, cleanly swept courtyard and a newer one with high eaves and smooth walls to the left. The doors of the houses faced each other and a person could walk from one to the other with a dozen leisurely strides across the courtyard.

A slender teenage girl was going from the older house to the newer one, carrying a green pitcher inside a red bowl. She greeted the visitors with a bow. After Abraham told her who they were, she said, "I'll be right back" and went inside the newer house.

"That is Lesim," whispered Abraham, "Zewday's daughter."

Desta tensed up, anxious to see what his seventh-generation relative and the Agew woman looked like. Several minutes later, Lesim emerged and invited Abraham and Desta to come in. Abraham tethered the horse to one of the eucalyptus trees near the courtyard, and father and son went inside.

Desta's apprehension and anxiety fell away the moment he stepped indoors and beheld the family around a dining table in the middle of the living room. The man, tall and willowy, had midnight-blue skin. Closely cropped, loose salt-and-pepper hair crowned his small but sturdy head. With his chiseled and refined features, he could serve as a model for a woodcrafter's masterpiece. The whites of his eyes, bloodshot at their outer corners, popped out against the sable of his face. All in all he resembled no one in Desta's family, causing the boy to question his father's claim that they were related.

The woman next to him was his antithesis: buxom, young, and fair-skinned, with big brown eyes and a loose halo of hair. Her high cheekbones and nose, with its slight kink in the middle, were superior to the man's. The third individual at the table was a boy three or four years old. He was halfway between his mother and father in the shading of his skin and his features.

The man and woman rose, and Abraham and Zewday greeted each other with three kisses on their cheeks. Mebet acknowledged the guests with a bow and then three kisses on the cheeks. Abraham dropped to the floor and kissed Tesfa, the boy. He finished this gesture by saying endearing words and giving a quick rub to his head.

Desta's eyes went from the man to the woman and back, entranced. He found his legs when Abraham whispered, "Go kiss their knees." The boy moved to the man, bent down and kissed his knee. When Desta came up, Zewday grabbed the boy's chin and kissed him on his cheeks. Mebet refused to be kissed on her knee and, instead, grabbed Desta, kissing him on his cheeks.

They all sat down, Abraham and Desta on the two spare chairs. Two glass tumblers partially filled with tella stood before Zewday and Mebet. Food crumbs and water droplets speckled the floral white plastic table covering, suggesting that the family members had finished their lunch and concluded it by washing their hands.

Mebet signaled to Lesim, and within a few minutes, the girl brought two glasses of the same brown beverage her parents were drinking. Desta was more hungry than thirsty, but he still drank a substantial amount of the tella. He put the glass tumbler on the table and wondered if their hosts were going to offer them any food, as Abraham had said they would.

"*Ager dehina new*—is the country well?" Zewday asked.

Abraham said all was well.

"How about your children, the animals, and the crops?"

Courtly and polite, Abraham acknowledged that they were well also and thanked Zewday for his interest.

Abraham in turn asked Zewday about his health, the health of his relatives, and his work. Abraham then offered the same courtesy to Mebet and her family.

Nobody asked Desta any questions and he did not feel important enough to be part of the adults' conversation. With butterflies in his stomach and sweat on his palms, he twiddled his thumbs under the table as he anxiously waited for Abraham to stop his mundane tattle and get to the main reason they were there. When his father didn't stop, the boy occupied his eyes with things around the house.

For starters, there was the circular wall, whose smooth plaster of mud and straw had been seamlessly covered with newspaper from ceiling to the floor. Two doors, one to the north that faced the second house and the other to the east, interrupted the flow of the wall. A few feet behind Zewday stood a block-shaped high earthen seat with a plush cowhide covering a grass pad. Beyond this area, the wall was broken again to create an outward-extending pocket that was the only bedroom.

On the wall near the bedroom hung a lovely white horsetail flyswatter and a leather-clad book. Desta thought this book was probably a *Dawit*—Bible. His brother Tamirat used to have one exactly like it. Next to it leaned a gleaming, yellowish walking cane of solid wood.

Lesim reappeared with the kettle of tella and refilled Abraham's cup. Desta refused any more of the brown drink but took the opportunity to study the girl a little more.

About sixteen years old, Lesim had dull cinnamon skin and a long symmetrical face that was neither notable nor exactly refined, except for her big soulful eyes, her most striking feature. Her long legs were not shapely or adequately defined and terminated in a set of flat ashen feet, whose little toes curled back, wishing to have nothing to do with the dirt the others walked on.

Lesim went out with the kettle, treading lightly across the large palm leaf mat that extended from the center of the living room to the entrance. The rest of the smoothed dirt floor was covered in cowhides. Near the entrance, a long sturdy table supported pots and pans, drinking glasses, aluminum kettles, a clay incense burner, food baskets, and a *jebena*—clay kettle—and small multicolored coffee cups on a wooden tray. There were no other furnishings in the room.

Mebet rose, excused herself, and left with the boy in tow.

"I know I have not seen you for quite some time," Abraham said.

Desta stared at Zewday's eyes and mouth, paying particular attention to any hints in his pupils, twitches at the corners of his mouth, or uncomfortable shifts in his body when Abraham finally broached the reason for their journey to his home.

"You don't have business that brings you to our town anymore?" Zewday asked.

"I have been busy with court cases and other things and have not had time to do anything else."

"What brings you this time?"

"We have an unfortunate circumstance involving this boy," Abraham said, glancing at Desta. "Having exhausted all our options, we thought we'd bring him here and see. . . ."

Desta clenched his teeth and held his breath.

"Is something the matter with him?" Zewday asked, his eyes on the boy.

"No, nothing like that. You see, he had relentlessly pestered us about putting him into modern school. We took him to our little town to live with his uncle and wife and go to school. Sadly, the couple died in a bus accident last September while going to Addis Ababa to see the wife's aunt. We have no other relative in the little town who he can live with to continue his studies. We approached complete strangers and found no one willing to take him.

"I am a believer in the old adage that blood is thicker than water, and I brought him here on the good chance he can live with you and pursue his studies. He is a very good boy and can earn his keep by bringing firewood, running errands, and doing other miscellaneous chores for you and *Weizero*—Mrs.—Mebet. Of course, we will also bring his supply of food by way of sacks of grains and other things."

Zewday shifted his eyes to the open door and thought for a few seconds. Then he turned and looked at Desta once again.

The boy kept his eyes on Zewday for a few seconds and then dropped them to the table. It was considered impolite to stare back at an adult for any extended time. He bit his lip and held his breath.

Zewday's eyes now shifted to Abraham. "You say he's a good student?"

Desta placed his hand over his heart.

"Tops. His teacher told me that he finished his lessons in half the time it took the other students," Abraham said with a tinge of pride in his voice.

"That's fine. The only personal service I'd need from him would be to accompany me when I go to church on Sunday."

Desta let his breath out and slowly removed his hand from his chest.

"Thank you. He could carry your cane, your Bible, or umbrella, and do any other task you wish."

Lesim came to ask if they needed anything and Zewday told her to tell Mebet to come for an important matter. When Mebet came in, Zewday shared Abraham's request to have Desta live with them while he went to school. She slightly crinkled her brow and narrowed her eyes, gazing at her husband.

Desta couldn't explain those expressions, whether they indicated surprise that she had not been included in the decision making or signaled her reluctance to have him in her home.

Zewday explained to Mebet the kind of services the boy could offer them, including bringing firewood and doing other errands. Her brow relaxed.

"I've also offered to bring sacks of grain and other supplies," Abraham chipped in quickly.

Mebet's face brightened. "I'm okay with my husband's decision," she said.

"I think we can use a boy in the family," Zewday said, smiling at Desta.

"Weizero Mebet, I think you will be happy with this boy. He is obedient and a hard worker," Abraham added, holding Mebet's eyes. He wanted both to reassure the woman of the house and be clear that she had accepted his son unequivocally.

"Like I mentioned," Mebet said, "if my husband approves it, I am happy to have your son live with us."

"Thank you. That's very kind and generous. I will entrust this boy to your care. In two months, shortly after we celebrate the Easter holiday, I will return with a good supply of grains that will help cover his food from now till then and for the months following, until school closes in June."

"It's not necessary to make that long journey with sacks of grain, Abraham. The boy will share whatever we have. Don't trouble yourself," Zewday said, getting up to go back to his office. Desta and Abraham could tell Zewday appreciated their offer, given his kind response.

"It's the right thing to do," Abraham said, rising to go. "I'm grateful that you've accepted him wholeheartedly. May God extend his blessings to you and your family as you've extended your kindness to my son."

He shook hands with Zewday and Mebet this time and headed to the door. Desta followed his father out. He felt no fear or abandonment. He had no feelings at all.

Abraham had just untied Dama's lead from the tree when Lesim came with a message from Mebet. "My mother said that when you come in April, she would greatly appreciate it if you could bring some butter." She crossed her legs and broke into a nervous smile.

"Tell her I'll be happy to," Abraham said, winding the horse's lead around his hand.

"*Melkam menged ingidias*—good journey then," Lesim said and left.

"Okay, son," Abraham said as he bent down. "Be strong. Study hard. Be a good, obedient boy to this family. If you do everything they ask of you, they will treat you like their own child."

Desta said nothing.

"Did you hear me?"

Desta nodded. "Don't offend them and disappoint me." Abraham bore his big eyes down on the boy. "If it doesn't work out here for you, you will have no choice but to come home and become a farmer."

"Yes, I will do my best. I will be a good student, work hard, and try to do everything they ask of me."

"Good." Abraham kissed him on his forehead and gave his head a little rub.

Desta wished his father would do it some more. He wished he had done that to him when was little, when he needed him the most. Tears filled his eyes but never fell.

TWENTY-ONE

After Abraham left, Desta leaned against the smooth, circular wall of the main house and tried to assess his feelings. He had no fear or apprehension about anything, although he was overwhelmed by the size and humming noise of the town. He felt in some ways as if he were in a jungle full of birds and noisy ground animals.

This was a jungle of houses: grass-roofed, circular structures, like those in the country, and rectangular buildings with pitched roofs of corrugated tin like some of the ones in Yeedib. There were the all-pervading eucalyptus trees that rose high, like some of the trees in the forest near his home, shielding much of the sun and the sky. Beyond the neatly swept path in front of him, the thick grove of coffee plants roofed over much of the property. On the north side of the property, just beyond a closed shed, was a high wooden fence bordered by a row of leafy bushes; it seemed to bar contact with whoever lived on the other side.

He wondered whether he would be happy living here, without seeing any mountains, clouds, or the sun. There was no one here he could share his feelings and thoughts with, and he was so far away from home. He knew he had no option but to get used to his circumstances, like he had gotten used to being an outcast in his family. Like he had gotten use to walking for four hours a day back and forth to school when he lived with his sister the previous semester. And he had nobody to miss. Kooli, his dog, was long dead. His beloved sister Hibist had married and moved away, and his vervet monkey friends had left the area. And Tru and Mekuria were dead. In that regard, he was free, not emotionally bound to anyone who would tug at his heart. He was glad about that. To accomplish his missions, he couldn't have anything or anyone like that who would get in the way.

Like his grandfather's spirit had said, his only companion in his new world would be the invisible image on his chest that echoed the coin in the sandalwood box—his guide and protector, his talisman. That he wouldn't lose. No one could take it away; it would not abandon him.

While standing outside around sunset, Desta heard a man shout in a loud, rugged voice from what seemed like the west side of town. The words "Allahu Akbar!" filled the air. The man sounded like he was hanging down from the sky because his vigorous voice floated over the din and the clamor of the town and the rustle of the leaves from the tall eucalyptus trees around where Desta stood. The man repeated the mystical words. It was unlike anything he had heard before.

Lesim came up when she noticed the boy standing still, his face down, riveted. "Are you okay?" she asked.

"I am. Who is that man and what's he saying?"

"He is *Islam*—Muslim; he is letting his religion's followers know that it's time to pray."

"Is he standing on top of a tree or hanging down from the sky?"

Lesim placed her hand over her mouth and suppressed a laugh. "Why?"

"His voice seems to come from above the trees. The only time it sounds like that where I come from is when someone climbs a mountain and announces the death of someone in the area. There are no mountains here."

"He is standing high up on the roof of their *mesgid*. It's a house where the Islamic people go to pray, like we go to *betechristian*—church."

Desta had a lot of questions about the Islamic people. What did they look like? Where did they live? Why didn't they wear a *mateb*—cord—around their necks? He remembered Hibist once admonishing him for not having one around his neck. . . . But he didn't want to start out the wrong way and be accused of asking too many questions. He would find the answers on his own over time. The lunch the boy had hoped to eat when he and Abraham arrived came at dinnertime, in the form of half an injera with a scoop of shiro wat. Although Desta was surprised by the skimpy meal and was still hungry after he finished eating, he dismissed the gesture as the family's probably not having prepared enough food that day.

The following morning, Desta rose from his sleeping mat on the living room floor in the main house. He put on his shorts and jacket and covered himself with his gabi. Lesim gave him a pitcher of water and a bar of orange-colored soap to bring outside and wash his face and hands with. He went around to the side of the house and put the pitcher on the ground. He tipped it with one hand

and poured water into the cupped palm of the other. He splashed the water into his face and then rubbed his face with his hands. The water felt icy cold, sending shock waves throughout his body. He tipped the pitcher and splashed cold water into his face several times, until his skin squeaked to the touch.

Minutes later, Lesim brought a towel, warm water in a kettle, and a blood-red plastic bowl. Desta was to take these to Zewday at the back of the main house. He found Zewday sitting on a wooden bench, his back against the wall, saying his prayers. Next to him was a folded book with a red cloth binding. He looked up and said, "Gosh, you brought my face water."

"*Awwe*—yes," Desta politely replied. He studied the man. The outer corners of his eyes creased like parchment, with fine dark lines that radiated out and vanished at the temples. His skin looked dusty, as if rubbed with ashes.

Zewday smiled, showing his alabaster teeth. He leaned forward and stuck his hands out so Desta could pour the warm water over them. "Aaah," said the midnight blue man. "This is just what I needed on this cold morning." His small carmine eyes twinkled with joy. He picked up the brown soap from the bowl and lathered his hands and face.

With a few rounds of water that Desta poured into Zewday's cupped hands, the man rinsed the soap from his face. He wet and brushed back his close crop of peppered hair. He dab-dried his hands and face with the towel he took from Desta's shoulder and then tossed it back to the boy.

"*Beka*—enough," Zewday said, waving Desta to go.

Desta threw the wash water into the trees and returned everything else to Lesim. He realized then that this was probably one of the services his father had said he could render to the family.

Zewday went inside the main house and dressed in long cream-colored pants, a light-colored shirt, and a dark coat, topping these with the wrapping of his gabi. He sat at the table and waited for Lesim to bring his breakfast.

Lesim came in with a tray of *firfir*—minced injera—in a hot spicy sauce of beef jerky and eggs. Soon after, Mebet came and sat with her husband to eat her morning meal.

"Give Desta his breakfast," Zewday said to Lesim. "I plan to take him to school to register."

The girl brought Desta a pristine white plate containing two tablespoons of the firfir on half an injera. Desta wondered if it would be enough to last him till lunchtime. He sat on the floor, placed the plate on his lap, and ate.

Remembering Ayénat's advice about the impoliteness of eating one's meal quickly, Desta ate consciously. He took tiny bites and chewed them deliberately. At the end he left a morsel of the food, again following his mother's advice: "When you are a guest in someone's home, no matter how hungry you may be, always leave something on the platter. That way the hosts won't feel they have not fed you enough."

Desta took his plate to the second squat house that the family referred to as *madd-bet*—kitchen—and returned with warm water, soap, a bowl, and a towel. He dispensed water for Zewday and Mebet, and one at a time they lathered and washed their hands. After they rinsed their hands, Desta poured more water into their cupped palms, and they sipped and washed their mouths with it and spat the waste into the bowl. The boy took the wash water outside and threw it away.

This, Desta thought, was probably a second activity he would be performing for the couple.

"Go get ready," Zewday said after Desta returned. "We will go to the school soon, and I have to go to work afterward."

Zewday and Desta exited the gate and traveled south toward the center of town. They then turned directly east. They crossed the sleepy Amin River and walked a wide pathway between columns of eucalyptus trees. They came to a set of three long one-story buildings arranged in the shape of a T. Classes had already begun and the buildings were quiet, save for one room where students loudly recited the alphabet in unison, following a lead boy.

A short, slender man with soft dark eyes and wearing a baggy jacket appeared out of nowhere. "Good morning," he said with a slight bow.

"Good morning," Zewday said, his head unmoving. "Are you the *zebegna*—custodian? I am here to register this boy. Can you show us where the director's office is?"

"Yes, I am Gizachew, the custodian. Follow me." Gizachew led the guests to the entrance of the middle building. He pushed open the corrugated tin door and they entered a short hallway with a clean dirt floor and two closed rooms on either side.

"Please wait here," Gizachew said, glancing at Zewday with a serious face. He knocked on the door to the first room on the left.

"C'mon in," said a man in a loud, booming voice.

Gizachew entered and returned shortly after. "Please come in," he said, stepping aside to let the guests pass. "Ato Tedla is hard of hearing," he whispered.

"You have to speak louder than normal to communicate with him."

Tedla rose the moment Zewday and Desta entered. The two men greeted each other with bows followed by a handshake.

Desta studied the man. Nearly a mirror image of Zewday, although his skin tone was closer to twilight than midnight; the all-black clothes he wore, save for the crisp cream shirt underneath, made him appear a shade or two darker than he really was.

He wore a long tongue-shaped garment, with horizontal black bands in a white field that looped around his neck and cascaded down his chest in two strips. *Is this man blind, too, that he needs a leash like a dog for someone to pull him around with?* Desta wondered. The man's eyes appeared normal.

"Please sit down," Tedla said, louder than necessary. He threw his hand out to one of the chairs before him. Zewday sat down but Desta remained standing.

"I am sorry but I cannot accept the boy this late in the semester," Tedla replied forcefully after learning the reason for Zewday and Desta's visit.

Desta winced and held his breath.

Zewday stared at Tedla for a few seconds, at a loss for words. "But you have to accept this boy. He traveled for two days with his father, hoping to live with us and attend your school," Zewday said, louder than necessary.

"I've no problem with him attending our school. It's just that it has been over two weeks since the semester started and it would be hard for him to catch up." Tedla glanced at Desta. "Where does he come from?"

"Yeedib, in the high country of Sekela."

"Oh, one of those rural schools," Tedla sneered louder than necessary. "That is another reason we cannot accept him in the middle of the school year. Those schools are often run by former priests. They have no formal training in modern education. This boy probably has not learned much beyond our alphabet. All our teachers are graduates of teacher training institutes. Not only do they know our written language well but also mathematics and English."

Desta could hold his breath no more. He let it out. He replenished himself with another inhalation and held that breath.

"That I don't know," Zewday said, his voice flagging. He turned to Desta. "Step forward. Can you tell Ato Tedla what you have learned from your country school?"

Before Desta had a chance to speak or exhale, Tedla interrupted.

"What we can do is put him in the first grade. That way he will learn all the basics—reading and writing, the English alphabet, and arithmetic. If he does well, we can promote him to the second grade next year. Then, if he ranks in the top three in his class, he can be promoted to the third grade after the first semester."

Zewday swiveled around and looked at Desta, once again trying to determine his reaction to Tedla's suggestion. Desta let out the air he had been holding. "I learned all those things at my school in Yeedib. I got good marks on all my tests. I became first in my class. I received a prize for it," Desta said with a firm and determined voice, louder than necessary. He reached into his cloth pouch and pulled out the book he was presented. He stepped closer to the table and handed the book to the still-seated director. "Here," he said, louder than necessary.

Tedla read Brook's inscription. He flipped through the pages. "From the way this book is worn, it seems you have spent a great deal of time with it." He looked up at Desta, studying him. Tedla pressed the top of a gleaming silver bell near the edge of his table. It rang with an intense reverberation, summoning Gizachew into the room.

"Please call Ato Betew, the homeroom teacher for second grade, in Section A."

The zebegna soon returned with Betew. Tedla introduced the teacher to the visitors, explaining why they were there and the reason for his bidding. "This boy has no certificate or grade reports. He says he was in the second grade last semester and that he passed his first grade at the top of his class. This is the book he was awarded for it."

Betew read the inscription, flipped through the book, and stopped at a page in the middle. He turned to Desta. "What is a female sheep called?" he asked.

"Ewe."

Betew leafed through some more of the pages.

"What do we call gathered sheep?"

"Flock."

"What's your name?"

"My name is Desta Abraham."

Betew closed the book and gave it back to Tedla. He shifted his eyes to Desta.

"What do you get when you divide one hundred by five?"

"Twenty."

What's seven times five?"

"Thirty-five."

Betew looked at Tedla. "I'm happy to take this boy in my class."

"Thank you for your help and for coming so quickly," Tedla said.

"My pleasure," Betew said and left.

The director looked up at the new student. "You spoke convincingly and answered all Ato Betew's questions correctly. We'll accept you for the second grade," he said.

"*Amesegnalhu*—thank you," Desta mumbled, bowing a little.

"So your full name is Desta Abraham?" Tedla asked, again louder than necessary, as he opened his register.

"Awwe," Desta replied.

The director picked up a blue inkwell, unscrewed the top, and placed it beside the register on his right. He reached for a long nib pen and withdrew it from its silver mount atop a square brass base. He dipped pen in ink and then hunched over the tome, writing Desta's full name. "Birth year and date?" he asked.

Desta replied and Tedla repeated as he wrote it down: "January 7, 1949." He returned the pen to its holder and firmly screwed the lid back on the inkwell. He left the register open.

"Well, very rarely do we accept transfer students in the middle of the year, let alone weeks after the semester has started. But based on our assessments, this boy appears to be exceptional and deserves an exemption." Tedla smiled at Desta.

"That is how we felt, too, when his father brought him and explained his situation and his dedication to his studies," Zewday said as he rose.

Tedla blew air over the area where he'd written in the register before he closed it. He rang the bell again and the zebegna reappeared at the door. "Gizachew, take Desta to Betew's class," he commanded in his loud voice. He then rose and shook hands with Zewday, saying, "Thank you for your visit and for bringing the boy."

"Thank you for making the exception and giving him a chance to attend your school," Zewday said, stepping toward the door.

Desta and Zewday followed Gizachew outside. Before the custodian and Desta walked off, Zewday said, "Wait a minute. Who is going to bring him home when the students are released for lunch? The directions are not complicated. . . ."

The two men talked a bit as Zewday explained the general location of his home.

"I know roughly where you live. I will send him along with one of the students who comes from your neighborhood," Gizachew said.

Zewday was thankful. He shook hands with the custodian and departed.

TWENTY-TWO

Near midnight on Saturday, three consecutive loud bangs at the corrugated tin door shattered the silence and woke everyone in the room, except Tesfa. Startled and frightened, Desta sprang to his feet and pressed his back against the wall. He had been dozing with his face on his folded and crossed arms over his bent knees.

"Am coming!" Lesim shouted as she groped for the matchbox on the floor. Finding it, she hurriedly pulled the box open and extracted a match. After two misses, she managed to strike the side of the box. Sparks flew and a bright yellow flame erupted at the matchstick's tip, giving Lesim fire to light the small kerosene lamp.

The brightened room put Desta at ease, making him less fearful of the unknown intruder.

Mebet sat up on the high earthen seat near the bedroom where she had been dozing with Tesfa. She threw her netela over her shoulders and dropped her feet to the floor. She sighed. Pensive and thoughtful, she placed her hand against her cheek and gazed at the cowhide under her feet.

Lesim opened the door.

"Have you been sleeping?" Zewday demanded, glaring at his daughter. He swayed a little as he walked across the threshold.

Mebet looked up and threw a long glance across the room at her husband. "We have not enough kerosene to stay up with the light going," she replied, answering for Lesim. "And our normal bedtime has long since come and gone."

"Didn't I give you money to buy a gallon of it a week ago?" Zewday barked, fixing his red eyes on Lesim.

"No, that was over a month ago," the girl replied.

Zewday grunted and staggered past Lesim to the living room and came crashing down on the high earthen seat.

Desta studied the midnight blue man from head to toe to see if he was wet. He couldn't understand how someone could smell so much of tej and not have been soaking in it.

"Do we have dinner? I'm hungry," Zewday garbled. He looked at Lesim first, then at Mebet.

"Our mealtime, too, came and went a long time ago. As usual, we waited for you, hoping you would come home early for a change," said Mebet, twisting the fringes of her netela between her fingers. "When you didn't, we napped. Now the food we prepared has gone cold."

"I'm not asking you for a hot meal, am I?" Zewday snarled.

"I just wanted to make you . . ."

"Some friends wanted to discuss a legal matter and they delayed me."

"The same story all over," complained Mebet. She hissed and shook her head.

Zewday fixed his eyes on Lesim as if he wanted to communicate something personal to her.

Desta had been standing with his back still pressed against the wall, afraid of Zewday and mystified by his behavior. Lesim said to Desta, "Please take the bowl and pitcher of water for their hands."

The boy had brought the water hours ago, right before the regular dinnertime, but when Zewday didn't come, he had left them under the big catch-all table by the entrance.

Desta had noticed from the beginning that Mebet wouldn't serve dinner until Zewday came home. This was because, according to Lesim, a married woman shouldn't eat her meal alone, especially if her husband was in town and expected to come home in the evening. Furthermore, it would be impolite to watch one's husband dine alone when he finally came home.

The children had to wait, too, because Mebet made only one pot of sauce and she couldn't siphon the *merek*—oily layer—and give it to them. Only adults are privileged to have this.

Once Desta knew this rule, he could only pray that Zewday would come home earlier so they could eat dinner on time. He would learn that Zewday rarely came home on time. During the week, he was at least two hours late and on weekends more than double that. And he always came home smelling as if he had drenched himself in tella or tej—those common, home-brewed alcoholic beverages.

The boy's hunger often was greatest around dinnertime. Once it was past that time, he didn't feel it anymore, as if his body had found an alternative supply of food within itself—his own flesh.

While Mebet was getting ready for dinner, Tesfa woke. He rubbed his eyes with the back of his petite hands. "Your son is up," Mebet said to Zewday. "Say something to him before he starts crying."

He turned to Tesfa. "I didn't even know you were back there," crooned the drunkard. "Come, come, my son." The boy placed his hand over his nose and shook his head from side to side.

"How so? You don't want to come near your Baba? Okay, I know you are not going to refuse what I got for you." Zewday reached into his coat pocket and brought out a white oblong package. "Do you remember what this is?" he asked, waving the item before Tesfa.

"I dooo. Give it to me," cried out the boy, his face breaking into a smile.

"Come and kiss your Baba first and I will give it to you."

Tesfa shook his head again and refused to come near. "You smell funny," he said, furrowing his brow and studying his father. "Have you been drinking tej again?"

"Just a little." Zewday dropped the hand on his lap that held the package. He sighed. He cast his eyes to the floor and stared absentmindedly. More than his son's refusal to come near him, the boy's incisive accusation had cut to the father's heart. "Okay, if you don't want it, I will keep it for myself," Zewday said finally, bringing the hand that held the white package toward his pocket. The boy rose and went for his father's hand.

He snatched it from his father and ran giggling to his mother. He removed the wrapping and inspected what was inside, turning it one way then the other. "Just the way I like it," the boy said, sinking his teeth into a white bun.

Desta had been curious about what Zewday had brought Tesfa. It looked like a piece of bread, but it was whiter than any he had seen before.

"Don't you want to save half of your *firno*—the oven baked white bread—for tomorrow morning?" Mebet said, grabbing the boy's arm. "Your father probably has spent all his money on tej and won't be able to buy you another one for a while."

"No, I want to eat all of it now." Tesfa pulled away from his mother; he clearly enjoyed digging in with his teeth, taking bite after bite.

"Desta," repeated Lesim, "please bring the soap and water to Baba."

Mebet fetched the kerosene lamp and placed it in the middle of the table, atop an oval clay holder.

After Mebet and Zewday had washed their hands and dinner was served, Tesfa came and clung to his mother with his loaf still in his hand. He had had enough of it. His mother took away the boy's bread and placed it on the tray with the extra injera. Tesfa now wanted to eat what the adults were eating. Mebet alternately fed herself and the boy.

Desta and Lesim sat on the floor, waiting until the adults finished their dinner. They ate afterward because if food was left over from the parents' tray, it would supplement their own dinner. As it was, though, no food was left on Zewday and Mebet's platter.

The smell of the spicy sauce and the sour injera bread had awakened Desta's appetite. His stomach turned over, his saliva drained into the cavity between his tongue and the floor of his mouth. Hoping the saliva would abate his hunger, he swallowed it.

To distract his attention from his hunger, Desta watched the flame of the lamp. He had sat behind Mebet and slightly to the right, where her shadow barely reached his toes. He directed his eyes to that sole source of light in the house and watched the flame as it nodded, swayed, and flickered in a continuous jet. He studied the gradation of color—white at the base turned into gold, brown, then charcoal gray at the top, and finally into nothing discernible. And he wondered how the liquid from the belly of the canister rose through the bunched threads of the wick and continued to give light.

Zewday and Mebet finished their dinner. Desta brought water, soap, and the towel for their hands. Once done, Zewday got up and crawled across the high earthen seat and into the bedroom.

Before Desta and Lesim had sat down to eat their dinner, the room was shaking with Zewday's sonorous nasal rattles.

"There he goes again," Lesim said, shaking her head.

"I am going to bed. I'll see if I can quiet him down," Mebet said hopefully.

"Please do. Otherwise we're not going to fall asleep tonight," Lesim said.

"It's always worse after he comes home drunk," Mebet complained with a sigh. She tugged on Tesfa's hand. "Come, let's go to bed." She lifted him onto the high earthen seat, and then mother and son vanished into the bedroom.

"Let's wash our hands and eat our dinner," Lesim said to Desta. She fetched the lamp from its pedestal on the table and set it on the floor near where they would sit and have their dinner. Then she brought a pitcher of water with glasses and a tray containing a full injera with two scoops of sauce on it.

After washing their hands, they sat on the palm leaf mat and ate, she perching on her bottom, with knees folded and poking her long dress like tent poles, Desta on his heels.

"Can I ask you a question?" Desta said.

"Sure."

"Why is that bread Tesfa was eating so white?"

"Ooh." She laughed.

Desta looked at her, puzzled and embarrassed.

"You have never seen it before?"

"I wouldn't have asked you if I had," he replied, annoyed at her for making fun of him.

"That's firno. It's made from flour, like our regular dabo is made from wheat or rye flour. I don't know why it's white, but you can go and ask the Arab man who makes it."

"That Arab man at the end of the street, at the corner?"

"Yes. He is the only Arab in the whole town. The bread costs twenty-five cents."

"Does it taste good?"

"Delicious!"

Lesim rose, walked over to the basket on the table and returned with two small pieces of Tesfa's partial white bread his mother set aside on their tray. "Here, taste it."

Desta tossed the morsels into his mouth. He chewed and chewed, smacking his lips.

Once they finished eating, Lesim put away the tray and the empty glasses. They washed their hands and were ready to go to bed.

Together they dragged the grass-padded mattress from against the wall and laid it on the floor. Desta brought a folded blanket and two old sheets from the same place. They spread one of the sheets over the mattress and tucked its corners and sides under it. Then they spread the second sheet and the blanket but didn't secure them under the mattress.

Lesim brought the matchbox and the lamp and placed them on the floor on the right side of the mattress where she slept. As she had done on many a night, she flattened her right hand to mimic the edge of a knife.

"Remember, this side is mine, that side is yours," she said, cutting an imaginary divide from the top of the mattress to the bottom.

"Do you have to keep reminding me? Have I ever crossed the border?" Desta would always ask, smiling.

"Just to make sure," she would reply, smiling.

They got under the covers, Lesim facing her side of the wall, Desta his.

Desta ran his hand over his stomach, his rib cage, and his pelvis. The curving lines of his ribs continued to become more and more noticeable, the pelvic bone sharper and more angular. His stomach had begun to curve inward and the muscles that connected the upper part of his body to his lower were more sinewy.

Lesim blew out the light. Desta closed his eyes and tried to go to sleep. Just before he drifted off, he wondered where and when he would find twenty-five cents so he could buy a whole firno bun.

TWENTY-THREE

Desta sat on the long wooden bench under the eaves of the main house and stared at the ribbons of sunlight that had penetrated the tall eucalyptus trees and fallen across the tidily swept footpath. He had come here seeking privacy and quiet so he could pray and recite the legends of the coin from the parchment and study his school lessons afterward. But that morning his bodily preoccupations were too great to immediately engage in either activity. He instead gazed at the view and wondered when he would have enough food to stop the gnawing in his belly and the weakening of his muscles.

The half injera with shiro wat he had been receiving at every meal had caused his stomach to turn, his body to double over whenever he sat, and his knees to sometimes buckle when he stood or walked. Thanks to the magical coin his grandfather had inscribed on his chest, he had managed to endure the deprivation he had faced since he came to live with Zewday's family over a month ago.

Yet the boy was unwavering about his objective and his purpose in life, to finish his schooling and find the coin. *No matter my circumstances.*

Desta took his eyes from the speckled earth, and he folded and crossed his legs. He placed the *braana*—parchment—on his lap. Staring down at the legends at the end of each channel, he closed his eyes and recited. "I must have courage with everything I do. I must be diligent in my studies and my efforts to find the coin. I must have . . ." Zewday appeared from the side of the house, startling the boy.

"I want you to accompany me to church this morning, Desta," he said. He had wrapped himself in a brown-checkered blanket and he wore his old faded green flip-flops. Their plastic strips resembled the antennae of a giant insect.

Desta was a bit flustered but remembered that what Zewday had requested was the kind of thing his father had told him he must do for the man in exchange for allowing Desta to live with his family. He replied, "*Ishee*—Okay." He folded the square braana and inserted it in its cloth covering.

Zewday lingered for a bit, watching the boy as he gathered his things and put them in the pouch. This gave Desta an opportunity to glance at the man's lower limbs. Although the arched part of his feet looked ashen against the dark footpad, the texture of the skin was velvety smooth. Desta wondered whether Zewday had ever walked barefoot when he was a boy and whether his own feet would ever become that smooth when he finally got a chance to wear shoes. The truth of Saba's comment about the danger of wearing shoes suddenly became apparent to the boy: would he ever be able to walk barefoot again if his feet became soft and smooth like Zewday's?

Zewday and Desta washed their hands and faces separately and got ready for church. While Desta waited for Zewday outside, Lesim came and said, "Baba said you're going to church with him."

"Yes, I am kind of looking forward to it."

"I hope you can last through the service," Lesim said. "It's very long."

"What made you think I couldn't?"

"Because you always seem to be tired."

"Yes, but what do you think is the cause of it?"

Lesim shook her head.

"It's because I don't get enough food."

"You receive a half injera with shiro wat with every meal—the same amount I get."

"Yeah, but I am sure you help yourself when you bake injera and make the shiro sauce."

"Not really," Lesim said feigning a smile. "You're too clever to think like that, aren't you?"

"I am not blind, you mean?" retorted the boy, incensed. "The difference in the way you and I look is so obvious, Lesim."

"No, I think the town food doesn't stick to your ribs," jeered the girl. "You're a farm boy and not used to eating quality foods like we have here."

"You're absolutely right," Desta replied, turning to go. He realized that Lesim either couldn't accept the truth or couldn't care less about his situation.

Lesim stepped close and grabbed Desta by the sleeve of his jacket. "I'm going to tell you something," she said. "Don't ever talk like this in front of any of the neighbors or anybody else in town."

"I don't think I am invisible to anyone around here or that they have lapses of memory," Desta replied, trying to jerk his arm free. "How I look now is so different from the way I looked when I arrived. I understand that there is not enough food in the house for all of us."

Lesim let go of Desta's arm and the boy walked off.

"Remember what I just said!" Lesim shouted after him. "Don't let Ma or the neighbors hear your complaints."

"*Atasbee*—don't worry," Desta said, heading to meet Zewday, who had gone out the back door and was waiting for Desta by the path.

Desta wondered if he could, indeed, make it to church, particularly if it was far. In the mornings he seemed to have energy and no problem walking to school. It was the walking at lunch and after school that tired him.

Zewday was wearing his old black leather shoes, a frayed woolen jacket and pants, and had draped himself with a newer white gabi. He carried his leather-clad book in one hand and his gold-colored cane in the other.

Zewday handed the book with its hanger to Desta. "Slip the handle up your arm and onto your shoulder," he ordered. "It's my Dawit."

The boy complied.

Zewday motioned with his cane. "Let's go. We need to get there before the priests start the mass." They walked down the dappled path and turned left at the main street.

The cool air nipped at Desta's toes and fingers. He put his hands into his pockets, but he could do nothing for his toes.

Eucalyptus trees rose to the sky behind the conical grass-roofed homes and pitched corrugated tin-tops that bordered the nearly straight and level street. Wooden fences surrounded many of the homes, their small yards strewn with leaves or dried corn stalks left over from the previous season's harvest. From a few of the houses, men and women emerged dressed in white, heading out to church, as many of the townspeople were doing.

Zewday always walked briskly, as if responding to an emergency or trying to get away from something. His tall slender frame made him light of foot, and he glided easily through space with long strides. Desta hurried to keep up and had to break into a trot when he fell behind. To Desta's relief, Zewday would slow to a leisurely pace when he met people he knew along the way.

Desta remembered what his father once told him: "A gentleman is never in a hurry. He has to cherish each moment as if it were his last, even while walking somewhere."

Abraham did often walk as if to make a statement with his movements.
His bearing was erect and dignified; his strides confident, purposeful, and
measured; his arms swung back and forth in rhythm with the cadence of his
steps—precise and harmonious. His limbs were well-calibrated instruments,
singing mutely to all who watched. His eyes engaged not with what was before
him but with whatever he was thinking about at the time.

Desta often found himself walking with a similarly relaxed gait as he imitated
his father and thought about his lessons or ways to pursue the coin. Additionally,
Abraham had told him not to talk glibly or excessively, lest he gave away too
much of himself. Desta was also mindful of these things.

As Zewday and Desta and other churchgoers continued along the leaf-strewn
road, more people emerged from their houses and joined them, all dressed in
their Sunday fine clothes and wearing leather, canvas, or Congo plastic shoes.
The men had donned jackets and bolalay pants and draped their shoulders with
their gabis. Most of the women wore traditional white skirts, whereas a few
dressed in modern floral or solid colors, all of them throwing their netela shawls
over their heads and around their shoulders.

"Who is this boy, Zewday?" asked one of the men. Desta had noticed the
man's puzzled, quizzical look every time their eyes met.

"He is the son of a relative who came to live with us and go to school,"
Zewday replied, matter-of-factly.

"How nice to have someone to accompany you to church," the man said with
a hint of sarcasm.

"He earns his keep," Zewday said casually.

A woman approached from the opposite direction carrying a live but tentative
fire in a clay piece. "Poor girl," Zewday said, changing the subject. The man's
questions and repeated glances at Desta seemed to bother him.

The woman occasionally blew into the fire, shielding with her hand the fragments of *kubet*—dried cow dung. The smoke, like tendrils of fine white hair,
obscured her face every time she blew. Her purple-bordered netela hung cockeyed and nearly dragged behind her in the dirt. She seemed oblivious to the
people around her or her trailing netela as she nudged and coaxed the precious
fire to keep it alive.

For a moment Desta was transported back home. Hibist and Melkam used to
do the same thing on their way back from collecting a glowing charcoal or two

from the neighbors when the fire they had buried in the ashes the night before had gone out.

"She probably couldn't afford to buy a box of matches," the man said.

"Do you feel like being generous?" Zewday asked, smiling. "I am sure she would appreciate it."

"No, I am sure she has many young friends who would purchase one for her if she really couldn't afford to spend fifty cents herself."

Zewday reached in his pocket. "Desta," he said, handing the boy a dollar bill, "take this and tell her to buy a box of matches with it."

"A true Christian you are, giving alms to someone in need," the man mocked. He looked down at Desta. "But I think charity should begin at home."

Zewday screwed his face and glared at the man, irritated and caught off guard by the neighbor's barb. But he simply said, "Go, Desta. Run, and tell her what I told you."

The boy loped away, Zewday's book thumping against his hip. "*Set'eyo, set'eyo*—lady, lady" he called out to the woman. She turned and looked at him with teary eyes. "What is it you need, boy?" she asked, clearly bothered by the interruption.

He held out the dollar bill. "That tall man in the middle of the churchgoers sent this so you can buy matches."

She cracked a smile. "Tell him I appreciate it. I will return the favor with a *birelay*—round narrow-necked drinking glass—of tej the next time he comes." Desta ran back with the message.

The group of churchgoers had just broken off from the main road and was walking on a narrower path that went through a grove of bushes. Zewday said nothing. Nor did the inquisitive man. The others were busy talking about something else. After a few hundred feet, they came upon an open space. At one corner stood a single building bound by a high stick fence.

"That is Saint Michael's Church," Zewday said, pointing with his cane.

Desta looked in disappointment at the circular structure with its tin roof. It was small, simple, and stark, lacking the majesty and mystery of his parents' grass-roofed country church. Its saving grace was that shiny corrugated modern roof. Like his parents' church, at the top of the conical main roof was a fixture like a little parasol, skirted by tiny metal flutes and surmounted by a metal hoop with seven spokes, five of which held ostrich eggs.

Within the church compound was a smaller building, probably a chapel,

Desta thought, and a lone tree of an unfamiliar kind.

The priests were chanting from deep within the church wall.

Outside the fence stood a number of women, most wearing white dresses, their heads veiled with a portion of their netela shawls.

Desta remembered that having physical intimacy with a man the night before a service is one reason women aren't permitted in the church compound. He surmised this was probably why these women stood outside the fence.

Zewday opened a rickety, ridged tin gate and they entered a dried grass interior. Desta followed his host to the south side of the church near the chapel. They stood under the canopy of the tree, behind a wooden bench that seated four. Zewday crossed himself three times, bowing after each action. Feeling awkward about crossing himself like an adult, Desta just bowed once.

All around the compound a scattering of men and elderly women stood silently, some reading their Dawit, others with covered heads bent in prayer.

"Let me have my Dawit," Zewday said, handing Desta his cane.

Desta held the cane in the crook of his left arm and slipped the hanger from his right shoulder. He passed the Dawit to Zewday. Zewday grasped the book firmly and slid off the outer jacket. He looked at one side then the other and flipped it over when he realized he was holding it wrong side up. He opened it and leafed through a few pages and then began to read silently.

Desta wrapped all ten fingers around the cane and planted it a few feet from his toes. He leaned forward slightly and rested his chin on his hands. He was grateful to Zewday for the staff. If his energy became sapped from standing too long, he could hang on to the cane. In an emergency, of course, he could always count on the coin on his chest for help.

"Stand up straight," Zewday commanded. "And put away the cane. You're too young to need a staff to lean on."

Desta stood it against the tree, disheartened. Having no Dawit of his own to read or prayers to say, he realized it was going to be one long, tedious morning. Somehow he needed to occupy himself so that, hopefully, the time would pass more quickly.

He attentively listened to Zewday's whispered reading, the rustle of the leaves overhead, and the chanting, singing, and recitals of the priests inside the church. He ran his fingers under his gabi and across his chest. He counted his ribs, stopping and pressing occasionally to feel the bones under his skin. There was less of him now than the last time he examined himself.

He gazed at the stonework around the bottom of the church wall and worried that he might die if he got any thinner. He slid his fingers up his chest and around his neck to confirm what he already knew. The deep holes between his collarbones terrified him. *Have I contracted a mysterious disease that's doing this to me?* There was nothing to indicate that he had. He had not even caught a cold or succumbed to a fever. Insufficient food was his real nemesis.

I should be cured of this when my father comes after Fasika—*Easter*—*with sacks of grain.* He counted the time until Easter on his fingers. Forty-five days. His father would come two or three days afterward, the mule and donkey loaded with different grains that would last his hosts and him for months to come. He would have plenty to feast on then. His body would return to the way it was when he lived with Tru and Mekuria. He would run home from school for lunch and back like the other giggling boys and girls. He smiled at the image of himself happy and running.

A creaking of the gate woke Desta from his daydream. A crippled man on wooden crutches swung across the threshold while one of the women held the gate open. The man's legs were folded as if stuck to the backs of his thighs. As he hopped, his feet dragged in the dirt, like toys a child might drag behind.

His hands, leveraged and protected by the pair of U-shaped wooden crutches, seemed to have taken over the role of his feet. He planted the crutches firmly in the dirt and raised and swung himself forward. A padded animal skin hugged his bottom and crotch. He wore an old, tight-fitting brown jacket and a soiled gabi. He carried a small book on a leather hanger across his shoulder and chest. After several of his simian hops, he came to one of the benches near the chapel and perched on the ground facing the seat. A dusty halo of hair framed his fine pale features and big eyes. His bare legs were ashen and dusty. He crossed himself three times, each time dropping his head down and kissing the bench. He then took his chunky book out of its case and spread it open on the flat stone surface before him. He started to read quietly.

Desta shook his head, amazed by this unusual man. He had never seen a person who walked on his hands instead of his legs. He had now forgotten his own problems. *Somebody has it worse,* he thought. *Thank God, I have all my limbs to do whatever I want with them.*

The activities inside the church took Desta's attention away from the man. The chanting, singing, and reading of the priests and deacons, and paying homage to God, had begun to absorb the boy. He closed his eyes and listened, enjoying the measured rhythms of the priests' reverent voices, the dignity and grace they imparted to each word and phrase.

Sometimes it was not even words they sang, just the *zemas*—notes—on their vocal cords. They twisted, curled, and stretched the tones, bringing out their many shades, like those musicians who could extract a multitude of qualities when playing a single-string instrument like the *masinko* with a bow. The sound was hypnotic, transporting Desta to another world, making him forget his misery and everything around him.

When the priests stopped, he felt the ache on the back of his heels. His stomach felt as if someone was clawing him with long fingernails. He held the folds in his belly with one hand and the image of the coin with the other. The discomfort in his stomach faded, and the pain in his heels dissipated. He sighed.

A priest began to read in a loud voice. Instantly, the congregation assumed all forms of supplication. Some of the men bent their heads and recited while gazing inwardly. Others kneeled—eyes closed, heads touching their clasped hands before them. Nearly all the women prostrated themselves on the ground with hands held open to the sky.

To Desta this moment was a welcome relief. He kneeled and rested his forehead on the bench in front of him. "God, give me the strength to endure this hardship. Take away the hunger from my stomach. Help me walk to school and back without feeling exhausted. Please don't let me die before I finish school and find the coin." Desta was surprised by how these words just rolled off his tongue.

Out of the corners of his eyes he saw the women rising one at a time. He waited until everybody rose and then he got up. His heels felt better and so did the rest of his body. A light breeze bathed the air, causing the leaves overhead to rustle and the tiny flutes up on the secondary roof to chime.

A single singing voice breached the church walls and poured into the compound—it was sweet, pure, and transfixing. The congregation fell silent, the tiny flutes ceased to tremor, the leaves above Desta became still. It was as if the wind, too, had paused to listen. He closed his eyes and wished he could sing like that and bring joy and comfort to himself whenever he felt sad or down. He wished he could ride that voice to another world where there was love and plenty to eat and where he could find the person with the coin.

This voice was young, reminding Desta of his brother Tamirat. He was sorry Tamirat had abandoned the priesthood and that he did not sing like that anymore, making people happy and causing everything around the church compound to pause—most of all, making their Baba proud like he had wanted to be.

After the singer stopped, a bearded priest in brocade of blue, green, and gold came through the eastern entrance, swinging an incense burner on long metal chains with tinkling trinkets. The priest swung and swooshed the burner, dispensing vines of smoke and sweet fragrance. For Desta the whiff of incense was the kind of emollient he needed to lift his spirit and numb his hunger. It reminded him to smell the rosemary seeds Saba had given him when he felt hungry or depressed. The priest went back inside but soon reemerged through the western door and delivered the same fragrance, smoke, and tinkling sounds.

This was followed by more of the priests' singing, chanting, and reading—and the congregation's praying and supplicating. Toward the conclusion of the mass, a bell jingled continuously inside the church, taking Desta back to the time when he took communion at his parents' church to cure him of the dog disease his family feared he had contracted.

At that moment he imagined couples with babies, older women and men, and young children lining up to receive the flesh and blood of Christ from a bearded priest. One young man tinkled the bell and a second dispensed liquid into the people's mouths immediately after the priest dropped the sweet pea-sized taste of God's flesh into their mouths.

"Here, take my Dawit," Zewday said, distracting Desta from his imaginings. He slipped the book's hanger up onto his shoulder and then looked around. As the communion went on, some of the women dropped to the ground while the men just bowed their heads as they stood or sat on benches.

A short, stocky man appeared at the eastern entrance of the church holding a fat book. He stood at a pulpit of wood someone had pushed out earlier. He greeted the crowd with a "good morning" and a bow as he set the tome before him. He proceeded to read from it, occasionally pausing to translate passages from the ancient language of Geez into Amharic and to elaborate on the meanings and purposes of God's words.

Desta listened attentively with his hand on his mouth and both ears wide open, trying to make sense of what the preacher was saying. He was fascinated by some of the messages—including that Christ was a shepherd of humans, like Desta had been of flocks and herds, along with the idea that Christ had died a long time ago and was destined to return. Desta had never heard that people, like animals, needed to be looked after and that a dead person could rise from the grave and be with people again.

And then this: the preacher said that when Christ comes again, all people would rise from the dead. *Could this mean I will have a chance to see grandpa again, this time in his own flesh and hair?*

Desta felt his own hair on the back of his neck stand on end. At this time, the preacher said that everyone's past lives and deeds would be examined and they would be separated one from the other, as a shepherd separates the sheep from the goats. Those who signified the sheep, Christ would make stand on His right, those who represented the goats, on His left. The priest said some more things about each group and the meaning of the group's position relative to Christ, those on the right having visited the sick and given food, water, clothing, and shelter to the needy and those on the left having given nothing. The reward for the sheep was an eternally beautiful place in heaven, whereas the goats would be punished, relegated to eternal fire and brimstone.

Desta put his head down and shook it, surprised and saddened that some of his favorite animals were considered bad enough to represent people who would end up burning for eternity. He remembered when he was herding the animals that the goats were among the naughtiest. They often got into thorn bushes and refused to come out until their bellies were full. *Still*, Desta thought to himself, *this kind of crime was not bad enough to deserve punishment by fire.* And he couldn't understand why the meek and docile sheep were chosen to represent those people who did good things for others.

While reflecting on these ideas, Desta had stopped listening to the rest of the preacher's sermon. He finally looked up to see the flourish of the man's hands and hear his excited, sharp voice. Shortly after, the man stepped down from the platform and vanished inside the church.

"There will be mekleft to break our fast with, so we'll stay put," Zewday whispered. This news was music to Desta's ears. He sat down on a stone bench behind Zewday. The boy realized his host had chosen their location strategically for its proximity to the chapel, which is where the congregation would gather to eat mekleft before going home.

A commotion ensued. The crowd milled for a bit and then moved toward the chapel. Many sat on the benches. Some remained standing. Some went inside the chapel. Desta and Zewday had a clear view of much of the interior of the building and its rows of benches that would seat three or four each on either side of an aisle. Up on a raised platform was a long wooden table dressed with a floral plastic cloth. Behind the table were three straight-backed chairs, with another six behind those. A row of seven covered baskets adorned the tabletop.

The preacher came out of the church, followed by an entourage of three deacons and two more priests. They headed toward the chapel. Men and women bowed as they passed, some stepping forward to receive the head priest's blessing: the sign of the cross.

Inside the chapel the priests scaled the wooden platform and stood before the rows of chairs, two younger priests flanking the head cleric. The deacons stood behind the three men. The head priest recited a line of text and then said the Lord's Prayer. The congregation stood and repeated after him. Once done, they all sat down.

A woman with patches of white hair above her brow stepped up, opened the first basket, and slid it before the head priest. He made the sign of the cross over the basket and cut through the layers of mekleft injera it contained with a long gray knife, making eight equal wedges. A second woman came and picked up the basket of sliced mekleft.

The priest peeled off two of the slices, placed them on the overturned basket cover, and gave it to one of the women. She took it to the crippled man. Another woman picked up the basket with the rest of the slices and distributed them to other church members. In this manner all the mekleft in all of the baskets was blessed by the priest and dispensed to the entire congregation.

Zewday noticed Desta staring at the disabled man and said, "That man received the first injera pieces to praise him and encourage others to follow his example. He gets up early and takes nearly two hours to get here. It will take him that long to get back home after the church services are concluded. There are many people who have properly functioning legs and yet they don't make the least effort to come to church on Sunday. Our neighbor, Aba Admass, is an example. He used to come to church with his wife and me, but he stopped attending over a year ago. The wife still comes with us by herself." Zewday shook his head sadly.

Desta had nothing to say in response. He just waited patiently until one of the women with a basket of the bread came around. When he received his, he stared down at it, hoping this blessed piece of bread would stop his body from emaciating further and allowing it to recover to the level it used to be. Then he took a bite and the mekleft tasted incredible. He began to chew on it, savoring its sweet flavor and soft spongy texture. When done his stomach was not full but he had a sense of well-being and comfort.

Shortly after eating their mekleft, the congregation departed. Some people walked leisurely and visited as they walked. Others seemed to be anxious to get home. When Zewday and Desta reached the gate of the house, Zewday told Desta to hang his Dawit on the wall indoors, as Zewday continued somewhere on his own.

Neither Mebet nor Lesim were at home. The slice of injera Desta had eaten at church had only awakened his hunger for more food. After hanging up Zewday's Dawit, he went out and stood by the door, thinking about how to sooth his gnawing stomach.

He remembered there often were whole and cracked peas, barleycorns, and wheat berries left in the dirt around the grinding stone under the eaves of the kitchen house. He sauntered across the courtyard and sat on his heels near the grinding stone and looked for any stray pieces. There were quite a few. One by one he picked up the lost peas and barley and wheat. He poked at the dirt with a stick and found some more, netting him enough of the assorted scraps to cover the palm of his cupped hand.

He took them inside the house and washed them in a cup. Then he dabbed them dry with his gabi and began to eat them, tossing one piece at a time into his open mouth. The barleycorns and wheat berries tasted like dirt. The peas were musty and hard to crack, but he eventually managed to chew them thoroughly and swallow. Now, however, his hunger was greater than ever. His stomach churned as if he might actually get sick.

Desta felt he might vomit, so he went out to sit under the coffee trees. Lesim suddenly appeared on the path that went to the neighbors' home, looking disheveled. Her hair was a mess, her skirt cockeyed, and her eyes looked sleepy. She stopped in her tracks and gazed at Desta cagily. "You and Baba came home early," she said, her eyes shooting past Desta to main house's entrance.

"Early?" Desta replied, mystified by Lesim's behavior.

"Baba is probably waiting for his lunch. I need to get it ready for him." Desta didn't have time to respond before the girl dashed past him and into the kitchen.

The boy's stomach had calmed a bit; the urge to vomit passed. He was leaning against the tall eucalyptus tree and thinking about his first trip to church with Zewday when Lesim came out. She had covered her hair with a scarf and straightened her dress. "Is Baba resting?" she asked.

"No, he is not at home. Gone to town," Desta replied, studying Lesim. Her face was washed and her eyes looked fresh and alive. But he noticed something he hadn't earlier. Her lips were pouty and ruddy, as if someone had pulled on them with a vice.

"Can you give me my lunch?" he asked.

"Mebet went to visit her sick uncle and I don't expect her till evening. So I am free to do what I can in the food department," Lesim said with a smile. "C'mon in."

Desta followed her into the kitchen, sat on the high earthen seat, and waited until he was served his meal.

"You can have my portion of food today, as I don't feel like eating," Lesim said, handing him a tray with a full injera. She had poured two full ladles of steaming shiro wat over the bread.

As he ate, Desta wished Lesim would visit the old couple's home next door every day if it meant he could have meals like this all the time.

TWENTY-FOUR

It was as if Desta's seatmates at school had discovered something horrific around the bench where they sat. The seat he usually shared with two other students was empty. At first he thought his mates were absent that morning, but when he looked around, he found them sitting with other students. Desta examined his bench to see if something was wrong with it. Nothing was apparent. He scanned the room once again. There seemed to be a conspiracy afoot. The students all glared at him in hushed silence, as if willing him to react.

The boy stood by his seat confounded. Perspiration broke out on his brow and moistened his hands. "What is going on here?" he asked, finally, in a nervous voice.

The monitor, a big-boned boy named Gebru, rose and came across the room. "Here is what's going on. . . ." Gebru looked down at his feet for a few seconds then he looked up and stared at Desta. "Your seatmates think you might be sick with something. They don't want to sit next to you anymore; they don't want to catch your disease. I can't blame them. You are looking more sickly by the day."

"I have no disease. I am okay."

"You're not okay. You look deathly, except for your eyes. Some horrific illness must be eating at you that you don't even know about. Do you have a family? Why don't they take you to the mission's clinic so you can get checked? We all discussed your possible health problem after class last Friday and we decided that the best thing is for you to sit by yourself until the teacher or the school finds a solution."

Desta felt sick, so sick that cold sweat suddenly began trickling over his brow and down the back of his neck. It streamed down his face and along his spine. His cheeks felt hot. He turned and stared at the door, contemplating leaving the room. Where could he go? Not home. Neither Mebet nor Zewday would care. He would have to endure this as he had endured so many other trials in the past.

Desta didn't want to say he had been deprived of food. He didn't want to put the family he lived with in a bad light.

"Don't ever talk like this in front of our neighbors or anyone else in town" Lesim had warned him once.

"Your father's reputation has been shielded for so long because nobody else is here at night to see how he behaves after he comes home drunk," he had wanted to say to Lesim at the time but didn't.

If he talked badly about the family and they found out, they would send him back home to the country, forever ending his dream of finishing school and finding the coin. He didn't want to take that chance. All he could say to Gebru was, "I am okay. I am fine. Please tell my seatmates to come and sit with me."

"I'm not going to force them to sit with you. Sit down until the homeroom teacher comes. Hopefully, he will have a better solution to your problem."

Desta bit his lip and sat down in the center of the bench, making sure he left enough space for his seatmates in case they decided to return. Part of him wanted to believe that this was some sort of practical joke and his mates would come and sit with him.

They didn't.

Some in the classroom whispered and stared at him with deeply suspicious eyes. Others looked at him with a detached, disdainful gaze. Some appeared to feel pity for him, but no one came to console and comfort him. He felt shame and disgrace as a new sheen of sweat broke out over his brow.

Just then he remembered what his real companion and source of comfort was supposed to be. He slipped his right hand under the jacket and touched the image of the coin. Instantly, he felt calm and serene. For a moment his classmates were virtually invisible to him. He shook his head and blinked, trying to assure himself he was not hallucinating. His classmates were there but they no longer snickered and stared. Everything felt normal. It didn't matter anymore whether his bench mates came and sat with him.

The homeroom teacher, Betew, walked in. The class rose and then quickly sat down at the teacher's gesture. Betew placed his attendance register and the English vocabulary tests he had graded over the weekend on the small rickety table near the blackboard.

"Looks like we have lost a few students," he said after scanning the room. "What happened to your seatmates, Desta?"

Desta looked at one corner of the room and then the other, where his mates were sitting.

The teacher followed Desta's eyes. "What happened? Why are you two not sitting with Desta?"

The two boys didn't have the courage to say what was on their minds. Gebru rose and spoke for them. The teacher crinkled his brow and narrowed his eyes as he listened to the monitor.

"Is that all?" Betew asked. "I want you two to immediately go to your regular bench. What makes you think he has a disease? He just happens to be thinner than you are." Betew was trying to minimize the obvious, but Desta knew he looked more than just thin.

He had seen his face in the water when he crossed the Amin River and in the pitcher that contained his wash water. Yes, he appeared unwell, but he didn't look like a monster.

The two boys grimaced as they contemplated the order. They knew they would get whipped if they refused. They gathered their notebooks and grudgingly walked over and took their respective seats at the bench, as far away from Desta as they could get.

The teacher did a roll call. Then he passed out two English books, one on each side of the room. One at a time, and alternating from one side to the other, each student was to read aloud a list of English words and then translate the words into Amharic.

These were the same words Betew had put up on the blackboard the previous week for the class to study. Now they would learn how to pronounce them. Many of the students stumbled over the words and their translations. Desta kept correcting them in his mind. He hoped he would remember how to pronounce them all when his turn came. This was his only revenge against those who had demeaned and shamed him. Being the best in his studies was always his saving grace, his defense against all those who tried to put him down, and one of the few things that made him feel he was somebody. It was one of the only means he had to prove to the world, to his family, and to himself that he was *okay*.

Desta never had a chance to read that morning because it took many of the students so long to read and translate the words.

When the lesson was over, almost as an afterthought, Betew said, "I have your tests from last week." He leafed through the pile and pulled out three papers and set them aside. After he passed out the other papers, he picked up the remaining three. He said, "These papers got the top scores in the class." The students looked around, trying to see who had not received their papers.

"Daniel, with two errors you got 90 percent. Nadew, with one error you got 95 percent. Desta, with no errors you got 100 percent." All the class turned and stared at the boy. Tears welled up in him, but he checked his emotions. He felt as if the pieces of him had emerged out of the dust and reassembled to make him whole again. This was the first test he'd taken since coming to this school. His body had become emaciated, but his mind had not wasted away.

TWENTY-FIVE

It was Saturday morning. Desta's heart fell when he saw Betew coming toward Zewday's house. The incident with his seatmates had occurred five days earlier. He watched from his perch on the bench under the eaves as Betew approached Lesim, who was playing with Tesfa by the walkway.

"Is Ato Zewday in?" He asked. She indicated that he was, and dashed into the main house. Moments later Zewday emerged, his face tense, eyes searching. "Good morning, Ato Betew," he said, extending a hand. "Is everything well?"

The two men shook hands. Betew seemed nervous. "I came to have a few private moments with you. Do you have time?"

"This is Saturday, our day of rest, so I do have time. C'mon in."

Betew followed Zewday into the main house.

Desta couldn't resist eavesdropping. *This is it! He's come to tell Zewday he should take me out of school.* His heart in his throat, the boy slinked to the back entrance and stood near the closed door, holding his breath. He could see their faces through the gap in the door, part of which was covered with Desta and Lesim's standing mattress.

After the two sat down at the table, Betew explained the reason for his visit. Some of the students as well as their parents had complained that Desta might have some sort of disease. "In a month's time we have seen his body atrophy so quickly. We don't know the history of the boy. He came in the middle of the school year. We wonder if he might have been expelled from his previous school for health reasons. I have no evidence one way or the other, but I wanted to find out firsthand whether he has health problems."

Zewday caressed his chin, his eyes gazing dreamily at Betew. "No, he has no disease that we know of. It's true that he has gotten thinner since he came. We have been at a loss ourselves. We thought it might have to do with the boy's new life in a strange town—perhaps it's the air or water here. He used to be a shepherd, you know. So we thought that, in due course, he would adjust and recover."

"Does he have any problem eating that you know of?" Betew appealed.

"Not that we know of. My wife tells me that he eats everything given to him."

"How about sufficient food?"

"That too. No problem. He and my daughter share the same meals. She looks very well but he doesn't."

"I'd try giving him extra food and see what that does for him," Betew said, rising to leave.

"Will do."

Desta let go of the air in his lungs.

After Betew left, Desta stepped away from the door and came back to his bench, where he struck the pose of a diligent student.

That evening Zewday and Mebet discussed what Betew had said. Mebet protested that Desta and Lesim received equal amounts of food. Lesim looked well but Desta didn't, and she was at a loss to explain the boy's problem.

As an experiment, they decided that Desta would get a full injera with his usual scoop of shiro wat, "just in case" his weight loss had to do with not getting adequate food. However, the proposed experiment wouldn't be conducted for another week because Mebet had insufficient teff flour to make more injera.

ON SUNDAY ZEWDAY DECIDED to go to church on his own. He feared the boy would be an embarrassment to him. He didn't want the congregation's scrutiny.

In the afternoon, Mebet sent Desta to fetch a tray a neighbor had borrowed. She was a single woman who lived with her little daughter in one of the two houses by the front entrance of the compound. Desta arrived to find the door open but nobody inside. Thinking they might be napping, he walked in without any announcement. No one was at home.

At the corner near the bedroom stood a covered basket. Desta bent over and took in the smell of its contents the way a dog sniffs a scent. Almost unconsciously, he walked over and opened it. It was piled with injera. He counted them. Six. He salivated. A prickling sensation gnawed at his stomach. For several seconds he debated: should he steal one? Would God be upset with him for breaking one of His cardinal rules? Would the woman find out Desta had stolen her injera or suspect someone else? If she did find out who did it, would she tell Mebet and Zewday?

His mouth drooled. His hand shook. His mind went blank. He reached for the bread. Wait! There should be a strategy for his crime. Instead of taking a whole injera or tearing one out, he should take pieces from around the edges. That way it would look like a mouse had eaten it.

He quickly went to work, breaking pieces of the soft bread from all around the pile and putting them in his pocket. He then returned the lid and ran to the door. He halted at the threshold and looked around to make sure no one watched him leave the scene of the crime.

There was no one. Relieved, he dashed out and walked home briskly. A couple of times he turned around and looked to see if the woman might be following him. He was safe. The whole neighborhood was hushed. He was sure that nobody saw him and he would never be implicated as the real thief of those crumbs of injera.

En route he remembered a similar moment when he lived at home. He had stolen a sheet of writing paper from his father's straw box. Although he knew it was sinful to steal, he had reasoned that he would take food if he were starving. Stealing the writing paper so he could practice his scripts on a sheet of paper instead of his dry thigh was the same extreme situation. If he could do one, he might as well do the other. He would make it up to God somehow. Desta smiled at another irony of his life: to find himself in this similar situation. It was as if his life had come full circle, like the figure of the sun and the coin.

After telling Mebet he couldn't find the neighbor, he gathered his books and went to his bench to study. He was eager to tackle his homework but much more so to dive into that bread. With the excitement of a boy just given his first toy, he reached into the big side pocket of his jacket and took out a piece of injera. As he opened his English book, he placed the bread in his mouth, chewing it slowly, savoring its spongy texture. He had just swallowed his third piece when he felt the presence of someone behind him. He dropped his book on his lap and turned around. It was a woman with a covered basket cradled in her arm.

"Did you do this?" she asked, tapping the basket top.

"Do what?" Desta retorted sheepishly.

She removed the cover. "This!" she exclaimed, tossing her chin down toward the bread.

"No, I didn't. It looks like a mouse got to it," he replied, trying hard to stay calm. He realized later that by this answer alone he had implicated himself.

"No, mice don't open baskets!" she sneered, building her case against the boy.

In his trepidation he had forgotten that critical element. He should have left the cover off. That way a mouse could have been easily explained as the culprit.

The woman could have forgotten to cover the basket.

Desta looked down and mumbled, "Then I don't know."

"What is it you're eating?"

"I'm not eating anything."

These desperate, mechanical responses were making him sick. He never liked to lie and he disliked those who did.

"Is Mebet home?"

"I don't know. Go look." After the woman left, Desta got up, dashed into the coffee bushes, and peed. He returned to his bench and waited for Mebet's wrath and verdict.

His accuser returned with Mebet, the person who had power over the boy. "Did you do it?" she demanded.

"No."

"What do you have in your pocket?"

"Nothing."

"Let me take a look," Mebet commanded.

"No." Desta rose and clutched his pocket.

The accuser placed the basket on the bench.

"Show us peacefully where the bread is, or we'll make you show us," Mebet threatened.

"No." Desta was prepared to flee if he had to.

"Here," said Mebet, turning to the woman. "I'll grab his hands and you reach in his pocket and take out whatever is in there."

With the swiftness of a skilled athlete, Mebet seized Desta's hands and twisted his arms behind his back. Mebet's power and speed astounded him.

"He is easy game. I used to take down much bigger and stronger boys when I was a girl in the country," boasted his captor.

Desta struggled to free himself but it was no use. Mebet's grasp was like a vice.

The neighbor herself seemed confused, afraid—and stunned.

"Reach in his pocket!" shouted Mebet.

The neighbor slipped her hand in as instructed and withdrew a handful of bread pieces.

Mebet let go of Desta. "Let me see," she said, tapping the woman's fist to open it.

"This is from my injera!" declared the neighbor, now having unequivocal proof of the boy's crime.

"Just as we suspected," affirmed Mebet. "He is a thief. He probably used to steal from the people he lived with before he came here. Obviously, that's why they sent him home. His father brought him here where nobody knew him. Put the crumbs here," Mebet ordered, throwing open her hand.

As the woman poured the injera morsels into Mebet's hand, a few fell to the ground.

"We didn't have to put him through this," the neighbor declared. "That he did it was not in question. My next-door neighbor saw him run out of my house."

"I just wondered if he might have stolen it from *our* basket," Mebet countered apologetically.

"No, this is all from my basket," the woman asserted, shaking her head.

"Do you want to take them back?"

"No, give them to him. Let him eat them if he's that desperate." The neighbor cast a sympathetic eye toward the boy. She seemed to notice for the first time Desta's emaciated frame.

"No!" Mebet barked. "You don't reward a thief. He'll have to learn a lesson! I am sorry you have been violated in this manner by this miscreant." Mebet spat.

"I certainly have no use for those handled fragments," the neighbor said with a hint of remorse.

"We'll give them to the birds then. . . . I will tell Zewday what happened and we'll see what we can do about it. I need to go now," Mebet said in a clipped, sharp voice. She threw the injera scraps into the coffee trees with such force that some of them shattered on the leaves. She turned to go to her kitchen.

Shaken and stunned as he was, Desta's eyes and heart went with those wasted morsels.

"I am sorry. I am partly to blame for failing to close and lock my door," the woman said as she stepped back onto the path to go home.

Mebet turned back. "Please don't apologize. It's he who should; it's he who dishonored the sanctity of your home."

Desta rose and staggered to the wall. He was dazed. Afraid. Shamed. He felt like the worst criminal on earth. From the way Mebet talked, he thought he was finished. He probably wouldn't be living with them anymore. They would probably kick him out in a few days. He had no place to go.

All his aspirations would come to a grinding halt. He could no longer hope of finishing school or finding the coin. He wished there was a private room where he could sleep off his misery, hide from his feelings and thoughts, distance himself from the people around him. He reached to his chest and pressed his fingers against his skin. Serenity descended upon him.

He went inside the house and brought out Saba's rosemary packet, deeply inhaling its perfume. The gentle aroma helped relax his nerves, allowing him to reflect on his deed. What he did was not by choice but out of desperation. He was not going to blame himself and he was not going to apologize to Mebet or Zewday, even though he saw the need to apologize to the neighbor. For now, to further preserve himself, he needed to disappear from this world.

He put the rosemary packet in his pocket and shuffled back to the bench. He pushed his notebook to the side and lay down on his back.

WHEN HE WOKE SEVERAL HOURS LATER, the sun had left and his legs were chilled. He found Lesim peering down at him. "You slept here all after-noon?" she asked, incredulous. "I bet you were mad at yourself," she said. The hint of sympathy in her words was a sliver of comfort to Desta's heart. There was something in the way she breathed the words and the lilt in her voice that reminded him of his sister Hibist. For a fleeting moment, this recollection of a happier time helped make him feel whole again.

"What made you do it?" Her voice was more accusative. The sliver of comfort faded along with the memory of his beloved sister.

"Lesim, please leave me alone. I don't want to talk about it."

"I want to prepare you for the bad news." She looked away for a long time as if waiting for his reaction or deriving pleasure from his heightened anxiety.

A sharp burning sensation radiated from the base of Desta's neck down to the tip of his tailbone. He didn't like the tone of Lesim's voice. He stared up at the eaves, his nerves recruited and cued for the message Lesim was about to deliver.

When Lesim didn't say anything, Desta rolled his head and gazed at her. "What is the bad news?"

"Mebet said that we can't give you dinner or breakfast. This is meant as punishment for stealing the neighbor's injera and for tarnishing our family's good name."

"Is that so?"

"That's so. She also said that you will sit with me and watch while I eat my dinner. I thought this was cruel, but that is what she said. I want to prepare you for what is coming. I was not even supposed to tell you this, but I didn't want you to be surprised when you found out there wouldn't be food for you at dinnertime."

Desta rolled his head back and pressed his lips. He bit his lip and stared blankly up at the eaves.

Desta thought to himself: *Ba inkirt lie jero gudif*—on top of her burgeoning goiter, she got a swelling under her ear—a common saying brought to mind to someone who has dual problems. He sighed and sat up. "Thank you for telling me this. I will very much miss having dinner tonight, but it's okay."

"I am sorry. I will make it up to you at lunchtime tomorrow. I'll save you a full injera and two scoops of wat." Lesim walked back to the kitchen.

When the evening turned dark gray, Desta put his notebooks into his pouch and went inside the main house. Mebet, needle and thread in hand, was hunched over some clothes. She suspended her activity briefly and gave the boy a hard, probing stare. Desta tried to discern the meaning of her scrutiny.

He decided that Mebet's stare was not one of hate but of distrust. He knew he was doomed. Desta dropped his eyes to the floor and shook his head. He knew that overcoming her hate would have been easier than regaining her trust, remembering Saba's advice: "A broken trust between people will take a long time to mend, if at all. Don't ever lose the confidence and trust that people have in you."

Mebet called him. When he went near her she said, "Don't expect dinner tonight. This punishment is meant to teach you a lesson so hopefully you won't steal again."

Desta studied her for a bit wondering whether or not he should protest his verdict but realizing he has no power to make Mebet change her mind, he simply said, "okay" and walked away.

Feeling low and miserable, he strode across the floor and hung up his pouch and then fulfilled his evening duties. He took the small round canister lamp from the corner of the food prep table, fetched the green bottle of kerosene underneath it, and went outside. Sitting on his heels, he wriggled and pulled out the lamp's thin flutelike top, leaving most of the long coiled wick of bunched threads in the canister's belly.

He unscrewed the bottle of kerosene and gingerly poured the chemical into the bottom of the lamp. He pinched and pulled up the charred tip of the wick and tapped it with his index finger so the tuft of threads would flare a little. He reassembled the lamp and returned the kerosene to its place under the table and the lamp to its half-moon ledge on the wall.

He went to the kitchen and gathered a pitcher of warm water, the orange

Martello soap, the crimson plastic bowl, and a hand towel. He brought these things to the main house and left them on the bench near the food prep table.

The aroma of shiro wat and freshly baked injera caused Desta's stomach to turn and his mouth to water. *Stop it*, he told himself, knowing he was not going to have his dinner that night. Like an obedient child, his stomach quieted and saliva ceased to seep into his mouth.

Zewday and Mebet washed and dried their hands and were ready for their dinner. The boy returned the washing implements to their place under the prep table. He then grabbed his pouch and went to the kitchen. He made a little fire of sticks and began to study.

After the couple and their child finished their dinner, Lesim stepped out and called Desta to come. "They've finished dinner. Bring water for their hands," she commanded. He fulfilled his duties again, put the washing items back, and returned to his reading. Several minutes later Lesim called him again, this time so he could sit across from her and watch while she ate her dinner.

"I will eat quickly," Lesim whispered. "I know it's cruel, but she doesn't want you to repeat what you did, or, worse, steal something bigger and end up in jail. *That* would be especially bad for you and our family."

A few choice words bubbled up into Desta's throat, but when they reached his tongue, he squelched them. With Zewday and Mebet within earshot, he didn't want to say anything provocative and aggravate his problem. Instead he just said, "I know. Thank you for the reminder." Tears welled up. *Stop it*, he scolded himself once again and whipped them away with the back of his hand. His emotions subsided.

Lesim brought a full injera on a platter with a ladle of shiro wat poured in the middle of it and set it on the floor. "Sit down," she said when she noticed that Desta was still standing, looking lost and forlorn. "Remember, you are supposed to watch me as I eat my dinner. You cannot look to the left, right, or straight ahead past me. Your eyes should be on my mouth and hand the entire time I'm eating. This is the instruction Mebet gave me," Lesim whispered.

The boy squatted on the floor across from Lesim, his left hand pressed against the loose skin of his stomach, for comfort, and his right on his chest, for strength. His sagging belly skin terrified him. He felt as though every morsel of food he'd eaten hours before had been washed out of him.

He could deal with the sight of Lesim's dinner. It was the aroma of the spicy sauce and sour injera that kept his saliva emptying into his mouth and his stomach writhing. "Stop it," he audibly said to himself several times. With this series of self-scolding, his stomach eventually quieted down and his mouth secreted saliva no more.

Soon after Lesim began to eat, Zewday retired for the night. Mebet followed after, picking up Tesfa and carrying him to the bedroom. She returned shortly after, sitting at the table and busying herself with the clothes she was mending. Every so often she glanced at Desta and Lesim, her eyes probing and checking to see that the criminal had not broken her decree.

Desta hated himself for what he had done. He hated his stomach for going hungry and causing him to steal. He hated God for making people depend on food to live.

Having finished her dinner—the entire injera, equivalent to what she and Desta usually shared at their meals—Lesim rose and brought her tray to the catchall table by the entrance. "Let's make our bed," she said after she returned. Stiff and haggard, Desta rose and followed Lesim to the back wall to help her pull down the mattress and bedding.

Mebet put her sewing aside. She took several steps toward the door, as if she were going out. Desta and Lesim were about to tip the mattress and drop it on the floor when they saw her pace over to the food prep table. The two young people suspended their activity and watched. Mebet removed the conical cover of the bread basket and set it aside. She dug both hands into the round-bellied basket and leafed through the layers of injera, counting them.

Mebet walked back to the dining table, gathered the clothes she was sewing, and tossed them into a box. She climbed the high earthen platform and disappeared into the bedroom. Desta was astonished by Mebet's level of punishment and mistrust.

"Let's lay down the mattress," Lesim said. They tipped the bulky thing onto the floor and spread the sheets and blanket. Still wearing his jacket and shorts, Desta crawled under the covers and hoped sleep would come soon and take him away to where there was no hunger and where people didn't punish him for stealing out of despair.

Lesim brought the kerosene lamp and set it to the side. She undressed, got into bed, and covered their faces with the sheets.

THE FOLLOWING MORNING, Desta had hoped things somehow would be normal again. He rose and began to perform his usual duties, warming Zewday's wash water and bringing it to him along with soap, a towel, and the other implements. He would then wash his own face and hands and be ready to eat his breakfast and go to school. But that morning was not like any other. As a continuation of his punishment, he was not allowed to have breakfast.

He simply gathered his books and left for school. He lingered near the coffee bushes, wondering whether the bits of bread were still there or the birds had gotten them. Desta fought the temptation to look. He didn't want to give his punisher the satisfaction in case she noticed. Instead, he walked down the path with dignity, as if nothing was the matter.

His stomach seemed to have gotten the message. He didn't feel hungry or particularly tired as he walked to school. Only during the mid-morning break did his desire for food resurface, and this was because he smelled *kolo*—roasted barley snack—which someone was eating outside. He knew in another hour and a half he was going home to eat the full injera and two scoops of shiro that Lesim had promised him.

The noon bell rang. The teacher gathered his things and left, and Desta and his classmates filed out. Walking home at the noon break was always the hardest for Desta. He envied the boys and girls who ran past him, excited to get home for lunch. He sometimes could hardly walk without assistance from the coin. Desta wondered if he could even keep his hand pressed to his chest without fainting or his fingers going numb.

He trudged across the Amin River and watched the crowd of students briskly march up the gentle slope beyond. The big meal Lesim had promised was a beacon pulling him home. All he had to do was endure the next two miles. He then would eat his lunch, be revived, and run back to school for his afternoon lessons.

A voice said: "You sickly creature! If the school won't kick you out, I can do the job for them!" Desta had barely turned to see the source of the threat when a boy lifted his foot and smacked him on the side of his torso. He swayed one way and then the other, trying to steady himself. The boy jumped and struck him with all the power he had in him, and Desta crashed down into the street.

Some other boys giggled as Desta staggered and fell, but nobody stopped to help or console him. He sat up and tried to identify the vicious kid who had attacked him, but there were way too many children around, all running or walking briskly. He tried to get up, but his emaciated legs were like tender reeds. His back throbbed. Desta knew then that he was not going to get home and eat his coveted lunch. He decided to let time be his healer and to remain where he was until the crowd had passed, and then drag himself to the shade of a nearby tree. After he had rested and felt better, he would go home and forget the idea of returning for his afternoon classes.

Curled up in the dust, Desta thought about the string of events since he came to live in Dangila. He surged with emotion. Tears threatened to well up, but he quickly nipped them. His chest ebbed and flowed with the racing of his heart as it tried to rescue him from his misery. Even as hazy and numb as his mind was, his very existence on the brink of extinction, he managed to contemplate the merits of his goals. He wondered whether he should abandon school and his search for the coin—whether he should go back to his birth valley and become a farmer.

He noticed a figure he had not seen before, looking down on him. "What happened to you?" the figure asked.

Desta raised himself on his arm. "Someone kicked me."

"Sorry to hear that. Do you need help?" The figure extended a hand.

"No, I need to drag myself into the shade and rest before I can even think of getting up and going home."

"Have you been sick with a disease?"

"No, I have just not been eating much."

"How come? You have a problem eating?"

"No, I have just not been getting enough food at home."

"Do you want to come along to my house?"

"No, thank you. I don't have energy to spare. I'll be lucky if I make it to that tree."

"Let's see if you can make it there," the figure said, extending a hand once more.

"That I would appreciate," Desta said, grabbing the figure's hand.

Once he rose, Desta put an arm around the figure's shoulder and felt an arm around his back. He hobbled to the tree. The figure, a girl—presumably a class-mate—leaned him against the trunk.

"My name is Eleni. What's yours?"

Desta cringed. His face darkened. He slipped his right hand under his jacket and pressed above his heart.

"What is wrong?" she asked.

"Now you come in the form of a girl?"

"I don't understand," Eleni said. Desta didn't respond. "Are you in a trance or something?"

"No, my mind is clear." Desta studied the figure. It occurred to him that it was no doubt just a coincidence that this girl's name was the same as that of the woman of the wind. "Never mind. Maybe you are not who I thought you were. Thank you for your help. My name is Desta. Please go home, Eleni, or you won't return to school in time."

"Okay. Don't try to go home. Wait for me here," she said.

Desta watched her as she ran off. He remembered what his father had said about coincidences. *Was this encounter with Eleni a preplanned event? An event with consequences?* He wished he had asked her who she really was, in case he never saw her again.

The cool grassy ground was comforting. The Amin River, gurgling quietly at a distance, was pacifying. He lay down on his back and his eyes went up to the branches. He wondered whether, in the face of continued hardship, he should stay in Dangila. Things had not gotten better. He was not sure how much longer he could endure without collapsing and dying.

If the only options he had left were death or going home and becoming a farmer, he'd certainly rather go home. If things didn't get better, he would return to his hole of a valley when his father came after Easter. There was always the possibility of attending the school in Yeedib once again if he still wanted to pursue his goals.

The more he thought about going home, the more excited he became. It would certainly be better there. If something like this happened to him in Yeedib, he at least could go home on Saturday morning, have plenty to eat, and return on Sunday evening. There he would have the added benefit of Saba or one of his other sisters bringing him dabo or other snacks to supplement his regular meals.

The tree-covered flat land with no mountains or sky to behold had depressed him. There was nothing he would miss from this town. Yes, it would be very disappointing to return home without traveling to Bahir Dar to look for the woman with the coin. That had been one of his reasons for coming to live in Dangila, but he realized that it could wait. He could go to the town by the big lake when his circumstances improved.

In Dangila he had no friends. His classmates hated him. The family he lived with had no feelings for him. Zewday—a relative—never treated Desta like one. To Zewday, the boy was like an *ashker*, as if Desta was there merely to provide him a myriad of services. Desta bit his lip and shook his head.

Then Desta was suddenly seized by a renewed desire to fight this adversity. He could endure and deal with anything. All he needed was to find a solution for his hunger. That way he could stay here until he got an opportunity to travel to Bahir Dar. With sufficient daily nourishment, he could stay on until he finished the eighth grade. Maybe Desta needed to find a solution to the problem of his hunger on his own. His father was coming with grains in a little over a month. That supply should last the family three to four months, depending on how much Abraham brought. After this supply was consumed, Desta would need a way to supplement the food he received from Zewday and Mebet. These thoughts made him feel a little better about his future.

To Desta's surprise, Eleni returned, carrying a yellow cloth bag with something heavy in it. "You're lucky," she said, dropping the bag before him. Eleni crouched and opened the bag. She took out an aluminum canteen filled with water and a beautiful silver bowl cradled in a basket. She removed the cover of the bowl and a pleasing, zesty aroma filled his senses. When he peeked into the bowl, Desta couldn't believe his eyes: two eggs, several white injeras of a kind he had never seen before, and two chicken legs coated with a thick, mouth-watering red sauce.

"My parents have gone out of town. I asked our servant to fix me lunch in a basket that I planned to share with someone who was ill and in need of food. I made sure this food came from the same pot as the white teff injera she serves my parents, not from the pot containing the shiro wat and her brown teff injera. She said it was a waste to give such good food to a complete stranger who might not appreciate it. I was amused by that, but that is how she talks. She thinks nobody else is entitled to the food she prepares for my parents."

Desta said, "Please tell her that this complete stranger was very appreciative of her hard work and generosity. She will go to heaven for this kind deed."

"I am sure she would like hearing that, particularly because it has to do with God and heaven. She goes to church every Sunday. . . . Let's have our lunch." She straightened the creases and pulled the edges of the bag, creating a flat, level surface. She took the silver dish out of the basket and placed it on the improvised table. She broke the injera into halves, spread them inside the basket, and poured some of the sauce on top.

Desta watched Eleni's busy hands, not believing his eyes or his good fortune. Her being here with such beautiful food was akin to the strange things that used to happen to him when he was a shepherd. *Did grandpa's spirit arrange all this? Is Eleni his messenger?*

"Come, let's eat," Eleni said with a wave of her hand.

With a torn piece of injera, Desta scooped the thick, delicious-looking sauce. His mouth and stomach had been cued from the moment the rich, savory aroma entered his nostrils and traveled to his brain.

He tilted back his head, opened wide, and placed the first piece of injera into his mouth. Like a drop of water falling on parched earth, it was palliative not just to his flesh but his soul. He tore another piece of injera and had another scoop of the sauce—then again for the third time and the fourth and more. He heard nothing, saw nothing around him, but he fully smelled and tasted every bite of the bread and sauce.

"Eat the egg, too, not just the injera and sauce," Eleni reminded, as she poured water into two plastic cups.

Desta broke the egg in half. The round yellow center rolled out and settled in the sauce. The remaining rubbery shell reminded Desta of a disemboweled animal. He picked up the entire trembling thing and placed it into his mouth, letting his teeth go to work. Next he broke the yellow yolk between his fingers, rolled it in injera, and ate it. He picked up his cup of water and drained half of it in one continuous gulp.

"So your name is Eleni?" Desta asked, putting his cup down.

"Yes, but I like my other name better because it used to belong to the most beautiful girl in the world," Eleni replied with a smile. She chewed on the half egg she had placed in her mouth.

"I like the name *Eleni*, but what's your other name?"

"Helen," she said with a whisper, as if the name would crumble into pieces if she spoke it with any emphasis.

Desta smiled. "That is even prettier."

"My father said Eleni is my Amharic birth name. Helen is the English version, but nobody calls me by that name. . . . I wish they did." The girl looked away wistfully.

"I will call you Helen," chimed in Desta. "I like that name, too."

Eleni smiled. Her lashes, long and curving, revealed the deep-brown hue of a setting sun every time she blinked and gazed at him. The tip of her precise and efficient nose rose to just the perfect height. Her blameless, full lips parted like the petals of roses. She had woven her lustrous hair into fine tapering ridges around the sides of her shapely skull. Her neck was long, her fingers elegant, tapering and beautiful.

Abraham had been right. If names are indeed picked by God, the King of heaven had certainly chosen the right name for Helen.

"Don't forget the chicken leg," Eleni said, pushing one toward him. "We each get one."

She picked up one of the drumsticks and daintily bit and nibbled at.

"What does your father do?"

"He is Colonel Asheber, head of the police," Eleni said with a hint of pride. "And he is one of the two people in the whole town who has a private car—a Land Rover."

Desta was wondering what a head of police does and what it meant to have a car in your house, when it occurred to him: "Do you go on the road with your father?"

"All the time! Particularly when I am not in school. We have gone to Debre Marcos, Addis Ababa, Bahir Dar, and many other cities."

"I've been hoping to go to Bahir Dar someday. It's one of the reasons I came to this town to study."

"Where did you come from?"

Desta told her.

"Maybe you can come with us the next time we go to Bahir Dar."

The first school bell rang. This meant they had to prepare to return for their afternoon classes.

"It would be an opportunity of a lifetime," Desta said.

"I'll ask my father."

"I will forever be grateful, just as I am for what you have done for me this afternoon."

"*Minim Iydel*—it's not much. This is something I have learned from my mother. She always gives money and food to the beggars she finds on her way to church and in the center of town."

"You're blessed to have a mother like that."

Eleni put the lid on the dish, its topside down, and placed it into the basket. She picked up the yellow bag, shook the straw from it, and dropped in the eating utensils while Desta held it open. "I will run to that house over there and be right back," Eleni said as she rose. "Our servant's mother lives there."

Desta watched as his lifesaver flew across the field and vanished into the trees.

After she returned, the two children gathered their books and walked back to school together. His ribs, where the boy had kicked him, were sore, but the pain was not bad enough to interfere with his ability to walk.

"I thank you so much for everything you have done for me this afternoon," Desta said as he was about to part with Helen and go to his classroom.

"Minim Iydel. I hope to see you again, particularly if you want to go to Bahir Dar with us."

"Thank you. I would forever be grateful to you."

"I will let you know," Helen said as she skipped toward her class in the building that was next to Desta's homeroom.

TWENTY-SIX

Desta didn't like the way Zewday looked at him as he brought the man his washing things that morning. His red, puffy eyes steadily and questioningly held Desta's until Zewday picked up the soap and began lathering himself with the warm water Desta dispensed from the green plastic pitcher.

Desta had decanted the wash water among the coffee trees and was about to go back to the house when Zewday stopped him. "What made you steal injera from that poor woman?" Zewday demanded, looking down from his height of six feet two inches.

Desta looked down at his feet and said nothing. He had not given a reason to Mebet for the theft and he was not going to give one to Zewday now.

"Do you not get enough food?"

Desta didn't want to reply yet until he thought of a safe answer.

"Did you steal food from the people you lived with before you came here?"

"No."

"Then why now? You have progressively gotten thinner since you arrived here. Do you have a disease you are not telling us about?"

"No."

"What is wrong then? Mebet tells me that you and Lesim eat identical amounts of food. She looks fine but you don't."

"That may be so, but I am just not used to eating a mere half injera with a scoop of shiro wat at mealtime. I go to bed hungry every night. And the food I receive for lunch is barely enough to get me to school and back."

"If not eating sufficient food is the only problem, then we can fix that. In a week or so we'll harvest the coffee beans and we should get a good amount of cash for them to buy teff, beans, and maybe even meat. We'll see how you fare afterward." Zewday got up and headed to the house, his slippers smacking his heels.

For Desta this promise was the glimmer of hope he needed to keep him going—to stay with the family, continue with his education, and go to Bahir Dar to look for the keeper of the coin.

THE STEALING AND THE SCHOOL INCIDENT brought positive changes to
the household. By his own decree, if Zewday didn't come home by seven o'clock
in the evening, the rest of the family could have dinner and go to bed. For Desta
it had been not only the hunger itself but also the waiting at night for Zewday
to come home that was hard to bear. He had often sat in the corner of the living
room, hugging his belly and battling sleep, while Mebet lay sleeping on the high
earthen seat with Tesfa. Lesim would remain by the entrance ready to open the
door when her father arrived, sometimes napping on the bench and other times
just leaning against the wall, bobbing her head as sleep played tricks on her. But
she never hugged her belly.

With the new rule came some logistical changes. The *merek*—the oil-rich
part of the sauce—was siphoned off and kept in a separate pot for Zewday and
Mebet's dinner. The children were served the bottom residue with their half
injeras. Desta thought that this instruction had been made by Mebet and not
Zewday. No matter, it was great news. It meant they didn't have to stay up for
hours waiting for the drunkard to come home so they could eat their dinner.

This new rule, which was meant strictly for the convenience and comfort
of the family, turned out to be a benefit for Zewday as well. He could stay out
longer without guilt or the pressure to come home early. The man of the house
took advantage of it. On weeknights he came home at eleven; on weekends he
returned much later than that.

One Saturday, in the middle of the night, a loud bang on the corrugated tin
door brought the sleeping family members abruptly to life. For a few seconds
Desta didn't know where he was or what had caused the booming sound. Lesim,
as if by instinct, got up and stumbled to the door. The kerosene lamp on the wall
was still going. They had forgotten to put it out.

"What took you so long to open it?" Zewday garbled, spittle discharging from
the corners of his mouth. Lesim didn't answer because she had heard the question so many times before.

Zewday staggered in, nearly tripping at the threshold. He reeked of tej. He sat
on the high earthen seat and ordered Desta to come and untie his laces and remove
his shoes. Zewday then ordered the boy to bring his slippers and the flashlight. He
needed to go to the bathroom and wanted the boy to accompany him. In the warm,
pitch-black night, Desta followed Zewday, aiming the light on the path to the

toilet shed.

But Zewday couldn't wait. He stepped off the path, unbuttoned his pants, and sent out a golden arc into the coffee bushes, framed by the circular disk of light Desta held before them. The dribble on the dry leaves and his seemingly endless stream was a curiosity to Desta. He tilted the flashlight to get a glimpse of Zewday.

"Keep the light away from me," slurred the midnight blue man, his cascade still going. It was as if he had imbibed several gallons of the yellow beverage.

After he had finished, Zewday buttoned his pants and continued to the toilet shed. He stepped inside. After several crackles, rattles, and groans, Zewday came out smiling. He rested his hand on Desta's shoulder and the pair walked back to the house through the coffee trees, following the light the boy shone before them. "My coffee beans, my coffee beans," Zewday sang.

Desta looked up at the man, not knowing what to make of this sudden reference to the purplish beans that glistened in the branches in front of them. Zewday continued singing:

My coffee beans, my coffee beans
First you bloomed and filled the
   air with your jasmine fragrance
   then your flowers withered
   and fell off as if in an instant
For months we waited
   as your budding fruit went
   from green to yellow
   to orange and then to red, a fiery glow.

Zewday pulled one of the branches down, parted the leaves, and studied the cluster, singing:

So alive and kicking
   At last you were purple
   and ready for picking.

The midnight blue man continued singing as if he were now bestowing private praise on the cherry-like beans. When he noticed Desta was looking at him curiously, he said, "Once we harvest and sell the coffee beans, we will have plenty of money to buy all types of grains and meats. And you will never go hungry again."

Desta was not sure whether he should believe what Zewday was saying, considering the man's state of mind, so Desta said nothing. But this alleged bounty from the coffee bean harvest gave him a flicker of hope just the same. Zewday resumed with his ditty:

> With baited breath we wait for that day
> When we will pulp and dry you
> and get you under way
> To bring and sell you on a market day
> to fetch us a barrel full of money
> To purchase teff, peas and barley
> butter, areqey, and kerosene, too
> And things that would bring gladness and peace   °
> in our household.

En route to the main house, Zewday stopped and said, "I want you and Lesim to bring your mattress with a clean sheet to the kitchen. I need to lie down by the fire so you two can scratch my back."

Desta tilted the light upward and studied Zewday's face, wondering whether he was serious. He had never asked for this service before. The man still was not quite in control of himself physically, let alone mentally. However, he appeared to remember perfectly the poem he was singing. Zewday didn't repeat the request and instead he went on with his song:

> As precious as honey
> You'll make us the money
> To fill our bellies and make us happy

> I love you, my coffee trees
> Shower me with your beans
> I love you, my coffee trees
> You're the best ever seen!

"Let me have the light. . . . Go bring the mattress," Zewday said again.

Desta scampered in the light Zewday cast toward the entrance of the main house. Zewday began harmonizing his song once more, this time in a low voice:

> My coffee beans, my coffee beans . . .
> As precious as honey
> You'll make us the money

To fill our bellies and make us happy.

"Not again," Lesim whined, rubbing her eyes to wakefulness. "I used to do this for him so often before you came."

The two children dragged the mattress out of the main house. When Zewday noticed Desta didn't have the strength to lift it off the ground, he handed him the flashlight and took over.

"Lesim, lift your side and let's go," urged the father, raising his side of the mattress off the ground. After they took a couple of steps, Zewday's feet got tangled somehow, and he lost his balance and fell forward, pulling the mattress out of Lesim's hold and bringing it down on the ground.

Desta and Lesim giggled. "What happened, Baba, are you that drunk?" Lesim asked, teary eyed.

Zewday planted both hands on the mattress and hoisted himself to a standing position. "No," he said, catching his breath. "I believe Desta pushed me."

Desta chuckled even more, surprised by the wild allegation. "No," he finally countered, "I didn't even touch you."

"I attest to that. He didn't do it," Lesim concurred, her giggles puttering out to snivels.

After Zewday caught his breath and steadied himself, father and daughter managed to transport the bulky bedding across the courtyard into the kitchen house. They threw it down by the side of the hearth.

Lesim wiped the remaining tears from her smudged cheeks and said to Desta, "Go get kindling and a few logs from the side of the house while I go fetch a clean set of sheets, a blanket, and a pillow."

"Turn off the light," Zewday ordered after Lesim left. Desta complied. He lingered before heading out to bring the firewood, watching Zewday and wondering what he was going to do in the near darkness. Zewday removed his shoes and then all his clothes. He wrapped himself with just his gabi and sat on the bench and waited.

Desta came first, cradling a few logs and kindling. Lesim arrived with the bedding and the little kerosene lamp.

Lesim spread out one of the sheets and tucked it under the edges of the mattress. Then she carelessly spread the second sheet and the blanket. This done, she dug out the fire-starting embers she had buried in the ashes a few hours earlier and with a handful of dry eucalyptus leaves and the kindling Desta had brought, she made a roaring fire in no time. Desta was exhilarated by the smell of the eucalyptus leaves and the fragrance of the smoke.

"Come and lie down, Baba," Lesim said, patting the bed.

Zewday dropped the gabi to waist level and wrapped his torso and lower limbs. He peeled back the top sheet and blanket and slid under them. He lay on his side, his back to the fire.

With the kerosene lamp in hand, Desta watched the unfolding ritual with fascination.

"Coffee beans, my coffee beans," Zewday droned absentmindedly, staring at Desta's feet.

"Baba, don't you want to turn around? Haven't you had enough of the fire?"

"Sure, my back is itching for your good hands, daughter," Zewday said and happily obliged.

Lesim lifted and folded down the top sheet and blanket until she reached Zewday's gabi wrapping.

Zewday's back and shoulders were lean, almost emaciated. On his velvety skin were scattered small islands of pimples. He had no hair on much of his back except for a thin arc that trailed down from the lush growth above his neckline.

"Coffee beans, my coffee beans," Zewday hummed again.

"What about your coffee beans, Baba?" asked Lesim as she crouched and studied her father's back.

"We are going to harvest them in a week or two. After they are skinned and dried, we'll sell them to merchants for a lot of money. We will then buy plenty of teff and other grains and meat so you and Desta will have plenty to eat."

"We would always have plenty to eat if you didn't spend your money on tej every night, Baba."

Zewday went silent for a few seconds and then said, "I don't spend my money. My friends buy me the drinks."

"I have heard that before. . . . The pimples on your back have returned. I am going to crush them with my nails," Lesim said as she ran her fingers over her father's back.

"That's why I came here by the fire, to see if you can get rid of them once more."

Lesim planted all ten of her fingers on Zewday's back and went to work.

She popped the bubbly outcroppings, as many of them as she could feel beneath her thumbnails. Zewday stopped singing and now just emitted hisses and puffs of gratitude, saying "ahhh" and "ooo." By the time Lesim was done, the man's back looked as if it had been cut up. Pale liquid streamed from all directions to Zewday's lower flank. He started to sing his song again.

Lesim went to a bamboo basket in the corner of the room and returned with a white cloth. She wiped her father's back and then massaged him with a bit of butter she had brought in a small glass jar.

"Ohhh, that feels sooo good," Zewday emitted again.

He twisted his arm behind and asked Lesim to scratch him where he pointed. Once she was done there, he wanted her to attend to the edge of his gabi wrapping and then his spine. He asked her to scratch him there, from top to bottom, and Lesim did, slowly and methodically.

"Ahhaaa." Zewday was in heaven.

Having done all he requested, she began to caress him with the tips of her fingers. These touches were hypnotic to the father. His eyes fluttered as if they were about to succumb to sleep. Lesim seemed to know just what to do. Zewday soon began to snore, forgetting his coffee beans and not knowing what exactly had happened to him.

Lesim unrolled the blanket up to his neckline. She buried the embers in the ashes. "Shhh," she commanded Desta, as they headed to the door with the kerosene lamp. Lesim slowly pulled the door closed and they scurried to the main house.

With no mattress to sleep on, Lesim brought the two skins and palm leaf mats and spread them on the living room floor. Desta, wrapped in his own gabi, and Lesim in her father's, went to sleep.

TWENTY-SEVEN

Two young men sat on the wooden bench outside the main house, their chins hidden in the turns of their gabis. One, with highly arched feet and small, deep-set eyes, reminded Desta of his brother Damtew. His skin tone and physiognomy too bore a striking resemblance to his sibling. The second, big eyes and circumspect disposition, reminded Desta of no one in particular.

He had just arrived home from school. Neither man said anything when their eyes met his. They just stared at him. Desta quickly went past them, thinking of Damtew and feeling queasy. He went immediately to Lesim and asked her who they were.

Lesim replied, "They are Mebet's relatives from the country. They came to pick the coffee beans tomorrow and Sunday. They are waiting for Baba."

Because Zewday had indicated that the family's economic status, and with it the amount of food they could buy, would significantly change after the coffee beans were harvested and sold, Desta had been checking the transformation of the cherry-like beans from green to yellow to orange to red, their best stage for picking, according to Lesim. Now that the time had arrived to harvest some of the beans, the boy was excited. He quickly went inside, put away his notebooks, and came back out.

He was debating whether he should go and talk to the men or wait until Zewday formally introduced him when Lesim called for him from the kitchen. Desta went to the door. "Give them these glasses of tella and tell them that father should be arriving soon." She handed him the brown drink, which had been prepared by Mebet for the guests.

En route to the men with the tella, Desta wondered whether Lesim might be dreaming about her father's early arrival—on a Friday? It would be a miracle. Maybe not, though, he realized. Zewday probably needed extra money as much for his habits as to provide sufficient food for his family.

The first man accepted his tella, saying, "Thank you." The Damtew look-alike took his with just a nod. Desta was talking with the first man, who introduced himself as Yirga, when Zewday walked briskly up the path. *Miracles do happen*, Desta thought to himself.

"Good evening, Yirga and Ashager," boomed the midnight blue man, smiling. The men rose and bowed. "Good evening."

"Desta, wait here with them. I need to go and change my gabi and shoes and will be right back," Zewday said and went into the main house.

When Zewday returned, the two guests and Desta followed him into the coffee grove. As they walked around, Zewday would pull a branch down, part the leaves, and point to the clusters of berries, each at different stages of ripening. "As you remember from last year," Zewday said, "we want just the red and purple berries picked. Not the greens, the yellows, or the oranges. Those will be picked at the next round, when they turn red or purple." He let the branch snap back to its original position.

"There aren't many that are ripe," Zewday added apologetically, as he surveyed more of his coffee bushes. "Still, we need to pick all that have matured."

Zewday headed to the north end of the plantation with his workers in tow. He opened the door to a shed and pointed to the many rolled palm leaf mats. "After you pick the berries, I want you to take these out—" Zewday interrupted himself. "Matter of fact, let's take them out right now."

They carried the rolls to a patch of land on the south side of the compound, near the sitting bench under the eaves of the main house, and piled them on the grass close to the coffee bushes. "Tomorrow," Zewday said, "I want you to unroll these mats and let them air first before you spread the harvested beans on them to dry. The berries can be skinned or left whole when they are drying. I'll let you know which option to follow."

YIRGA, ASHAGER, AND DESTA rose early on Saturday morning and went to the plantation, each with a basket for collecting the beans. They started at the street and worked their way back. Desta collected the ripened berries from branches that hung low and those that had fallen on the ground. The men picked those the boy couldn't reach.

Desta worked intently, knowing that harvesting the beans would directly benefit him. But he was curious and intrigued by these fruits that clung together like the best of friends along the branches and how a single cluster sometimes had green, yellow, red, and purple berries at their various stages of ripeness.

He wondered what they tasted like. He wiped a plump berry and squeezed it between his thumb and index finger, trying to eat the skin. He found the tart- to bitter-tasting outer layer unpalatable and resorted instead to gnawing the meager but sweet pulp he found underneath. Gnawing through these layers to reach the birthplace of the bean was an adventure in itself.

First there were the twin kernels, nearly identical in shape but mirror images of each other. They were curved on their backs but flat where they conjoined— separated by thin parchment. With another pressing the pair fell apart, their membranous skin intact. His exploration and discovery complete, Desta tossed the bean into his basket. "Fascinating."

After he filled his basket, he took it to the palm leaf mats. He poured and spread the berries like Yirga and Ashager had already done. He then hopped and skipped back to the grove.

At midday, Lesim showed up. "How is it going?" she asked when she found Desta busily picking the berries.

"Great!" he replied.

"Glad to see you so excited by this work."

"This means there will be more food for you and me, and I am happy about that prospect," Desta said, smiling broadly.

Lesim pretended not to have heard. "You should have seen this place back in September when these bushes were in bloom. The whole compound smelled of jasmine."

"Is that right?" Desta was glad to hear about the flowers that gave birth to the fruits he was busily collecting.

"Yes, some warm evenings we'd roast and grind coffee, invite neighbors, and sit at the porch, letting our nostrils fill with the rich aroma of the fresh coffee we had made along with the wonderful jasmine fragrance," Lesim said longingly. "The bushes blossom for two or three weeks, although each flower wilts and falls after just a day or two." She pulled a branch down and studied the cluster of beans on it. "You know, these berries, which father sometimes called cherries, are like human babies. It's nearly nine months from the time the petals fall until the berries ripen."

"Fascinating."

"It is! You think I am joking, huh?" Lesim said, annoyed by Desta's one-word response.

"I didn't mean to give you that impression. I am really fascinated. I found out coffee beans are not beans at all but fruits with big seeds inside them."

"Who told you this?"

"One of the teachers. He comes from Kaffa, the birthplace of coffee. Also, the berries have all these amazing shades of color. The exterior skins on the ripened ones are so smooth and glossy that you can see your face in them. Then I discovered the different layers of skin. This pale green pair, with winding canyons on their faces, looks so innocent and adorable. And now you are telling how they develop and grow. What can I tell you? I am sincerely and genuinely fascinated! Now do you believe me?" Desta grinned at her.

"Okay, okay, I believe you. I came to tell you guys that lunch is ready."

"Oh! Do you have enough for all of us?"

"Mebet bought a kettle of tella for Yirga and Ashager, and we borrowed a few injeras from the neighbor, to be repaid with coffee."

Desta was not sure whether Lesim was telling the truth, especially about the repayment idea, but he didn't want to press her.

The three workers sat on folding chairs that circled a mosseb. They were leisurely eating their lunch when Zewday walked up. He had left when the three laborers started early that morning and was returning from wherever he had gone. His rugged brow glistened. "How is the picking going, fellows?" Zewday asked, looking down at the group.

"Going good," piped up Yirga. "Take a look at what we have gathered so far. We have spread them to dry on the mats."

Zewday walked over to the mats, studied his harvest, and returned. "*Dinknew*—terrific," he said. "Just remember that all the over-ripened ones need to be pulped today or they will ferment and go bad."

"Oh, I don't remember you telling us that," Yirga said. "No problem. We'll dedicate two hours to do just that before the day ends." Ashager acknowledged with a nod. Desta was thrilled to get to spend more time pressing and prying open the fascinating beans.

Zewday said, "I have been talking to the different merchants in town, trying to see who will give us an advance based on the coffee you've picked so far. Ato Abdullah said he would come Monday afternoon to take a look. We should make sure we have the best-looking beans for him. It will take ten to fifteen days for the cherries to dry and before all of them are pulped. He will have a good idea about the quality of the beans from looking at the raw harvest.

"We'll do our best," Yirga said.

"Good job. Keep going!" Zewday scampered away to the courtyard and vanished into the main house.

In mid-afternoon the three workers brought the last baskets of their pickings and poured them onto the mats with the others they had spread to dry earlier. Over the next two hours they selected all the purple-colored cherries, spread them on hides, and pulped them with the use of paddles. They pressed and kneaded by hand those that got missed.

They then poured the mushy mixture into a bucket of water and separated the floating pulp from the beans that settled at the bottom.

Desta continued studying the beans. He pressed the plump berries between his thumb and index finger to release the slippery, membrane-coated beans. He broke the parchment-like skin with his thumbnail to expose the oval-shaped twins clinging together face-to-face. He pried the pair apart with his fingertips and looked at them apologetically. He found a common thread between these beans and himself.

He said to them: "You who have been together since birth with the bond of twins: 'I for you, you for me'—or is it 'one for two, two for one'?—are now disconnected from each other. Soon you will be thrown onto a heap of other beans that have met a similar fate. Where each one of you will end up, in whose cup or on what ground you will fall, nobody knows. My life is the same. And with me, there is no telling where I am going or where I will end up living— whether I'll finish my education or find the magic coin. My future is uncertain, just as yours is." Desta shuddered.

After their two full days of effort, Yirga, Ashager, and Desta had produced the equivalent of 120 pounds of quality grade beans. It was going to take ten to twenty days for all the beans to dry. Zewday had ordered Desta and Lesim to take turns stirring the beans several times a day during that time.

On Monday evening, just as Desta finished raking the drying beans, Ato Abdullah arrived. He was a stocky man who wore a tightly woven fishnet skull-cap and greasy jacket with oversized pockets. He stood by the harvested coffee beans and eyed them critically.

Zewday arrived shortly after the merchant. The two men shook hands and chatted as they walked around the mats and studied the beans. Every so often, Ato Abdullah crouched, scooped a handful of the polished beans, and examined them. Then they toured the orchard to see the beans yet to be harvested.

Zewday led the way, parting the branches where the bushes grew densely.

They returned to the drying beans and talked prices. Zewday wanted 150 birr for the two sacks of beans he soon would have ready. Ato Abdullah wanted to pay twenty-five birr less. They talked some more. Zewday decreased the price by ten birr. They continued negotiating. Zewday came down an additional five birr, and said, "No more."

Ato Abdullah crouched near the beans once again and scooped and studied them, as if to convince himself unequivocally that the coffee beans were worth 135 birr. That money, plus a handsome profit, would be returned when he sold the beans out of his shop or shipped them to Addis Ababa.

Zewday watched the businessman with confidence and a glint of triumph in his eyes. Desta studied them from his perch on the bench, fascinated by the ritual of bargaining.

Ato Abdullah sprang upright. "Okay," he said. He reached into his breast pocket and took out a wad of red and orange bills. Clipping the layers of bills between the fingers of one hand, he peeled away the first thirteen red sheets. He pulled out an orange bill from the bottom of the stack, added it to the first set, and handed them to Zewday.

Zewday counted each bill and then folded and stashed them in his breast pocket.

"Amesegnalhu," he said, shaking Abdullah's hand. "I will have these beans ready for you in a week and a half."

"Let me know when and I'll send a couple of porters to pick them up," Abdullah said as he stepped onto the path to go.

"Will do."

The midnight blue man had just received the equivalent of two months' salary. Zewday hadn't even reach the threshold of the main house before Mebet, who obviously had been watching the men haggle from a distance, came running. "How much, how much?" she asked anxiously.

"Not much," Zewday said casually. "Here, I will give you sixty-five birrs to buy two sacks of teff, enough for two months, and all the other things you need for the kitchen, plus two hens."

"Is that all?" Mebet cried. "How can I buy a two-month supply of teff, peas, butter, condiments, and two chickens with sixty-five birrs?"

They haggled. Zewday gave in. He peeled off another red bill and handed it to his wife.

"Easter is coming in another week," Mebet said. "Seventy-five birrs will not be enough to buy all the things we will need for the holiday."

Zewday took the orange bill out of his pocket, slapped it in his wife's hand, and dashed into the house. Mebet, flustered and angry, gazed at the door as if expecting Zewday to come out with more money. She wrapped her fist around the eighty birr worth of bills and stomped toward the kitchen.

Desta envisioned himself in a week or two. He'd be running to school and back like the other students, chasing and kicking the soccer ball in the field with his classmates. His ribs would be filling out and he would be looking a lot better when his father came after Easter with the grains and butter he had promised Mebet.

TWENTY-EIGHT

Almaz Beyene was a hair braider. She braided hair all day, five days a week. Sometimes even on Saturday, and she probably would have worked on Sunday, too, if she had not been afraid of offending her Christian God or concerned about her neighbors' criticism for working on a holiday. Her clients wouldn't have minded, though, because their God permitted them to work all seven days of the week if they so chose. They were Muslims.

Almaz's "salon" was in the open air, framed by Zewday's wattle fence on one side and closely grown rows of eucalyptus trees on the other three sides. The roof was that portion of the sky outlined by the tall eucalyptus trees, which she saw every time she looked up. Her furniture consisted of two hand-carved stools, one slightly taller than the other. The taller stool had legs that flared out for stability—Almaz was a tall, heavyset woman. The smaller stool, made from simple blocks of wood, was the seat for her clients.

Next door to her salon was a grass-roofed hut with perhaps two hundred square feet of living space. This hut was Almaz's residence and she was the only one who lived there. The door to her hut faced Zewday's fence and her workstation. Although the little courtyard where she sat was neatly swept, farther down was overgrown grass and fire logs piled high along the fence. A few feet from her entrance lay a large, round clay pot with many holes in it. Weeds had grown through the holes and peeked freely at the sky. A broken wooden box filled with dead eucalyptus leaves had taken shelter under the hut's eaves. A mousetrap coated with rust leaned between the wall and the box.

The footpath from the street to Zewday's residence went past Almaz's compound. There were big gaps in the fence posts through which Desta could see just about everything going on in Almaz's compound. Almaz could see the passersby with just a slight turn of her head.

"Good afternoon, young man," called out Almaz one evening as Desta came home from school. Almaz was braiding the hair of a round-faced, middle-aged woman, who was perched on the smaller stool.

Surprised by this unexpected greeting from the old woman, Desta paused and acknowledged her with a bow.

"How much of the coffee beans did you pick?"

Desta's face twitched in surprise. He had never before talked to Almaz or as much as exchanged a casual greeting as he came and went past her salon. "I don't know, but a lot," he said finally.

"Step closer to the fence. I want to tell you something."

Hesitant, Desta took two steps toward the fence and stopped.

"Be right back," Almaz said to her client and came to the fence.

"Your name is Desta, right?"

Desta nodded that it was.

"Can you give me some coffee in exchange for food?"

The boy gazed at the woman, astounded by the bold and unexpected question.

"Can you?" She repeated.

"No!" Desta exclaimed.

"I love Zewday's coffee. He used to sell me a year's supply every year until we had a silly feud over nothing."

Desta stared at Almaz. Her lined face appeared to have once had the smooth texture of granite. Her tired and sleepy eyes must have once been the talk of the town's young men. Her symmetrical, sunbaked nose, full but now-peeling lips, and slender yet wrinkled hands must have been, in her youth, pretty to behold. Almaz smiled.

"Don't you want some food? You were such a handsome boy when you came. Look at you now. . . . They must be starving you. It's a shame. . . . A family that owns all that land and a coffee plantation . . . a secretary of the judge earning good money . . ."

"No, I will not give you any coffee regardless of what you say, unless Aba Zewday says so. Besides, Ato Abdullah has bought everything."

"How about for money?"

Desta looked around. "No, ma'am, no," he said and walked home briskly.

Later, as he sat on the bench with his notebook, he thought about Almaz and what she had said. *Food she prepared with those hands? No way. Even if I was starving to death. Her hands are always greasy and she looks as if she bathes in oil with her clothes on.* The woman's once white cotton gown was now shadow gray. And he had always been told that hair was one of the most unsanitary things one could have lying around the house or on anything. Hibist used to throw out food if she found a single speck of hair in it.

Desta had never seen anybody else around Almaz's yard other than her clients. *This explains why the old woman lives alone and has no family visitors.* Desta flinched in disgust.

Money, on the other hand, was a different matter. He could always use money, and the first thing he would buy would probably be *firno*—the white puffed oval bread the Arab man baked. But that offer came with its own set of problems. To sell coffee beans to Almaz, he would have to steal it first and this he wouldn't do. *If I do that, I will forever be labeled a thief and would probably be sent back home.*

Of course he was not going to gamble his future and reputation for a piece of bread. Once when he had been really, really hungry, he was sent to buy white bread for Tesfa. He remembered fantasizing how one day when he gets his first job, he would spend his first month's salary on a whole sack of that bread. For now he just needed to endure his problems.

Besides, things were already looking up. With the new infusion of cash in the household, Zewday and Mebet would purchase sacks of teff, lots of peas to make shiro wat, and beef, lamb, and chicken to make *tibis*—cubed sauté meat—and stew. Then his father would come with more supplies of teff and butter and other things. He didn't need to sell coffee beans to Almaz.

Having suppressed this unexpected and unwanted temptation, he picked up one of his books and began to read.

THE SATURDAY FOLLOWING the pre-delivery sale of the coffee beans, there was excitement in Zewday's family. Desta was particularly looking forward to the grains Mebet was going to purchase so he could have full meals. Zewday had given her most of the money she needed, and Saturday was the day farmers brought their grains to market. Mebet left at mid-morning to get there at peak time, when most of the farmers had arrived, so she could have a greater selection and better bargaining opportunities.

At mid-afternoon Mebet returned with two porters, each carrying a sack of grains. They unloaded them in the courtyard first and then carried each sack between them into the kitchen house.

"Uhhh, I am pooped," Mebet said after the porters left. "I need to go rest for a while." She hobbled to the main house.

"I wonder if she bought all brown teff or if one of these is white," Lesim said anxiously. She untied one of the sacks. "Ahh, this is brown," she said. "Let's hope the other is white. Knowing her, she probably bought another brown." Lesim slowly untied the second sack, building her own anticipation and surprise. The moment the leather sack fell open, her face went dark.

"What's wrong?" Desta asked, coming closer to look. "What kind of teff is this?"

"It's not teff but dagussa!"

"What's dagussa?"

"It is a grain some people give to animals. Others use it to brew areqey. It's the only food most poor people can afford."

Desta reached into the sack and felt the small round grains. "This is like sand!"

"It's a dry grain and not very tasty."

Desta's mouth went dry and his stomach knotted.

Noticing his reaction, Lesim said, "Of course, it doesn't mean it's for our meals. She probably plans to make areqey with it."

"I hope you are right." He went outside with his books and around the main house to his bench.

On Monday the grains were taken to be ground at a mill house.

On Wednesday when Desta came home for lunch, Mebet gave him a folded full injera soaking with a steaming sauce. *My hunger days will soon be over,* he thought. He took the platter and sat on the high earthen seat. He tore a piece of the injera and grimaced when the unusually thick and heavy bread crumbled as if made of fine sand. He dropped the piece on the side of the platter. He looked up for an explanation, but both Mebet and Lesim had gone to the main house.

He broke off another piece. Perhaps this one would be softer and more edible. It was just the same. He scooped the shiro sauce with it and put it in his mouth. It tasted gritty and mildly tart. But he was hungry and the food was tolerable enough once he began chewing it. The generous amount of sauce Mebet had given him made the bread easy to chew and swallow. When he finished the whole injera, he was full but felt as if he had stuffed himself with a mixture of sawdust and sand. Given the way the food sat in his stomach, Desta wasn't sure he would ever digest it.

Lesim entered and asked, "How did you like your lunch?"

"Tolerable."

"Let's see how tolerable it will be when you go to the bathroom."

Desta eyed her.

"Maybe not with you," she said. "Some people have a harder time with it than others."

"I don't know what you're talking about. I certainly don't want any more surprises."

IT WAS AS IF HIS BODY had decided to conspire with Mebet against him, with intent to trick, tease, and humiliate. The second day after consuming the exotic food, Desta went to the shint bet three times, each time with nothing happening but threats and gas.

A voice within him said, *You have never seen anything like this, boy, but this is another lesson in life you have to learn to endure. Your limitations will be tested, and painful it will be. Your body has the ability to stretch, expand and grow, and adapt to new circumstances. The price for this is pain, and you have to endure it. What is happening within you now is a metaphor for the life you have come to know.*

The voice was uncanny. He went to the shint bet for a fourth time. He pushed and pushed: there was some progress, but it was ever-so slow. He realized he was not going to do it on his own. He needed leverage. There was nothing around except stacked pieces of paper for normal trips to the shint bet.

He had an idea. He needed to attach a rope to the crossbar on the corrugated shint bet door and then pull on the rope while he pushed. He went inside the house and looked for a rope, but there was none. He looked around outside. By the well was a bucket attached to a long cord, which was used to pull water out of the shaft. He removed the cord from the bucket and went back to the shint bet. He closed and latched the door. He inserted one end of the cord between the crossbar and the groove in the corrugated tin and looped and tied the end on itself. He walked over to the opening in the toilet, squatted, picked up the slack of the rope, and wound it twice around his hand. Overlapping his hand with the other, he went to work, pulling and pushing at the same time. Tears oozed, and in agony, his bottom felt as if it were pulling apart and clamping shut at the same time. For a brief moment he thought of a dream he once had about his sister Saba in labor and everybody in the room saying, "push, push, "and Saba saying "kill me, kill me."

But Desta had nobody to root for him. He was alone—locked up in the dingy, smelly shint bet. When he was finally done, it was a relief, but he was determined never to go through that again.

When he told Lesim what had happened, she smiled and said, "I told you so. It seems you had it bad. I'll tell Mebet and see if we can do half 'n' half—half teff, half dagussa."

"Do something, or I am not going to eat that food anymore. . . . Or I may be forced to take my option." He gazed at Lesim. "I may be forced to take my option," he repeated.

"What are you talking about? Like I said, I will tell Mebet and let's see if we can do something."

Desta limped back to his books.

TWENTY-NINE

A week after Easter, Abraham came.

"Era!" the father exclaimed, throwing his fingers to his mouth the moment he saw Desta. "Have you been sick?" He studied Desta from his head to his feet to assure himself the mid-afternoon sun was not playing tricks on him.

"Quite the contrary. I have not had even a single cold."

"Then, why?" Abraham's eyes began to brim.

"*That* you will have to ask my keepers."

A single tear slowly streamed down Abraham's cheek.

"Why cry?" asked Desta, staring at his father. "I am still alive. My skin is still attached to my bones and I can still walk, thank God for my image of the coin." Desta rested his hand, gratefully, over his heart.

Abraham tilted his head and wiped off the lone tear that clung to his cheek, as if refusing to let it fall any farther.

Desta stared at his father. "That tear you just wiped is no consolation to me. Weren't you the one who told me that, as gold is tested with fire, a man's will and strength are tested with hardship? I guess you can say I'm trying to live up to your expectations, not really by choice but by circumstance."

"We can talk about that later. Let me kiss you first." Abraham kissed Desta three times on the cheeks.

Abraham had three animals with him, his horse Dama, a mule and a donkey. The horse snorted. The mule with the load on her back stood unmoved. The donkey sauntered to the mound of dry grass by the garden patch. He seemed to treat what he was carrying like it was a bag of feathers.

Mebet dashed toward them. "*Tena-yistilegne inquan dehina metu*—may you have had good health, welcome back," she said in her heavy Agew accent.

Abraham hesitated for a second and then said in a distant, forced tone, "*Tena-yistilegne, indeman aleshi ehitay*— may you have had good health, how are you, sister." 'Sister' was not appropriate, and Abraham knew this. Mebet was not Desta's aunt and didn't merit the esteem such a title conveyed. Also, she was a lot younger than Abraham's older children, certainly much younger than Saba. Abraham went through the motions of the ritual three alternating kisses on Mebet's cheeks.

"Lesim, please bring chairs," Mebet said, noticing the girl was standing right behind her.

Lesim ran to the main house and brought out two chairs, setting them against the wall.

"Please have a seat," Mebet said with a wave of her hand. She dashed to the main house and returned with two birrs. "Lesim, here, go and buy a kettle of tella." She turned to Abraham. "Please have a seat."

"I need to unload the animals first." Abraham's hands and feet moved animatedly. He was too absorbed with his son's condition to do anything naturally. He unloaded several of the smaller sacks and an *agelgil*—leather-clad basket—and then the heavier sacks of teff and barley from the animals' backs. He piled the offering against the wall.

Mebet dashed to the kitchen house and returned with two washed drinking glasses on a tray and set them on the bench.

"Please take a seat, Ato Abraham," Mebet said again, after he hitched the animals. "Lesim should return soon with a kettle of tella. You must be awfully thirsty on a hot day like this."

Abraham took his seat. "April is always our hottest month, and today felt as if we were walking through a desert."

"Oh, I know. Even for us who live surrounded with so many shading trees, we have been toasting. . . . Be right back." Mebet ran back to the kitchen.

Desta couldn't help but smile at the absurdity of Mebet's excitement.

"Come," Abraham said with a wave of his hand.

Desta strode over and stood near his father, for a moment lost in thought.

"Your teeth and smile are all that have not changed."

"My teeth had nothing to lose," Desta said, suddenly overtaken by emotion. He tapped his chest and clenched his teeth. The waves of anger that surged through him quickly subsided. "The teeth never lose their smile, even after everything else is gone," he added, remembering his grandfather's shining teeth in his remains.

"I am just sorry and sad to find you in this condition. . . ."

Lesim returned with the kettle of tella, some squirting out of the spigot, wetting her skirt and feet. Perspiration had dewed her brow. She poured the tella into the glasses. She handed one to Abraham and left the other for Mebet. She then set the kettle on the ground and was about to return to the kitchen when Abraham stopped her.

"Thank you, Lesim. *Dehina nesh*—you're well? Let me kiss you before you go," he said, putting down his glass.

"Dehina," Lesim replied, tossing her head down into a bow.

His eyes on Lesim's rebellious little toes, Desta thought about the strange adult world he lived in.

Abraham gave the girl the three ritual kisses. She bowed once more and dashed to the kitchen.

"Come," Abraham said, tugging the boy toward him and standing him between his legs. "We can talk later about all that has happened to you," the father whispered as Mebet returned.

She said, "We expect Zewday for lunch shortly. Would you like *koors*—snack—till then?"

"I am fine, thank you," Abraham said sharply. "The drink is good enough for now." He picked up his glass and took a sip. He cleared his throat and said, "Have you all been well?" His voice was craggy. He enfolded Desta in his arms.

"We have, thank you . . . except for your son." Mebet's eyes darted from Desta to the animals and back to the boy and father. What Abraham was feeling was not lost on her. "For a few weeks our town food was not agreeable to him and as a result he lost quite a bit of weight. He has steadily improved, though, as he got used to the food."

"Is that so?" Abraham gazed at her, trying to ascertain the truth of her report.

"We didn't know what was wrong with him at first, but like I said, he is getting better." Mebet was struggling to sound sincere, but her eyes betrayed her. "Ohh, here comes Zewday!" she said, grateful she wouldn't have to continue fudging the truth.

"Look who is here!" Zewday boomed.

Abraham pushed Desta aside and rose. The two men kissed ceremonially. Zewday dropped his eyes onto the things Abraham had brought.

"Everything well with the family and all? C'mon, let's go inside," Zewday said, waving his hand.

Mebet folded and picked up the chairs, followed the two men indoors, and opened and placed the chairs at the table. "Come sit, please?" she said.

After lunch and coffee were served, Abraham signaled to Desta to bring the agelgil inside. The boy staggered back, cradling the basket. He placed it on the table in front of Abraham and stepped aside. Abraham untied the straps at the apex of the conical top.

"I want to thank you both for accommodating my son for the past three months. I brought him without advance warning and you were kind enough to take him. As a token of appreciation . . ." He realized *appreciation* was the wrong word, considering the condition he had found Desta in. He removed the top of the basket, revealing an object wrapped in banana leaves. Gingerly peeling off the layers of leaves, he said, "I've brought this butter in the hope it will be a good supplement to you."

"This is wonderful," Zewday and Mebet said almost in unison. "Of course, we always appreciate butter. We thank you very much."

"In addition," Abraham said, glancing at Zewday, then Mebet, "I have brought two sacks of grains, one teff, another barley, and smaller bags containing peas and fava beans."

"That is very generous. We thank you so much. . . . Whether you brought these things or not, you know that we wouldn't have let your son go to bed without food. But again, we thank you."

"As you know, cash for us farmers is a premium, so I am happy to have the option of bringing food supplies instead of money." Abraham closed the box and prepared to leave.

"Have some more tella, please," Mebet said.

"No, I better go. I want to arrive at my sister's while it's still light; plus, I haven't had a chance to visit with Desta. He can accompany me to the center of town and we can visit there."

Desta winced. Abraham was not going to spend the night?

Everybody went outside. Abraham said, "I need to transfer these sacks into something. Do you have a bag or large container?"

Mebet and Lesim dashed to the kitchen and returned with a canvas bag. "All we have is this," Mebet said awkwardly.

"I will transfer the grain from one of my bags into this bag, and I will collect my other container the next time I come."

"It would have been nice if you could have spent the night, but I understand," Zewday said, watching Abraham untie the teff bag. "We have no place where you can keep the animals overnight."

"That's just it," Abraham said, as he poured the teff into Mebet's canvas bag.

The two men shook hands. Abraham thanked Mebet and Lesim, gathered the leads of the animals, and left with Desta.

At the center of town, Abraham tethered the animals to a telephone pole and the two went into a nearby teahouse. Drinking tea, Abraham and Desta talked for nearly an hour. Abraham was upset and disturbed by what had happened to his son and hoped the food he brought would make things better for him. Desta learned that Lesim's mother had been Zewday's servant and that the woman was from a lower class. Her father announced this fact with the choice of "Lesim," which was considered a demeaning name. To him she amounted to nothing more than someone who would carry his name.

Desta was saddened by this revelation and realized why he liked the girl. The two had something in common. Just as he grew up being told he was inferior because of his premature birth, Lesim's father conveyed to the world that she was insignificant.

Abraham was concerned more about Desta's story than the meaning of Lesim's name. "If it has been as bad as you are telling me, do you want to come home?" Abraham asked, after they left the teahouse.

Desta paused. "You mean, I should abandon my dreams?"

"Something worse could happen to you. Do you want that?"

"I'm a survivor. No matter what, I could never go back on the promise I made to grandpa's spirit or leave my own aspirations unfulfilled."

"Okay. It's only two months before the school year finishes. I will come get you then. We can talk more about your future when you come home." Abraham kissed his son, rubbed his head endearingly, and left.

As Desta walked home, he thought about his mother, the mud, and the horse manure that would be waiting for him back home at the end of the school year. The thought made him shiver.

THIRTY

Despite the infusion of food supplies and money from the sale of coffee beans, Mebet still used the dagussa flour in Desta's daily meals. She continued to give him injera prepared with a fifty-fifty mixture of teff and dagussa. However, Desta was grateful for the added ladle of shiro wat, which improved the palatability of the dry injera.

From a private conversation with Lesim, Desta found out that Mebet had decided to save for the upcoming rainy season all the food Abraham had brought. This was because many basic food supplies were more expensive and harder to get at that time. She bought new canvas sacks for Abraham's grains and beans and peas and stored them away. She melted the butter with many different spices, filtered it, and stored it as well.

Desta understood then that Mebet was a selfish woman; she didn't seem to care at all about him. Before, he had blamed Zewday and his drinking for the lack of food. Now he saw that Mebet was also to blame. She had no heart or sympathy for Desta. He realized that he needed to fend for himself, even if he had to break one of God's cardinal rules—even if he had to steal. But he would make it up to God with acts of kindness. And, hopefully, this time he would have better luck and avoid getting caught.

Despite Abraham's suggestion that Desta come home after school closed in June, he decided to stay in Dangila and find ways to go to Bahir Dar to look for the magic coin. As Mebet had prepared herself for the rainy season with Abraham's food supply, Desta needed to make backup arrangements for himself.

Throughout May and into early June, the coffee bushes continued to produce beans. Because Mebet's relatives in the countryside were busy with their own farm work, Desta and Lesim were enlisted to pick the remainder of the coffee beans. Desta picked beans for two or three hours every evening after school. He raked them when he came home during lunchtime, and he uncovered them to dry before going to school in the morning. On the weekends he picked and pulped the cherries.

The side benefit to this was that, seeing that she could get more work out of the boy, Mebet continued to give him more food. With the infusion of cash from the sale of the coffee beans, Zewday bought a large lamb. Its meat fed the family for a whole week. Mebet gave Desta a generous amount of lamb meat. "It is because of your hard work picking and harvesting the beans that we're able to get a big lamb this year," Mebet said one evening as she dished out lamb sauce. Interestingly, however, Mebet's apparent generosity yet belied her fundamental stinginess as she still continued to give him the teff-dagussa injera.

One afternoon Desta went to the fence near the hair braider's salon. He stuck his face between the fence posts. Almaz was weaving the hair of a young woman with big beautiful eyes. "Emma Almaz, do you still need coffee?"

"I told you I would pay with food or money, whatever you prefer. As much as I like Zewday's coffee, I feel obliged to help you, too, because it seems you have been deprived of adequate nourishment."

"How much coffee do you need?"

"I used to purchase a year's worth from him, paying him once a week."

Desta thought about how he could save that much coffee without it being noticed.

"How much is that?"

She excused herself to the girl, went inside her home, and came back with a clay cup.

"This cup full of coffee is enough for a week."

Desta thought that four of his fistfuls would fill the cup.

"How much would you pay for that?"

"One birr and twenty five cents."

"How much food can I get for that?"

"Depends where you go. If you go to Khadija's restaurant, which I recommend, you can get a full meal for twenty-five cents. Other places charge more. With what I propose to pay, you will have enough money for five meals."

Desta looked around to see whether there was anyone who might have overheard their conversation. They seemed only to be in the company of Almaz's beautiful client, who was not close enough to hear the details of their conversation. "Let me think about all this for a while and I'll let you know." He started for home but then changed his mind. He needed to take a long walk instead and ruminate on what Almaz had proposed.

The boy took a long deliberate stroll to the center of town. As he walked, he realized that the arrangement he was tempted to strike with Almaz was not going to be an easy one. There were a lot of things to consider.

First, there was God to worry about. Stealing was one of the things He frowned upon. God's punishment could be severe once Desta eventually died and went to heaven. Also, Desta associated stealing with being dirty, like having mud on his feet or muck on his clothes. He didn't want to feel like that every time he fetched Almaz's weekly supply from his storage silo.

Furthermore, he worried about being discovered, since he would be storing the beans on the family's property. If he gave any of the family members reason to be suspicious, they might secretly follow him and find out about the hidden beans. If the family found out that he had been stealing and selling their coffee beans, he could forever be labeled a thief. Worse still, he could be sent back to his country home, ending all his dreams.

On the other hand, there were compelling reasons for stealing and selling Zewday's coffee beans. One, there always was a shortage of grains in the market during the rainy season, and the prices were high for those that were available. Two, according to Lesim, the time of the coffee harvest, with the extra funds it brought in, served only to increase her father's drinking bouts and squandering of money, which decreased their food supply all the more. Three, if Mebet was going to save Abraham's bags of food, Desta could rationalize doing the same with the coffee beans and selling them to Almaz. This way he could use the money to buy meals that Mebet should've been making with Abraham's food all along. With these thoughts, Desta returned home.

The decisive moment came that night after Desta went to bed and noticed his body. Starting from his thigh, he traced a path with his fingers to the cliff of his pelvic bone, down to its base, and up along his waist. He crossed the flank of his ribcage, skidded over the ever-protruding ribs, and up around the neck to the big crater that lay at the craggy summit of his shoulder, between the splitting collarbones. This deep-recessive topography always stopped Desta's fingers in their tracks, causing his heart to skip beats, his nerves to tense, and his stomach to lurch in fear.

If his body had become emaciated like this during the relatively easy dry season, he shuddered at the thought of what might happen during the rainy months. Desta made up his mind, unequivocally—no matter the consequences—to steal some of Zewday's coffee beans.

THE NEXT DAY, as he was preparing to go see Almaz, Desta considered the terms she had proposed. If he gave her a week's worth of coffee, she would give him one birr and twenty-five cents, enough for just five days of supplemental meals at Khadija's restaurant. The exchange was not equal. He wanted her to cover him for an entire week of meals. He also wanted her to give him an extra fifty cents a week. With this money, he planned to buy tea and white firno bread at the teahouse. What's more, Desta thought he might have the opportunity to meet other children there.

With these ideas in mind, Desta went to see Almaz. As usual, she was at her station braiding a woman's hair. Desta stuck his face between the fence posts. "Emma Almaz, do you have a few minutes?" he asked, raising his voice a little higher than normal.

The old lady excused herself and walked over to the boy. She lowered her oily, wizened face and asked, "What have you decided?"

"It was no easy matter. I have decided to go along with your proposal, but we need to modify it a bit."

"Oh?" croaked Almaz, placing her greasy hand on the fence railing. "Tell me." Desta told her.

They went back and forth discussing the payment the boy sought for his weekend meals and pocket money for tea and the firno bread. At the end, Almaz asked, "Where did you learn how to negotiate?"

"From people in the market and stores."

"You're a smart boy. Okay, you bring me the amount of coffee I need once a week and I'll arrange with Khadija to give you one meal a day for the full week. But I cannot give you the extra fifty cents; there are two reasons. One, if Zewday or any of his family saw you coming and going from teahouses, you would have a hard time explaining how you got the money. Two, for me to pay the extra fifty cents, you'd need to match my money with your coffee. I don't think you want to do that because you would run out of your coffee reserve sooner. I just think it's better that you don't go to a teahouse for now."

Desta bit his lip in disappointment. He eyed Almaz pensively.

"On the other hand," continued the old woman, "if you need a meal a day for the whole rainy season, you need to save me enough coffee for all or most of the three months."

Desta didn't like the idea of not receiving any extra money, but knowing the circumstances, he heeded Almaz's warning.

Having agreed on the terms, Almaz gave Desta a clay jar in which to store the coffee beans and from which he would bring her weekly supply. "Make sure to hide it at the farthest corner in the compound where the bushes are thick with leaves," Almaz advised. Then she added, "Next Saturday, come to my place shortly after the sun has filtered through the trees and you and I will go to Khadija's restaurant."

"I CANNOT BELIEVE THIS," Desta said, rubbing his burning calf where Zewday had whacked him with his cane. Not even a full day had passed before Desta witnessed the manifestation of his fears. The very day the boy cemented his agreement with Almaz to supply her with Zewday's embezzled coffee beans, the coffee plantation owner demonstrated his capacity for violence.

He had come home inebriated as usual but there was something more sinister in his bearing. Wet from the rain, he stood in the living room supporting himself with his cane. Zewday demanded to know which one of the two children stole money from his pocket the previous week. He said that he had forgotten to bring up the matter until that night, having just remembered the infraction on his way home. Desta and Lesim looked at each other, baffled.

"But Baba, nobody stole money from you," Lesim said, stepping closer to help him to the chair. From the mud on his pants, shoes, and gabi, it appeared he had already fallen several times.

"You deeed; I know you deeed," Zewday slurred, glaring at his daughter. Lesim was not sure what to do. She returned her father's gaze, wondering what was really going on with him that night.

"Are you all right, Baba? I mean, you're not imagining things?"

Zewday didn't answer, instead saying, "Are you going to return the money you took from my pocket or not?"

"I have no money to return, Baba, because I didn't take any from you."

"Let me see if this makes you confess." The drunkard lifted his cane and whacked his daughter on her midriff as she leaned and raised her hand to protect herself. She gave out a sharp, pained cry as she scrambled toward the door. Zewday managed to hit her once more, this time on her back, before she could undo the latch and run out of the house and into the rain.

Desta watched, frozen. He had never seen such sudden outburst of brutality from Zewday.

Mebet watched from the bedroom, herself shaken.

Zewday bore down on Desta. "Did you steal the money from my pocket?"

"No," whimpered the boy as he eyed the door.

Zewday grabbed Desta by the arm. "Tell me the truth before you receive a piece of this cane, too."

"I . . . I . . . I'm telling the truth," Desta stammered. He struggled free but Zewday still managed to hit him on the calf as he ran to the door.

Lesim had run to the kitchen, braving the rain. Desta stood by the door and watched Zewday, who then had managed to trip over his cane and fall on the floor. When he didn't get up, Mebet came out of the bedroom and assisted her husband to his feet. "Help mee take my shoes off," he garbled to his wife. "I'm not feeling well. I need to go to bed immediately."

"Please bring me a bowl. My stomach feels funny," he said leaning to the side of the high earthen seat. Mebet looked up and didn't seem to like what she saw on Zewday's face. She dropped his foot and dashed to the table and returned with a bowl. She placed it under Zewday's face on the side of the high earthen seat. Immediately Zewday's chest heaved, his head jerked forward and a slurry mixture of food and liquid hurled into the bowl. Two more motions to the chest and head and two more retches and he was done. He wiped his mouth and hands with a cloth Mebet had given him. He pushed down the back of each shoe he still had on with the toes of the other and quickly climbed the seat and disappeared into his bedroom.

Mebet took the bowl and its contents and threw it out of doors through the back entrance. The rain had tapered, allowing Desta to scamper across the courtyard and into the kitchen. Mebet came to the door of the main house and called out for both children, but they refused to go back. They made fire, and then laid down Zewday's newly bought scratch mattress and slept on it in their clothes.

THIRTY-ONE

On the appointed Saturday, Desta went to see Almaz. She was draped in her netela and wearing a pleated, ankle-length gray nylon dress and sling-back black plastic shoes. She was perched on a tree stump by the rickety gate to her property, cane in hand.

"Good morning! Good that you didn't make me wait too long," she said.

Desta greeted her with a bow. "I have been thinking about this day since I saw you last. I am glad it has finally arrived," he said with a smile.

"No doubt. Khadija is looking forward to seeing you," Almaz said, casting her soft brown eyes on the boy. "Let's go quick, though. I've a woman coming for braiding later this morning." They stepped through the gate and she closed it behind her. They walked up the main road toward the center of town, Desta behind Almaz. The neighborhood was redolent with the aroma of roasting coffee and there was excitement in the air. It was always that way on a market day.

"I want to share something with you about Khadija and her restaurant," Almaz said in a low, deliberate voice.

Desta trotted closer, realizing the confidentiality of the information Almaz was about to share.

"Khadija is a Muslim, like nearly all my clients are. All her customers are Muslims and you will be among the very few Christians who eat at her restaurant. I'm taking you to her because there will be less chance of Zewday's family finding out about you eating outside the home. You never know who you may run into in the Christian restaurants, even Zewday himself.

"You should know that Christians don't usually eat meat that comes from animals that Muslims have killed, and vice versa. It's up to you in this matter. I have eaten their meats before. It never bothered me. Khadija Lugman is a good person. I have told her about you, as much as I know from what I have observed and the brief conversations you and I have had.

"Be careful as you go in and out of her restaurant. If the news gets to Zewday, you will have a hard time explaining both where your money came from and why you ate at a Muslim woman's restaurant."

Desta was quietly processing this cryptic information when Almaz turned around. "Do you understand?"

He shook his head. He didn't understand. "What is a Muslim and why is it wrong to eat their meat?"

Almaz explained who Muslims were. "Christians and Muslims don't eat each other's meats because . . ." Almaz paused, searching for a good answer. Not finding one, she just said, "Because their religion does not permit it."

"Why not?"

"That you have to ask the priests."

Khadija was a rather heavyset woman. She smiled broadly the moment she saw Almaz and Desta walk in through the open door. She was sitting in the front part of the restaurant fussing with the leg of a long bench-like table. "Sorry, I forgot it was today you were coming," Khadija said. She dropped the table leg and rose. "Let's go to the back."

In the back was a somewhat subdued room. There were five tables, each with six chairs. To Almaz and Desta, having just come in from the bright morning light, the room appeared dark at first.

Khadija led her visitors to the far corner of the room. "Sit down," she said, pulling out chairs from under the table first for Almaz and then for Desta.

"You have explained to him the potential problems, haven't you?"

"Yes, he knows. Don't you, Desta?" Almaz asked, glancing at the boy.

Desta nodded yes. "But will anything bad happen to me if I eat your meat?"

Both women laughed. "Nothing bad will happen to you if you eat my meat," Khadija assured the boy, still chuckling a little.

"That's right," Almaz agreed. "But it's not necessary to tell anybody else if you happen to eat her meat."

"Obviously, he is concerned. The meat dishes we serve mostly to our high-paying merchant clients. For the rest it's mostly potatoes and shiro wat—and tomatoes and salad when they are in season."

"He will be fine with that. Certainly, much better than what he has been getting at home."

"But you get to sit in the merchant's section, in the back," Khadija said to Desta with a smile. She shifted her eyes to Almaz. "That is because the front door is always open and the front part of the restaurant is viewed by every pedestrian who passes by."

"Thank you. As you know, I have to protect myself, too," Almaz said. "My intentions are good, but if this arrangement somehow gets exposed, my reputation will be ruined."

"Not to worry. I will have one of my children's tables set up for him here," Khadija said.

"It will be good for him to be in the company of business people—world travelers," Almaz said, smiling at Desta.

"They are all gracious people. They will be kind to him."

Desta felt as if a new world was opening to him already—free from Zewday's cramped, isolated, dull compound. He had learned little from the family and they had no interest in his education or well-being and certainly no concern for his aspirations or dreams.

Khadija said, "Would you have time for coffee? I can have one of my girls make one quickly."

"Ohh, no, thank you. We have to go. In fact, Medina might be waiting for me at my station already." Almaz got up to go and motioned Desta to get up, too.

Desta wished they could stay longer so that he could talk more to his future provider.

At the door, Almaz said to Khadija, "Just occurred to me. This area has one of the highest concentrations of tej and tella houses—two of Zewday's favorite drinks. . . ."

Khadija patted Almaz's shoulder. "I know, but don't worry. Everything will be fine."

The two women said good-bye. "See you soon," Khadija said, pressing on Desta's shoulder.

Almaz walked briskly. Desta hopped and trotted behind her, excited by his new prospect.

THIRTY-TWO

By the end of the school year, Desta finished as one of the top three students in his class and was promoted to the third grade. This was in 1960. School closed on the last day of June. Abraham had promised to come and take Desta so he could spend the two and a half months of break at home. He instead sent his nephew Alem-Seged, a son of Aunt Zere, because he had a court case that week and couldn't come to fetch him. Desta had long before made up his mind to stay in Dangila through the rainy season. He was not missing home and he didn't think home was missing him. Living with Zewday's family was hard, but having been assured by Almaz of getting one good meal a day through the end of September, he felt he could weather any further hardships he might face.

He had a number of things planned for those two and half months, the most important being a trip to Bahir Dar to look for the holder of the coin. He also wanted to visit with the merchants in town. Because these businessmen traveled to faraway places, he thought that if he became friends with a number of them and made them aware of the person he was looking for, they would spread the news for him. He wanted to spend time exploring the town, particularly the Muslim section on the west side of the main road. That booming voice of the man he heard five times daily announce the Muslim prayers had been a constant reminder.

So when Alem-Seged came to fetch Desta the Saturday following the end of school, he said he wouldn't go home because he had other plans during his school break. However, he sent a message to Abraham. He asked his father to come and see him after the rains had stopped in September. Desta wanted him to sell any grains he had planned to bring and send him the cash instead.

When Desta came home after parting with his cousin, he learned about a month-long project Zewday had in mind for him. Some of the fence posts on the north side of the property had rotted and fallen. Zewday wanted to take down the 150 foot-long fence and replace it with a new one. This meant that the jar Desta had stashed his coffee beans in was going to be exposed. The following morning he rose early and moved it to the south side, near Almaz's home.

Zewday hired two young men, Dinku and Aberra, to do the job, and Desta was to be their helper. At the beginning of the work, Desta dragged posts and carried bundles of the thinner lattice material from the dismantled fence and piled them behind the kitchen house for use as firewood. Dinku and Aberra concentrated their efforts on cleaning up the fence line and freeing it from weeds, vines, and debris. After this work, they dug two-foot-deep holes, separated by three feet, for the posts. These activities took the three workers a full week.

Meanwhile, a man named Daud and his son had brought, in multiple trips, new solid wood posts loaded on donkeys, and left them in small piles at several locations along the fence line.

The second week, Dinku and Aberra placed the posts in the holes, pushed back the soil they had dug, and pressed the dirt in with their feet until the posts felt firm to the touch. Then they nailed three eight-foot rails to each post, the ends of the rails touching. It was Desta's job to provide extra nails when the men needed them and to drag the rails near the posts.

The final stage of the fencing job was the most dangerous and hardest for the workers. This task involved weaving thorny branches between the railings. These branches were delivered, wrapped with hides, on the backs of donkeys and then piled at different locations along the fence. Desta had to separate the thorny branches and drag and hand them to Dinku and Aberra.

By the end of the first day grappling with the thorny branches, the three were haggard and fatigued. Scratches of all sizes, shapes, and depths traced their hands, arms, and legs. Blood had oozed and curdled into tiny droplets from several of these scratches. Besides the ghastly scrapes, the soles of Desta's feet had been pierced and bits of thorns become embedded. The men had tough, old, and gnarled leather shoes that helped shield their feet.

"My goodness," Zewday said after studying the men's bodies. "You guys look as if you had battled with a bunch of cats. Who won?" He grinned.

"*They* did, of course," replied Dinku with a half-smile. "We just managed to survive." He studied the backs of his hands and then twisted and turned his arm as he traced his eyes over it. He bent over and examined the white lines on his shins. He then lifted his heel and twisted his leg to have a better look at his calf.

"Yeah, you're right. I didn't feel all these nasty scratches at the time because we were so busy with the work."

"I never had this many scratches and thorns in me when I was a shepherd roaming the fields and looking after the animals," Desta said.

Aberra shook his head, disturbed by the many gashes and tears in his skin. "We need to be extra careful tomorrow."

"Wrap some sort of skin to shield yourselves," Zewday said. "It can be your best weapon—against those cats." The midnight blue man grinned.

"That's a good idea," Dinku said.

"Good night," Zewday said. The men left and Desta limped to the house.

That night, after Lesim and he laid out their bed, Desta sat on the edge of the mattress and tried to pry out the thorny bits from the bottom of his feet with a safety pin. Lesim held the kerosene lamp close and watched. She studied the landscape of Desta's sole and toes and nails.

"How did you get all those other tiny splinters?"

"Some parts of the field where I looked after the animals had a lot of thorns."

"Do you want to take them out?" Lesim asked, running her index finger over the tough skin. "I can help you."

"No. They are reminders of my past, as the keeper of the animals I tended." Lesim stared at him.

"That's right. Removing those bits of thorn is like wiping out my history. These new ones," Desta said, pointing, "I must take out because they hurt."

"You're strange. . . . but it's up to you. For tomorrow's work, I'll see if I can find Baba's old shoes."

Desta smiled at Lesim and then looked away as he imagined what it would be like to walk in a pair of shoes, not to mention Zewday's old shoes.

"What's funny?" Lesim asked, glancing at the boy.

"First, they'd be too big for my feet. Second, I wouldn't know how to walk in them. Third, I'd rather wait until I can put on a brand-new pair of shoes that fit me perfectly. That will be a very special moment and is worth waiting for. I'd then celebrate by throwing a big party for all my family and friends." He smiled again.

Lesim laughed. "Don't be ridiculous."

"I know you all take wearing shoes for granted. My feet have been needled with thorns and straws and scraped with stones and splinters all my life. I have walked barefoot in mud and muck and flood and dust. To finally wrap my feet in something warm and protective would be meaning enough to celebrate the event in a big way."

"Okay, I see that you are serious about your intentions. Will you invite me to the party?"

Desta remembered what Saba had said about people whose feet become smooth from wearing shoes and who therefore have problems walking barefoot. He looked at Lesim and said, "Yes, of course I will invite you, assuming it happens sometime soon. If I'm gone from here when it happens, I will think of you when I romp around in them."

Desta took out the last of the new splinters from his feet.

"Okay," said Lesim, taking the lamp away, "Let's go to sleep now that you're free of your thorns." She placed the light by her side, got undressed and slid under the covers.

Desta pierced the collar of his jacket with the safety pin and pinched it closed. Then he removed his jacket, got under the covers and slid off his shorts.

Lesim blew the light out. "Good night. I hope your dream of wearing your first pair of shoes comes true soon."

"Thank you. Wearing shoes is not as important as my other dreams, but thank you just the same."

As Desta tried to fall asleep, he wondered what Lesim's chest felt like.

THE FOLLOWING MORNING, after the routine task of bringing Zewday's warm face water and then eating breakfast, Desta prepared to join his coworkers by the fence. When he went outside, Lesim was waiting for him. "Come," she said, waving her hand. "I've found Baba's old shoes." Reluctantly, Desta followed her to the back of the house. In front of the bench stood a pair of old, stiff black shoes, their toes banged and dented, evidence of the many hits they had suffered every time their owner came home drunk.

Desta said, "You brought these out for me to wear?"

"Yes, they will protect your feet from the thorns. There is nothing else you can use to shield yourself."

"I thought I made myself clear last night. I will not let my feet touch an old pair of shoes. I will wait until I can afford to purchase brand-new ones for myself."

Lesim looked disappointed.

"Besides," continued Desta, "they are way too big for me and I'd trip all over even if I was fool enough to wear them."

Lesim sat on the bench and pulled out the fabric she had stuffed inside the shoes so Desta's feet would fit snugly. She folded the fabric multiple times and replaced it in the backs of the shoes as padding. She quickly inserted one foot and then the other, pulling the laces tight and tying them. She rose and took a wobbly step forward. "They feel strange," she said, looking at Desta.

"That should have been apparent to you before you even put them on," Desta retorted.

Lesim took another step. "I don't know how Baba ever walked in these," she mumbled.

Desta just stared, anticipating her fall and cueing himself for a hearty laugh. Lesim took more steps. With each stride she gained confidence and soon felt secure walking in the gnarled shoes. She began walking almost normally. When she felt completely sure and safe, she lifted her feet higher and romped in the courtyard, her hands flailing wildly in tandem with the movement of her legs.

"See, it's not hard to walk in them. If I can do it, so can you."

"You look absurd. No, thank you," Desta replied sharply.

She went off to romp again, this time going around the perimeter of the courtyard.

"I need to go," Desta said.

"This was for your benefit. If that is your attitude, go get riddled with thorns. Don't ask me to help you take them out tonight."

"I won't. Obviously, you have never had shoes either and are taking this moment to live out your dream. I am happy for you." One of the men called Desta. "Thank you just the same. I need to go." He parted the branches of the lush coffee bushes and made his way to the job site, wondering when, if ever, he would have his first new pair of shoes.

THIRTY-THREE

When Desta arrived at Khadija's restaurant for his first meal, he was not sure if he was at the right place. "Priests?" he wondered after seeing the turbaned men who packed the back room. But there was Khadija, just a few feet away, speaking to a turbaned man who had tried to sit at the small table in the corner. "That table is reserved for a special customer," she said.

The man crinkled his brow. "A special customer?" he asked, scanning the room for another table.

"A friend of a friend who will be with us regularly for a while."

He spotted an empty seat at another table. "Okay," he said curtly. "You should've put a sign then."

"I'm sorry. I didn't think customers of your size would bother to sit there. Thank you for your advice. Will keep that in mind for the future."

Khadija turned toward the kitchen and saw the boy. "There you are, Desta. Been here for a bit? Did you see that man who wanted your little table and chair?"

Desta nodded.

"Well, it looks like it's going to be a popular spot. I am not sure how I am going to protect it for you." She smiled sweetly. "I will have to put a sign on it."

Desta smiled, too, but only in his heart. In Khadija's flashing, evenly grown white teeth and radiant face, he saw kindness and comfort. He felt at home.

"Sit down," Khadija said, patting the boy on his shoulder. "Farah will bring your lunch."

She walked to the front room and Desta was left to study the gathered men. They didn't look like priests, exactly. And they *couldn't* be priests, of course. What was he thinking? It was their appearance, more specifically, their white hats and head wrappings, that aroused the fleeting interpretation of Orthodox Christian priests.

But there were some obvious as well as subtle distinctions between these men and the Christian priests. The priests he knew, such as Aba Yacob, wore their turbans to make a statement, declare their status, and demand respect and reverence, albeit implicitly. It was as if to say, *My shash*— white head covering —*is neatly wreathed around my head because I am a member of the clergy and we have standards to abide by. My shash commands your respect and supplication before me, as I am the agent of God's scripture. I have the power to lighten your burden and abate your sins. I carry the cross and I can bless you. I am here; you are there. We are not equal.*

The men at Khadija's restaurant had no pretensions about anything. Their turbans seemed swathed around their heads without care, without meaning or purpose—a mere custom dictated by their culture. The priest's *shash* sometimes referred to as *timtim*, on the other hand, was a symbol of his power and prestige.

From some heads, the end of the turban hung like an oversized belt. On others, the wrapping itself looked crooked. The rest of the men wore simple, tight-fitting white hats that were creased at the crown. Some of them wore soiled jackets with shadows of grease here, spots of dirt there, and stains of sweat around the collar and under the arms. Others wore casual but clean clothes, and many swaddled their gabis, folded once and thrown over the shoulder, to make room for their arms.

Some were busily eating. Others, who had finished their meals, were talking volubly, much of which Desta couldn't hear well. Once in a while, someone would say *wallahi*. What that term meant he would have to find out, from Khadija perhaps. Some had beards, others were clean-shaven or had salt-and-pepper stubbles.

Farah, the waitress, brought Desta's lunch, a full injera opened and spread on a red-and-white floral-patterned tray, loaded with shiro wat, tomatoes and lettuce, and a boiled egg. The green and red mounds at the corner of the platter were things he had never seen before. He asked Farah what they were. She smiled. "You have never eaten *selata*—salad and *tima-tim*—tomatoes—before?"

"Where I come from, they don't serve these kinds of foods."

"Try them. They are good for you."

Khadija waved at the girl and she ran to the front of the restaurant.

"Wallahi" filled the void Farah left.

Desta ate, savoring the soft, freshly baked injera and steaming shiro wat. He'd almost forgotten how wonderful food could taste. The beautiful texture of the bread and the rich flavor of the sauce had him swooning. His mouth lingered on the sauce-soaked egg. He almost felt his strength returning with each bite. He nibbled at the tomatoes but didn't touch the leaves. *Only goats eat this kind of food.*

As he walked back home, feeling almost like new, Desta ran into a group of children playing some sort of game by the side of the road. He stopped and studied them for a bit. They seemed so absorbed in their game that they didn't feel threatening. He took a few steps closer.

A cat's eye in a small glass sphere rolled over level ground and came to rest outside a scratched circle roughly two feet in diameter. The boy who had thrown the sphere walked over pensively and looked down at it. Two other glass balls—one with green, red, and blue spiral traces, the other inlaid with gold and swirls of brown—had found their positions outside the circle, about a foot apart. Another boy got up and tossed his glass ball. Floating clouds were trapped inside.

Desta was transfixed. Within the bounds of the circle were more of the orbs, huddled in a smaller ring, like sheep herded in their pen. These contained colorful images reminiscent of blades of grass in green, blue, red, and yellow hues. The afternoon sunlight, shining through the glass, projected the patterns of color onto the ground.

"What are these?" Desta asked one of the players. The boy looked at him quizzically. "They are *biyee*—marbles." He then tapped the shoulder of the player next to him. "You go first. Yours is the closest to the big circle, although just a tiny bit away from mine."

The other boy complied. He picked up his marble with the spirals in it and wrapped his index finger around it. He placed the knuckle of the hand that held the marble on the ground where it had rested, aimed at the marbles inside the smaller circle, and flicked it with his thumbnail.

The huddled marbles dispersed and two came to rest outside of their home base of the small ring. The incoming marble rolled to the side but remained within the big ring. The boy who had shot picked up the two marbles he knocked out of the inner circle and put them in his pocket.

The next player aimed at the remaining marbles. Three of them flew out of the inner circle but his shooter remained within. He took a regular marble from his pocket and swapped it with his shooter.

A third player shot at the remaining marbles in the inner circle. He knocked all of them out and gathered and pocketed his winnings.

There were no more marbles to win, so the fourth boy didn't have a chance to play. He wanted another game, but the others said no. He asked them again, but each said, "Wallahi," they had to go home. They left, saying they would come to play another time.

"Wallahi, I need to go to my job," Desta said to himself. The novel term was ringing in his head.

As Desta walked home, something bothered him: how so many things that people took for granted as commonplace were new to him. He felt like a baby who was just beginning to learn new things every day. He was tired of the surprised looks on people's faces every time he asked for an explanation of something that was new to him. He promised himself he would not ask any questions again. He would just pretend he had eaten it, seen it, and heard it before. *'Oh, those timatims. Of course, my mother grows them in her garden. That selata, too . . . and those biyees—I used to play with them in my village every time I had a break from watching the cows. . . .' Just pretend until I learn on my own or hear about things from others.*

THIRTY-FOUR

With anything new and educational, Desta went to the extreme. When he first wanted to learn the alphabet, he neglected his responsibility as a shepherd and nearly paid for it with his life. Then when he first saw the sunset, he refused to go home, preferring to stay at the top of the mountain so he could see the sun every day as it went home.

Coming to Khadija Lugman's restaurant had the taste and feel of those previous experiences. Every day he couldn't wait till he got there, to sit quietly and observe the Muslim merchants as they chattered, haggled over deals they were making, and talked about places he had never heard of before. Coming there had revived his imagination and heightened his dream of travel and adventure. The unlimited possibilities of going farther and farther away from his place of birth, of seeing things he'd never witnessed before, of discovering places he'd never been to, and of coming closer to finding the Coin of Magic and Fortune had taken a new hold on him.

Since he had come to live with Zewday, Desta's imagination and aspirations had been stifled. His hunger and difficult living situation contributed to his inability to pursue his studies with passion and his tree-shrouded surroundings to his sense of isolation and disconnection from his hopes and dreams.

Because he was small and sat in a dark corner of the room, the merchants hardly noticed him. Or if they did, they probably thought he was the owner's son or a relative. Desta loved that feeling of secrecy, of being incognito. Nobody stopped to say hello or ask questions.

During peak time, around noon, there was a lot of chatter—the merchants' conversations became difficult to make out. These people talked on their way to the washbasin outside and on their way back. They continued to chat after they all sat down around the nicked, scratched, and greasy tables, as they waited for their orders of injera with meat and shiro sauces, salad and tomato. There were two trays served to each table. Three or four people would share a tray and eat out of it with their hands. They kept talking, even with their mouths full, but their conversation always petered out mid-meal. After they finished eating, some left right away. Others lingered over tea or coffee.

At the end of the meal hours, there were always a few men who remained. These were the deal makers, most of whom, as Khadija had indicated to Desta, had no shop. They worked out of their homes. The sellers would bring out some merchandise and show it to potential buyers. They would haggle back and forth and finally settle on a price.

The traders in watches were always the most fascinating to Desta. The seller would bring out a dozen or so from his case and arrange them on a solid blue, black, or green cloth. Specks of light scattered in the room from the burnished surfaces, making Desta wonder where these objects came from and what hand or machine could make the metal shine like that. But the merchant's interest was not the nature of the making or maker of his merchandise but rather the deal he wished to strike with his buyer that afternoon.

"How much?"

"One hundred birr each."

"Too much."

"My profit is not much considering the distance I have gone to buy these."

"Where did you go?"

"Dire Dawa."

"Probably contraband that you paid a pittance for."

They haggled.

The seller yielded. "Ninety-five."

"Eighty."

They haggled some more.

"Ninety. The best and final," said the seller, gathering his watches.

"Wait," the buyer said, pressing a hand on the seller's arm. "Okay, we are not strangers to each other; I will pay what you're asking."

Desta couldn't quite see how many watches the man bought, but he thought probably around twenty, because he gave the seller twenty of the red bills or 200 birrs.

"Don't double their prices if you want to sell them faster," the seller said, smiling.

"I know you want me to get rid of these sooner so I can come and buy more."

"In the future you should go all the way to Djibouti. You could save half of what the contraband man charged you, and give me lower prices."

"No, I won't do that. I don't want to risk my life. . . . I will see you next time."

THEN THERE WERE the big merchants. These were shippers of many of the locally produced goods: animal skins, honey, grains, and *kat*—narcotic leaf. They had their own trucks or rented trucks to transport their wares, mostly to and from Asmara and Addis Ababa. Smaller merchants who wished to ship their goods along with those of the bigger merchants would wrangle to pay less to take more of their goods.

The trucks returned with clothing, yarn, pots and pans, salt, sugar, tea, and many other goods—and the merchants haggled over prices again.

The merchants talked about the towns where they stayed overnight and where their trucks had broken down. These discussions sparked Desta's imagination and he dreamed of someday seeing these places and meeting the people who lived there. This detailed knowledge of geography he was absorbing from the merchants both stimulated his sense of adventure and brought to life his classroom lessons. More than ever he wanted to travel, find the coin bearer, no matter how long the journey or demanding the effort.

THIRTY-FIVE

By the time the fence project was finished at the end of July, Desta was nearly finished, too. He had bruises on his shoulders, arms, and legs, and thorns and wood splinters in his feet. Although Dinku and Aberra had been hired to do the job, they made Desta, who was not paid by them or Zewday, shoulder much of the miscellaneous and menial work.

Although Desta was sufficiently fed during the project, he was just as skinny as before. Not only had Zewday told Mebet to make sure the boy got adequate food, Desta had been getting an extra meal each day at Khadija's little restaurant in town. He made sure he got his one restaurant meal a day by going there at noontime or after work in the evening. Yet he scarcely gained weight. All that he ate seemed to sustain his daily physical exertions and nothing more.

He slept very well at night, especially after he got used to the work, and the initial soreness in his legs and feet and hands went away. The patter of rain on the roof, his fatigued muscles and bones, and the mental concentration he put himself through during the day, all enabled him to easily fall asleep the moment he lay down. When he awoke in the morning, he was well-rested and ready to put in another full day's work.

Desta now had a lot more time on his hands and was ready to pursue his dream of going to town and meeting a lot of the Muslim merchants to ask them a favor.

He realized that it would not be easy to randomly ask his favor of the merchants who went to faraway places, like Bahir Dar and Addis Ababa. He needed to get to know one or two of them.

For some time Desta had been curious about the Muslim *mesgid*—mosque. He wanted to make friends with someone who would take him to see that place of worship. *Khadija could play a key role in this*, Desta thought. She was a Muslim, and she knew a lot of the Muslim merchants.

He told Khadija about the relative he was looking for and she was happy to help. "I can empathize. I lost a cousin years ago and nobody knew what had happened to her. I'll introduce you to friends of mine. They are successful merchants who travel to different cities. Make yourself presentable, wash your clothes, and I'll take you to their store one day."

One Saturday afternoon, after he ate lunch, Khadija prepared to take Desta to the store of Masud and his father, Sheik Ibrahim. She gave him a brief introduction about the owners and their shop. It was the largest clothing establishment in town. Sheik Ibrahim was a well-known and well-traveled man, having gone as far as Mecca to receive his title of "sheik." The story about Mecca and the importance of Ibrahim's title had no meaning and was of little concern to Desta.

When Desta and Khadija arrived at the store window, Masud was opening some boxes of clothing on the floor, a few feet from the counter. He looked about thirty or thirty-five. He had a handsome face, marked by a well-proportioned straight nose, a neatly cropped mustache and soft and kind eyes. His skin, like most of the population, was not exactly *tikoor*—black, neither was it *teyim*— dark olive nor *keyee*—fair, but the deep brown hue of the earth. When he rose he commanded a height of six feet. "Good afternoon," he said, showing an even set of white teeth.

A boy named Hassan, so Khadija had told Desta, was helping customers at the far corner of the counter. "*Gibu*—c'mon in," Masud said, walking over to open the door.

Khadija put her hands on Desta's shoulders and said, "I need to go back to the restaurant, but you and Masud can visit."

"You're always in a hurry," Masud said, smiling genially.

"That is how it is when you're running a business—you know it." Khadija bent her head down. "Go in," she said, lightly pushing Desta forward. "I will see you both later."

"Come," Masud said, leading Desta to his desk. He pulled a chair out for the boy and then walked around the desk and sat across from Desta.

Several feet away, an older man with a colorful turban sat on a red plush rug with a design of birds and fruit trees. Surrounding him was a pile of freshly cut leaves, a kettle, and a cup filled with brown liquid. The man snipped the leaves near their stalks, put them in his mouth, and chewed them. He seemed to be in another world, almost in a trance.

"That's my father, Sheik Ibrahim," Masud said. "He is on his kat and tea break."

Although Desta knew what tea was, he had never heard of kat. Nor had he seen people eat leaves like animals. Pensive and circumspect, he pursed his lips and nodded.

"You and I share names with a similar meaning, and our fathers have similar surnames," Masud said, trying to make Desta feel at ease.

"Is that so?" Desta said, pleased by the associations.

"In Arabic my name means 'happiness,' just like yours does in Amharic. *Ibrahim* is 'Abraham' in Arabic."

Desta smiled.

While the two were talking, he kept sneaking looks at the old man, who never seemed to stop snipping the leaves and putting them in his mouth. He chewed on the green things continuously but never seemed to swallow or spit them out. He appeared to bury them in one cheek like a squirrel.

"Have you ever eaten leaves like what my father is chewing?" Masud asked, intrigued by Desta's fascination.

"I never have. Where I come from only goats eat leaves, not people."

Masud burst into a laugh. "Where do you come from?"

Desta told him.

Masud shifted to his father. "Baba, Baba."

The father lifted his face and glanced at Masud. "What is it, son?"

"This boy likened you to a goat." Masud laughed again.

Desta's forehead felt hot and his mouth went dry. *There goes my chance of getting to know these people.*

Sheik Ibrahim rose slowly and trudged over with a few strands of the leaves.

"So you think I am a goat, huh, young man?" His mouth showed a filmy green residue; it was pale and dry on the periphery and wet and frothy on the inside of his lips. Sheik Ibrahim now reminded Desta not of a goat but a cow chewing its cud.

"I didn't say that, Aba." Perspiration dewed Desta's brow. He wiped it with the back of his hand.

Sheik Ibrahim chuckled. "Do you want to try what the goat is eating?" He snipped a leaf and gave it to the boy.

Out of respect for the old man and as an apology for his offense, Desta placed the leaf in his mouth and tried to chew it. It tasted so bitter that he immediately spat it out into his hand.

"Do you want to try it with sugar?"

"Stop it, Baba. Don't you see he is uncomfortable?"

Sheik Ibrahim chuckled again as if pleased with his reprisal. He pulled a chair beside Masud and sat down. He said, "Weizero Khadija tells us that you live with a family that cares little for you. She says that although she doesn't know the details, you supposedly have a very close and caring relative you're looking for. Is that right?"

Desta flinched, surprised by how much the information he had shared with Almaz and Khadija had gotten distorted. "That's right," said the boy, realizing this was to his advantage.

"So what can we do for you?"

"Khadija said that Gashé Masud goes to Bahir Dar regularly and I was hoping he could take me with him so I can look for my cousin."

"What's her full name and description?" Sheik Ibrahim asked, taking out a black pocket notebook.

Desta groped for a bit. He knew this answer was always tricky.

"That's the other problem," Desta said, looking at Masud and then at Sheik Ibrahim. "You see, I don't have an exact description of her or what she is called. I only know what her name means. . . ." Desta stopped and looked again at one man and then the other, afraid he'd elicit more guffaws.

"And that is?" Sheik Ibrahim asked.

"Sweet and sour."

"What?" blurted Masud, leaning a little forward as if he had missed something.

Desta repeated.

Father and son laughed.

"How do you expect to find this woman if you have no actual name? People are not known by the meaning of their names. These meanings are often personal. The same name could mean different things to different parents," Sheik Ibrahim said.

"The other thing is—" Masud began to say, stopping to clear his throat. "There is no name in Amharic or Arabic we know of that has that meaning. Don't you agree, Baba?"

"That's right!"

"There could be a name that means sweet and sour in another language, but we don't know what that language is," added Masud.

"It couldn't be in another language, for an obvious reason," the father corrected. "She is his cousin, and if the name exists, it has to be in our language."

"True. I was just thinking aloud of other possibilities."

Desta said, "I know it's complicated, but it's very important that I find her, no matter how difficult it seems or how long it takes me."

Sheik Ibrahim said, "Look, son, this is what you should do first. You come to our mesgid one day and we'll introduce you to a number of merchants. There are many who travel to different cities and who might have heard of the woman. I realize that this is going to be very difficult, but you can try. Maybe we can make a sign for you, and you can stand outside so that everybody who comes through will see you with it."

"Actually, that is an excellent idea, Baba. If nobody comes forward with knowledge of her, then you and I can go to Bahir Dar," Masud reasoned.

Desta thoughtfully twirled a piece of cord in his fingers. "So when can I come to your church?" He had long wanted to see the man who announced *"Allahu akbar"*—God is great—five times a day. Now he had another reason to go see where the man practiced his religion, and it would be a lot easier than going on his own. Desta's heart fluttered with excitement.

Father and son grinned. "Our place of worship is called mesgid," Masud corrected. "As to when, it has to be on a Friday."

"That's right. We have the most attendance on Fridays," the father concurred. "Need to go back to my tea and leaves." Sheik Ibrahim waddled back to his rug.

USING A FOURTEEN-BY-SEVENTEEN-INCH piece of cardboard—Desta had specified the dimensions—he and Masud made a sign that read:

> I Need Your Help!
> I'm Looking for a Lost Relative!
> Her Name Means "Sweet & Sour."
> Have you heard of such a woman?

ON A FRIDAY AFTERNOON, Masud and Desta crossed the main road at the center of town and went to the west side. They walked on a narrow path between groves of tall eucalyptus trees. While they walked, Masud explained that the man who announced "Allahu akbar" five times a day was the assistant imam, and the announcements were to remind the Muslims in the area to come for prayer. Then he told Desta what Muslims must do before they come to have personal moments with God. First, they removed any trace of filth from their bodies. Then they performed *wudu*—the ritualized cleansing of the body—and showered as needed.

Masud said that wudu involved three washings of the hands, the mouth, the inside of the nose, the face, and the arms up to the elbow, starting with the right hand. It also meant cleaning with a wet cloth the areas behind the ears and the sides of the head and all around the neck, and then cleaning the feet three times using both hands, starting with the right foot.

Desta listened intently, surprised by the rigor of the cleansing process—of all that was required before Muslims could pray. He thought about the Christian women who were not allowed on church grounds when they were unclean— when they had given birth recently or were menstruating or had been intimate with a man the night before.

Masud continued, "When we pray, we always face in the direction of the Kibla, the cube-shaped house of God in Mecca, our holy city in Saudi Arabia. And there are *very* specific patterns to our prayers. . . ." They reached the mesgid gate and went inside. Other people, mostly adult men and a few veiled women, were arriving from all directions. Weeds and a spattering of yellow daisies and other flowers hugged the outside of the fence.

"Let me finish telling you about our prayers before the services start," Masud said, retreating to the side of the entryway. "Our prayers are simple but done in a cycle of ten steps known as a *ra'ka*. There are five obligatory prayers, said at noon, at four in the afternoon, at sunset, at any time between sunset and sunrise, and at dawn. Some prayers require two ra'kas and others as many as four ra'kas.

"Every prayer begins and ends by reciting 'Allahu akbar.' The recitals are in Arabic, no matter what language people speak, and all Muslims everywhere go through the same cleansing process, follow the same steps, and recite the same phrases and lines of text from the Qur'an, which is equivalent to your Christian Bible. That all Muslims use the exact same practices is one of the most power-ful, unifying forces of our religion."

In the center of the spacious compound stood a building with a pitched, corrugated tin roof. It was a much less elaborate building than Desta had imag-ined. On the right side of the building, as seen from the gate, rose an open stair-case with a platform at the top.

Masud pointed to the platform. "That's where the imam or the assistant imam calls the prayers throughout the day." Desta craned his neck. Now he knew where the mysterious announcer stood and shouted, "Allahu akbar!"

More men and partially veiled women filed in through the gate. The women walked around the building. The men went through the open door at the front. Masud and Desta entered into an anteroom where people took their shoes off and lined them on racks on either side of the entrance.

Then they walked into a large room with several roof-bearing wooden posts. Over the compacted smooth dirt floor were laid several palm leaf mats, roughly twelve feet by four feet, placed in a row and oriented to the east. At the front of the room was a small platform with curving banister.

Desta looked around, trying to find any pictures similar to those at his parents' church: the woman with a baby, the winged man, or the horse-riding figure. There were none. As stark as everything was, though, there still was an enveloping serenity in the room.

Robed men with tightly fitting bleached hats and multicolored turbans—and some with no headdresses—milled around the room or talked in clusters. By and by, the room became packed with people. An older turbaned man signaled and everybody lined behind the mats in long rows, facing east. The man turned and faced the wall, his back to the others.

"That is Imam Muhammad. He will be leading the prayers," whispered Masud to Desta. "You can wait here with me or stay outside by the entrance and hold your sign up. The prayer will be over in ten minutes. I will join you then."

Desta lingered by the entrance and watched as people stood straight up, bowed and prostrated themselves, sat on their heels, went down on the ground, and then rose again. He was amazed at their precise and nearly identical postures and actions. When people bowed, all of them rested their hands on their knees; when they went down on the ground, their foreheads, their knees, the pads of their toes, and their palms pressed on the ground in unison. And when they sat, their bottoms rested on their left heels while their right feet were supported on the pads of their toes.

When the prayers ended, Desta went outside and stood by the gate with his sign. The women came out first, from around the back of the building. Just about all of them pushed back their veils and glanced at him as they walked by, but nobody said anything. Then the men came out, four or five at a time. Some of the older men stopped and stared at Desta's sign. They struggled to read it but couldn't make sense of it. Desta told them what it said and why he was standing there. Some chuckled, obviously amused by the contradiction in meaning. Others simply eyed him at a distance and walked past.

Soon Masud returned with a group of men, among them Imam Mohammad.

"This young friend of mine—his name is Desta—is looking for a long lost cousin whom he must find. I invited him here to see if you business folks who travel to distant lands may be of help to him. He has no name or exact description of the person. As you can see on this sign, her name means 'sweet and sour.'"

"Do you know when and where she was last seen?" the imam asked.

"I don't know for sure, but I know she lives in this world, somewhere. I know this because my grandpa, who knows everything, told me so." Desta blamed himself for forgetting to ask that very question when he last saw his grandfather's spirit. "Unfortunately, my grandpa is dead and gone and can tell me no more."

"It will be difficult to find her without any more clues—without the names of other relatives or a location," the imam explained. He turned to Masud. "The best we can do is to remember to ask people we run into if they have heard of a woman designated as 'sweet and sour.' If each of us talk to the people we know and each of them, in turn, talks to the people they know, we could end up reaching the whole world." He smiled at Desta.

"That's exactly what I am hoping," Desta said, smiling back, excited by the possibility. The imam had made it sound so simple.

A tall bearded man said, "You have a good friend in Masud. He told us all about your problem. We'll do the best we can to help you."

Desta and Masud went back to the store where they found Sheik Ibrahim looking upset and dejected. "Zewday was here with a policeman," announced the old man. "He wanted to know what we are trying to do with Desta and demanded to know where you two went."

"A policeman? And what did you tell him?"

"I said we are not doing anything with Desta other than befriending him. And that I didn't know where you went. He apparently had gone to talk with Khadija, too."

"Isn't it a bit too much to bring a policeman here just to find that out?"

"That is what I thought, too. He is making us look like criminals."

"He is probably thinking we are trying to convert him to Islam," Masud said.

"That, plus I think he suspects some sort of shady activity involving Khadija."

"What sort of shady activity?"

The sheik looked at Desta. "I don't know."

Desta's stomach knotted. He felt woozy.

"Do you know anything about this?" Masud asked the boy.

"No . . . I . . . I don't," Desta said, feeling the tension rising within him.

"That's strange. We'll find out soon what Ato Zewday is up to," Masud said, his face pensive and far away.

"I guess, but I hope it's not anything serious," Sheik Ibrahim said. He looked away thoughtfully. "You know, at first I thought somebody must have told Zewday that Desta had gone to our mesgid with you. It is not a good idea to take a Christian boy without the permission of his parents or guardians. And then he mentioned theft, which explained the presence of the policeman, and I became less concerned about my earlier thought."

"Desta," Masud said, "Baba has a point. Don't ever voluntarily mention you went to the mesgid with me. Of course, if he asks you, tell him the truth."

"So long as you have not done anything wrong, everything will be all right, Desta. Allah will protect you," Sheik Ibrahim said.

"Baba is right, Desta. See you soon. Come tell us when you find out what happened."

Desta didn't want to go home. He went to Khadija's restaurant, but she was not there, and the merchant's room was nearly empty. Desta was scared. The waitress gave him his meal but he barely touched it. He rose and left after apologizing to her for not eating. He had to find out what was really going on with Zewday.

The walk home was not easy. The road got longer and longer with every step he took. When he finally arrived, Lesim asked, "Where have you been?" She looked distant and cold.

"Oh, just in town."

"Is that all?"

"What do you mean?"

"I don't know. Baba was looking for you earlier."

"What for?"

"I am sure he will let you know when he comes. Just to warn you, it's not very good news."

"Tell me," Desta said anxiously. A cold sweat ran down his back.

"Like I said, you will find that out from Baba."

"Do you derive joy from tormenting me?"

"Huh?"

"I mean, you tell me there is bad news concerning me, yet you are unwilling to tell me what it is."

"It's something he has been accusing me of, and sometimes you—stealing money from his pocket when he comes home drunk."

Desta closed his eyes and sighed, relieved it was not what he thought—the stolen coffee beans. Confident that he would be exonerated of the suspicion, he didn't think much about the possible accusation.

"I have never stolen money from his pocket, so he cannot blame me for such a crime."

"I hope that is the case," Lesim said and went inside the main house.

That is right! I've never taken money from Zewday and I have nothing to worry about.

That evening, because it was Friday and Zewday was probably not going to come home early, Mebet decided they would eat their dinner and go to bed.

Desta went to bed but not to sleep. The things he observed and heard at the mesgid had brought back the confusion and arguments he used to have with his mother about heaven and hell and her many Gods.

To Ayénat, besides the One that was in control of everything, there were the saints, the angels, and Jesus and Mary, all of whom she worshiped like they were God. "If God is the ultimate decision maker on the lives of humans, what's the point of worshipping all these others? Doesn't God get jealous or upset for being left out?" Desta remembered asking.

"No, He doesn't," she had said, "because they are all messengers of God. Why so many? Because some are better listeners than others for purposes you wish fulfilled."

His questions about Jesus and Mary used to get Ayénat mad. He was always stumped in understanding Jesus's overall role in the lives of the people in his valley, and in many respects it seemed that Jesus was more powerful than God or Mary.

Every year Jesus's birthday was celebrated—people killed big animals, like cows or bulls—while God's and Mary's birthdays were never even mentioned. People always talked about Jesus, prayed to Him, and swore by His name, but not often to God or Mary.

He once screwed up his courage and asked his mother who Jesus was. She said He was the son of a holy woman named Mary but had no real father. Desta asked what kind of person was it who didn't have a father. She said He was conceived by the will of God.

"Conceived by the will of God?" Another mystery!

Every time Desta wanted to ask more questions about Jesus, Ayénat put an end to it by saying, "You are not supposed to ask too many questions about the Son of God. We accept everything as given to us by the priests."

"The Son of God? I thought you said he didn't have a father."

"Blasphemy! Didn't I tell you that we don't ask those kinds of questions?"

Desta walked away angry and even more confused.

Now he had gone to the Muslims' mesgid and found out they worshipped none of the people his mother did—no Jesus, no Mary, no saints and angels. Only God!

A loud and angry knock on the door caused Desta to sit up.

Lesim got up and dashed to the door.

"You came home early tonight, Baba, what happened?" Lesim asked jocularly. She was trying to humor her father, but Zewday was in no mood for humor.

"Nothing," he said gruffly.

"Is everything okay?"

He went past her without a reply and leaned his cane against the wall. He unbuckled and pulled out his belt, folded it, and put it by his side where he sat on the high earthen seat.

That's strange, Desta thought, noting Zewday's unusual behavior.

Mebet and Tesfa were fast asleep.

"Desta, come here. Let me talk to you," the drunkard cried.

Shaken, Desta walked over. *Is this what Lesim warned me about?*

Zewday grabbed his slender right arm with such force that Desta thought it might break. He glared down with his bloodshot eyes. "Tell me. How long have you been stealing money from my pocket?"

The smell of tej on Zewday's breath wafted into the boy's face.

"Ne . . . ne . . . never stole money from your pocket."

"Who gave you the money you have been spending at Khadija's restaurant?" Zewday squeezed Desta's arm even tighter, bringing his face right down to the boy's.

"No . . . nobody," Desta said, trying to hold his breath to avoid inhaling Zewday's fumes.

"You mean to tell me then that it dropped out of the sky into your hands?" Zewday picked up the belt with his free hand and waved it before Desta's face.

"Now are you going to tell me?"

"I didn't steal your money," he replied sheepishly, his eyes darting about like an animal caught in a snare.

Zewday drew back his belt and whipped Desta across the spine. He struggled to get free but it was useless. The drunkard whipped him once more, demanding an answer. Realizing Zewday was not about to accept his denial, Desta said nothing. With his right hand locked in Zewday's iron grip, Desta had no way to lay his hand on his chest to stop the beating and the barrage of questions. Still, he pulled and pulled to get free.

"Let me see if you can answer another question. Why did you go to the mesgid today? Are you planning to become a Muslim? Did your father entrust us with you so that his Christian son could turn into a Muslim and a thief—that is, if you were not already a thief before you came to live with us?"

Desta bit his lip firmly to ensure no word accidentally came out of him.

Zewday shoved him facedown onto the floor. He tried to turn over and reach for the coin on his chest, but his right arm was numb and immobile from the man's grip and he could get no leverage.

The drunkard continued to whip him as if he had found his archenemy and was not going to spare a single square inch of his skin. Desta didn't emit a whimper or shed a tear. He had been through this before—having remembered the beatings by his father and his brother—and he didn't want to give Zewday the satisfaction of seeing him weaken. He curled into a ball, hugging his head with his left hand and covering his face with his arm.

Mebet was yelling, "Stop, stop!" When he wouldn't, she rushed over and wrapped her arms around him. Zewday tried to get free, and they tottered and crashed to the ground.

Lesim dashed over and snatched the belt out of her father's hand.

For a brief moment everything was calm. Mebet rose and helped her husband to get up and stumble onto the high earthen seat. Desta remained curled, listening to the pain of his body and watching through the crook of his arm.

"Here I have been blaming my daughter for stealing money from me, while the real culprit was this visitor friend of ours. What's more, he has been spending my money in a Muslim restaurant, eating meat from a cow they killed. For a Christian boy, this is taboo. He should have known by now." Zewday stared disdainfully at Desta. In a calmer tone that was somewhat apologetic, he continued to justify the beating.

"How did you find out all this?" Mebet asked.

"From Abdullah, the merchant who bought the coffee beans."

"Although it doesn't call for such severe beatings, I agree with you about his going to a Muslim restaurant and eating unblessed meat. I am sure his parents would be very upset about this. Regarding the money you accuse him of spending for his meals, it's possible his father gave him some when he came last May. I think it is *verry* possible you're blaming the wrong person." Mebet looked away.

Zewday turned and stared at his wife intently. "What do you mean by 'verry'?"

"I mean that you stay out drinking and you could never know who might have stolen it, if you really believe you have lost any. If you had lost any around here," she said, dropping her gaze, "it was probably me, not your daughter or this little boy you savagely beat up." Mebet lifted her eyes and stared at her husband without a blink. "Now that you know who the real thief is, perhaps you can learn to give me enough money to buy our food supplies—so I won't have to steal it from you again."

Zewday's faced turned into a metallic mask. "You kept mum all this time while I complained so often about my missing money?"

"Yes, I did, because if I told you, you would hide it somewhere, denying me the ability to buy even the most basic of things."

Desta was now angrier with Mebet than Zewday. Not only was she the cause of his beatings, but she had said nothing when Zewday began whipping him.

"I know you didn't get the response you were seeking from Desta. I will give it to you. It was me who took one or two birr or whatever I could find from your pocket. Either you give me sufficient money or I will continue to steal. If you dare threaten me with physical punishment, I will gather my son and belongings and go live with my family."

Zewday writhed in rage. His midnight blue face turned to the hue of the beetle's wing. His brow glistened and steamed with sweat. "How could you wait this long, saying nothing when I spanked and dressed down my own daughter—and tonight when I exacted punishment on a boy who didn't deserve to be whipped?" He started to weep.

"You're not in a good state of mind to talk about this tonight. Tomorrow when you are sober we can. I am going to bed. If you want dinner, Lesim will serve you." Mebet rose and went into the bedroom.

Zewday wiped his tears with the back of his hand. He stared into space and shook his head.

Lesim walked over to her father. "I am sorry about everything that happened tonight. I know you are mad at yourself for your actions. I think it's better that you eat something and go to bed. You can think through things tomorrow with a cleared mind. . . . Can I bring you water for your hands?"

"No, I am not hungry. I am going to bed," he said. "But you can untie and help me remove my shoes."

Lesim fulfilled her father's request. He rose and scrambled to the bedroom. Lesim walked over to Desta who was still curled on the floor. "I am sad about what happened to you, Desta. I knew Baba was up to something the way he was talking and behaving earlier. I never thought he would be this violent. . . . Get up, help me bring the mattress and we can make our bed. . . . Oh, my God, you're bleeding. So much of it on the floor."

Desta lifted his head and looked down. "Ehe ehe ehe," he whimpered, horrified by the blood. He tried to move his arm and get up but the pain was too excruciating. He shook his head in sadness for finding the physical violence here that he thought he had left behind in his country home.

He wished he could cry to feel better after such an assault. But no tear came to him. He uncurled himself and tried to get up, but his lower limbs were too painful. He looked on the floor where his head had rested and cringed at the drops of blood where he had fallen. He inserted his index finger into his mouth and groped to see if any teeth were missing. He found a chipped molar. His finger came out soaked in blood and he flinched again. For reasons he couldn't explain he had no soreness or any other sensation in his mouth. Just blood and the puffiness to his cheek.

He rose slowly. Using the hand water he had left for Zewday and Mebet, he rinsed his mouth several times and spat into the bowl. Involuntarily, his tongue kept finding the jagged chipped tooth.

Lesim made their bed by herself while Desta cleaned up the blood on the floor with a towel. He found the tooth fragment and placed it in his pocket. He didn't tell Lesim. He didn't want more drama. As he drew the blanket over his face, he realized that going to Bahir Dar with Masud would remain just another dream. He choked with passion but no tears flowed. Sleep came instead, saving him from his misery.

THIRTY-SIX

Despite everything that had happened, the upcoming New Year's celebration brightened Desta's spirit, particularly when he learned there were opportunities for him to make money.

The beating by Zewday had left him physically and emotionally debilitated. Fortunately, neither were there scars nor was his chipped lower molar visible to others. Still, that he had been violated and punished for something he had not done was upsetting to him.

At the same time he was relieved that the accusation had nothing to do with the hoarded coffee beans he had been selling to Almaz. Zewday never pursued the matter of where Desta got the money he was spending at Khadija's restaurant. Mebet's simple explanation seemed to have satisfied him. No matter, though, he had to be more careful about everything involved with his eating arrangement.

Two days after his beating, Desta went to share the incident with Masud.

"What happened to you?" he asked. Masud was visibly upset.

"The swelling and the scratches will heal. Let me show you something that perhaps I will never recover from." Desta parted his lips and showed Masud the chipped tooth.

Syncopating waves first of shock then disbelief traveled across Masud's handsome face. "How did all this happen?"

Desta told him as much as he could remember, although some of it he wished he didn't have to repeat.

"It's horrifying to see . . . . that this family man is capable of assaulting a fragile boy like yourself. What's equally a surprise is that there are people like him in the Christian community who still see Muslims as outcasts, not to be associated with at social settings."

Desta didn't exactly know what Masud meant by "outcasts," but he got the general idea just from the tone of his voice.

Masud stared into space for a few seconds. "You know, in actuality, when I was a child, my mother used to do that to me. She didn't want me to play with Christian boys. She never beat me, though, but she scolded me, sometimes severely. The last vivid incident in my mind is when I brought home a piece of meat given to me by my Christian friend. Once she found out its source, she snatched it out of my hand and gave it to the dog. My father was the complete opposite. He encouraged me to be friends with everybody."

Desta said, "Where I come from there were no Muslims and we had no such problems. I don't know why it should be a problem. The day I arrived in this town I was so curious to find out about the man who announces the prayer times. I was so happy when you invited me to come. I never thought there would be any consequences to my coming to your mesgid."

"Don't let Zewday influence you in any way. You'll grow to be a better person. That way you will also have more friends."

"Masud, I do need more friends! I have never met anyone I can call a friend in this town. You have come the closest and I'm thankful for it."

"Oh, my pleasure. For whatever reason we met. Maybe we both are meant to learn something from this experience."

"I don't know, but I am not blaming you, nor do I regret coming to your mesgid. I have a greater understanding of who God is now. Perhaps this experience is going to help me understand and appreciate my religion better. My visit to your mesgid left me with the same feeling I had when I first climbed the mountain behind my parent's home and discovered a much bigger world."

"That's what I mean," Masud said. "Never limit yourself. Never listen to anything but your heart. Never be shackled by the beliefs or prejudices of others. You have a beautiful spirit. Don't let it be tarnished because of what others do to you.

"Let me give you an example. I have a young cousin, Saleem Nuru, in Begemider province. A similar thing happened to him as to me, when his mother found him eating meat given to him by a Christian family. She snatched the meat out of his hand and threw it away. He was only two years old then, but this incident started him on life-changing course. By the time he was four, he began asking questions that wouldn't be expected even from many adults—about religious hypocrisy, the inequality of the sexes, violence against children, the often unfair and dishonest dealings between people. He asked many question about these things and others, and when people couldn't answer them, they began labeling him a mentally sick boy. Just recently, I heard that his family threw him out of the house. I have a feeling this boy is destined to change not only his own life but also the lives of many others."

Masud continued, leveling his gaze, "So what I can tell you is this: don't stop being as independent a thinker as Saleem Nuru. Luckily, you grew up in a place where you were free of the harmful labels parents infect their children with here in the towns. That you were never exposed to this is a blessing in itself. Don't let other people's way of thinking influence the way you relate to people in your life."

"That's amazing about your cousin. I had a very similar experience and I can relate to what he must have gone through. It was not fun to be ridiculed and shunned by adults."

Sheik Ibrahim walked in from the back room, the end of his turban dangling from the side of his head. He had a bundle of kat leaves. At the edge of Sheik Ibrahim's sitting rug was a steaming blue kettle of tea as well as a white cup and saucer.

Sheik Ibrahim greeted his son and Desta and went to his place of comfort. He dropped the leaves next to his pillow, took his sandals off, and sat down on the rug. He folded and crossed his legs. He picked up the kettle by its bowed handle and poured the tea into the cup. Steam rose both from the cup and the spigot of the kettle. The brown liquid was transporting. The tea's mingled aromas of cloves, cinnamon, and cardamom filled the room.

Sheik Ibrahim took a couple of sips and placed the cup back on the saucer. He untied the string from the kat bundle and picked out two twigs with lush leaves. He begun to snip the leaves and stuff his mouth with them.

Desta rose and prepared to leave. Masud followed him to the door. "Come see me again."

Desta turned around and said, "Soon I hope."

As he was heading home, Desta saw the marble-playing boys again. They hovered around their marbles like bees on a flowering bush. One boy was perched on a rock, busily scribbling something in his notebook. Desta walked over to him. With the boy's permission, he stood and watched. The boy was drawing beautiful flowers on vines and the branches of bushes. The boy said the drawing was to be presented to people he knew on New Year's Day and who, in return, would give him money. Desta saw an opportunity for himself. He left after thanking the boy for letting him watch what he was doing.

That evening he practiced drawing flowers in his notebook with a pencil. To his surprise, drawing came naturally to him. The only other time he had seen anybody draw something artistic was years ago when his grandfather's spirit had re-created the coin image on the goatskin parchment.

One afternoon a few days later, as Desta was leaving Zewday's compound, Almaz came to the gap in the fence. "Khadija said Masud wants to see you," she whispered.

Instead of going to watch the boys playing marbles and, hopefully, ask the one with the notebook where he got all those colored pencils, Desta went directly to Masud's shop.

"Masud is not here," Hassan, the shop assistant, told him. "Come inside and wait. He should be back pretty soon."

"Good, you got my message," Masud said the moment he saw Desta. He was cradling a big box in his arms. He took it to the counter and returned to his desk after telling Hassan to open it and place its contents on the shelves.

"Here is what we can do," Masud said. "Three of us, Almaz, Khadija, and I, have decided that you should continue to eat at Khadija's but instead of coming through the front door, go through our store and enter her restaurant through the back door. That way nobody will see your comings and goings. Also, instead of coming at noon as you used to, come at mid-afternoon. I know it will be later than your usual mealtime, but we'll have to compromise the inconvenience for your safety. That way you will avoid running into Abdullah again."

"Thank you so much for your efforts," Desta said. "I will follow your instructions. I probably could survive on the meager food I receive at home if I could not come to Khadija's, but I am not going to stop out of fear of Zewday. I'll never give him that pleasure or give up my freedom to do what I please."

"Good to hear it! That is how all of us felt, too!"

"Something else I want to share with you," Desta said in an urgent voice.

"Tell me."

"I heard that New Year's Day could bring a bonanza of money for children like me who make drawings of *enkutatashi*—a new year's salute—flowers and present them to neighbors and friends. I understand that they give you money for them in return."

"Oh, yeah? Who told you? I have a bunch of colored pencils I can give you and blank sheets, too."

"Do you?" Desta smiled broadly. "One of the marble-playing boys told me. I have been practicing after seeing how he was doing them. I'm already getting good at it."

"Very well, I will tell all my friends to expect you." He went to the front of the store and returned with a dozen colored pencils and a sharpener. "Take these and start drawing your flowers. Hassan will give you a box of blank sheets at the counter. Keep being strong! Don't let Zewday break your spirit. You deserve better."

Masud's words and kindness were like honey to Desta, sweet and soothing to his senses.

Loaded with his box of paper and pencils, he arrived home. Neither Mebet nor Lesim were in the main house. Pleased that he didn't have to explain his art supplies to anyone, he deposited his windfall in the corner of the room.

For the following five days he drew his flowers. Starting with the circular top of a bell-shaped basket similar to a mosseb, Desta traced lines that spread out above the basket like the stems of blossoming flowers. He drew in luxuriant leaves around and between the stems, and he capped the ends with blood-red roses, yellow daisies, and sky-blue forget-me-nots. The more he drew, the better he got, and in the end he had illustrated a total of one hundred pages with his artistic creations.

The next challenge was how he could distribute that many Enkutatashi drawings on New Year's Day. He could probably distribute twenty or twenty-five easily because, thanks to Masud, he knew at least that many people. Then he realized that he didn't have to wait till New Year's Day but could start two or three days in advance.

So beginning at one end of the huge rectangular business complex, he started passing out the drawings, calling, "Enkutatashi!" He passed out his artwork to kiosks, big shops like Masud's, tailors' stands, teahouses, small and big eating places, tej and tella establishments—practically to anyone whose place was open and willing to accept his beautifully drawn flowers.

Some teased him, saying the new year was not in yet. Others smiled and said, "*Ba ye ametu yamtashi*—may you come every year—every time he said, "Enku-tatashi," and handed them the drawings. Most people gave him ten or twenty-five cents. The owners of the bigger shops, especially those he met at Khadija's restaurant, gave him from one to five birrs.

Masud had an idea. "Bring me fifty or so drawings and I will pass them out here and collect the money for you."

By noon on New Year's Day, Desta had given out all his drawings. When he went home and counted his money, he found he had made seventy-five birrs and fifty cents. He wrapped his coins and bills in a piece of cloth, the way Abraham did with his money, and put it away. The next day he collected his bundle and went to see Masud. Desta could hardly contain himself as he walked up to the shop. His friend was with a couple of customers. He winked at him the moment he saw Desta. After the people left, Masud walked down to the section of the counter where Desta was standing. "How did you do?" he asked, smiling broadly.

"Not too bad," Desta replied, matching Masud with his own grin.

"Tell me."

"Here, count them," Desta said, dropping the bundle on the counter. The clatter of the coins was muffled by the cloth.

Masud untied the strings, opened the cloth, and spread it on the counter. Glints of light shone from the silver coins, only barely so from the copper pieces. "It looks like you made a fortune."

"Thanks to you, I feel like that, too."

Masud separated the coins and bills by denomination. Desta took note of how much easier this made it to count the money. "Wow, you made seventy-five birr and fifty cents! Now let me show you what I have for you." Masud lifted the lid to a wooden box on the counter and brought out a small bag. He opened it and poured the money on the counter, which he counted after again separating the coins and bills by denomination. There was a total of fifty birr and fifty cents for Desta, including ten birr from Sheik Ibrahim and Masud.

"That means you have a total of—get this—one hundred and twenty-six birr. Very good!" Masud smiled with genuine surprise. "Forget this school business. Come work with me and Baba if you're this good. Seriously, for someone who has never done anything like this before and all through his own effort, this is very impressive."

Desta had never had that much money in his life. One hundred twenty-six birr! He felt like the richest person in the whole world. "Thanks," he said. "You had a lot to do with it."

"What do you want to do with all this money?" Masud asked, putting the bills and coins all together in Desta's cloth.

"I have not thought about that. The first thing I want to do is to travel to Bahir Dar to look for my cousin. I can save some of it for food. I'll definitely need money for my books when school opens. And it would be nice to have a change of jacket and shorts. I have been wearing the same ones every day for two years, but I don't think I will have money left for that. So I will probably have to put off buying new clothes for now."

"How about shoes?"

Desta laughed, remembering Saba's remark about people who wear shoes. "Shoes for me right now? No. I cannot afford to ruin my feet yet."

"Ruin them? Who told you shoes ruin your feet?"

"My sister. But seriously, I have no means of purchasing another pair once the first pair becomes old and unusable. I would rather wait until I have that luxury."

"This is what we can do," Masud said, holding Desta's eyes. "I can give you the fabric—in your choice of color—enough for your shorts and jacket, and you can pay for the tailoring and buy your shoes."

"I appreciate it very much. I will take you up on the fabric, but regarding the purchase of shoes, I would rather wait."

"You're one determined boy, Desta! That's admirable. Okay, we'll do it your way."

A husband and wife with two giggling girls came to the window. They had come to look at material for dresses for the girls.

Masud tapped the counter. "We can talk about this some more later," he said, and turned to the couple. Desta grabbed his money and left, giddy with excitement.

A FEW DAYS LATER Desta returned to Masud's store with his money. School would reopen in a week and he needed to buy his supplies and, hopefully, have his new shorts and jacket made. After touching, eyeing, and pulling on different textiles, Masud and Desta chose a dark brown fabric.

"Now we need to go to a tailor for your measurements," Masud said, lifting the countertop to go out. They crossed the huge market grounds and entered the store of an old man, in the middle of which stood a Singer sewing machine. On the walls hung clothes the man had custom-made. He rose from his seat and greeted each of them with a handshake. At Masud's request the tailor measured Desta quickly. Now they knew the amount of material they would need to make the boy's jacket and shorts.

Back at the store, Masud said, "We'll cut the material and deliver it to him. Do you need anything else?" He seemed in a hurry.

"Nothing other than my school supplies," Desta replied, taking money out of his pouch. He bought two notebooks, two pencils, a fountain pen and a pencil sharpener for eight birr. He had one hundred eighteen birr left. Desta hoped it would be enough to pay for the tailoring of his clothes, for a trip to Bahir Dar and back and for extra meals through the first semester of school.

THIRTY-SEVEN

On Saturday, a few days before school opened, Aunt Zere's son, Almaw, showed up at Zewday's house. Desta, who was sitting on the bench outside with his notebook, was the only one at home. Mebet and Lesim had gone to the market. Desta didn't know where Zewday had gone.

After the ritual kisses, Desta invited Almaw to sit on the bench next to him. The cousin had a message from Abraham. He said that Abraham had cut and damaged his leg while splitting wood and was in bed recuperating. He hoped to come after Christmas; better yet, he hoped that Desta would come home so the rest of the family could see him.

Desta didn't know how to react to this news. Lately, he had forgotten he had a family. He couldn't remember a moment during the rainy season when he had thought about them. So he kept quiet.

Several minutes later Zewday arrived. Almaw rose and greeted him with a bow and a handshake. "Is nobody else home? Why are you sitting out here?" the midnight blue man asked.

Desta told Zewday where Mebet and Lesim had gone.

"Come inside and wait till they return. Then we'll have coffee and something to eat."

"I actually need to get back to the market," Almaw said. "I have people waiting for me. I came to pass on a message to Desta from his father. He was planning to come see him and your family in September, but he couldn't because of his health."

"What's the matter with him?"

"He cut his leg with an ax while splitting wood. As a result he is not mobile at the moment, but he's getting better," Almaw said with good cheer.

"Oh, sorry to hear it. . . . Give him my regards."

"Will do," Almaw said, preparing to leave.

"Let's go to one of the local tella houses," Zewday said. "I will buy you a drink or two, and I have something important to share with you."

"I was hoping to take Desta with me to the market so he can see a couple more of his cousins."

"That is fine. He can come along. He can stay out with his friends nearby while we have a conversation."

The three went to the main street and headed south toward the market. Zewday and Almaw went into a tella house. Desta waited outside, leaning against the wall and watching the pedestrians.

Not long after the two men went into the tella house, they came back out. They shook hands and Zewday departed.

Almaw was cold and distant.

"Is everything okay?" Desta asked, puzzled.

"I am not happy about what I heard, and I don't think your parents are going to be happy either," Almaw said, sucking the air between his lips.

"What's the matter?"

"I think it is not a good idea for a Christian boy like yourself to eat at a Muslim restaurant, go to the mesgid, and spend much of your time in the company of Muslims. And your parents are not going to like the idea either. We feared that you, as a country boy, would be corrupted by the town's way of life. We never expected you to go to such an extreme and become a Muslim. What do you know about religion that you dare to make such a monumental decision?"

"I've no idea what you're talking about. I am not becoming a Muslim just because I became friends with them. Please don't ever say that to my parents or anyone else because it's not true."

"Don't worry about your parents or anyone else. Do worry about your future, and your soul, if you indeed have become a Muslim," Almaw said gravely.

"I don't know what else I can say to convince you that I have not become a Muslim."

"I just want to warn you of the potential consequences. The personal relationship you have with God will be affected and also the bonds you have with your own family and the relationships your family has with other families, with friends, and with the community at large in the valley you come from."

"Almaw, I'm going," Desta said, wheeling around to head home. Seconds later he turned around and shouted, "I hope you have conscience enough not to sell out your cousin for the glass of tej Zewday bought you."

LATE THAT AFTERNOON Desta went to the tailor's shop to pick up his new jacket and shorts. They were only his second set of new clothes in a year and a half and he had been looking forward to the joy of wearing them.

"Good afternoon, young man," Berhe, the tailor, said. "You here to pick up your clothes?"

Desta nodded.

"I think you're going to be happy to get rid of those old and torn ones you have been wearing."

Desta didn't appreciate Berhe criticizing his old clothes. They had served him well for the past eighteen months and it was not their fault that they were old and torn.

Berhe took down Desta's new clothes from a hook on the wall by the entrance and gave them to him. "Try them on. Let's see how they look on you."

Desta sat on the bench by the entrance and thought for a few seconds. This was another watershed moment in his life. He had exchanged his cotton gabi for a khaki jacket and shorts when he started modern school eighteen months ago. Now he was going to exchange the clothes that had given him his persona and identity as a modern student for new garments. If he had remained a church school student he wouldn't have had this luxury. He would have worn just his gabi and sheepskins for his entire school life. Desta tipped his head down and thanked providence for his good fortune.

He knew he was going to feel good and look better when he put on his new clothes, but he wanted to express his gratitude to the old and tattered set he was about to part from. He felt now as he did when he buried his dog Kooli's skeletons or when he watched his brothers entomb his grandfather's remains. The emotion was deep and visceral.

The old man returned. "You've not tried them on yet?"

"Give me a few more minutes."

The man's brow crinkled. "I am curious to see how they look on you. Be back in a few minutes."

Desta examined his old clothes as if seeing them for the first time. He noted all their defects: the tears, holes, and stains he had ignored or been ashamed to look at before now. That he would never see again these, his first modern clothes, made him sad.

His eyes traced down the right arm of his jacket. At the folds he could see skin beneath the bare threads. The cuff was frayed. He folded his arm and his elbow jutted through a hole in the fabric. He looked down at his front and saw where the buttons used to be, along with stains and more holes. It was apparent he had worn these clothes every day for the past five hundred-fifty–plus days.

He slid his jacket off and set it on the bench. He picked up his brand-new jacket, brought it to his nose, and drew in the pristine smell. The smooth, clean feeling was refreshing to his senses. His frayed and hole-ridden shorts were next. Desta unbuttoned and slid them down and stepped out of them. He picked up his new shorts and smelled them, too. He inserted one leg, then the other, and slowly and thoughtfully pulled them up and buttoned them. The old man's measurements were masterful. The jacket and shorts fit him perfectly.

Berhe came out. "How do you like them? . . . What a transformation!"

"Thank you."

"You make me look good."

"It's the other way around. I cannot wait to show these to Masud. How much do I owe you?"

"Thirty birr."

Desta picked up his old shorts, took the money from the pocket, and gave it to Berhe. "Thank you, again."

"What about your old clothes?"

"*Weeyee*—I didn't mean to forget. I need to keep them." Desta bent down to pick them up. "Do you have something I can carry them in?"

"Here! Roll them in this," Berhe said, handing him some brown paper. "I could just as easily throw them out for you."

"No," Desta said thoughtfully. "You don't part with something or someone that has meant so much to you for so long."

Berhe shook his head, mystified. "Good luck to you."

Desta ran across the market ground to Masud's store. Gasping and breathless, he asked at the counter, "Is Masud in?"

"No," replied Hassan. "Anything wrong?"

"No. I wanted to show him my new clothes."

"Congratulations. I'll tell him you came by."

Disappointed, Desta strode through the alleyway into the main street that took him home. On this road, every kiosk owner, tella and tej bet owner, and all their customers had seen him in his old and torn clothes. He wondered if anyone would say anything to him as he walked past in his new clothes. He strolled at a leisurely pace, hoping that anyone who looked out to the street would notice him. He glanced from one side to the other to see if there were any eyes on him. There were none. He wondered whether these people had ever really noticed him before. After all, he had been walking the same street every day. He wondered if they thought he was a completely different boy. Although he didn't know them by name, he was familiar with many of the inhabitants along his daily route.

Then it happened. Just a short distance from the entrance to Zewday's compound, a woman he had never seen before came out of a tej house and said, "Are you Desta, Zewday's ashker?"

"Yes, I am Desta, but I am not Zewday's ashker," he replied, miffed that she had referred to him as a houseboy.

"I am sorry. I didn't mean to offend you. I am only repeating what your master told us."

Desta was trying to figure out how to answer this obnoxious woman when she continued. "He's finally bought you new clothes, as we had encouraged him to do in the New Year. . . . You look becoming in them."

Desta realized then that this woman obviously took pleasure in wounding his ego. "Thank you for your compliment and support," he said. "You certainly are a good mimicker." He felt as if doused with a cold bucket of water. Desta continued walking home, trying to be strong. But by the time he pushed open the gate and began walking the path to the main house, he was on the verge of tears.

LATER, WHEN THE EVENING turned ash gray, Desta took a shovel from the little storage shed at the side of the kitchen, gathered his old clothes still in their paper wrapping, and headed to the northern section of the coffee grove. Lesim came out and asked, "Where are you going with those things?"

"I'm going to hold a funeral service. Wanna come?"

"Who died?" she said, chuckling.

"You think I am joking. Do come if you can."

"You sound serious. What've you got in that paper?"

"The deceased. ...Don't ask so many questions. Just come and you will find out."

On the north side of the property, near the spot where he used to keep the coffee jar before he moved it the opposite side, Desta dropped the wrapped clothes and began digging with the shovel. When he looked up, Lesim was standing in front of him.

"Those are your old jacket and shorts! Why do you need to bury them?"

"Because they mean so much to me," Desta said, talking as he dug. "They are my first modern clothes. They deserve more respect and dignity than just to be thrown away. I'll be happy knowing where they lie."

"Talk about being ridiculous," Lesim said, remembering what Desta had said to her when she tried to walk in her father's old shoes.

"Here," Desta said, handing her the shovel so he could wipe his perspiration. "I'm not being ridiculous. I'm just paying respect to a set of clothes that transformed me from a country shepherd boy into a modern town boy. They protected me from the cold and the sun, and they were there for me for the past eighteen months. This is the least I can do for them."

Desta sat down on his heels and unwrapped the paper. He lifted and shook the old clothes, brushing and straightening them. He carefully lowered them into the hole, lengthwise, orienting them to the east—the jacket first, followed by the shorts. He took the shovel from Lesim who was watching him, transfixed. He gently tossed a scoop of the fresh soil as his emotions rose in his throat. To check his intensity of feeling, he scooped and tossed as fast as he could. When the hole was nearly filled with dirt, he stopped.

"Here," he said, handing the shovel to Lesim once again. "Do you want to throw the last scoop of dirt?"

She took the shovel and awkwardly dug, tossing a small amount of the soil.

Desta crouched on his heels, head bent and eyes closed. He whispered, "Thank you for giving me warmth and protection for the past year and a half. I'll forever be grateful to you."

Then he rose, took the shovel from Lesim, and said, "Let's go."

When they reached the center of the courtyard, Lesim glanced at Desta and said, "You know, I always suspected there was something strange about you. After witnessing what you just did, I have no doubt." She smiled.

"Rest assured, you aren't the first to feel that," Desta said, heading to the storage shed with the shovel.

THIRTY-EIGHT

"In the time of your ancestors, Zewday would have been your ashker, not the other way around," Eleni, the Wind Woman said, showing up in front of him out of nowhere. Desta was leaning against the school building during his mid-morning break, watching the students play ball.

"What're you talking about? You have a way of always showing up in unexpected places, don't you?"

"I'm aware of how badly you felt when that rude woman referred to you as Zewday's ashker the other day. Because of your grandmother's decision to go live in that isolated valley, you all grew up not really knowing who your ancestors were. And your father, astute as he is about many things, never attempted to learn his family's background. What I'm about to share is something I've had in mind to do for quite some time.

"As you already heard from the spirit of your grandfather, you are a direct descendant of King Solomon and his pharaoh prince, Tashere. What he failed to mention is that you also descend from the royalty of Gonder, and for this you deserve the title of prince and other associated accolades. Instead, because of where you grew up, you have been called just another shepherd.

"Regarding your family's isolated existence, however, this is in keeping with the tradition of the Gonder monarchs. In the old days, to ensure the safety of their families, the Gonder kings sent them to live in the remote and isolated valley of Wehni. You should someday learn about it—it's fascinating. Your grandmother's decision to go live in that remote and secluded valley was in the tradition of her ancestors, although whether she made that decision instinctively or knowingly is hard to say. And life turned out to be what it was for her children and grandchildren, who became animal herders and farmers. . . . Walk with your head up. You're not an ashker and you don't come from ashker stock."

"How did you find out all this?" Desta asked, happy to hear that his ancestors were kings, like Haile Selassie, Emperor of Ethiopia. It meant that were it not for the mistake of his grandmother that led to his current lot in life, he could have appeared on the covers of notebooks like the emperor's children did.

"It's common knowledge among the Winds. We have done our research. We are as curious about where your search for the second coin will end as you are." Eleni smiled furtively.

Desta was puzzled by this statement and by her secretive smile.

"Just know that we care about you. I personally care about you. I didn't want you to be hurt by ignorant and stupid people's comments like that woman made. . . . There is a man at a place called Zegay who has a record of your family line. You and your father should go there someday and talk to him. You'll be pleased to know who you really are. I've got to go now. You go back to your classes." The Wind Woman vanished.

Desta walked to his class not knowing exactly how he felt about the strange woman's comments. That his ancestors were this or that didn't matter to him. He just wanted to be strong enough to accomplish his goals.

THIRTY-NINE

Desta's dream of meeting the woman with yellow hair and milk-white skin was about to be fulfilled. He had his new jacket and shorts, he was feeling well and looking good, and he was ready to meet any dignitary in town, including the lady who was unlike any he had ever known before. He was anxious and excited about this trip—he couldn't wait.

His third-grade class was assembled outside the classroom. They were preparing to go get vaccinated for *wetetay*—smallpox. Betew, the homeroom teacher, had explained to the students what they should expect. The children were giddy to be out of doors and taking a walk to the missionaries' clinic.

They walked east across the school's soccer field to the main traffic road and then cut south on a dusty footpath that ran parallel with the roadway. They braved the strong heat and the long walk to the clinic. Trucks threw up plumes of dust and scattered gravel at their feet, causing them to turn their heads away from the road every time a large vehicle passed.

After walking for nearly three-quarters of an hour, they arrived at the mission where they'd meet the woman with yellow hair and milk-white skin. Inside the closed gate stood a man with twinkling brown eyes, his face shadowed by the top hat he was wearing. A woven wire fence circled the huge rectangular compound. Betew walked up to the gate and knocked. The man cracked it open. He and Betew exchanged a few words.

Betew turned around and commanded, "Form a single line!" The children pushed and shoved, but, eventually, everyone got into line. Desta stood seventh from the front. He wanted to study the woman before she pierced his arm with the needle.

The guard swung open the gate and the students entered noisily. Betew admonished them to be quiet. Following the guard, they made a beeline toward the white building, which had a small porch at the front. The guard opened the door. Their teacher turned around and placed his index finger over his mouth. "Sshhhh."

Some of the students turned to their classmates and mimicked the teacher with index fingers over their mouths. "Sshhh."

Wide eyed, they shuffled in, one by one. Desta noticed that the floor, smooth as his mother's baking pan, was cool and immaculately clean. He saw that the walls and ceiling were milk white and spotless. The room was large enough to seat thirty people and was arrayed with rows of brown folding chairs. Before the chairs were three white tables on which lay three trays of sealed white bottles, needles attached to some kind of holder, and pieces of white cotton.

The children filed in and were directed to sit down in the rows of folding chairs. A flurry of activity overshadowed the scene before them, with people coming and going through the hallways. These people were no different from anybody Desta knew. He asked one of the boys next to him, "Have you ever seen the woman with yellow hair and milk-white skin?"

"I live not far from here. I see her walking outside all the time on the weekends."

One of the women stepped forward and announced to the students what was happening that morning: they were to receive a *kitibat*—vaccination. She reached down to the first boy in line, grabbed him by the hand, and led him to the tables. Tentative and hesitant, the boy followed. The woman rolled up the sleeve of the boy's left arm and rubbed the skin with something white. A stern-looking woman next to her picked up a horrific-looking needle seated in a thick, grooved holder. She pierced his skin and in one swift motion plunged the needle deep into his arm. The boy winced when the needle punctured him but stood stoically afterward.

"Keep the sleeve up for a few minutes," the woman said, letting his hand go. Holding the rolled up sleeve, the boy walked back to his seat. The woman with the needle signaled for the next boy to come up.

The vaccinations continued, the woman changing the needle each time. The first boy was still holding his sleeve up, occasionally glancing at his arm. Otherwise, he kept his attention on the table, as if looking to be told to unroll his sleeve. The sound of whispers, muffled coughs, and shuffling feet accompanied the activities at the table.

Desta's attention was cued to any sign that the woman with yellow hair and milk-white skin might appear. His eyes shuttled between the activities at the table and the hallways. His ears were angled for any footsteps. He began to wonder if she was even around.

Just before the boy next to Desta got up for his shot, she appeared, as if out of thin air, briefly taking Desta back to the times his grandfather's spirit had come to him. The room hushed. Desta stared. *Is she a spirit or a real human being?* Strangely, her refined features reminded him of Eleni, though this spirit had a much lighter skin than the Wind Woman.

The vision before him said something to the other women that he didn't hear clearly and couldn't understand. The boy next to him went up for his vaccination. Desta prayed that the strange-looking woman wouldn't vanish into thin air before he could see her up close. The women had suspended their activities while she was talking to them. The next boy stood with his arms crossed over his chest, seeming also to be transfixed by the specter-like woman. Now Desta wondered whether he would have the chance to get close and really hear the woman's voice and study the details of her face.

Hurry up! he wanted to shout to the other women. There was a muffled giggle in the back and Desta turned. Two boys and a girl, their faces close to one another, were chattering, their eyes stealing away to the teacher occasionally. Betew also seemed transfixed by the apparition at the table.

Desta turned around and the vision was gone. He gasped. His stomach lurched. He shook his head and stared down at his feet. *Was she a spirit or a human being?* He was almost convinced she was a spirit because spirits in folklore were described as having golden hair and very fair skin. She certainly came and left like one, too.

It was Desta's turn. He rose and hurried across the floor to the tables, cursing his luck for missing the opportunity to see the woman up close. The first woman had rolled up his sleeve and the second woman had just pierced his skin when the woman with yellow hair reappeared, cradling a box in her arms. Desta jerked in shock, causing the needle to penetrate deeper in his flesh. He would have screamed under normal circumstances, but instead he froze and gawped at the woman.

"Keep still, keep still," the woman said as she pushed the grooved holder forward. She then withdrew the needle and gave him a wad of cotton to hold against his pierced skin.

The apparition placed the box at the table and opened it, again suspending the activity of the other women. She was talking while her hands were busy taking vials out of the boxes. None of her words made any sense. She talked as if taking care not to break the words she uttered. She seemed to caress each word that came out of her mouth. She spoke like a spirit, speaking spirit language.

As she talked, her thin lips vibrated as if made of parchment, her pale blue eyes gliding gently over the things before her. Her face seemed a network of silken thread, like a spider web. Her features were simple and precise, accented by a small brown mole on the right side of her chin. Her skin wasn't exactly milky white, nor was her hair precisely yellow, as he had imagined them to be. Rather, her skin was the color of freshly fired clay, her hair, saffron.

Desta continued lingering there, holding the swab to his arm and dreamily tracking every movement the woman made. She said something to her assistants. They turned to Desta and said in unison, "Go back to your seat!"

Startled by the unexpected command, Desta scuttled back to his seat. Too preoccupied to watch where he was going, he tripped and stepped on the foot of the boy who sat to his right, causing the boy to flinch and whimper.

"Where does this spirit come from?" Desta asked the boy sitting to his left.

"She is not a spirit. She is a *Ferenge*—a white woman—*where* she comes from, you ask those women at the table."

"Do you know if she has a husband?"

"I don't know. This is my first time here, like you."

"She does," replied the boy with the hurt foot. "A big, tall man." He eyed Desta critically.

"Do you know where their country is?"

The boy glanced at Desta severely. "You ask too many questions. I don't know. If you are that curious, ask the teacher."

The vaccinations over, the students filed out of the ivory white building. As they walked back to school, Desta trailed behind, his mind transported to the Ferenge woman's imagined country. He wondered whether the God that created her and people like her was different from the one who created him and others like him. He tried to imagine what it would be like—whether he could be happy—living in a place where everybody was the same as her. No matter what, he would want to go to such a place if ever he had the opportunity, just to see what it was like.

When he lived in his walled-in valley where the sky appeared like a dome overhead, any time the adults mentioned others places, he always thought they must be on the other side of the sky. Now he no longer thought that. At any mention of a place, he immediately thought it was here on earth but far away. Desta wanted to know what the earth—and plants and grains and animals—

looked like where that lady came from. He thought the land was probably like his country but that the animals and plants and grains were different. What exactly they looked like, no image came to him: his mind was completely blank. "Good," he said to himself, smiling. "I would rather be surprised when I eventually go there." He said it with such certainty that he was startled by his bold declaration.

"Desta, you're falling farther and farther behind. Are you tired?" Betew asked, after having stood and waited for him.

"No. I was just thinking about stuff."

"Like what?"

"That Ferenge lady, for one."

"What about her?"

"I was just amazed by how she looks, so different from us. At first I thought she was a *zarrh*—fairy."

Betew laughed. "No, that's a Ferenge and that's how all the Ferenges look."

"Where exactly does she come from?"

"I am not sure. She must come either from America or Canada."

"Where are those places?"

"I'll get a *yalem karta*—world map—from the storage closet and show them to you."

What the teacher said was as blank in Desta's mind as were the animals and plants and grains he was thinking about earlier. Yalem karta? Desta was not going to ask what that was. He would wait and be surprised.

When the students got back, it was lunchtime. The bell rang and the rest of the students spilled out of their classrooms. All rushed toward the main walkway that brought them to town. Desta sprinted home, excited to think about the America and Canada he would be seeing in yalem karta when he returned from lunch, God willing.

Betew didn't come back after lunch. Another man taught the class for the rest of the day. Desta's thought of yalem karta never left him through that whole afternoon and evening and into the morning of the next day, when Betew walked into the classroom with a rolled paper in his hand. Right after the bell rang for the morning break, he said to Desta, "Come, let me show you where America and Canada are."

Desta followed him to his rickety table. The teacher sat down and unrolled the paper, holding it open with his elbows and hands. A bunch of students congregated around them. "Here," Betew said, handing an edge to one of the boys. With the eraser end of a pencil, he pointed out different places. "Here is America. . . . Here is Canada . . . England . . . Italy . . . France . . . Israel . . . *Gibtse*—Egypt," he said, placing the eraser every time he called out a country.

"And here is Ethiopia," announced one of the boys proudly, pushing his index finger into the right corner of the map. The other children pointed to the few countries they had heard of and seen before on the map. Other than Ethiopia, Egypt and Israel, Desta had never heard of many of the places that the teacher and the students were calling out. He was impressed, but he also felt very behind in his knowledge of the world.

After the students ran out of countries they knew, Betew started again. He randomly hopped his pencil across the open map, stopping at the straw-green patches to call out more names. "Here's the Red Sea . . . and Mediterranean Sea . . . and Indian Ocean . . . and Atlantic Ocean," Betew said, as if these seas and oceans lay just next door and he knew them intimately.

Desta was actually disappointed by Betew's show-and-tell. It had no meaning to him. He had thought the teacher was going to bring Canada and America to the classroom, albeit indirectly, like with a picture.

The bell rang. "Do you feel like you know something about America and Canada now?" Betew asked as he rolled up the karta.

"A little."

Betew smiled. "That's how it is. You learn everything little by little."

Desta pressed his lips together absentmindedly and wondered what Canada and America were really like.

FORTY

One Saturday afternoon after Mebet and Lesim went to the market, Desta brought out his money jar, the same jar he had hoarded the coffee beans in. The spring season was in full swing. Roses, daisies, and daffodils in the lot adjoining the vegetable garden smiled at the world around them.

Tiny white blossoms dotted the coffee bushes, imbuing the air with the fragrance of jasmine. Alone and feeling like he owned the world, Desta sat down on the long bench under the eaves to count and enjoy the money he had made in exchange for his flower drawings.

He pushed his notebooks away to make enough space to lay out his paper money. There were seven of the red ten-birr bills, three of the pink-orange five-birr bills, and three of the straw-green one-birr bills. Because he had never owned money before, he didn't really know all of what was depicted on the bills. He straightened a one-birr note by pressing it away with the palm of his hand. He studied its details.

There was that man, the *Negus*—king—in the far right-hand corner of the bill, his head tilted up and staring into space but seeming to look inwardly as well. The collar of his coat was studded with a woven relief of gold leaves; a similar intricately woven metallic fabric ran along the ridges of his shoulders, and there were strips of ribbon arrayed at his chest. Before him were three luxuriant coffee bushes, one embowered with green berries. *Ye Ethiopia mengist bank* was printed in Amharic at the top-middle portion of the note. *Aned ye Ethiopia birr*—One Ethiopian birr—it said directly below. There was a string of numbers beneath the man and another set on the left, above the coffee beans. The opposite corners of the bill identified the numeral one, both in English and Amharic.

Much of the note was engraved with a tapestry of fine fabric, causing Desta to wonder about and admire the fine work that had gone into creating it. He couldn't help but remember what his sister Saba had complained about when the policeman's wife purchased her sack of teff with such paper money. He could understand Saba's misgivings. How was it that a piece of paper like he was holding could buy so many things—a sack of teff, sheep, clothes?

After he thought about it, he realized it was not his business to be pondering and questioning such things. He should accept them, as his mother accepted everything the priests said about God, Jesus, angels, and the saints. He was happy he had that much money in his possession so he could buy so many different things with it.

After accounting for the ten birr his father sent him and what he paid for his jacket and shorts and school supplies Desta had ninety-eight birr. He planned to use six birr for his supplemental food and twenty for his round-trip to Bahir Dar. The remaining seventy-two birr he would save.

He put the piles together and rolled them up. He tied the roll with a string and wrapped it in its cloth. He knew this was a lot of money. He was grateful to Masud and to Khadija and Almaz who had helped him sell his drawings. More than the money itself, the discovery that he had the power to earn it and not be dependent on anybody for anything, now that he had a livelihood, brought him joy. It was akin to the feeling that had filled his heart when he first stood atop the mountain above his home and discovered there was a much bigger world than the one he had been living in all his life: he now had the freedom that came from venturing beyond his realm, into the far-flung universe.

If he could earn a living for himself, he would no longer be at the mercy of others, including those who gave him food and shelter in exchange for services he must render. He would not have to beg his father for precious cents. As fragile and small as he was and as big and frightening as the world was for him to tackle all alone, that he had it in him to earn money for his food and clothes and school supplies was freeing and exhilarating.

He didn't know what to call the feeling that blanketed him at that moment, but it was like having a solid rock to stand on, not outside but within him. He knew what he could do for himself through his own efforts. The coin was his protection. He could go with courage as deep and wide in the world as required to achieve his goals of finding the other coin and finishing his education. It was empowering to discover that the world had a lot more to offer than all his family and relatives combined could offer. There was kindness in complete strangers, more so than in his own family, and all he could hope was to find more of them.

With his rolled bills in hand, Desta walked to the plot where he had hidden his coffee bean supplies, parting the lush leaves of the bushes with his hands and wading through overgrown weeds. His tracks of a few weeks ago were already covered with newly grown wild plants. Once he got there, he removed the top from the jar and pushed his wad of money deep within the remaining coffee beans. He put back the lid and then straightened the tousled grass and bushes to leave no hint of his presence and to ensure the safety of his treasure.

As he walked back by a new route, Desta was once again comforted by the knowledge of his own security—he would not be starved again in the months to come. He pressed his lips and moved his head up and down, acknowledging his thoughts.

FORTY-ONE

Having decided to go home for Christmas, Desta wanted to make an all-out effort to first go to Bahir Dar. After all, going to the town by the lake was one of the two reasons he had readily accepted his father's suggestion to attend school in Dangila. He had scrapped the idea of going there with Masud because Zewday would surely forbid it. He had money to pay for the trip but nobody to go with. He didn't feel close or comfortable enough to ask Zewday. It was not worth even a try with a man who had no interest in him and who chose his tej and tella over his own family.

For days he thought about ways he could get there on his own. He couldn't come up with any workable idea. The longer he went without finding a solution to his problem, the more anxious and determined he became. Then one morning on his way to school he remembered the girl Eleni, or Helen—the name she preferred to be called by. She had mentioned that her father had a car and that he went to Bahir Dar often. Maybe he could go with her father the next time he went.

During the mid-morning break, Desta went looking for Helen. She had said she was in the fifth grade. He remembered she had a pretty face and big brown eyes. With so many students milling around the school grounds at recess, he realized it was not going to be easy to spot her. He scurried through the crowd looking but didn't see Helen. He began randomly asking the students but no one seemed to know her.

He heard more kids playing ball on the other side of the building, where her class was located. He ran down the side of the building and went to the back. After catching his breath, he scanned the group. Some of the boys were kicking a ball. The girls were huddled together and chatting in the shadow of the building. He couldn't see their faces. He approached them. One of them turned around and stared at him intently.

"You look familiar. Do I know you from somewhere?"

"Are you Helen?"

"Yes, who are you?"

"I am Desta. You helped me one time when you found me lying on the ground during the lunch break. You brought me food and water. You were so kind."

"Now I remember. What's going on with you? You look very well since the last time I saw you."

"Thank you. Things have changed since the last time you saw me. *Egzi Ab'hare yimesgen*—thank God. . . . Can I talk to you privately for a moment?"

Helen excused herself and walked over to Desta. "What can I do for you?"

He led her a few more steps away from the other girls. "The reason I came looking for you is because you said your father has a car and he goes to Bahir Dar often. Do you think he could let me ride with him? I have money to pay for the trip."

"I don't know. I have to ask him first. Why do you want to go there?"

"I'm looking for a cousin who is supposed to be living there. . . ." The bell rang.

"I'll ask my Baba. I'll have the answer tomorrow." She dashed toward her homeroom.

"Thank you!" shouted Desta as he ran toward his own classroom.

The following day at the mid-morning break, Desta went looking for Helen again. He located her in the same area with the same three girls. This time she excused herself and came to Desta the moment she caught sight of him.

"Let me quickly tell you before the bell rings. My dad—if you remember, is Colonel Asheber—said we can take you with us when we all go there one week-end. He needs to talk with the people you are living with first. He wants to know the names of the people you live with so that he can talk with them directly for their permission to take you with us. He also said he wants to meet you before we do anything else."

After Desta wrote down Zewday's name on a piece of paper and gave it to her, Helen said, "I will let you know when you can come to meet my dad, *ishee*? I've got to go. Our teacher is unforgiving if we are late."

A few days later Helen came straight to Desta's homeroom before the after-noon session began. "Desta, I want to bring you home tomorrow evening after class. Can you do that? My father wants to talk to you," Helen said the moment she saw the boy.

"Yes, that would be fine," he said somewhat ambivalently. All of a sudden, meeting the head of the police, who put people in jail, frightened him.

"Okay, I will come here right after school finishes. Wait for me in case our teacher goes past our release time." Helen flew off like a butterfly.

That night, when Desta got in bed, the meeting with Colonel Asheber was in the forefront of his mind. He had to remember to bring twenty birr for the round-trip to Bahir Dar. He thought one of the reasons the colonel wanted to meet him was probably to see if he had enough money to pay for the trip. Desta had never been in a car and didn't know the normal arrangements people made to travel in those moving machines.

He rose early, before anyone else, and went to the coffee grove. He unearthed the jar and counted out exactly twenty birr. He folded and rolled the birr notes and stashed them in his breast pocket, where he could see them at all times. The rest he put back in the jar, which he buried, and set off for school.

COLONEL ASHEBER was sitting at a table on the porch and smoking a cigarette when Desta and Helen arrived. He was a short, thin man and far less intimidating than his name or title. He wore glasses with circular lenses so thick that, when he peered at Desta, his eyes looked like gray marbles in a deep dish of water.

"So you want to go look for your cousin in Bahir Dar? How do you intend to find her?" He puffed a plume of smoke, sending it straight up into the air above his nose. The smoke momentarily obscured part of his face.

"I have to go to places where people gather, like the church and the market-place," Desta said, holding his breath. The smell of the cigarette was choking him. "I'll make a sign to let people know who I'm looking for," he added when he finally could breathe out.

"I don't think you will have much success, son, because the people that come to the marketplace are farmers. They don't know how to read." With his index finger, Colonel Asheber tapped ashes into a small silver tray. He brought the cigarette into his mouth and took a long pull. He sent a plume of curling smoke up into the air again. "For that matter most of the townspeople can't read. Your sign will not draw many people's attention. If you lived there and could talk to people daily, you might have better success."

"I will explain to those who can't read who I am looking for. Or I'll simply talk to everybody I see."

"Yes, but you are just not going to have time to do all that. We'll stay there just Saturday and part of Sunday. You better go when you can stay longer, like during your Christmas vacation."

Desta ran out of other convincing reasons. He reached into his breast pocket and pulled out his twenty birr. "Look," Desta said, unrolling his bills. "If it's a question of my ability to pay, I have enough money for the round-trip."

The colonel smiled. "You don't need to pay to ride with us. That you're so determined and prepared to go to Bahir Dar is reason enough to bring you along. I'd hate to disappoint you. I'll talk to Ato Zewday and you talk to him, too, if you have not already done so, and you will go with us."

Desta wished he could jump to show his gratitude. Instead he said, *"Betam amesegnalehu!*—Thank you very much!"

"Once we get Zewday's approval, Helen will let you know when we will come to pick you up."

"Amesegnalehu," Desta said again. He restrained himself, walking normally from the colonel's compound, and then he ran home at top speed.

Once Desta talked with Zewday, and Zewday with Colonel Asheber, the boy had permission to travel to Bahir Dar. The night before, Desta made all his preparations. Using his leftover Enkutatashi colored pencils and sheets of paper, he made a big sign with boldface letters, pressing hard and tracing his colored pencils multiple times on the letters. It simply read:

DOES ANYBODY KNOW A WOMAN WHOSE NAME MEANS SWEET AND SOUR?

He tacked the 8½-by-11-inch paper on cardboard using hot, liquefied dough paste. He bored holes at the top and bottom of the sign and tied it with string to a stick he had cut from a eucalyptus tree branch.

In the morning he rose early. He washed his face. He recited the legends found in the coin. He brought his sign out and fixed to go.

"Don't you want something to eat?" Lesim asked, stepping out of the kitchen.

"They are coming to pick me up soon. Better wait for them by the gate."

She returned to the house and came back with a wedge of a loaf. "Here, have something in your stomach."

Thankful, Desta munched the wheat loaf as he walked to the gate and waited for Helen and her family to arrive.

The hunter green Land Rover came, stirring the street dust to life.

The colonel rolled down the window. "Been here long?"

Desta didn't even have a chance to respond before Helen opened the door and commanded, "C'mon in!"

Tentative and apprehensive, Desta put his sign in the car and climbed in. This was the first time he was going to be riding in a car and he wasn't sure what would happen to him when the car began to move. Then a strong, unfamiliar smell entered his nose and went directly to his stomach, causing it to roil. Though it seemed the strong odor had subsided once he was in the car, Desta remained apprehensive.

He sat beside Helen in the back seat. Helen's mother, Tigist, sat with her husband in the front. "Close the door," the colonel ordered, looking back. Desta pulled the door shut but the latch had not engaged. "Open it again. This time slam it hard," Colonel Asheber said. Desta followed the order but the door still had not latched.

"Let me do it," Helen said, as she opened her door. She ran around the car, opened Desta's door, and swung it shut with all her power.

"That's how it's done," the colonel said, smiling. He cranked the engine and brought it to life. He pressed on something with his foot and the car roared. He moved a lever from his right side on the floor and the Land Rover began to roll, slowly at first but then faster and faster, picking up speed.

Desta clutched the side of his seat every time the colonel shifted gears or went over a rock or an uneven or potholed surface. Helen said, "The car will go smoother once we get to the main road. Is this the first time you're riding in a car?" Desta nodded his head, indicating yes.

The main road was no better. The car swayed and shifted every time it went over bumps and potholes. Gravel flew to the sides, and it felt to Desta as if the bottom of the car was being pelted with a shower of pulverized rocks.

Helen reached over and picked up Desta's sign. "This is clever," she said. "I like your neat letters and the colors you chose to make them."

"Thank you. I hope it will get a lot of people's attention."

"Where do you plan to use it?"

"Today, in front of the main entrance to the market. Tomorrow, outside of the church grounds."

"You're going to be burning in the sun," Helen said, smiling. "Bahir Dar can be hot at times."

"No matter. This is something I have to do."

"Does a woman you have not even met mean that much to you, to make these kinds of sacrifices?"

"Not her so much but something she holds, an ancient family treasure. . . ."

Helen furrowed her brow and narrowed her eyes. "A family treasure?"

"It's a bit complicated to explain. Just understand that any sacrifice I make regarding this matter is worth it to me." Desta said this with such firmness that Helen decided to drop the subject.

Desta looked out the window. The nearly table-flat land was a monotony of farm lots, cattle fields, and acacia trees. Rust-colored soil mantled some of the agricultural lots, while white stubble was strewn over those lots that had not yet been tilled. Clusters of squat grass houses huddled behind bush fences or within eucalyptus groves.

The green boxy machine devoured the road. The smell of gasoline, and the constant rocking and shuddering as they rode over rocks and potholes, caused Desta's stomach to heave. Colonel Asheber sped through small towns without heeding the boys and girls who hoisted baskets of fruit for sale as they ran toward the car.

The temperature inside the car rose steadily, as if someone had made a roaring fire beneath the passengers. The interior of the vehicle became stuffy and oppressive.

Helen tapped her father's shoulder. "Papa, can we roll the windows down? It's really getting hot in here."

"If you can put up with the wind and dust," replied the colonel.

Helen rolled her window down and told Desta to do the same. Clouds of dust wafted in and out of the car, pelting their faces and causing them to cough. For Desta there was another, more offending problem the colonel hadn't mentioned about cars with open windows: the noxious exhaust from the trucks and cars zipping past from the opposite direction.

Desta's stomach could take no more. He rolled up his window and asked Helen if she wouldn't mind doing the same. Not long after, he asked the girl if her father would mind stopping the car. He was about to retch and he needed to step outside to do it.

The colonel didn't have to wait until his daughter asked. He overheard and had noticed Desta's desperate look in the rearview mirror. Immediately after the car stopped, Desta unlatched the door and dashed to the ditch. He sat on his heels, his stomach heaving in syncopated motions. His throat was raw and his stomach a washed—out bowl. The retching ceased. He wiped his eyes and mouth with a corner of his gabi and returned to the car. He apologized to the others.

The colonel and his wife minimized the problem, saying these things happen when one is traveling in a car for the first time. Tigist added, "I often get sleepy when I'm in a car, particularly on hot days like today."

Helen look worried. "If your body can't take car fumes and dust, what are you going to do when we get to Bahir Dar? There are a lot more cars and dust in the streets there."

"Now, now, Helen," Tigist scolded. "I am sure he will get used to it."

"How long before we get there?" Desta asked, now more than anything else concerned about the climbing temperature in the car. When Helen groped for the answer, Colonel Asheber replied, "We should get there in another hour."

At a town called Beekolo Abayi, the colonel stopped the car in front of what looked like a popular buena bet. "Let's all get out and have something to drink before we continue." They all got out of the car and followed the colonel. Strings of multicolored beads hung like a curtain across the entrance of the café. The strings swooshed and their glass adornments glinted in the sunlight when people parted them with their hands as they went in and out.

The colonel's party sat around a low table and ordered drinks. Tigist was served an orange-colored drink in a tapered glass bottle. The label read FANTA. Helen chose a mahogany-colored beverage that came in a tall bottle that struck the figure of a shapely woman. Its exterior announced COCA-COLA in loud letters. Colonel Asheber ordered a bottle of St. George Beer. Desta settled for something familiar: a glass of tea with three cubes of sugar in it.

They drank their refreshments and left. Desta came out of the buena bet and flinched when he thought he saw the familiar Eleni walk by with a young man at her side. He blinked and looked again, but there was no sign of the Wind Woman. With so many people around, it could have been anybody.

They got into the car and the colonel roared the engine to life. He waited a few seconds until the people ahead finished crossing. Then he slowly rolled the car back onto the road. After a couple of quick presses on the horn to warn pedestrians, he took off at full speed.

"Do you feel better now, Desta?" Colonel Asheber asked, glancing back briefly as he drove. The boy said he did and thanked him for asking.

It seemed their trip to Bahir Dar had to have some drama before they reached their destination. After they had driven for several miles, Desta noticed wispy smoke streaming out from around the edges at the front of the car.

"Is that normal?" he whispered to Helen, pointing with his finger.

Helen gasped. "No. It's not normal." She tapped her father's back. "Papa, something is smoking under the hood."

"Era!" cried the colonel.

"By God," Tigist said, waking from her nap. "You need to pull to the side. Immediately! The car might be on fire."

"No," the colonel said calmly. "It may have something to do with the cooling system."

He pulled over, got out of the car, and walked to the front, apprehensively. Helen and Desta spilled out and stood around Colonel Asheber with their hands on their mouths. Tigist stayed in the car.

Asheber opened the hood. Steam belched and sputtered from under a metal cap. He let the car cool down for twenty minutes and then unscrewed the cap, protecting his hand from the heat with a rag he had brought from the trunk.

"Yup! Like I suspected," he said. "The radiator water is low. Luckily, I have enough in the car to get us to Bahir Dar."

Everyone was relieved.

The colonel reached in the compartment behind where the children had sat and pulled out a square metal container filled with water. He bent under the hood and poured water into the radiator, but the cavity seemed bottomless. The radiator kept gurgling and spitting with the continued pouring from the jug. After nearly three-quarters of the water was added, it backed up and spilled out of the radiator opening. "This is not good news," Asheber said, standing straight. "There must be a leak in one of the hoses or the radiator itself."

What the colonel talked about was foreign to the children.

"Let's see if we can make it to the town of Merawi. It's only fifteen kilometers from here," he said, jumping into the car. The children followed suit. By the time they reached the little town, the car was steaming again. The colonel drove off the road onto a level spot and stopped.

"I don't think we can find a mechanic in this godforsaken little place," Colonel Asheber said as he stepped out of the car. Helen and Tigist got out but Desta stayed, thinking about what this problem would spell. He rolled his window down and looked across the dreary bare earth, which evidently was the town's plaza.

Asheber paced for a bit and then said, "I don't think it's wise to take a chance on driving the rest of the way in this condition."

Desta didn't like what he heard. He unlatched the door and got out.

"So . . . what's our option?" Tigist asked.

"I think you should all go home, assuming we can find a *berrari mekeena*— shuttle bus—that goes back to Dangila. And I will catch one going to Bahir Dar. Tomorrow I will return here with a mechanic to get the radiator fixed. Without the car it's pointless for all of us to go to Bahir Dar."

Tigist clamped her lips and shook her head in dismay. Helen wore her disappointment all over her face. Desta felt as if the ground was shifting beneath his feet. *I have come so close to the place of my dreams, how can I possibly return without reaching it and making some sort of attempt to find that woman?*

Children and a few adults of all ages materialized out of the thin air and stood around the worried family, curiously eyeing them and the Land Rover.

"I guess you're right," Tigist said, finally finding her voice. "We cannot go to all the places we had planned to visit without the car."

Colonel Asheber said to Desta, "I'm sorry to disappoint you like this, son. Sometimes there are things humans have no control over. This is one of them. . . You can come with us another weekend. We should have a more reliable car by then."

Pensive and thoughtful, Desta just made lines in the dust with his big toe as he listened to the verdict.

A policeman was the next to arrive. When his eyes met the colonel's, he stood erect and quickly threw his right hand to his temple, fingers extended and stiff. Just as quickly, he dropped it when the colonel extended his hand to shake the policeman's. They walked away from the crowd—which had swollen quite a bit now— talked for a bit, and returned.

"As we said," the colonel declared, "you three go home and I will go to Bahir Dar. The policeman here will arrange for someone to look after the car. Tomorrow, once it's fixed, I will drive home. The policeman said there should be a berrari coming any moment that goes to Dangila."

A porter climbed to the top of the Land Rover and brought down the family's two suitcases and a carry-on bag. Desta, fighting hard not to show his disappointment, took out his sign and carried it on his shoulder. The four travelers, accompanied by the policeman, the porter, and a spattering of curious children, walked to the bus stop. Shortly after, a green bus arrived, its horn blaring. The policeman dashed over, talked to the driver, and returned having secured seats for the colonel's family. Desta removed the sign from the stick and wedged it under his arm. He left the stick on the ground.

"Mine should be arriving soon as well," Asheber said, as he kissed his wife good-bye. Helen reminded her father not to forget to bring her new pair of shoes.

The colonel put his arm around Desta. "Be strong. You will come with us on one of our future trips to Bahir Dar. Between today and tomorrow I will tell people I know to look for the woman of your description."

Desta felt comforted by the colonel's warm hand on his shoulder as much as by the promises he gave.

The driver of the bus blew the horn, reminding people to get on board. The porter had already placed the family's luggage on top of the bus and secured it with a rope. A middle-aged man gave up his seat at the front to the colonel's wife. Desta and Helen squeezed between two smelly farmers behind the driver. The colonel waved his hand as the driver cranked the engine, causing it to purr like a contented cat. The driver disengaged the brake and did something with his foot to cause the engine to whine first and then purr again. He pressed something else on the floor that made the bus sway and lurch forward. It was soon at top speed, leaving behind a billow of dust and a deafening roar.

They reached Dangila at dusk. "We'll try to go to Bahir Dar again another weekend," Tigist said when they were about to part and go their own way.

"I'm sorry. It just wasn't meant to be," Helen said, tightening her lips.

"I guess not, but thanks just the same," Desta said. "I'll see you at school."

Tigist stepped close. "Cheer up. This won't be the last time. We'll have many opportunities to go to Bahir Dar. You can come with us soon."

As he walked home, Desta wondered whether the car had really broken down or whether someone at tampered with it, especially since he thought he had seen the Wind Woman walk away from the car with a man.

FORTY-TWO

On Sunday Zewday didn't go to church because he had come home drunk in the wee hours and still felt groggy and sleepy in the morning. This meant Desta didn't have to go to church either. Once Desta had started eating at Khadija's restaurant, and got his strength and hardier appearance back, he had been going to church every Sunday with Zewday.

The botched Saturday trip to Bahir Dar had been like a bad dream that wouldn't go away. He couldn't concentrate on anything else without its sneaking up and stealing his mind away. In these kinds of circumstances in the past, Desta would go to the center of town and walk around, seeing things and talking to people—to take his mind off his troubles. Sometimes he preferred to be alone. He would stand leaning against one of the shop walls and study people as they came and went to the store windows or scurried across the open plaza.

That day, though, Desta had barely cleared the corridor between two buildings when he saw the Wind Woman. She was leaning against the wall where he usually stood, between the popular teahouse and the big merchandise store. It was as if she was waiting for him.

Desta shuddered at the sight of her, stopping in his tracks.

"Oh, Desta, Desta," Eleni sang. "Why do you always behave like that toward me, after all the nice things I've done for you? Remember all those animals I used to create to keep you company when you were a shepherd?"

Desta just gazed at her.

She took a few steps toward him. "Come, let's go sit some place, like one of those farmer's benches in the market grounds. I've very important information for you regarding the magic coin and who has it. My Wind associates have gathered many details about them."

Desta perked up a little but still wouldn't move a foot. "Tell me," he said, probing deeply into Eleni's winter-gray eyes. "Did you have something to do with what happened to Colonel Asheber's car on our way to Bahir Dar yesterday?"

"Who is this colonel? What are you talking about?" Eleni asked indifferently. "Why would you suspect me of doing something to this man's car? As I've told you before, I'm not allowed to talk about anything I do, but I can tell you that I was in a completely different part of the country all day yesterday."

"I thought I saw you and somebody else walk away from the colonel's car after we came out of the buena bet."

"You must have imagined things, as you used to. Come! Let's go." Eleni grinned slyly.

Desta followed her hesitantly. He looked up at her back. The round object above her neckline beneath her veil was not visible this time.

She turned around. "For your information, I am not revealed to anybody but you. And nobody else can hear our conversation."

Once they sat down, Eleni said, "You'll be glad to know that our team of researchers has identified who has the coin. It is neither a he nor a she but a *they.* I am afraid this is going to be even more confusing as you continue your search for the coin.

Desta lifted his face. "What?"

"Yes. That's exactly the reaction you will get from just about everybody as you search for the coin bearers."

"You mean they are two people? One is called sweet, the other sour?"

"Yes and no. Yes, because sweet refers to one and sour to the other. No, because the two people actually live in the body of one individual."

"I'm not following this." Desta looked away, trying to make sense of this bombshell.

"Let me give you a little related information about these individuals you have come to know as 'sweet and sour.' The parents of the two beings who are living in the body of one person had tried for years to have children. Those they conceived never made it to term; a total of six children were lost to miscarriages. The seventh child was carried to term and the parents were thrilled. Upon close inspection of this baby, they discovered it was a boy *and* a girl, having both female and male parts between its legs. They were devastated but at the same time happy to have a healthy and strong baby.

"They named this child *Marva and Kamala*, which means *sweet and sour*. It was sweet that they eventually had a child and sour because the child was not normal, not capable of producing offspring that could inherit their ancient Coin of Magic and Fortune. Later, the parents merged the two names, calling the child *Marvakamala*, and then eventually shortened it to *Marka*. In documents, this person is still referred to as Marva and Kamala. This is the name you'll look for if you continue to search for the coin."

Desta slowly let out his breath. He let his eyes wonder the market grounds, thinking about how, if they met, he could deal with a person who is both man and woman, living in one body. He had never known of a relative like that in his family.

Eleni said, "Now you know what kind of person you're looking for. The information is specific enough to make your efforts a little easier."

Desta shook his head vaguely. He was not sure how to take this news. He crossed his arms over his chest and stared into the distance.

Eleni continued. "In the country I come from, people like Marva and Kamala are referred to as hermaphrodites. In your language they are called *finafint*."

To Desta's ears these words sounded like sawdust, something he couldn't chew or digest. He tried to pronounce the first word, but only a fractured, awkward scrap of it remained in his head.

Eleni came to his rescue. "It's pronounced 'her-maff-row-dite.'"

Desta repeated, "Herma-frodit."

Eleni slowly pronounced the term again.

Desta repeated it after her, getting it straight this time. He said it again and again, as if the novel term was stuck on his tongue.

"I hope this new information helps, even though I know it will be more confusing as you ask people about Marva and Kamala," Eleni said, rising to go.

Desta rose to go home, too, ambivalent about acknowledging what she had told him. "I hope you're right."

The Wind Woman walked down the roadway for a short distance before leaning forward to let the air inflate her baggy clothes. She lifted and flew westward over the eucalyptus trees and vanished.

AS DESTA WALKED HOME, he found himself angry with the Wind Woman. *Why did she tell me all that information now that she knows I may not go to Bahir Dar any time soon and have no other place to look for this strange person?* Desta had a strong suspicion that Eleni knows just about everything that is going on with him. He was even angrier with himself for being swayed like this by information he had no way to verify.

Then he caught himself: did he have proof about what his grandfather's spirit had told him? No. He was going on mere belief and trust in the Cloud Man. This had been good enough for Desta. His grandpa's spirit would not lead him astray; he believed that Desta would eventually find the coin out there somewhere. At the moment it didn't matter if it was held by two people or one. He just needed to find it.

FORTY-THREE

The emperor was coming to town. They said he was going to Bahir Dar for some event and he was scheduled to make a stopover in Dangila. They said he was going to bring a caravan of trucks full of clothes and money to be given to the students throughout the province of Gojjam. The school officials said that no student should ever miss this once-in-a-lifetime opportunity to see up close Emperor Haile Selassie, King of Kings, the Lion of Judah.

This was a major event in the rather tranquil town. Since the news began circulating, the townspeople had been preparing in a big way. The town's administrators had decreed that all those who lived along the route the emperor was going to travel paint their houses. Most people complied with the mandate—at least by painting those areas of their homes that were visible from the street. The townsfolk were also expected to line the streets, dressed in their best attire, before the king arrived. They were to bow and clap their hands as his motorcade passed through.

The head of the school had issued a directive that all the students were to appear in their best clothes. Desta had washed his only clothes and was eager to see in person the emperor he had seen only on the cover of his notebooks and on birr bills. And of course he was looking forward to the fifty Ethiopian birr that all the students were supposed to receive along with new clothes—shorts and a jacket for the boys and a dress for the girls.

It was a Saturday in mid-October and the bright spring-season days were in full swing. The last batch of jasmine-scented coffee blossoms had permeated the air of Zewday's compound. Zewday wore his wool suit, the first time Desta had seen him in this black fabric, and Mebet her modern but traditionally white dress, instead of her usual homespun country gown.

The old couple that lived in the adjoining property was invited for coffee that Lesim had prepared. The neighbors were also dressed in their fine clothes.

Desta had just served the dabo kolo snack to the couple and was setting the tray on the bench by the door when he heard a snarling and snapping sound outside. Everybody stopped talking and listened.

"It sounds like we have some dogs outside. Could you please chase them out, Desta?" Zewday asked.

What Desta found when he went outside astounded him—a female and a male dog, locked intimately, the male looking helpless and in pain, the female grim-faced and looking determined not to let go. A dozen other male dogs danced around the two, baring their teeth at one another as if fighting over who would lose this battle of the sexes.

Desta watched them, mesmerized and wondering how long the conjoined canines would remain this way. Zewday came to the door and said, "Are you afraid of them? Here, use my cane to drive them off."

How can I drive off a pack of dogs, and with two of them in a fierce tug-of-war? Desta moved closer and waved the cane. The male and female moved sideways, like a snake, but they traveled only a few feet. A few of the other dogs retreated to the coffee bushes, but the rest were unfazed by Desta's threats. One black dog bared his ferocious teeth and glared at him disdainfully.

Desta raised his cane high in the air, intending to whack the beast. He didn't have a chance. The beast was swifter. He shot into the air and knocked Desta to the ground. The dog went for his neck, but Desta defended himself with an arm. Then the animal attacked whatever he could sink his teeth into, which was Desta's thigh. The dog locked his teeth onto the boy's flesh so firmly that the canine nearly lost his balance. Desta pressed his hand to his own heart and the dog immediately let go of his thigh.

The others had come out, shouting and cursing, but grew silent as they took in the unbelievable scene. The dog that had bit Desta so severely was now docile and repentant. It began licking Desta's wound. The rest of the dogs had vanished. Zewday tried to chase the black dog away from Desta, but it wouldn't leave. It stood at a distance and stared sadly at the boy.

Desta, still traumatized by the event, was helped up by Zewday. With Lesim and Zewday holding Desta by his arms, the boy limped into the house. They laid him on the mattress Lesim had spread in the corner of the living room.

Everyone gathered around him. They wanted to see where and how badly he was bitten. Desta rolled onto his belly. Streaks of blood led their eyes to the bite on the back of his thigh, near his buttocks. Zewday rolled up the leg of Desta's shorts so they could have a full view of the bite. He had four deep wounds where the dog's teeth had pierced him.

"My goodness, that's one vicious dog," said the old woman. "He could have taken a chunk of his flesh if he had had more time."

Zewday said, "The strange thing is, after he bit him, why did he stop? The dog could've done a lot more damage. Instead I found him tenderly licking Desta's leg."

"Desta must have a guardian angel," replied the old woman.

"He is very lucky to escape with just bite marks. Dogs chasing a bitch in heat can be very dangerous," chipped in the old man.

"Desta, do you think you can walk to school and march with your classmates to see the emperor?"

He rolled onto his back and tried to sit up. It was too painful.

"Let's see if you can walk," Zewday said, extending a hand.

Desta rose, took a step, and stopped.

"He'd better stay at home," said the old woman. "In this condition he won't make it to the gate, let alone to the school."

Desta collapsed back to the mattress, sad and disappointed to miss a once-in-a-lifetime opportunity to see the King of Kings and to receive money and clothes from him.

"We better get ready to go ourselves," Zewday said. "Lesim, bring him extra covers and give him his breakfast."

Everybody left to line the streets where the emperor would be driving by. Desta lay on his back and stared at the gold bamboo ceiling. He was angry with himself for accepting Zewday's walking stick as his protector, instead of relying on the much more potent weapon he had on his chest. Had he touched his chest to begin with, he would be out there singing and cheering with his classmates as the emperor arrived in town. He took this experience as a lesson. Never again would he rely on external aids.

His mind drifted back to the people in the streets, his classmates lined up and waving their hands or bowing as their teacher had instructed them. What was more hurtful, he might never receive money or clothes like his classmates would. Who would care to remember and walk up when his name was called? Nobody!

He decided the best thing he could do was banish this whole experience from his mind. By midday, Desta was treating the day's events like a foggy dream.

He closed his eyes, hoping to go to sleep and forget everything that had happened.

When he awoke in the afternoon, Zewday and Mebet were sitting at the dining table and talking.

"You didn't miss much, Desta," Zewday said when he noticed the boy was awake. "The emperor decided to drive straight through to Bahir Dar. But the school has received its share of clothes for the students."

Desta raised his head and cocked his ears. "Say that again."

"After all that preparation, the emperor and his entourage decided to skip the visit to our town. But your school received clothes and other things."

Desta placed his head back on the pillow. "I guess the emperor's visit to our town was not meant to be. What a disappointment it must have been for everybody who so anxiously waited to see him."

"They said for security reasons they needed to get to Bahir Dar in daylight."

"What would happen to him?"

"Who knows? Even kings have enemies. They have to be very careful all the time."

Desta didn't understand how a powerful person like a king would have to fear anything, but he didn't feel like pursuing the discussion. He covered his face and rolled onto his side. His hope of receiving his share of clothes and money had been renewed.

His injuries didn't feel any better the next day, which meant he missed a second day of classes. On the third day he could walk well enough to go to school. He discovered that the emperor had given only clothes and not money. The students who came to school the day after they were delivered had selected all the best clothes. When Desta went to the storeroom, the guard showed him the leftover selection and everything was either too big or too small.

He picked one of the larger jacket and shorts sets assuming he would get it altered to fit him. They were made from a cheap cream-colored fabric and Desta didn't enjoy looking at them let alone wearing them. He ended up giving them to one of Mebet's farmer relatives.

The enigmatic emperor had come and gone. After witnessing the rehearsal the school went through, Desta thought that, yes, the students and townsfolk might feel disappointed, but they had been saved from having to bow until their backs cracked and clap until their hands burned. For him, the scars on the back of his thigh would be persistent reminders of the emperor's visit that never was.

FORTY-FOUR

Desta thought he was hallucinating. He walked west, parting shrubs and tall grass as he went. He moved along the path that went to the neighbors' property and then he ambled back to where he started. Mystified, he scuttled to the eastern length of the same fence, walking to the far corner and then returning to the spot that was as familiar as the back of his hand. He thought at one moment that he might be on the wrong side of Zewday's property and then that he might be in an entirely different coffee grove. It was the kind of experience that only happens in dreams—like people flying in the air and landing in a new location. But he was not dreaming and he was not on the wrong side of the fence. He was in the same familiar place; it was just that the familiar object was gone, the clay jar, which contained what was left of the coffee beans and was now the safe place for his money—all ninety-eight birr he had worked so hard to earn and he had kept to pay for his supplemental food and anything else he might need.

He felt sick all over. He felt naked and vulnerable. He couldn't stand going hungry every night and not being able to go home from his midday meal. He hated the idea of standing at the edge of the field during breaks, watching his classmates play ball, and feeling envious of their energy and strength while he preserved his own so he could make it home at the end of the school day. These images flashed in his head and he got scared.

He closed his eyes and breathed deeply. He placed his right hand on his chest. By degrees he calmed down. As he walked back to the house, he was gripped by fear of a different kind. Who had found that little jar and taken it? Lesim? Mebet? Zewday?

While he could explain the source of his money, there was no plausible reason or explanation for the coffee beans, although only a couple pounds remained.

He saw Lesim in the courtyard and studied her face. No cold, hard look. This was a good sign. He walked into the main house. Mebet was playing with

Tesfa on the high earthen seat. She briefly glanced at him and said nothing. No suspecting or accusative look.

Two down, one more to go, he thought, remembering the line from his English book about the six green bottles on the wall.

If Zewday didn't come out and question him in his sober state, he would most certainly in the evening when he came home drunk. Only one dark cloud left on the horizon. Desta would know by midnight, give or take an hour, whether he was to suffer Zewday's wrath. The waiting was so nerve-racking for Desta that he decided to turn in early. Zewday returned home at his usual time. The alcohol on his breath and clothes filled the air around him. He walked unsteadily across the floor, clambered onto the high earthen embankment, and vanished into the bedroom beyond without saying a word to anyone.

Desta sighed. *Then who found the jar?*

DESTA'S FEAR HAD GRADUALLY but surely begun to bear fruit. The hunger that nearly debilitated him before had returned. He had stopped receiving supplemental meals from Khadija because he had no more beans to sell to Almaz or money of his own.

October and November were pre-harvest months and there was always a shortage of food supplies during this period. Desta's meals were reduced from a half injera to a quarter, with shiro wat poured over the bread only some of the time. In the morning he occasionally received dabo kolo snacks with tea. Other times he got nothing. Then breads and injera prepared from the nutritionally poor dagussa became more prevalent.

One day, Mebet pulled Desta aside and said, "Since your father has not brought any food for you, you will have to earn your keep. Every Friday you will have to go out of town with the neighbor's housekeeper and bring firewood. If you can't do that, you will have to look for your relatives when they come to the market and go home with them."

Mebet might as well have punched him in the stomach. More than even the words, it was her cold, hard stare and the unfeeling and metallic tone she used to deliver them that crushed Desta. He had already felt alone in this tree-shrouded town. Although he had lived with Mebet and the others for nine months, Desta felt as if he had met the woman for the first time. It was not as if the meager food she was giving him was all for nothing. He ran every manner of errand for her and Zewday. He escorted her husband to church every Sunday, babysat her son when she and Lesim went to the market, pulled weeds from underneath the coffee bushes, brought warm water for their hands and face in the morning and evening.

He was not going to stop his school in the middle of the semester and go home. He would have to brave his hardship until Christmastime, and then return home and see what other arrangements for going to school his father could make for him.

Per Mebet's order, he took Friday off and went with the neighbor's servant, Mebrat, and brought firewood. As much as he didn't want to miss his Friday classes, there were some incidental benefits to this arrangement. Mebet fed him well in the morning, saying, "We'll give you enough for both your breakfast and lunch because you won't be returning until late in the afternoon." In the woods where they went to collect dead and dry firewood grew a variety of berries and wild tomatoes. And many of the surrounding crop fields were ripe with barley, wheat, and corn. Desta applied what he had learned from his vervet monkey friends and raided these fields. He collected two or three ears of corn. He snipped the spindles from some wheat and barley stalks, removed the husks, and ate the grain.

He brought some of this bounty home and hid it for snacks that lasted him two or three days. During the week, when his hunger was at its worst, Desta would rise in the middle of the night and go outside with Zewday's flashlight, pretending he was going to the bathroom. He would in fact detour to the grinding stone under the eaves of the kitchen house. With the flashlight he searched for stray beans and peas left after Lesim or Mebet had ground them for sauce— an opportunity he rarely had during the day as either Mebet or Lesim was always around.

Desta kept what little skin he had on his bones through December 1960 by consuming anything he could get his hands on. He still would have liked to go to Bahir Dar to look for the bearer of the coin. He knew that Masud would be willing to take him the next time he went to the city by the lake. However, considering that Zewday frowned upon Desta's associating with the Muslim villagers, he would be creating another problem for himself if he decided to go. Desta still had a standing invitation from Helen's mother, but even that option wasn't appealing to him considering his state of mind and his relationship with his host family. Although he felt the sting of having to put Bahir Dar on hold indefinitely, he was happy when Christmas was at long last around the corner.

He could go home, eat as much as he wanted, and finally say, "I'm full; I've had enough," a luxury he rarely had since coming to live in Dangila.

Desta was equally hungry for the people at home who would give him a hug, show him tenderness, put their arms around his shoulders, and say that everything would be okay—that he would make it one day. He could find one or two people who would extend to him this kindness and affection.

When his first-semester results came, Desta was declared one of the top three students in his class and was therefore privileged to go on to the fourth grade after the Christmas break. He knew he might not return to Dangila to take advantage of this privilege, but he also knew that he could continue his fourth grade lessons at the Yeedib school, assuming he could find someone to live with.

A few days before his anticipated trip home, he went around and said goodbye to Masud, Khadija, and Almaz, who gave him a one-birr note so he could buy breakfast and lunch at Khadija's restaurant. He visited Colonel Asheber and Tigist and Helen and wished them a merry Christmas and thanked them for their attempt to bring him to Bahir Dar.

Desta rose while the morning was still gray. He gathered his belongings and put them in his cloth pouch. Lesim offered to make a fire and warm something for him to eat. Desta declined the offer. He needed to be on the road before the sun got hot. Now that he had decided to go home, he was anxious to part with this family and the town and get to the open spaces—to smell the fresh and clean country air.

He had already said good-bye to Zewday and Mebet the night before. He owed nothing to anyone and he was ready to leave. Lesim hugged and kissed him. He walked briskly out of the compound into the graphite-gray morning.

Home was not where Desta would have liked to go under the circumstances. He didn't want to prove Teferra right by "coming running back home when you can no longer stand the hunger and deprivation that come from living in town."

He was disappointed he hadn't made it to Bahir Dar. But he had made progress with his studies. He was now in the fourth grade. He got to experience living in a big town. He had met many good people, and he was not *running* back home. He was *going* back home, with one broken tooth, to regroup and make plans for his future.

He reached Aunt Zere's home at noon. "Have you been sick?" Almaw asked when he saw the boy. "You look awfully thin since the last time I saw you."

"No, I have not been sick."

"What happened then? . . . You must be hungry and tired." Almaw patted Desta's shoulder. "Mother will be happy you're here."

When they went inside, the house was half dark. Desta was grateful. The last thing he wanted was to be an object of curiosity and the recipient of a barrage of questions. Aunt Zere could only touch him and hear his voice. Her eyes had gotten worse since he saw her nearly a year ago.

Almaw's wife brought Desta food and drink, which he ate appreciatively. After his meal, the boy shared his plans with Almaw. He needed to go to bed early and get up early as he intended to make it home the following day, a journey that he knew would take at least ten hours. This intention also lessened the chances of his meeting more of Aunt Zere's children and having to answer too many questions about his condition.

That evening, Desta went to bed right after his meal, although it was far from his usual bedtime. The following morning, he rose half an hour before dawn and ate his breakfast of injera with freshly made shiro wat.

"This is the only meal you will have until you get home tonight," Almaw reminded him after seeing he had left a full injera and some of the wat. "Make sure to fill yourself up well."

"I have not had this much to eat in a long time. Thank you so much."

Desta gathered up his things and left after he kissed Aunt Zere's knee and she kissed his cheeks. Almaw escorted him out of the compound. "Give your parents, brothers, and sisters our best wishes for the holiday," Almaw said. He hugged and kissed the boy, and Desta got on his way. The sky above the eastern horizon was veiled with ribbons of gray and crimson that progressively morphed into fiery red. When the yellow disk of the sun finally emerged, splashing the sky in white and gold, Desta turned and took one more look into the gray haze that smothered Dangila, where only the day before he had left his sorrow, disappointment, hunger, and pain.

FORTY-FIVE

January 1961

When Desta finally reached the cattle field below his home, the sun had just touched the ridge above. He was happy to come to familiar terrain, to his stomping grounds and the site of his childhood memories. The cattle had their faces turned toward home, and the hired shepherd stood on the edge of the field.

Desta was hungry and thirsty. Although the boy didn't usually like his mother's cooking, for once he was looking forward to it. The last mile seemed to get longer and harder to travel. When he turned the final corner, he saw Ayénat coming out of the house with something in her hand.

Desta smiled at her.

"Era," she said with a cold, hard stare.

Desta's smile instantly vanished. *What is that supposed to mean?* he thought to himself.

As he walked toward his mother, Desta sensed an invisible barrier rising, ready to bar him from coming nearer to her or the entrance to his home. The hard ground beneath his feet was turning into quicksand. His mouth went dry and his stomach tightened as if trying to squeeze out his hunger and stop his mouth from salivating. At this moment he was unable to feel his tired limbs; they had become immobile. It seemed Ayénat's gaze had put the boy into a kind of trance.

"How are you, mama?" Desta asked, finally, when he came to his senses. With these kind words, he had hoped to break her icy stare. He had never seen his mother behave like this before. He feared she might even harm him physically, that the anger she had been harboring had finally gotten the best of her and was now flowing out at the mere sight of him.

She took a couple of steps toward him. "I suppose you expect me to receive you with open arms after you abandoned our family in search of a Saytan education and after you cast aside Christianity, the religion of your family, and adopted Islam. Our friends have been telling us we committed a grave sin for allowing you to get that kind of education, and now your father's soul and my soul are going to burn in *Isate-gomera*—fire and brimstone."

Desta was numb and at a loss for words again. He realized that nothing he could say would convince her of his innocence.

Ayénat took two more steps closer to the invisible barrier between them. "If I didn't fear God or the criticism of the valley people, I would send you back to the people that converted you to your new religion. Tomorrow is Christmas and you probably came to celebrate it with us. This is what we need to do: I cannot accept you into the house or even touch you because by becoming Muslim and eating Muslim food you have defiled your body and your spirit. We need to invite a priest here to recite biblical verses and bless you with the cross. Then you can come into the house and be a part of the celebration tomorrow."

She continued in a more conciliatory tone. "For tonight, we'll see whether you'll be accepted at Saba's house. Early tomorrow morning I will send for one of the priests from across the river, even if I have to pay him for the inconvenience this presents on our Lord's holiday. Doing this will also immunize us from scandal, since many of the people in the valley have already heard about you."

Desta's nerves eased a little. "Can I tell you something?"

"What? Deny that you have gone to an Islamic church and have been eating the meat of animals they killed?" When Desta didn't reply, she said, "That you look so emaciated indicates your new religion and food do not suit you. Perhaps it is even the result of God's punishment for abandoning Him and your faith."

"I've not converted to *Islam*. . . . Their church is called mesgid, by the way," Desta said, appealing to her with beseeching eyes and voice.

Ayénat tilted her head one way and then the other as if searching for something in Desta's appearance. "Pull down your gabi from your neck!"

Mystified by this unexpected request, Desta complied.

"See!" she shouted triumphantly. "You have not a single mateb."

By Ayénat's test of a person's Christianity, Desta was unequivocally Muslim because he didn't wear a mateb—chord—around his neck. He realized it would be futile to engage in any further dialogue. "Okay, can you at least give me a cup of water? I'm very thirsty."

"I cannot afford to throw away my *tsiwa*—clay cup. We certainly can't use it again if you drink out of it. Didn't you cross the Davola River?"

Desta still couldn't believe his ears. "Okay, I hope Saba will accept her Muslim brother. Merry Christmas!" he said, walking back to the path that had brought him home.

At a section of the fence where a few posts had fallen, he entered his mother's now-empty vegetable garden, crossed it, and headed toward Saba's house.

Saba was gathering clothes she had left to dry in the sun. When she saw Desta, she dropped the clothes in a basket and rushed to him. She embraced and kissed him three times on the cheeks. "When did you come?"

"Just a short while ago."

"How wonderful! Yihoon and I have been talking about you often, particularly in the last few months. . . . Come inside. . . . You must be hungry and thirsty, and exhausted, too, I am sure. I have walked the road you came on more than once." She clutched him by the hand and they walked toward the house. "Anyway, we were planning to come see you after the Christmas celebration. Now that you're here, you've denied us the pleasure of surprising you." She smiled.

Desta said, "It would have been a huge surprise indeed, considering I did not have any visitors from here other than father, who came with grains after Easter."

"We wanted to see you because it had been nearly a year since you left home and we hadn't heard much news about you in all that time. . . . We can talk about these things later. Get something to eat and drink first."

Once Desta was inside, Saba brought food and tella, and water for his hands. She perched on a stool next to him. "How has everything been with you?" she asked.

"Not as well as I have wanted it to be, but I have managed."

"We heard conflicting stories about your condition and the things that have been going on with you." Desta looked at her questioningly. "Go ahead and eat first. We'll have plenty of time to visit."

Saba's son, Destaye, woke. He rubbed one of his eyes as he stumbled toward his mother. Saba engulfed him in her arms. "Do you remember Desta?" she asked, pointing to her brother.

Destaye shook his head no.

"You should always remember Uncle Desta. It is because of him that you're here. . . . The short memory span of children." She smiled at Desta. "I've told him many times about you and the role you have played in his life."

"I've done nothing. . . ." Desta replied after he swallowed his bite. "He has grown so big."

"He has been fed and cared for well," Saba said. She brushed off lint and grass specks from her son's hair while he stood between her legs. "You might want to take a nap before Yihoon comes. That way you two can visit for a longer time. I am sure he has a lot of questions about your life in Dangila, as do I for that matter."

"I'm afraid if I lie down, I am not going to wake until tomorrow morning. I'll stay up as long as I can. And we have many days ahead to spend time with each other." He placed another bite in his mouth.

Saba fussed with her son's hair, and rubbed and caressed his neck and shoulders. After Desta finished eating, she brought him water for his hands and collected the serving platter. She then came and sat next to him. "If you're not going to nap, we might as well visit for a while." Saba said.

She first asked him about the well-being of Aunt Zere and her children, their animals, and their crops. After hearing Desta's response, she segued into something personal. "Anyway, the other reason we wanted to come see you was to confirm for ourselves some of the wild rumors we had been hearing."

"Which are . . . ?"

"When father returned from seeing you, we heard that the people you were living with had not been feeding you well. Then when Almaw came to report after he saw you last June, he said the town's food and water had not been suitable to you and that you had lost substantial weight, which is very apparent from looking at you. And then came the rumor that sent shockwaves throughout the valley. We don't know where it came from or who let it out of the family circle—whether perhaps Almaw shared it after seeing you. For all we know it could have been Damtew, or Teferra, or even your mother. If it indeed is true, why did you do it?"

"You have not been clear about the matter that shocked the valley, but having just come from talking to mother, it's not hard to figure out what you are referring to. To give you my simple answer, I've not become a Muslim." Desta would have liked to add, "And why should it be a problem if I did choose to become one?" but he didn't say it. He didn't want to confuse the issue.

"What is this story of your going to their church and eating their meat and spending a lot of time with them at the expense of your schoolwork?"

"Their church is called mesgid. I did befriend a couple of Muslims but not at the expense of my schoolwork. And let me say it one last time: I've not become a Muslim. If you don't mind, I would like to take you up on your earlier offer. I'd like to lie down for a while. As you know, I have been on the road all day."

"I'm sorry. I didn't mean to bother you with it. It's just something that's been on my mind. We can talk about it more another time."

Saba rose and made Desta's bed in Astaire and Zena's old room, spreading a plush cowhide over a pad of dry grass and a heavy cotton blanket. Desta washed his hands, thanked Saba, and clambered up to his retreat for the night.

WHEN DESTA WOKE the following morning, Saba's hand was on his shoulder. She shook him a little. Desta turned over. He gnashed his teeth and stretched his arms, brushing against Saba's arm as he did. "There is a young man who wants to see you. Can you get up?"

"A young man? To see me?" Desta asked once he was fully awakened.

"A young priest."

Desta groaned. "I know who sent him. Tell him I am not feeling well and I cannot get out of bed."

"Is there something I should know?"

"Saba, just tell him what I told you. I will share the story with you later."

Saba went out, but to Desta's surprise, she returned with the man trailing behind her.

Desta tucked the blanket around him and covered his face.

Saba tapped him again. "Desta, can you pull the blanket down? He wants to talk to you."

"No, I'm not talking to anyone. I need to sleep."

"Desta," the priest said, "I am here because your mother wanted me to say some prayers and bless you with holy water and the cross. She wants you to come home and be a part of the Christmas celebration."

Desta felt the hair stand on the back of his neck. His horrid experience with the head priest's holy water treatment years ago flashed in his mind. He peeled the blanket from his face and sat up. The man who peered down on him was not more than twenty-five years old. A thin white timtim wreathed his crown. He had soft, soulful eyes and a kind and pleasant face.

"I'm not going to let you touch me with your cross or holy water, and I certainly don't need your prayers," Desta declared. "I am not going to let my mother pull a fast one on me again."

Saba told the priest. "He had a traumatic experience once with holy water and the cross. Obviously, you have touched something painful in his consciousness. It is better we leave him alone."

"I'm sorry he feels this way. I certainly am not experienced to handle matters like this. The head priest sent me because he couldn't come, today being Christmas."

Saba led the man to the door. They chatted for a bit outside, and when she returned, she said, "I'm mystified by all this. Can you tell me what exactly is going on?"

Desta told her about his mother's refusal to come near him or let him into the house because she believed he had become a Muslim, and she had promised to send a priest to bless him.

"She did that? She said that? She called you *erkoos*—defiled, dirty, untouchable, unapproachable?" Saba said as Desta narrated his experience with Ayénat. "Your mother certainly is a good proponent of our uncompromising religion. As you know, the church treats us women as if we are dirty and untouchable when we are having our periods or have just given birth. If we do go to church then, we are relegated to the fringe of the church property. Father told me that in some of the ancient churches on the islands of Lake Tana, women cannot set foot on the dry earth let alone come near the church precinct.

"It certainly is not pleasant to feel unwelcome or be treated like an outcast. . . . I share your sentiments. I can understand if you don't feel like celebrating Christmas under your mother's conditions. You can celebrate it with us and stay here as long as you want. Now let me ask you this. Are Muslim people like us or are they like Ferenges?"

Desta was not quite sure how to answer this pointed but sincere question. He thought for a few seconds. "They are like us," he said finally. "They just happen to have a different *haimanote*—religion."

"All I know about them is that old expression people use whenever they want their wish or promise fulfilled: If you don't come to my wedding . . . or if you don't give me such and such . . . or your mother saying, if you don't comply with my demand to be blessed by the priest, you and I will be like Islamist and Amhara." Saba tried to smile at her sarcastic joke.

Desta replied, "She doesn't amount to anything in my life. . . . Just to correct you though, whoever started the expression probably meant 'Muslim and Christian' because Muslims can be Amharas or from other tribes."

"Now you go back to sleep, or get up and keep me company. I need to get started with all the things I have to do for the holiday."

"Okay, I will sleep some more. I could sleep for another full day and still not have enough. This is one of the few nights I have slept eight hours without being awakened.

"Good! Please make yourself comfortable. I am sorry you have not seen Yihoon yet. He left before you woke. He went with Baba across the river to kill a cow for the holiday. He should return by noon." Saba walked off to her chores. Desta scurried to the door and went outside for his morning rituals. After he returned, he went straight to bed.

When he woke at noon, Yihoon and Abraham were at his bedside. He dismounted from the high earthen bed and kissed the two men. Yihoon said he was very happy to see him. He had been in his and Saba's thoughts for some time. Abraham apologized for not having gone to see him; the damage he had sustained to his leg had left him disabled for long trips.

Abraham invited Desta for a private meeting outside. They sat side by side on a bench and talked at length, touching on the topic of Desta's alleged conversion to the Islamic faith. Desta told him the full story, hiding and editing nothing. Finally, the conversation turned to his refusal to receive the cross blessing and the holy water treatment by the priest who Ayénat had arranged for him. Desta gave his account firmly, giving no indication of changing his mind or showing a willingness to compromise. "I will talk to her and send someone to inform you when you can come and spend the holiday with us," Abraham said finally and left.

Late in the afternoon, Yihoon and Saba dressed in their finest clothes and prepared to go for Christmas dinner. Saba approached Desta. "Will you change your mind and come with us? It's a shame you have to be here by yourself while everybody is gathered at your parents' to celebrate *Lidet*—Christ's birth."

"Today is my birthday, too, if any of my family cared to remember it." Desta held back the sudden emotion that surged through him.

"Oh, that is right," Saba said. "It's that much more important you come with us. We can celebrate your birthday."

Desta didn't like Saba's scrambling for anything credible to persuade him to go with them. Her voice and words sounded hollow, attributes he wouldn't usually have ascribed to her. But he understood. His family had never celebrated his birthday before, and he did not expect them to now. "No, Saba. I have long lost my interest in family gatherings. I won't miss a thing. Don't worry about it." He waved at his sister to go.

Saba wiped a lone tear from the corner of her eye. "Okay," she said, her voice cracking. "You have done things your own way since you were little. And there is nothing I can do to make you change your mind. Yihoon and I will be back as soon as dinner is finished. In the meantime, if you are hungry, I have left you food in the mosseb by the kitchen. Otherwise, go back to bed and rest if you still need it."

"Thank you. Have a good time." He watched as Saba followed Yihoon and Destaye with a halting gait.

At that moment, Desta saw Ayénat's refusal to let him into the house as a veiled blessing. He didn't want the rest of the family, particularly Damtew and Teferra, to see his emaciated frame and snicker. Even more humiliating to Desta would be for one of them to turn to Ayénat and whisper, "See? I told you so. Let's see what he can do next. He will have no option but to stay put like he should have."

Desta decided to take a walk. He needed to think. He felt helpless and alone now that he was back at home with very few options left to him for pursuing his education and searching for the magic coin. Finding someone to live with so he could go to school was something he didn't want to bother himself with for the time being. He still had two weeks before school resumed. First he needed to think through the unexpected problem with his mother.

He wanted to go to the Davola River, lay next to it, and listen to the water tumble over the granite rocks, gurgling, bubbling, and frothing as it went down the crevasses and climbed over stones big and small. He wanted his vital force to be in sync with that of the water, hopefully relaxing his nerves and lulling his mind into reverie.

He walked down a path Yihoon had created and linked up with the caravan route at the valley floor. Two long fences bordered the path. The valley was eerily quiet. There was nobody on the main thoroughfare by the river or on any of the footpaths, which traversed the slopes like termite tracks, and there was no movement of animals in the fields or in the trees along the creeks. The only sound was the thin whisper of the waterfall high up in the eastern mountains.

Desta's eyes brimmed as he thought of all the bad things that happened to him in Dangila, his frustrated attempt to go to Bahir Dar, and his problem with his mother that kept him from being a part of the Christmas festivities. Then when he thought about having no one to live with when school opened in two weeks, his tears flowed quietly.

At that moment all he wanted was his grandfather's spirit to be there by his side—to counsel him and tell him that things would work out, that somehow he would finish his education and find the coin. *That would be*, he thought through his sniffles, *a great holiday family reunion and a special birthday gift.* The idea was so exciting that instead of going to the Davola River, he decided to visit the sholla tree in the field below his parents' home and the ravine where his grandfather's remains used to be. His heart leaped at the idea that by some miracle he would meet the Cloud Man again today. He wiped his tears with the pad of his palm and his nose with his fingers.

He crossed the rocky field first and then the creek and the wooded section of his parents' property. When he finally emerged into the open field, the old sholla tree loomed on his left. It was this tree that had provided Desta comfort and shelter from the rain and the sun. It was under this tree that his grandfather's spirit revealed so much about his own past, the family treasure, Desta's future and the coin, and in the process freeing Abraham from his emotional shackles.

It was here under the great tree that Desta had spent some of his happiest moments. He wanted to sit on the same granite rock under the leafy branches and try to reclaim some of the joyous moments of his past, to find comfort, happiness, and freedom from his fears.

So he came and perched on the rock. He scanned his surroundings and noticed there were fewer trees along the river and the creeks beyond, obviously cut down for firewood or home construction or because his family needed more fertile land. Nonetheless, to arrive here was like coming full circle, as round as the sun and rolling as the coin on his chest.

The day was so hot that the air shimmered around him outside the shadow of the tree, screening much of the farther view. It was while Desta kept his eyes on this pale, dust-like phenomenon, thinking about the happy moments with his grandfather's spirit, that he saw a familiar figure emerge, draped in white cotton chiffon from head to toe.

"Good afternoon," Eleni said, parting the cloth from her face. She tucked a small shy smile into the corner of her cheek.

"Good afternoon," Desta said guardedly. As much as he had come here to be alone and think through his problems, he didn't mind having someone to talk to. It would divert his attention from his dilemma for a while. "You have an amazing ability to show up at unexpected places and moments, don't you?"

"I understand that things have not been good since you arrived here. I thought you might need company since you're all alone while your family gathers to celebrate the holiday."

"You're wrong," Desta snapped. "I am never alone. I have my thoughts for company." He gazed at her.

Eleni flinched. "Well," she said, "I certainly didn't mean to upset you. I just stopped by to explain things to help you deal better with the situation with your mother."

"What're you driving at?" the boy asked.

"I think if you realized what exactly is going on, you could be forgiving, even sympathetic, toward your mother. This realization could help you deal with her moods better and accept the things you have no power to change. You could then have peace of mind. . . ." Eleni sat on the grass next to him. "What I have to share will need a little time and a careful explanation."

Desta shifted on his seat, uneasy and baffled. He stared at her like he was awaiting a verdict.

"How your mother and most of your immediate relatives treat you is described in the records that tell your story. In other words, many of your problems with your family are a consequence of the ambitious journey your grandfather's spirit said you're destined to take. If you could abandon the idea of looking for the other coin, I think your relationships with most of your family would change dramatically for the better."

"I don't exactly follow what you're saying."

"Let me explain differently. King Solomon had the two magical coins with their twenty-one encoded legends made as gifts for the descendants of his two children. It turns out, although not many knew this, the two coins became a symbol of duality, the two-ness that exists in the universe. These are things like night and day, hot and cold, love and hate, boy and girl. In fact, everything we see around us is held together by this fundamental balance that exists in the world.

"If you find the second coin and unite it with the one you own—thereby creating one coin—that balance will be violated. For this reason, a team of Winds was assigned to try to influence the births of the last destined coin bearers, the seventh child in each family. As it turns out, the Winds were unable to affect the births. Therefore, they were directed to get to know the coin bearers and explain to them the consequences of their efforts. I was assigned to work with you.

"Influence our births?"

"Yes. Things are a bit more complicated than you think. The Wind who was assigned to work with the other family inadvertently caused the seventh born to be a hermaphrodite. This is Marva and Kamala who inherited the coin but can't reproduce and so will have no heirs who can pass it on to the next generation.

"That you were born two months premature and still survived was not an accident. It was because your intended abortion was somehow averted. I suspect your grandfather's spirit, who lived in this valley those many years, waiting for your conception and birth, may have ultimately influenced the outcome. You eventually inherited your family's coin and now search for the second coin. I tell you again that this is a dangerous thing to do—uniting the two coins. It would violate the balance of things."

"But my grandpa's spirit said it's for good reasons why the two coins must unite," Desta whimpered.

"Yes, but there are a lot of things your grandpa's spirit didn't know. He didn't even know who had the second coin or what this person looks like. . . . We do. All the problems you have had from your conception to your birth to the present are connected to this coin-finding mission he told you to pursue. . . . Worse things could happen to you yet," Eleni said, arching her brow.

"But I have my protection here," Desta said, pointing to his breast.

Eleni recoiled. "Don't continue to be fooled. . . . For now, cheer up. You have no control over your mother's behavior, as she has no control over it herself. As you must know, I care for you. That's why I came to see you, hoping to cast a positive light on this otherwise dismal day. I must go now. See you sometime soon." Eleni rose, shook her garment, and flared it out with both hands, waiting for the force of the air. She soon levitated and vanished.

AT MIDAFTERNOON Desta retuned to Saba and Yihoon's house. He felt peaceful and clearheaded after spending much of the day out on his own, but he was also sad that the Cloud Man had not shown. *Would he ever?* Desta wondered. The last time they saw each other he said he would never appear again except in his dreams, but even that had not happened.

He ate the food Saba had left him. Then, feeling fatigued from the long hours of walking in the sun, and having not much else to do, he napped until his sister and her family returned. Saba found Desta wide awake on the high earthen platform bed and invited him to come and eat his share of the Christmas dinner, which Ayénat had sent.

A sudden tide of emotion rose within him, causing his nerves to tense and his mouth to go dry. He wanted to say something, but the right words didn't come fast enough. "Glad you guys are back. I was getting a little bored," he said instead, out of the sheer need to acknowledge his sister.

"I'm sorry things turned out the way they have between you and your mother, and before you even set foot in your parent's home after being away for so long. And that you couldn't be a part of the family on such big holiday." Saba's voice took a brighter tone. "Get up. I have brought a good amount of food. There's beef and a lamb leg from Baba. The beef cubes and injera are from your mother."

Desta rose and followed Saba to the fireplace.

"Come, sit here," she said, pulling her husband's seat forward. "Yihoon is out gathering the animals and putting them in their pens."

Saba fetched a can of water and a straw tray from the back room and placed them on a wooden pedestal near Desta. She removed the lid of the basket that contained Desta's Christmas dinner and took out the two folded injeras, spreading them on the platter. With a long wooden spoon, she scooped sauce onto the injeras. She then served the cubed beef and the leg of lamb.

"Here, wash your hands and eat your dinner," said Saba, bending a little as she offered the can of hand water.

"You can give me the can," Desta said.

Saba hesitated. "I will not feel insulted by pouring the water over your hands while you wash them. I know I am much older than you, but that's not relevant here."

"It's not that," Desta said, his voice trailing. "Let me have it."

She gave him the can of water and he set it aside.

"Please sit down, Saba."

"Something wrong?" Saba asked, her brow knitted in confusion. She sat next to Desta on the skin mat.

Desta turned to his sister. "Do you think I will eat this dog food?" he asked, gazing at her. "She treated me like a dog—erkoos—who's not allowed to come inside the house and who receives his food outdoors."

"You've lost me," Saba said, batting her eyes.

"I can't believe she bothered to send me food if she wouldn't allow me to come inside the house. This is adding insult to injury. When we were children, most dogs couldn't come indoors because they were considered erkoos or dirty. In her mind, I am like one of those dogs. Please take the food away and cover it."

"This is Christmas."

"Not for me."

"Have the leg of lamb. It was meant for me, but I saved it for you."

"I appreciate it, Saba. I am not hungry. After spending most of the day outside, I got back a while ago and filled up with the food you left me. So I am fine."

"It was not much and had no meat in it."

"It certainly was a lot more than I was eating in Dangila." Another wave of emotion surged through Desta, this time of fear. He had just realized he would not be going back to Dangila. His education and the search for the coin were on indefinite hold. He knew that in a few days he was going to feel like he was starting all over again. He had been in exactly the same spot last year, trying to find someone to live with while he continued with his schooling, a circle that was too familiar to him.

Saba said, "Let me make some *tibis*—sauté cubed meat—from our share of the cow meat Yihoon brought this afternoon. Tomorrow is our turn to host the family dinner. You don't have to wait until then to eat our holiday meat dishes."

"No, Saba, no. I don't feel like I'm missing anything. We can visit for a while, though."

Saba tipped her head sideways and wiped a tear from the corner of her eye. She rose and took the food to the back room.

Yihoon came in and while he and Desta chatted, Saba remained in the back room preparing things for the next day's dinner party.

When Yihoon went to bed, Desta remained seated partly because he was wide awake and partly because he wanted to visit with Saba some more. She finished her chores and came to the living room. "You still awake?" she asked.

"I slept well last night and napped some this evening, so I'm okay."

"In that case, let me finish what I'm doing and then I've things to ask you."

Saba returned. Her face and eyes looked thoughtful, as if she had been cogitating over things that bothered her. She sat next to her brother and said, "Tell me, if you say you have not become a Muslim, how did the whole rumor start? In a way I don't blame your mother for demanding you get blessed by the cross and receive a holy water treatment before you entered her house. Shortly after the rumor began, the head priest visited your parents. Apparently, he was very upset at them for sending you to such a faraway place and exposing you to the impure and depraved town life. He said that one of his parishioner's sons had become a Muslim and that was very unacceptable. If father had not had that accident with his leg in September, he would have come to get you. So your mother was probably following the priest's advice when she refused to come near you or let you into the house. You know how devoted she is to her faith." She glanced at Desta to check if he was listening.

Desta had listened quietly, staring at the fire. He sighed. "That's a lot you threw at me, Saba. Let me just say that I'm sure father didn't take the priest seriously and that I have no empathy for mother, allowing her aba to drum fire and hell into her head on my account. And I cannot accept the excuse you're making on her behalf for treating me the way she did when I arrived yesterday and like a dog this evening. If she were as devoted to her son as she is to her religion, she would have come to Dangila and found out the truth for herself."

Desta cleared his throat. He picked up a charred piece of smoking wood and dropped it into the glowing embers. It flamed immediately.

Desta looked at Saba, who seemed deep in thought, and said, "I'll tell you my side of the story."

The boy proceeded to tell Saba what actually happened in his association with the Muslims. That a kind woman named Almaz, who had noticed his emaciated body, arranged with Khadija, the Muslim restaurateur, for Desta to get supplemental meals from her. That through Khadija he met the father and son merchants, Sheik Ibrahim and Masud, who offered to help him find the woman with the coin. That because many of the Muslim merchants traveled to faraway places, Sheik Ibrahim and Masud had suggested he come to their mesgid so Desta could meet more businessmen who could help him spread the information about the woman he was looking for. And that he was at the mesgid just one time.

Then he told her how nice and helpful Sheik Ibrahim and Masud had been in other ways. That they helped him with materials for the Enkutatashi flowers he wanted to draw and present to people so he could collect money in exchange. And that Masud passed out his drawings to other merchants and collected money from most of the people who took them. Finally, how Masud gave him fabric of his choosing from which Desta had his shorts and jacket made. And that what he had on was made from the fabric Masud had given him as a gift. Desta had paid for their tailoring.

Saba said nothing. She stared into the darkness past the fireplace, her lips firm, waiting for the right moment to ask the questions that flowed through her head.

"How do you know they didn't do all those things for you so it would be easy for them to convert you to Islam?"

"They did all these things for me out of the goodness of their hearts. They were not trying to buy me. The subject of religion never even came up the whole time I was with them." Desta was disappointed with Saba.

"Let me ask you something else," Saba said, withdrawing her gaze and glancing at him. "Did you ever eat their meat?"

"What do you think would happen if I did?"

"Well, the animals they kill are probably not blessed the way we bless ours before we slaughter them."

"Actually, they do bless the animals they kill. Do you know what they say right before they kill an animal?"

Saba looked at him.

"*Bismillahi*."

"What does that mean?"

"In the name of God."

"That's what we say—*besimam wold*."

"Yes. We say the same thing. The only difference is the language."

"We don't eat each other's meat because of words that sound different but mean the same thing?" Saba echoed, surprised.

"In a nutshell, yes."

"What do we do about this?"

"Nothing," Desta responded. "We individuals have no power to change things. But have to learn not to let ignorance influence our thoughts and the feelings we have toward other people. I say this because although the belief and attitude I have toward my own religion hasn't changed, the time I spent with Khadija, Masud, and Sheik Ibrahim was a great education."

Saba studied Desta's face. "I must say, you think and talk like you have been around for many years, not just—how old are you now?"

"Today is my twelfth birthday."

"You always talked like an adult before, but now even more so."

"Thanks, Saba. It's getting late. Let's go to bed. We can continue our conversation later," Desta said, getting up.

"Okay," Saba said, also getting up. "Sleep well. Thanks for clarifying all the questions I had."

Because she was the eldest of Desta's siblings, Saba always gave the second Christmas dinner. All the relatives were expected to attend. Since dawn Saba had been bustling to get everything ready for the dinner party.

To avoid another rejection by his mother and the slew of questions from his brothers and sisters-in-law about his rumored conversion, Desta decided to skip the dinner. Much to his sister and brother-in-law's chagrin, he decided to go across the Davola River and spend the day with Awoke—his cousin and teacher.

Awoke lived with his parents, Yisehak Worku, Desta's great uncle and his wife Shashay Bedilu, at the foot of the eastern mountains. All the grown children from Yisehak's previous marriage lived far away and rarely came to celebrate the holiday with them. Awoke was the only child to his mother, Shashay, and the last progeny of his father.

Yisehak was eighty years old, but with his halo of completely white hair, wizened skin, and missing front teeth, he looked more ancient than his years. Yet he was healthy and strong, blessings he attributed to eating wholesome foods, drinking milk, and walking the fields all day looking after his large herd of cattle.

Yisehak draped himself with a large gabi, its open skirt allowing fresh air to drift up and bathe his body, another contributor to his healthy life. His only companion during the day, other than his cattle, was his long solid-wood walking stick, which he leaned on when he got tired. Also, he threw it across his shoulders to balance his arms on and used it to drive and gather his animals.

Awoke's mother, Shashay, was about fifty years old, with jet-black silky hair that she kept short and oiled with butter. Her skin was the lighter color of the earth and etched with very few visible lines. Shashay was a homemaker, although not exactly famous for it. Desta's sisters always complained that Shashay's living room was often cluttered with pots and pans and clothes and sacks of things.

About noon, after helping Saba and Yihoon with some miscellaneous tasks, Desta left to visit Awoke and his parents. He felt happy and peaceful as he walked down the cow field, his old stomping grounds. He was relieved that he wouldn't have to pretend and force a smile—kiss and be kissed by people who meant little to him.

Awoke's eyes popped when he saw Desta. His feet stopped in their tracks. He put a hand to his brow and stared at Desta, trying to determine whether this was an apparition that stood before him.

Desta had rarely visited his cousin when he lived at home. He was too busy with the animals. Now he had materialized out of thin air when he was supposed to be in Dangila, and come on the second day of Christmas, when children are usually with their family, all of which was a shock and a surprise to Awoke.

"Era! Are you Desta?"

"Awwe," replied the visitor, smiling broadly. Desta was pleased to see the stunned look of his mentor and teacher.

"This is hard to believe," Awoke said, stepping forward to kiss his cousin three times on alternating cheeks. "When did you come?"

Desta told him.

"Just yesterday we were talking about you and wondering if we'd ever see you again. It's just about a year since you were here, right?"

Desta nodded his head in acknowledgment.

"Come in. We were about to sit for lunch. My parents will be stunned, too." Awoke led Desta toward the entrance of his home. He said, "Just follow behind me. I'll keep quiet. Let's see how my mother reacts when she sees you." Awoke smiled. "My father's reaction will be delayed by a minute or two, until we tell him. His eyes are not good anymore."

"Who do you have behind you?" Shashay asked, tipping her head to see around Awoke for a clearer view of the figure following her son.

"We have a visitor; can you guess?" Awoke asked, grinning.

Shashay squinted some more at the visitor, turning her head one way then the other. "Not one of your nephews, is he?"

Awoke said he was not. Shashay rose and took a few steps toward the figure before her. "This is Desta!" she cried out, lunging toward the boy. She hugged and kissed him several times on his cheeks. She ran her fingers through his hair and asked him about his health, his life in town, and his schooling.

"Desta? Abraha's son? He is here?" Yisehak asked, shooting a glance across the fireplace. Yisehak always called his nephew *Abraha*.

Awoke told his father that the visitor was in fact Desta. Shashay let go of the boy so Desta could kiss his great uncle. He kissed the old man's knee first and then he thrust his head forward so Yisehak could kiss him on his cheeks.

Desta settled on a stool, on the plush cowhide, between Yisehak and Awoke. Shashay got busy with the lunch she was about to serve. Yisehak asked Desta about his general well-being, his schooling, the town of Dangila, and his relatives in Kuakura. He answered each question, glad that they had nothing to do with his becoming a Muslim.

Lunch consisted of injera with a *siga*—meat wat and tibis, both from the same cow that Desta's family had feasted on. Yisehak's family was part of the group that annually killed a cow and shared its meat.

After the meal, Desta and Awoke went out. The cousins were excited to catch up with what had happened to them since the last time they saw each other.

Desta gave a summary of what happened to him in Dangila, leaving out some of the more horrific details. Neither Awoke nor his parents had mentioned the rumor about his conversion to Islam, so Desta was happy not to bring it up. They attended a different church and probably hadn't caught a whiff of the gossip that had been milling around his parents' church and had circulated in the rest of the valley.

Awoke shared with Desta that he was now a bona fide farmer. He still read his religious books and transcribed letters and court cases for people. His parents had arranged that in four months' time he was to be married.

Desta told him he was happy for him and wished him well for his upcoming wedding. He looked away for a few seconds and then looked up, his eyes landing on his cousin's prominent nose. "Do you know it was because of you that I am in asquala temareebet now?" he asked, looking at Awoke with gratitude.

"No, it's because of your own drive that you're in asquala temareebet," Awoke said humbly. "I only got you started to learn the Amharic alphabet."

"Without that beginning I wouldn't have discovered the power of reading and writing. I thank you for that. I never had a chance to say this before. By the way . . . do you remember those strange characters at the bottom of our alphabet?" Desta asked thoughtfully.

"Yes," Awoke said, searching Desta's face.

"They are the English alphabet. If you still have your fidel I can teach you how to say them."

Awoke dashed to the house and retuned with his old, now tattered booklet containing the alphabets. He gave it to Desta.

They sat on the grass and leaned against the fence that ran along Shashay's vegetable garden. Desta snipped the longest straw he could find from a tuft of grass near the fencepost. Desta opened the pamphlet to the second page, his head nearly touching Awoke's. Using the straw as a pointer, he began to recite, "A, B, C, D . . ." Awoke repeated after his new teacher. They repeated the letters several times, taking breaks in between, then Desta closed the fidel and asked his cousin to recite them back. To his pleasant surprise, Awoke remembered more than half of them.

When he felt that his cousin knew enough of the alphabet, Desta started showing him how to combine the letters to form words and names, starting with their own. Awoke was pleased to discover that there were fewer letters in English—26 as opposed to 256 in Amharic—and they were easier to remember.

The sun had tipped into the western sky above the shadowy mountain. "I need to go," Desta said. "Keep practicing. Come and ask me if you have any questions. I will be around for two more weeks."

The two cousins parted and Awoke remained standing, lost in thought. Then he ran after his teacher. "Wait, wait," he shouted. Desta stopped and waited for his cousin.

"What am I going to tell people if they ask me why I am learning these strange letters and words?"

"Tell them you plan to go to *Amarika* one day," Desta said with a smile.

"I don't know if people will believe me, but I will keep studying them anyhow. Knowing something new is always better than not knowing."

Desta surprised himself, telling awoke he would be in the valley for just two weeks. He hadn't even thought about it when he said it. Having left Dangila not to return and with no promising family in Sekela to give him shelter and food, he might not be going anywhere come the end of Christmas break. The problem was his to solve—that is, if he still wanted to continue his studies and try to find the Coin of Magic and Fortune. His father had done the best he could. He had searched for willing families in Sekela. Finding none, he had sent him to Dangila and that had not worked out. But staying at home and becoming a shepherd and farmer was the absolute last thing Desta wanted.

When he arrived at Saba's home, all the guests had left, except for Abraham, who had been waiting for his son. The two greeted each other. Desta didn't really want to get into a discussion with his father, but he had no choice. He knew that his father probably wanted to find out for himself about his rumored conversion to Islam. Desta sat by the fire next to him.

His father was nursing his tsiwa of tella. He gunned his big eyes into the fire for several minutes. Then he turned to Desta. "Saba told me about the false rumor that had been swirling in the valley for several months. I didn't really believe it myself because you are too young, and I didn't think Ato Zewday would allow a boy I entrusted to him to go out and adopt a new religion. So I won't ask you about that. What I want to ask you about is the other story Saba shared with me—that you will not be going back to Dangila to continue your education?"

Desta gazed at his father. "Would it be a pleasure for you to see me die of hunger?"

"No, I just wondered what you plan to do with your education if you are not going back to Dangila. I know that Agew woman starved you. I am sorry you suffered by her hands."

"Don't blame just Mebet. Your relative is also to blame. You were wrong to believe that because he was a blood relation he wouldn't let me go hungry. 'He will share his last piece of bread with you if that was all he had in the world,' you said. The fact is, Zewday is a drunk. He spent all his money on tej and tella, even at the expense of his own family. So I am not going back. What my next options are, I don't know yet. For the next week, I just want to recover, gain some weight, and rest. I really don't want to talk more about that now, Baba. I will be going to bed very soon."

"All right then. We can talk about it another time, "Abraham said. He picked up his cup, drew his tella, placed it back on the floor, and rose to go home. Desta was surprised by Abraham's abrupt parting, but it was just as well. Saba followed him to the door and returned after escorting him out.

"I overheard your conversation with Baba. I hope to God you find someone in our town to live with so you can continue with your studies. It would kill Baba to see another child not complete his education. You have no idea how disappointed and hurt he has been by Tamirat not becoming a priest."

This added pressure from Saba was the last thing Desta needed. He stared at a smoldering log near the edge of the fire pit, wondering if he should get up and push it in. Then a thought he had entertained before came back to him. "Let me ask you this, Saba," he said, turning toward her to get her attention. "How can a grown-up boy like me have a closer relationship with complete strangers?"

"What do you mean?"

"Have a closer, more committed relationship with them as you would have with your own parents or godparents."

Saba thought for a few seconds. "One of the ways a child could be 'adopted' by another adult was through a 'Father-of-the-Breast' or 'Mother-of-the-Breast' ceremony. The relationship was similar to that of a godfather or godmother, but this unrelated guardian tends to look after children who have no living parents or have severed their relationship with their natural parents." Desta looked at his sister. *Was she serious?* He was surprised not only by the possibility of having a second set of parents but also by the nature of the association—'Parents of the Breast.' Might he actually have to suckle at their breasts in order to adopt them as his parents? Saba didn't know exactly how the adoption might occur, but Desta held to the literal meaning, and this unsettled him greatly.

"Yes," Saba said, "through this ceremony, a man and a woman can express the desire to adopt you and vice versa, and afterward you have a new set of parents."

"You mean a grown boy like me can do that?"

"Yes, someone of your age or even much older than you can do it."

Desta's heart leaped at the possibility of having a mother who would love and care for him like her own.

"Of course, you have to find people who would be willing to have you for a son," Saba said almost as an afterthought.

Desta's heart quieted just as quickly. "That is true. Where I might find a couple like that is a big question."

"It's getting late. Let's go to bed."

That night, Desta placed his hand on his chest and prayed that God might help him find people in Yeedib who would give him shelter and board when he returned to school. He also prayed that God might help him find a couple to be his Parents-of-the-Breast.

FORTY-SEVEN

Desta's relationship with his mother, Ayénat, had been fragile and strained at best. Yet, he never thought he would do what he was about to do. He thought about how miserable she was to him that Christmas Eve when he arrived home from Kuakura tired, hungry, and thirsty. And now she persisted in her refusal to allow Desta in the house without his being blessed by a priest. He decided to disown her.

Desta saw it as a relationship that was doomed from the start. His mother had wanted a boy instead of a girl—as if Desta had had a choice when it came to his gender. And then her selfish, unrelenting demand that he abandon his schooling and stay on the farm, which had often made his visit home unpleasant and uncomfortable. Secretly, he had hoped she would stop pushing her demands so that they could have a more loving relationship.

Now all her unfulfilled wishes and petitions were being manifested in various forms of anger and resentment.

Instead of continuing with such a dead relationship, he might as well part ways with his mother once and for all. He thought this would be for the best. One, this action would give him a clear and free mind. Two, if and when he found a family that would want to have him as a Son-of-the-Breast, it would be easier for him to establish a new relationship.

Abraham had always been supportive of his decisions. He never pestered him about anything. He didn't have to disown his father and their relationship would remain as it was.

When Desta told Saba and Yihoon about disowning Ayénat, they discouraged him from doing so and asked that he reconsider. She was his mother after all.

"How can I be obedient to ignorance? And to someone who insults and vilifies people whom she has never set eyes on, people who have been more kind and helpful to me than she has ever been? Until she is willing to hear my full story about these people and she drops her priest, cross, and holy water business, I will remain motherless. What she had the head priest do to me those years ago was unforgivable."

Desta's worry for the following two weeks was not Ayénat—or the cross or holy water treatment. It was where he was going to go to school and with whom he would live.

He had no option about the school in Yeedib, as there was only one in the whole town. But he had no relatives he could live with there. So he left the problem of Yeedib to Abraham. Every night Desta prayed while pressing his hand on his chest and over his heart, and envisioned the kind of people he wanted to live with.

AFTER A WEEK OF EFFORT, Abraham came to Desta with a glimmer of hope. "A new chief of police and his wife in town were looking for live-in help, a boy who could run errands and look after their milk cow."

The glimmer of hope quickly turned into doubt. "Look after a milk cow?"

"Yes, but not all day. Take her out to the field in the morning and bring her home in the evening."

"What do the people look like?"

Abraham described the policeman and his wife with such precision that Desta wondered if Abraham had known them for a long time. When his father told him where each was from, Desta groaned.

"What's wrong?"

"How is it possible that another couple exactly like Zewday and Mebet could turn up here in our little town? And you said she is an Agew?"

"Yes, but friendlier than Mebet," Abraham insisted.

"You know what they say about Agew people," Desta replied.

"They say it's hard to find their heart. . . . I am not sure why people say that, but there are going to be individuals like that in any group. So take that expression with a grain of salt. Stay as open-minded as you've recently proven you're capable of."

"But the similarity between this couple and Zewday and Mebet is uncanny."

Desta stared up at the smoke-stained ceiling, lost in thought. *At least I will be close enough to come home if something happens or I get hungry.*

"I think you will be happy. I have good feelings about them."

"And they are not relatives, although that blood-is-thicker-than-water notion doesn't really mean much, as I found out in Dangila."

"Considering we have no other option, I think you should accept the offer. Tell me 'yes' and I will go see them tomorrow."

THE FOLLOWING EVENING Abraham returned home having cemented the arrangement for Desta to live with the Negasu Lecho family and go to school in Yeedib. "They are very eager to meet you," Abraham said with a broad smile.

"I am very curious about them and anxious to find out if coincidences are such common occurrences."

"And what's more," Abraham said, "we don't have to bring any grain to them. They will provide your room and board in exchange for the small chores you do."

"I hope that's a good sign," Desta said, returning his father's smile.

THREE DAYS BEFORE SCHOOL OPENED, Abraham brought Desta to the Lecho family. Their compound shared fences with the courthouse buildings on one side and the jail on the other. It was a grass-roofed, circular, and squat home, neatly kept and properly furnished with chairs and tables, plush skin and palm leaf mats on the living room floor, and an arching high earthen seat.

Negasu Lecho was a six-foot-tall man of the *gala*—one of Ethiopia's major tribal groups—from the province of Shoa. He had broad shoulders; a long, lean torso; and strong legs. If Zewday Tessema's face was a sculptor's masterpiece, Negasu Lecho's was the master sculptor's perfection. He had plump high cheekbones, a handsome and distinctive nose, and firm, full lips that framed a corn-row of white teeth. His smooth skin was the beautiful deep hue of the night and his crop of curly hair was jet-black and lustrous. He looked splendid in his neatly pressed khaki police uniform and round woolen hat with a silver star, which he wore tipped to one side of his head.

Negasu's wife, Tshai, a full-figured woman, was his exact opposite in skin tone. She looked like the moon by night but shone like the sun by day. Her round face showcased her elegant and dainty nose, sensuous full lips, and big expressive eyes. Her neck was not long and elegant but appeared handsome adorned with the big silver cross she wore on a black silk cord. She wrapped her hair with a colorful scarf, the loose ends springing from the back of her neck.

Negasu and Tshai assigned Desta the small room next to theirs as his sleeping quarters. His bed was a straw mattress with an old, cream-colored sheet and a leather pillow, all draped with a thick wool blanket. This was the first time Desta had a private room since he left home, and he was thrilled.

Negasu and Tshai explained his task of taking their black cow to the pasture and bringing her home in the evening. Smaller errands he would do as needed. This meant Desta would have spare time to focus on his studies and plan his future.

AT SCHOOL, BROOK TOLD DESTA that he was disappointed when Desta hadn't returned after the Christmas holidays the previous year. He didn't want to see a promising student's career cut short because of domestic problems, as had happened to so many of his students.

Yitbarek, the only other teacher and head of the school, peered at him through his thick glasses. "You decided to give it another try, huh?" he asked with a half-smile.

"I never quit. I was in Dangila for the past year. I am already in the fourth grade."

"Good to hear it. Do you have your certificate?"

Desta's face went blank.

"We need to have proof that the school had promoted you to the fourth grade," Yitbarek said firmly.

"I don't have one. I didn't know I was supposed to . . . ," Desta mumbled in a low voice.

"Well, we need to put you in the third grade then," Yitbarek said.

Desta pursed his lips and touched them with his fingers, his mind a whir, searching for any good reason to convince the teacher. He had none. He finished his thoughts by just shaking his head.

"It won't make any difference," Yitbarek said in a softer voice. "If you're like most farm boys without relatives in the bigger towns, you're more likely to stay in fourth grade for one or two more years—until you find someone to live with in Finote Selam or Burie, or you decide to go back to your parents' farm. So don't worry, son."

Desta thought about this. He bit his lip and shook his head, saying, "I guess that's okay then."

"Good. It's only five more months before you get promoted to the fourth grade, assuming you do well with your lessons," Yitbarek said, smiling. He patted Desta on the shoulder.

Fenta was all smiles when he saw Desta. "Where have you been? You got tired of herding animals and you came back to give yourself a second chance?" he joked.

Desta told him what he actually had been doing.

"You're just one grade behind us then. . . . Who knows, you and I might actually be in the same grade next year if we don't find someone to live with in Finote Selam or Burie. This is Sayfu's and my second year in fourth grade." He looked away sadly.

Desta's stomach knotted at the thought of being in the same predicament after he finished the fourth grade.

"By the way," Fenta said, "there was a man and his son who came several times looking for you."

Desta's mind went blank wondering who they might have been. "A man and his son?"

"The father said you did some incredible thing for them, but they wouldn't tell us what that was."

It dawned on Desta. "A cross-eyed boy and his father?"

"No, the boy was not cross-eyed."

Desta smiled. "Did they say if they would come again?"

"No, but they've been back every three months or so. I am sure they will."

"I know where they live," declared Desta.

That evening, as Desta went down the hill to look for Negasu's cow, he realized how much he had missed the open spaces, the clean and fresh highland air, and the view of the endless sky. How much he had missed the brilliant, lurid sunsets like the one forming right now above the western horizon. The sun, like the coin, was a part of his life. He hadn't realized how much hunger he had for it.

FORTY-EIGHT

"POINT FOUR . . . a gift of the government of the United States of Amarika is what it says," Brook told the class. On the khaki-colored carton were a few other declarations. There was a field of stripes arrayed with a neatly laid-out block of stars. Below the benevolent statement, two hands clasped firmly. Farther down, an overfed spotted cow looked up proudly as she displayed her engorged teats.

"What does it mean?" asked one of the boys.

Brooks gave the Amharic translation.

The kids tried to grasp clearly the connection between Amarika and this *sitota*—gift.

Noticing the puzzled look on their faces, Brook explained that Harry Truman, the former leader of a nation called Amarika, thought that for a country like Ethiopia to grow and prosper, it needed assistance with money, equipment, and sometimes products like those found in the box.

"What's in it? What's in it?" shouted the students, craning their necks and standing on their toes, their weather-beaten faces peering over Brook's hefty arms.

"I don't know. Let's open it and find out." Brook turned the box over, inspected the other side, and then turned it back again, teasingly drawing out the suspense and curiosity that was building around him. He tried to pry open the glued down flaps of the carton with his nails but wasn't able to.

"Let me try it," said one boy, reaching for the box. To everyone's amazement, the boy quickly lifted the flaps and flared them out. All eyes poured into the box. A plastic bag containing white powder seemed to stare, like a wide eye, back at them.

A chatter of questions erupted. "This is milk," Brook said, when the noise subsided.

Giggling incredulously, the students looked at one another and the teacher. Another chatter of questions: "Milk?"

"Yes, powdered milk."

The identity and the physical appearance of the white substance didn't connect for many of the students. The only milk they knew was white and flowing.

"What do the cows that produce this milk look like?" Desta asked, trying to make sense of Brook's claim.

Brook explained, "They took the ordinary milk from the cow and dried it to make a powder. You turn it into regular milk by adding water to it." He got up and walked to the pile of similar boxes. "Who would like to take this milk and try it at home?"

No one moved. Desta looked around to see if anybody else wanted to accept the offer. The teacher asked again. Desta raised his hand and said, "I will." Two more boys followed. Then three more. Pretty soon the whole class wanted to try the powdered milk from Amarika.

Brook gave a box to each student until they all had one. Desta was ecstatic. He was as much looking forward to inspecting it with his fingers as learning whether it really tasted like milk.

"You can boil it with sugar or salt if you don't like the flavor," Brook told the students as they shuffled out of the room with their cartons.

Desta cradled his gift from Amarika in his arms like a puppy he was bringing home. He was anxious to open the plastic bag, feel the powder, dissolve it in water, and taste it.

Nobody else was there when he got home from school. Desta placed the box on the living room floor. Remembering how hard it was to loosen the flaps, he fetched a knife from the back room. He inserted the tip of the knife under one of the flaps and wiggled it in. He pressed down on the knife's handle and heard the cardboard crackle; the blade slid sweetly in. He loosened the other flaps as he had the first and then flicked them open like the petals of a flower.

He drew out the plastic sack and tore a two-inch hole into it. He then poured the powder into an aluminum pot. He took a pinch of the dried milk and pressed it between his thumb and index finger, feeling it disintegrate into a fine paste.

The next step was to find out whether it really tasted like milk. He quickly made a fire in the charcoal burner. He added water to the pot and placed it on the fire. He threw in a few pinches of salt and stirred it with a wooden spoon the whole time it was heating.

He took the pot off the fire and set it aside to cool, twiddling his thumbs and wiggling his toes, impatient to taste this foreign milk. He had one of the columnar glasses standing by the pot.

Tshai walked in. "What have you got there?" she asked.

"This is milk from a cow in Amarika. Do you want to taste it?"

"What?"

"Yeah, milk from a cow in Amarika. It's a gift."

Tshai looked confused and mystified. "Where did you get it?"

"From school. The teacher gave it to us."

This answer clarified nothing for Tshai.

"Do you want to try it? It should be cool by now."

Tshai crouched to watch Desta pour the curious liquid.

She took a sip. "Ughh."

Desta was disappointed. "You don't like it?"

"Here, taste it."

Desta took a sip. "I am sorry. I put in too much salt."

"Who told you to put salt in it?"

"The teacher. At home, my mother puts salt in coffee, too, sometimes."

"Only people who don't have sugar use salt. We have both."

Tshai brought an old yellow canister from the small table in the corner and opened it. "Next time use these," she said, pointing to the white cubes.

Desta took a sip again and shook his head, surprised by the amount of salt he had put in his novel milk. "Sorry," he said, as he walked out to throw it away.

FORTY-NINE

Getting stuck in Yeedib after he finished fourth grade had been a growing concern for Desta. He knew that finding the coin was intertwined with his education. If he didn't advance in his education, he would not come close to finding that ancient treasure.

He needed to plan his future starting right now. He quickly realized that living with the head of the police and his wife could lead to some great opportunities. Through his job, Negasu traveled regularly to Finote Selam and Burie. This meant that once Desta completed the fourth grade, Negasu might help him find another living arrangement in either of those towns. To develop such opportunities, though, Desta must first make himself appreciated by both Negasu and Tshai.

After school he would come directly home and help Tshai with anything she needed. On weekends he washed clothes for her and ironed Negasu's uniforms. When she went to the market on Saturdays, he carried anything she couldn't handle. And he looked after their daughter, Sihin, when the couple went out to visit friends. They, in turn, began to treat him more and more like a family member. Tshai gave him his breakfast of tea with dabo or a portion of the firfir—minced injera mixed with sautéed onions, garlic, butter, and red pepper sauce—which she also prepared for herself and her husband. He never felt slighted by them the way he had often felt with Zewday and Mebet.

Because of these niceties, Desta liked them both. Abraham had been right about Negasu. He was a very intelligent man. He didn't speak much while at home because he was often preoccupied with his work. There were cases of murder and robbery or the occasional remote area uprising. And it was his job to make sure that the prisoners received the meals their relatives brought them and that they got their routine exercise.

He was also very kind and generous, inviting acquaintances and even complete strangers to lunch. Then there was Shetu Balew, a tailor by occupation and a single man with two teenage boys. Shetu had a great knack for showing up wherever Negasu was in the hope of getting invited over for lunch. Negasu never resented this man and Tshai never complained to her husband about the constant parade of uninvited guests.

After Tru and Uncle Mekuria, Desta never believed he could find another couple—certainly, not complete strangers—who would be this kind to him. But they were such good people that Desta thought Negasu and Tshai would be worth having as Parents-of-the-Breast. He had lived with them from late January to June—through the completion of his third grade and the onset of the rainy season.

After several days of mulling over the idea, Desta wrote a letter to Negasu and Tshai. In it, he formally asked them whether they'd accept him as their Son-of-the-Breast:

> The kindness and support you have extended to me since I came to live with you is something I have not found even in my own family. I sleep well at night and am happy when I wake up every day. I have told myself that if I had a chance to be born again, I would want you for my parents. Since that is not possible, would you be willing to consider me as your Son-of-the-Breast?
> With great appreciation,
> Desta
> P.S. I want you to know that my decision regarding this matter was not made on the spur of the moment. I have thought about it for quite some time.

TWO DAYS LATER, Negasu asked Desta to join him for a walk. It was evening. The sun had been lost to the world, although there was still plenty of light. Out of the gate they turned left and strolled toward the courthouses. Negasu said he was touched by Desta's heartfelt letter and that it would be an honor to have such a good student for a son. Because it was a very serious decision for him and Tshai, they would have to think and talk about it. More important, they wanted Desta to talk to his parents and the rest of his family.

One market day Abraham had come to town on court business and went to Negasu and Tshai's home to check on Desta. Finding his son, he asked him to come along on a walk. Abraham wanted to know how everything was going. During the visit, Desta broached the idea that he was considering adopting Negasu and Tshai as Parents-of-the-Breast, explaining his reasons for this momentous decision. To Desta's surprise Abraham thought it was a wonderful idea. He added, "From the many times I have seen him in court, I've been impressed by Negasu. From the few times I met his beautiful wife, I came away feeling good about her, too."

Desta had not seen or spoken to his mother since Christmas. He didn't feel he had to consult her about this. Anyway, it was his father who had the final say. Once Desta had his blessing, he was free to pursue his plan.

A WEEK AFTER DESTA'S conversation with Negasu, his host prepared to lead a dozen soldiers and forty paramilitary personnel on a whirlwind expedition into a very remote and rugged land called Adama. The locals there had refused to pay taxes or comply with some of the country's laws. The men were believed to be armed and dangerous. Negasu was going there risking not only his own life but also the lives of the men he was taking with him. He needed an ashker to carry his rifle and holster. He asked around town if there was such a boy. Finding none, Negasu asked Desta whether he himself was interested. The boy readily accepted, knowing this would be another opportunity to see more of his new world. And Desta had no fear of the potential danger; the coin image on his chest would protect him and the trip was going to take place during his break from school.

The district governor, Girazmach Belie, was also a part of this expedition, as were a few of his strongest men. They were to travel separately and meet Negasu en route.

Negasu's group planned to stop along the way to investigate some cases of murder and cattle theft. The cattle thief had been spotted at a local market. Negasu stopped there with a few of his soldiers while the rest continued on to Adama.

After traveling half a day, they reached the Wednesday market in Talia, a hot lowland town south of Yeedib. The appearance of the police at the market sparked chaos. Those market-goers who didn't use the country's paper money thought the police officers were there to confiscate their Maria Theresa silver thalers. The market turned into a confusion of people scrambling to hide their silver. Some shoved their coins into sacks of grains, others under the rocks they were sitting on.

Desta had watched one farmer woman untie the knot of her girdle, unwrap her two silver birrs, and then crouch as if she had dropped something, pushing the coins under a rock. She got up and walked away without looking back. Desta noticed a man who had also been watching the woman.

Without hesitating, Desta walked over to the rock and retrieved the two silver thalers. The thrill of having those coins in his hands quickly gave way to a sense of guilt. He was taking something that didn't belong to him. It amounted to stealing, which is very wrong in God's eyes, and Desta didn't want to offend the King of the heavens.

Then knowing that cash is hard to come by for farmers and that those two silver thalers were probably the woman's life savings, he felt doubly guilty and ashamed. He scurried in the direction the woman went, hoping to find her and return her coins. However, he had not seen her face well enough to know what she looked like. Not finding her, Desta returned to the group of men feeling awful about the whole thing. He had no choice but to keep the two coins. He put them in his pocket.

After the group left the market and got on the road, Desta was hit by another wave of excitement regarding the coins. Maybe he was meant to have them, to remind him of what ultimately should happen to the two ancient gold pieces when he finds the second coin. That he came on this expedition was probably for this purpose. And he didn't think that his being at the market and the woman hiding her coins under the rock was merely coincidental. It must have been preplanned and for a reason. He reached for the coins and rubbed them together, imagining himself doing the same when he finally finds the second Coin of Magic and Fortune. A thrill of unimaginable depth passed through him.

ADAMA WAS NEARLY a day and a half's journey from Talia. Negasu decided to take a detour of about two hours in an attempt to capture a man who had killed someone at a wedding *fukera*—a form of skit to demonstrate bravery. According to witnesses, the killer was a man often referred to as *melaga*—lazy. The victim had used the term during his fukera, in an obvious reference to this man: "The time of the brave men who fought in wars and defended their country against foreign invaders like the Italians is long past. Now we are in the days of the *Melagas*." When the man's turn came to enact a battle scene, he aimed his gun at the man who insulted him and shot and killed him.

The governor with three men and Negasu with three of his were to rendezvous at the area where the melaga man lived. After walking for three hours on twisted rocky paths through rugged terrain that overwhelmed the eye, taxed the feet, and jarred the knees, they finally reached their destination. An informer who had accompanied them pointed out the house and left.

The wanted man had just come home from work and was about to sit and have his meal when Negasu with his three men walked through the open door. The man's wife, who carried a breast-feeding toddler, froze. The man tried to rise but one of the policemen drew his gun and told him not to move. The three others leaped at the man. Two of them grabbed and twisted his arms behind him while the third fettered him with a set of handcuffs. The wife, stunned and speechless, showed no emotion as they led her husband out of their home. Negasu stayed behind and explained to the wife the reasons for arresting her husband and that she could come and visit him at any time. He was sorry he had to do this to her family, but it was the law that a person who committed a murder must be brought to justice.

Negasu left the house and instructed two of his men to bring the killer to the police headquarters in Yeedib for processing and booking.

THAT EVENING, THE GOVERNOR SENT three of his men to seek accommodations with willing farm families. Desta and Negasu stayed at the home of a well-to-do farmer who offered to kill a goat for dinner but was dissuaded by Negasu. He explained that they were leaving early the next day and it was not necessary; however, the farmer could kill a chicken if he so wished. The chicken and the doro wat the wife prepared with boiled eggs, minced onions, and spices were a pleasure to Desta's palate and satisfying to his stomach, especially after the day's journey.

After dinner, the homeowner ordered his daughter to wash the guests' feet. Negasu hesitated at first, but the man insisted. "After all, you've come walking through this tough and rough terrain of ours and you're going to do more of the same tomorrow. I think you'll be better served if our daughter washes your feet, sir. Besides, you will sleep better that way."

Negasu sat on a stool in the corner of the living room and took off his shoes and socks. The sweat drenched socks and feet reeked. The couple, who were sitting around the fire several feet away, tightened their lips and held their breath. The girl came with an empty wooden bowl and warm water in a round clay pot. She involuntarily wrinkled her nose and squinted her eyes as she gazed down at Negasu's feet. Embarrassed by the reaction of the girl and her parents to his stinking feet and wanting to kill the odor as quickly as he could, Negasu rolled the socks in his handkerchief and put them in his knapsack. "What a lovely girl you are," he said, feeling obligated to distract her from the unpleasantness he was causing. "Do your parents often make you wash the feet of strangers like us?"

"Not that often. Only when important people come," she muttered without looking up. She poured the warm water from the clay pot into the wooden bowl. He eased his feet into the water. The girl discarded the dirty water from this first wash and returned with more. She scrubbed and rinsed Negasu's feet again, this time admiring the man's baby-soft skin. Having finished, she brought an old cotton cloth for Negasu to place his feet on until they dried.

Desta washed his own feet, although the girl had offered to do it. He had discovered one more reason why he shouldn't wear shoes—to avoid embarrassing moments like Negasu's. He would rather walk naturally than be encased and trapped in those leather or plastic things.

Negasu slept on a raised earthen bed that adjoined the couple's sleeping quarters. They had spread a plush cowhide over a straw pad and supplied him with a grass-filled pillow of soft leather. Desta slept by the fire on a piece of goatskin, but he was not envious of Negasu. The heat from the fire was heavenly.

The next morning the wife and daughter rose early and prepared breakfast—shiro and doro wat with freshly baked injera. Just about the time they had finished eating, one of Negasu's men came to say they were ready to get on the road. "Finish eating quickly," Negasu said to Desta, who had just begun eating from a separate tray. He wolfed down what he could and then rose when he noticed the chief had gathered the knapsack, the rifle and the pistol in its holster and was standing by the entrance waiting for him. After apologizing to the farmer and his wife for having arrived at their home unannounced and thanking them for their gracious provisions and comfortable sleeping arrangements, Negasu walked out to join the other man outside. Desta washed his hands and dashed out the door.

Once all of the men were accounted for and had begun walking along the caravan road, each told of how he spent the night. The governor, who appeared to have hardly slept, boasted how he had made a wealthy farmer kill one of his *mookit*—castrated goats—and that they had spent nearly all night feasting on its *choma*—marbled meat—which they ate first raw with red pepper and then in a stew with freshly baked injera after midnight.

The man spoke with such bravado that Desta began to feel sad. He imagined the same thing happening to his father with of one of his precious mookits. He thought how devastated his father would have been and how sad and upset the governor's hosts' must have been for someone to come without forewarning, make them kill their goat, feast all night, and leave in the morning without paying for any of it. By comparison, Desta's respect and admiration for Negasu was raised many notches higher, for his having refused his hosts' offer to kill their goat for dinner.

The others complained about their meager meals, hard beds, and the fleas they battled all night. Some laughed, others gloated, but Desta simply listened, at times upset by the callous and wanton things that people with power were capable of doing. From time to time he touched the coin on his chest and thought about what he would do if there arose a confrontation with the people in Adama.

Negasu raised his voice over the chatter, saying to the men, "No matter your circumstance last night, you will be lucky if you even have shelter tonight. We'll not be welcome where we are going, and I hear the place is always windy and cold. So brace yourselves."

The conversation sobered. "We have the governor with us, so perhaps that will help," said one of the men, glancing at Girazmach Belie.

"These are lawless communities and I don't think my presence will matter. We just have to wait and see," the governor replied somberly.

"Our goal is to engage in a dialogue without confrontation," Negasu said.

"I'm not sure about that," the governor said. "I think they are going to be up in arms the moment they hear of our arrival."

"Either way, Governor," Negasu said, smiling, "please don't even ask for a chicken if we're fortunate enough to have accommodations with one of the farmers."

"I should not refuse if a good farmer offers to kill one of his nice mookit goats, should I?" Belie grinned, in anticipation of Negasu's reaction.

"We'll be fortunate if we get food. Please don't ask for anything. Decline if they offer any animal for a meal. That is why these people refuse to pay taxes. They think the government is after everything they own." Negasu's voice was serious and firm.

The party was serious, too. Nobody spoke for a long time. Desta caressed the coin on his chest and those in his pocket.

They reached Mount Adama just before the sun touched the hazy western horizon. Desta's memory of his first trip to the mountains with his sister came rushing back. He remembered seeing the tips of Adama when he and Saba were atop the peak above their home. Saba had said, "That land in the east where you see snatches of hills through the pass is Lij Ambera. . . ."

One of those hills Desta had snatched a glimpse of turned out to be Mount Adama, the highest peak in the whole of Gojjam province. The sparse vegetation on Mount Adama clung for dear life to the rocks and craggy cliffs. The wind whipped around the men ferociously. It was raw and stinging. Desta thought this force of nature alone would be protection enough for the villagers and that they would have no fear of intruders.

Some of the men pulled their gabis over their heads and under their jackets. They kept rubbing their hands together, blowing their frosty white breath over them to keep them warm. From others the chattering of teeth could be heard. Desta, with his fingers over his heart, was the only one who seemed immune to the harsh wind and unworried about finding shelter.

A few of the men went scouting for any farmer willing to give them accommodation. The governor and the chief of police were discussing their options when the men returned. Negasu's men delightedly reported that some of the farmers could provide shelter for two or three people.

Only as they walked toward the farmhouses did one of the men notice Desta's tolerance for the brutal wind. "What's Desta wearing?" he asked Negasu. "He seems the only one who is braving this godforsaken place."

"He is just a tough kid. I'm proud of him."

Desta felt a surge of emotion. This was the first time he had heard from a male figure in his life talk about him like that. With his family he was the one possessed by Saytan, the one to be shunned. To Zewday and his family he was an adventurous enigma they couldn't relate to. Now Negasu said he was proud of him. If he had been in a private place, he would have cried tears of joy. Instead he turned to Negasu and just said, "Thank you!"

At the various farmhouses where the men were staying, everything was meager: the food, accommodation, and hospitality. Considering, though, that they had dropped out of the sky into this hostile environment, all the men were grateful to their hosts. Everyone was worried about the next day, however. They planned to meet with the local population and they had no inkling what the reception would be like.

THE NEXT DAY, SHORTLY AFTER DAWN, all the people in the party gathered near the main road in the foothills of Mount Adama. Some had invited their hosts. It turned out the problem was not with the farmers who lived here on the west side of the mountain but with those who lived on the east side.

The governor and the chief of police agreed to send a few of the local people they had met to speak with the leaders of the communities on the other side. In the meantime the men remained huddled to keep warm until the sun fully rose and began warming the air.

By noon, some of the emissaries had returned, but they didn't bring with them anyone from the villages they had visited; the people there refused to engage in any dialogue. Furthermore, they had warned that Negasu, the governor, and his men had better return to wherever they came from or there could be trouble.

One of the scouting parties did returned with an elderly man, but he had no power or influence on the rest of his community. After learning that the governor and the chief of police were part of the group, he agreed to go back and see what he could do.

By mid-afternoon, other local people began arriving, but they were not what the officials had expected or wanted to see: mostly young people in their twenties and thirties, armed with stones, guns, and spears. They kept coming and coming. By the time this influx ceased, the men stood several people deep in front of the visitors. The governor told everyone in the party to put down their guns. "We should not make them feel threatened," he whispered.

From among the locals, a young man with a gun stepped forward. "You either leave this place peacefully or get decimated," he warned. The others chimed in agreement.

"Can we talk briefly with you since you seem to be the leader?" the governor asked in a strained but earnest voice.

"No talk. We want you to get off our backs. We are tired of paying for your comfort while we get nothing in return," the young man said.

"That is why we want to talk, to hear your grievances," the governor said.

"The less we talk, the better—and the sooner you leave," the man warned again, this time vehemently.

Negasu and Belie looked at each other. Negasu turned to the man with the gun. "Look, young man, we are a country of laws. Laws have to be complied with for us to give protection to you and your family. . . ." Negasu panned his eyes over the crowd. "And to the rest of you."

Another young man with a sharp-edged stone in his hand navigated his way through the crowd and stood in front of the man with the gun. "Either you leave us alone or we'll break your legs and maim your bodies so you will be a feast for the mountain hyenas." He appeared ready to unload the dangerous-looking rock

on Negasu. A few of the policemen looked at each other as if waiting for someone to be the first to run. Others in the back of the group were checking the open
space behind them to make sure none of the locals were in the way if they made
a run for it.

The man with the gun stepped in front of the man with the stone, glaring at
him. The crowd, edgy and nervous, crept closer. "Look," Girazmach Belie said,
his voice cracking, "if you're unwilling to cooperate with us, we will depart
peacefully and this will be the end of our trip here."

Desta felt the intensity of the crowd—the men's emotion. They appeared like
dogs that had gotten a whiff of blood and were going in for the kill. He slipped
his hand under his gabi and reached for the coin above his heart. He pressed on
it firmly, stepped out of Negasu's shadow, and walked toward the crowd.

To the policemen's astonishment, the threatening young men moved backward. The more Desta walked toward them, the more they retreated. Their
stones dropped from their immobile hands with clatters. Those with spears and
guns had lost control of their fingers. Their weapons remained frozen in their
grasp. None of them said anything.

To everyone in Desta's party it was like a strange dream. The young men
continued to retreat as if blown by a strong wind.

Once the crowd was at a safe distance, Desta withdrew his hand from his
chest. He asked the young man with the gun, "Now would you be willing to
negotiate with the chief of police and the governor?"

"Can you explain to me who you are?" the man asked, awed.

"It matters not who I am, but I think you better negotiate with these people or
you and your community will be in real trouble."

The rock-wielding young man stepped out of the crowd again. "Who is this
ater—munchkin? Why not take him out first?" he said to his companions.

"You're not convinced?" Desta countered. "I can do it again, but this time you
won't be around to ask the same question." Desta was not sure whether the coin
had the power to kill, but he was emboldened enough by what it had done so far
that he felt he could get away with saying that.

"No, no," the gunman said. He raised his hands.

Desta signaled to Negasu to come and talk to the cooperating young man.
The governor followed right behind. "We didn't know what we had. It's a
miracle, obviously meant for us to reach a peaceful resolution to the problem,"
Negasu said sheepishly. He was still confused and baffled by what he had just

witnessed.

The young man said, "I think it's better if this discussion is between our elders and you. We came because they didn't want to turn the meeting into a confrontation. If you had told us you were coming, we could have started on a better footing."

"Okay then. Please send the key leaders in your community for a discussion. We'll accomplish as much as we can till darkness falls and continue tomorrow morning if we need to."

With this agreement, the crowd went home peacefully. Negasu's men kept shaking their heads every time they looked at Desta. To their many repeated questions, all he said was, "I prayed for the outcome I sought, concentrating on what it would be, and that's exactly what happened."

Almost all the men patted Desta on the shoulder and thanked him. "We're just glad you were with us," some said. "Thanks for saving us from major disaster," others declared.

THE LEADERS OF THE COMMUNITY, seven of them, came an hour before sunset. Perched on rocks, they engaged in discussion until nightfall. They all agreed the farmers' tax burden would not increase this year or for the next five years. With that, they parted.

Negasu and Desta took a walk before dinner. The chief of police thanked him privately for what he had done. Desta credited prayer and God as the power behind their ability to ultimately resolve the problem. "I'm glad things were resolved without incident," he said. "Could you now be my Father-of-the-Breast?"

"I will be very delighted to have you for my son. I had wanted to wait until this problem was behind us before giving you my answer," Negasu said. He smiled and hugged Desta and thanked him again. Desta thought, *this is what a desert must feel like when a cold rain washes over it.*

Later in the evening the local negotiators sent food and drink for the visitors. Everyone ate and drank to their heart's content. Some came and thanked Desta again.

The moment the governor saw Desta, he came to him and showered him with his gratitude. After listening carefully, Desta lifted his face and said, "I am happy I could somehow contribute to the peaceful conclusion of the matter, and I'm touched by the kind words you have extended to me. Can you do me a favor?"

"Sure," the governor replied eagerly.

"On future trips, would you stop asking farmers who host you to kill their mookits for you? I died a million deaths yesterday as you boasted about the feast at your host's house. My father raises goats and has several mookits. His animals are very precious to him. He spends a lot of time and money to grow them until they are of a size that will fetch a good price. As I heard you describe your experience with the farm family, I kept thinking that could have been one of my father's goats you ate, and I knew how devastated that man and his family must be. Would you never do it again? And will you send money to the man to pay for his goat?"

Girazmach Belie was moved by Desta's passionate appeal. He was saddened by his irresponsibility. He promised he would never do it again and would pay the man for his goat.

Everybody was happy as they got on the road. They had accomplished their goals. Desta had gotten Negasu to promise to be his Father-of-the-Breast. The governor and the chief of police had persuaded the villagers to follow the laws of their administration. And, hopefully, Girazmach Belie wouldn't again force poor farmers to kill their precious animals without payment.

FIFTY

"Desta, someone is at the gate looking for you," Tshai said. Desta was in the back of the house, combing Sihin's hair.

"Someone is looking for me?"

"I think it's your brother and some lady. Go find out."

Desta handed the green plastic comb to Sihin and left.

He took halting steps toward the gate, keeping his eyes on the couple. "Mother?" he mumbled under his breath.

Ayénat was the last person he expected to see.

"Surprise, surprise!" Teferra said.

"*Dena Aderih*—good morning," Ayénat said in a measured voice.

"Dena," Desta replied pensively. "What brings you so early to town?" On market days his family generally arrived around midday. Ayénat and Teferra had arrived well before noon.

Teferra answered for her. "She has important things to talk to you about."

Desta crinkled his brow. "About what?"

Teferra turned to their mother. "I think you two should go to some place private, like behind the *kab*—stone wall—and discuss it. I need to get to the market and set up," he said, and left.

So behind the kab Ayénat and Desta went to discuss these so-called 'important things.' They sat on the loose stones below the wall, overlooking the flat, expansive valley below.

"Your father told me you are planning to adopt the people you live with as your Parents-of-the-Breast," she said in a grim, rugged voice.

"I am," replied Desta unhesitatingly.

"What about your natural parents?"

"What about you?"

"Aren't we good enough?"

"Of course you are, Mother, but I am not going to get into a lengthy discussion about that. I made up my mind to have Negasu and Tshai as my Parents-of-the-Breast for personal reasons. I like them a lot. They have been very giving and caring, the kind of people I would like to have in my life for a long time. We have exhausted our search for relatives I can live with while I go to school. You and Baba cannot afford to support me. I need a couple like Negasu and Tshai as my Parents-of-the-Breast, and they are happy to have me as their Son-of-the-Breast. Rest assured that your place and Baba's in my heart will not change because of this." Desta cleared his throat. He realized this discussion was not going to be easy or short. He was feeling all the pent-up anger he hadn't had a chance to express when he came from Dangila for Christmas.

"Another thing," Ayénat said, gazing at Desta with her small eyes, which now seemed further diminished as her face darkened. "I understand that the man is a Gala and the wife is an Agew."

"So?"

"If you have gone insane enough to abandon your natural parents, why don't you at least choose an Amhara couple to be your Parents-of-the-Breast?"

Desta couldn't believe his ears. "What is wrong with having Negasu and Tshai as my Parents-of-the-Breast?"

"Nothing. . . just that it would have been better for you. . ." Ayénat trailed off.

"I get it. Mother, for you, anybody who is not Christian or an Amhara is not good enough to associate with. What do you know about Negasu and Tshai or the Muslims I was connected with? Or the Ferenges, for that matter, whose education you refer to as Saytan learning? You have never met a Gala, a Muslim, or a Ferenge in your life, yet you slight and criticize them for no reason. You have been limited by these barriers—"Prejudices," my Muslim friend Masud called them—you have put up before yourself. You have denied yourself the opportunity to learn about people who are different from you, and it's a shame."

"By virtue of being born to you I have inherited all that makes up who you are, and I have no choice about that. But I do have a choice not to inherit your beliefs, attitudes, and prejudices. I will not allow myself to be shackled by them. I cannot afford to!" Desta looked away. Seconds later he turned around and looked at his mother. "You know what, Ma? People like you measure their self-worth by how much they can elevate themselves above the people they see as inferior and therefore worthy of disdain. People like you end up merely 'flaunting their ignorance and arrogance,' as Masud, the Muslim merchant I befriended, used to say.

"Thank God there were no Muslims around here when I was growing up. Otherwise I would be like those Christian boys and girls who would never dream of playing with Muslim children because of the attitudes and beliefs they inherit from their parents. The sad thing is that the parents don't know what they are doing to their children and the children have no idea what's happening to them.

"Me, I have been free and happy ever since I broke loose from those mountains." Desta pointed in the general area of the peaks that circled him and his mother. "I plan to go far and wide in the world. I plan to enjoy myself and the people I meet wherever I go, without judgment or prejudice. And this is true freedom.

"In retrospect, I do want to thank you for one thing." He turned to Ayénat once more to see if she was listening. "I want to thank you for not sharing yourself with me. I have been hurt by your coldness and by the space you always kept between us while I was growing up. Now that I have a bit of perspective, I want to acknowledge my gratitude for that aspect of our relationship."

Ayénat tilted her head and squinted at Desta. "What are you talking about?"

"If I had been emotionally attached to you, it would have been harder for me to leave the valley and easier for me, as Teferra once said, 'to come running back' if life became difficult to bear. Hunger and hardship I could endure, but missing your love and comfort would have been harder to overcome. This I know from what happened to me when I lost Kooli and the vervet monkeys, and later when Hibist got married and left."

"You make it sound like I mistreated you," she said, knotting her brow, her voice flagging.

"I didn't say that."

Ayénat shook her head slightly. She snipped a blade of grass and flung it away. "If that is what you think, I hope the good Lord will forgive you in the end." Her face darkened; her small eyes dimmed. "I just want you to know that it's not the right thing to do."

"Why is it not the right thing to do? Are you concerned about who their ancestors are or losing me to a new set of parents?"

"Both your natural parents are still alive. They have done nothing wrong that you should, all of a sudden, want to have new parents."

"It's not something I decided on as a whim, Ma. I have considered this for a long time. My decision to have Negasu and Tshai for parents is to make it easy both for you and me."

"Easy? What *easy*? It will make things even more difficult for us at church. People have questioned the wisdom of our letting you get a modern education. They told us our souls would be punished. Now, by your adopting new parents, you will shame your father and me. Gossipy women will snicker behind our backs and we won't have a simple answer whenever someone asks why."

Desta planted his elbows on his knees, pressed the pads of his hands over his eyes, and thought. There was no other reason he could give his mother to convince her to support his decision.

She said, "I fear for you, too. God will punish you for making life difficult for your parents and for disobeying your mother. I don't like it and I don't approve, even though your father does." She got up.

Desta rose, too. "It's not out of disrespect for you or to imply that you have done me wrong that I am doing this. I cannot count on you and Baba or anybody in the family to support me. This was proven by what happen to me while I lived in Dangila."

Ayénat stared at Desta. "The problem with Dangila was the distance. It was all your father's fault. He should have found you someone locally where we'd get to see you and bring you food if you didn't get enough from your host."

"We tried doing that and found no one. What you're suggesting is not that clear-cut. What I am trying to do *is*."

"It *isn't*. All you see is your side, not our side, of the problem."

"If your concern really is what people might say, don't worry. You will get over it. If it's something else, I can't help you. Sorry. I have made up my mind to go forward with my decision, Ma. There is no more discussion of it." Desta sought Ayénat's eyes. She seemed lost and confused as she stared far into the distant, hazy mountains. "Ma, did you hear me?"

Ayénat's face was now a mere mask. It never wavered, nor did she blink her eyes.

"I need to go," she said, finally coming to life. Her brown face had taken on a smoke-gray hue.

Desta braced himself for a hug, but her arms never moved.

"You know how to get to the market, don't you?" he asked, minimizing her snub.

"Of course," Ayénat said curtly, and she strolled away.

Desta watched his mother until she vanished behind a cluster of huts. He felt sorry for her.

Before long, he started to feel nauseated. The conversation with his mother about Negasu and Tshai and the consequences of their becoming his Parents-of-the-Breast roiled in his head throughout the day and into the evening. He was so confused and anxious that he went to bed much earlier than his usual time of nine o'clock. He hoped sleep would heal him. He hoped that when he woke up, he would be in a better frame of mind and able to think clearly about the merits and consequences of his plan to adopt new parents.

Desta didn't have to wait until the break of dawn. He stirred into consciousness midway there. Everything that had clouded his brain the day before had dissipated, or so it seemed to him. Yet shortly after slumber had cleared from his head and he opened his eyes, his mind began to churn with the same thoughts again.

His refusal to comply with his mother's requests might sour his relationships with the rest of the family, particularly if it meant their reputations would be tarnished. The stigma of losing her son to adoptive parents, in addition to the tittle-tattle about his alleged abandonment of his religion, would be devastating to his mother, he thought. Equally worrisome was that, if the arrangement with Negasu and Tshai didn't work, he would have no place to go.

As if shifting the position of his body would solve what he feared, Desta switched from his back to the fetal position. When this didn't calm his spirits, he rolled to the other side and lay there for a while, and then again on his back. In the end, none of the positions mollified him.

He remembered the silvery full moon over the eastern sky when he had come home with the cow the previous evening. Assuming there were no clouds, the grounds outside would be draped with a yellow light, ideal for taking a stroll and contemplating. Yes, how about taking a walk instead of thrashing in bed trying to fall asleep? The night air on his face, the cool earth beneath his feet, and the soft, gentle light of the moon could be good emollients to his concerns.

Desta rose and ambled to the door. He stealthily unlatched the metal bar from the hook and stepped outside. "Perfect," he said the moment he strode into the yellow light that revealed his surroundings. Everything around him was hushed, except the metal-on-metal grinding of the prisoners' shackles from the jail next door, a sound so familiar that Desta no longer heard it.

He sauntered along the stone walkway to the gate. He turned left, paced twenty feet, and turned left again. The courthouse on his right and the office of records on his left stood mute, quite a transformation from the daytime, when they teemed with people who came to process their court cases. The heavily trodden and pulverized dry grass in the courtyard glowed in the moonlight. Desta felt he was in another world.

He continued walking along the path, the conversation with his mother filtering through his mind. When he reached the southern entrance to the compound, he stopped. Shrouded with tall eucalyptus trees, the town beyond the stone walls looked dark and foreboding. Now feeling more like a lost and confused little boy than a normal person out on a private stroll, Desta turned and walked toward the northern end of the courtyard. By the time he reached the stone barrier, he had addressed to his own satisfaction all the concerns his mother had brought up during their conversation, including his punishment by God for not obeying her requests.

Although his mother's concern about the gossip surrounding Desta and his Parents-of-the-Breast didn't bother him, the possibility of being alienated from his family did concern him some. The air had gotten a bit nippy, causing his face to chill and his feet and hands to go numb. Desta pulled up the hem of his gabi and covered his head, leaving enough of an opening for his eyes and nose.

As he doubled back and walked home, the boy considered all the benefits of having Negasu and Tshai for parents, the greatest of which was having a secure home while he pursued his education. He thought it would be nice to have a mother who cared for him and a father who was there all the time and with whom he could converse rather than being treated as someone insignificant, the way Desta felt Abraham had treated him when he lived at home. Both Negasu and Tshai had made him feel like their own son, and at times he felt closer to them than to his own parents. Then again, he had only known them for six months. He had no idea how they might change in the future.

Desta broke off from the path and made his way to a wooden bench near a bunch of rocks by the piled stone embankment. He needed to recline on this bench, close his eyes, and listen to his feelings and any messages that might come to him. He placed his hand over his heart and said, "God, you know what I want. Please help me fulfill it." When he opened his eyes, he noticed a small, rolled-up white paper sticking out from between two nearby rocks. Desta at first thought the paper belonged to one of the farmers who would sit on the bench to dictate cases to a hired transcriber. But there was something portentous about the way it was placed, tucked between the rocks so wind wouldn't below it away.

Desta rose, clipped the end of the paper between his thumb and index finger, and gently pulled it loose. Nervous and anxious, he held the rolled paper in his hands. Having had many similar preternatural experiences before, Desta knew what might be going on, yet he had no idea what the paper contained. Whatever it was, he prayed it would be something he could live with.

Fingers shaking, eyes fluttering, Desta carefully and slowly unrolled the document. It was inscribed with firm and bold letters. It said:

- Make your decision based on your feelings of today and not on those of the future!
- Don't worry what people will think, but think what will be good for your overall purpose!
- Your life mission must take precedence over anything else, or it's not a life mission. Trust your numbers and have faith in the information you have been given.
- Always do things when they feel right for you and not when you think they feel right for somebody else!

"Thank you!" Desta said aloud. He felt a big burden had been lifted from his shoulders.

FIFTY-ONE

Abraham didn't come for Desta's Parents-of-the-Breast ceremony, but he sent a beautiful gold-colored lamb for the event. Tshai said that the person who brought the lamb left quickly after handing her the animal and saying it was for the family's upcoming ceremony. Ayénat didn't come either, though Desta was not surprised by that. However, Desta was puzzled by Abraham's absence from such an important occasion and one in which a new family was going to relieve him of his responsibilities by adopting his son.

Maybe he didn't want to see the odd and awkward scene of Desta suckling at the breast of another man and woman. Maybe the idea of losing his son to another set of parents suddenly frightened him. It was also possible that his pride kept him away. Enlisting strangers to help support his son couldn't have been easy for Abraham. Of course, there could be other reasons entirely for his absence. No matter, that Abraham and the rest of the family were absent on this special day made Desta feel like a castaway again, like driftwood that had washed up on a riverbank. He swallowed hard, trying to hold back his emotions.

In the days leading up to the ceremony, Desta had his own concerns and questions. How much closer would Negasu and Tshai be to him after the Parents-of-the-Breast ceremony? How enduring would their relationship be? He thought both Negasu and Tshai were capable of loving him, genuinely and unconditionally, more so Tshai because she was more expressive of her feelings.

Then he thought about the extremely awkward moment of suckling their breasts. How could a grown-up boy suckle at the breasts of a woman and a man, and for how long? Imagining himself suckling at Tshai's large breasts was so odd that he covered his face and shook his head. He pictured himself clasping the fleshy part of her breast while he shot the onlookers a sidelong glance. . . . Desta chuckled uneasily at the bizarre image. But thinking about these things, Desta was glad his mother was not there. It would have killed her.

Tshai had bought *kettema*—pulpy deep green grass—and had just sprinkled it all over the living room floor when a one-eyed priest named Tewahade arrived. Negasu and Tewahade shook hands; Tshai bowed and stepped forward so the priest could bless her with his cross. "Is this the boy?" Tewahade asked, throwing his one-eyed glace at him.

Negasu acknowledged that he was. Tshai stepped back and started puttering with things in the kitchen.

Desta didn't like the priest's question and the way he sounded. It was the exact same question that Priest Yacob, from his parents' church, had asked when he came to perform the exorcism. That awful event was haunting him again. And there was something ominous about the man. Was it that one eye that seemed to look straight through him, instead of at him, that bothered Desta? Were the man's disproportionate and exaggerated features the source of his unease? Tewahade had a long face; a prominent but narrow nose; light-colored, pimply skin; and ears big enough to catch rainwater. Or was it simply that Desta didn't trust or like priests anymore? He couldn't say. He had to wait and see whether the aspect of the man that bugged him revealed itself. No matter, Tewahade was the last person Desta would have invited to conduct so important a ceremony as this.

"Please have a seat, Aba," Negasu said graciously as he led the guest to the high earthen bench. The two men sat side by side and talked.

In a wrought-iron pan, Tshai washed coffee beans, rolling them between her palms to remove the membranous skin and residual dirt. She decanted the murky water into a bowl and then rinsed the beans once more, ultimately placing the pan of beans over glowing charcoal. After the remaining water in the pan had sizzled off, Tshai stirred the beans with a long wooden spoon, spreading them out so that they roasted evenly. She absentmindedly watched as the beans popped, spattered, and smoldered, the emerging gray smoke obscuring her handsome face and filling the house with the rich aroma.

"Why don't you move the burner away from the draft," Negasu said, watching Tshai wipe the tears from her eyes.

"I'm almost done. . . . I wanted the charcoal to burn faster," said Tshai casually, her face grave and distant.

When the straw-green beans turned to a dark burnt sienna, she removed the pan and set it on the floor. She spread the smoldering beans and watched the fumes fizzle into wisps of fairy's hair, and vanish.

She fished out a few embers of charcoal from the burner and placed them in a tall clay cup with round leg. She set it by the entrance of the house and dropped a few crumbs of incense over the embers. The incense hissed when it touched the fire and blossomed into a cloud of white fragrance, causing Desta and the rest to revel in contentment.

The golden-brown lamb Abraham had sent for the ceremony was tied to a post outside. The sheep's continuous bleating was making Desta feel queasy. It was at events like this when Desta hated his father the most, when he felt sad for every lamb that was killed to celebrate a holiday. Now that another one was going to lose its life on his account, he felt doubly sick. He went outside and stared at the animal.

Part of him wanted to caress and pacify the lamb. Part of him knew how duplicitous that would be! So he just stood there, leaning against the wall, trying to hold back the emotions that coursed through him. *If your passage is going to bring me loving parents who can help me advance in my education and in my search for the coin, then your blood will not be spilled in vain.* He wiped his tears with the back of his hand. *You will hold the same esteemed place in my heart as Kooli and the vervet monkeys.* He wiped a few more tears from the corners of his eyes and took a long, deep sigh. He felt better. He stomach calmed and his spirits lifted.

Negasu stuck his head out of the door. "Desta, come in." When he stepped back inside, he found the priest and Negasu standing around the table in the middle of the living room. The priest was reading something from an open book. On the table were two small porcelain coffee cups, each partially filled with honey and milk. Tshai perched on a stool several feet away, pounding the coffee beans with the pestle in the wooden mortar, the steady popping sound reverberating throughout the house.

Negasu waved at Desta to come and stand next to him. The boy's mind began to whirl when he looked down on the milk and honey in the cups in front of him. At first he thought he was going to be asked to drink them, but drinking was far removed from suckling. Another thought: maybe the priest was going to coat their breasts with honey at some point and then wet them with milk before Desta began suckling. That, he thought, was more like it.

After several minutes of reciting and reading, Tewahade closed the book, inserted it in its leather case, and slipped the case's strap over his shoulder. *This is it.* Desta's heart raced and his nerves tensed with every passing second. It was going to happen in a moment. He was wondering whether he should close his eyes while suckling, when the priest signaled to Negasu to invite Tshai to join them.

When her husband called her, Tshai bent her head down and refused to look up. Negasu stepped to her, took her by the hand, and brought her to the table. Her face was expressionless, her lips stiff and clamped, her eyes distant and cold. To Desta Tshai seemed suddenly possessed by spirits. "You agreed to do this—what happened?" whispered Negasu. Tshai didn't reply.

Husband and wife stood around the table with the priest and Desta behind them. "Put your right hands straight out and hold them parallel with the floor," Tewahade ordered.

Desta and Negasu did as told, but it took several nudges from her husband before Tshai complied. Desta felt as if his dream of having a new mother was slipping away with each passing moment.

Confused and bewildered by Tshai's behavior, he wondered what he might have done that would cause her to change her mind. Now it seemed that no matter what happened, Tshai would no longer offer him unconditional love. The priest recited something that no one understood. He placed Negasu's hand over Desta's and asked him to hold the boy's wrist. After a few promptings from Negasu, Tshai held her husband's wrist. Tewahade said some more prayers and told the family-to-be to let their hands drop. Desta felt a knot in his stomach and a chill in his heart.

Tewahade picked up the cup of milk and told Negasu to dip in his thumb. The priest then asked Desta to take the milk from Negasu's thumb. Desta was relieved. Sucking their thumbs was certainly far more manageable than their breasts. Still, everything seemed like a dream. Desta felt Negasu's thumb in his mouth only after Negasu had coated it with the honey. Desta had immediately forgotten the first exercise with the milk.

When the priest held the cup with the milk in it and told Tshai to do what her husband had done, she broke away and sat down on her bench by the boiling coffee. Desta felt as if somebody had punched him in the stomach, awakening him from a long dream. The Tshai he loved and hoped was going to be his mother had vanished upon his waking.

Dazed and crushed, he slowly headed for the door. Negasu dashed up and grabbed him. When Desta refused to come back to the room, Negasu put his arm around the boy's shoulders and they went outside and sat on the bench under eaves. "It's not to you that Tshai said no, it's to herself, for reasons we don't know . . . yet. I know you're disappointed, but don't let it get to you. I have no doubt that she still loves you. Maybe the thought of being a mother for a grown-up boy like you is too difficult for her."

"I think it's just that I am not meant to have a mother. . . ." His own words reached deep within him and tears filled his eyes. Desta felt he was now forever cursed; he would never have a mother.

"I don't think that is the case," Negasu said, wrapping his big arms around the boy's slender frame. "First, let's start from the good side of things. You have a new father who loves you. You're intelligent and good looking, which means you will have women in your life who are going to love you for those qualities. Second, you're not going to need a loving mother, or a loving father for that matter, to do what you plan to do because they are not going to travel with you. . . ." Out of the corner of his eye, Negasu saw two men coming through the gate.

Desta dabbed at his tears. What Negasu had said hit home with him. If he had had a loving mother, it would have been difficult for him to leave home and even harder for him to stay away once he did. That was exactly what he had told his mother a few days ago.

Why was he so disappointed with Tshai's refusal to be his Mother-of-the-Breast? That was something he couldn't quite articulate to himself amid his mixed desires and needs. His was a deeply emotional reaction, although intellectually he had accepted not having emotional attachments to his family. He cherished his freedom and he certainly wouldn't trade it for maternal love.

Negasu rose. "Nadew and Mengistu, my colleagues from work, are here to help kill the lamb. We'll celebrate our Father-of-the-Breast ceremony—you and I. Of course, everybody else will join us, but you and I know this is special between us." Desta's new father patted him on the back. "Okay? Cheer up!" He gave Desta a quick, warm glance before he stepped away, which made the boy feel better.

This is more than I had at home. He was touched by Negasu's thoughtfulness and care. Desta never had any form of embrace from his father when he was growing up, let alone such loving support. *I'm not going to let this disappointment ruin my day. I have had worse things happen to me. I can live through it.* And no matter what, he would never allow Tshai to feel she had done him wrong. He would not change his behavior, manners, or attitude toward her. If the question of why she did not want to be his mother ever came up, he would simply say, "I understand. Sorry for troubling you."

Nadew and Mengistu took the sheep to the back of the house. Negasu went inside to keep the priest company until the animal was slaughtered and the *dulet*—mixture of raw liver and spices—was ready.

After the customary dulet meal, Nadew and Mengistu left. The priest invited Desta to escort him to the gate. "Listen," the priest said, resting his heavy hand on Desta's shoulder and glancing down with that one eye of his. "You wanted two Parents-of-the-Breast, but you ended up with one. There could be a reason God didn't want you to have Tshai for a mother. Our Father in heaven may think she doesn't deserve a sweet boy like you. . . . I know exactly how you feel about having just one parent. Sometimes one good parent is all we need." The priest looked away for a few seconds. "I'll share a personal story. I lost my eye when I was your age. After the initial shock and then the adjustment period, I got over it quickly and have done very well with my life."

Desta said, "I feel like a one-legged person. But how can you advance in life with just one leg?" He was surprised at himself for coming up with this question.

"By persistence and determination. What happened to you today is just another lesson, son. So . . . good luck . . . and good-bye."

Desta watched the one-eyed man until he vanished in the knot of eucalyptus trees past the stone wall. Then he turned around and hopped on one leg from the gate to the house.

FIFTY-TWO

After the disappointment of the Parents-of-the-Breast ceremony, Desta didn't find he was any closer to Negasu, who was now his nominal father, nor did he feel any distance from Tshai. This congenial relationship between Desta and Tshai continued partly because he made a conscious effort not to make her feel she had done him wrong. He showed it with his actions. He performed promptly any task or errand she asked of him and always with a smile. Over time, he even felt closer to Tshai than to his new father, again disproving Abraham's theory about the importance of a blood relationship or a symbolic relationship, such as adoption.

The milk cow, who Negasu had named Neuffa, was as important to Desta, if not more so, as the people he lived with. To start with, she was a milk cow only in name. She had no calf and she was not producing milk. The couple had bought her hoping that the beautiful auburn heifer would find a ready and willing bull to mate with, eventually producing a calf and, consequently, milk.

One of Desta's jobs every morning was not only to drive the animal to the field at the outskirts of town but also to ensure that she mingled with the farmers' cattle from the surrounding areas. As it turned out, Neuffa didn't like spending her days with the other cattle. She preferred instead to ally herself with the horses. Every evening when Desta went to fetch her, he found her grazing with the steeds, which exasperated both Desta and Negasu.

"Do you know if she is going for size and not compatibility?" Fenta asked, laughing when Desta told him his frustration.

When it finally dawned on him what Fenta was referring to, Desta said with a smile, "I don't know, even that is not happening."

Neuffa was a very independent and self-assured cow, and Desta liked her for that. He liked her also because she was cooperative and responsive to certain basic commands. She came to his call readily and happily, although there was nothing for her to really come for—no calf to nurse or hay or grains to eat.

Desta secretly thanked Negasu and Tshai for having the animal because she was the reason he was living with them and going to school, and because of her he could stay out until the sun set. Often, after he collected and brought her near town, he sat on a knoll or rock and watched the sun as it edged toward the horizon—a series of hues unfolding along with the births and deaths of colors—and then slid toward the distant peaks, until it eventually vanished from his world, leaving him alone and in awe.

AT THE END OF THE SCHOOL YEAR, Desta ranked first in his class and was promoted to the fourth grade. He stayed in town for the rainy season—June through September—although Abraham asked him to come and help out on the farm. None of his relatives came to see him except for his father, when he came for the sake of his court cases, and Saba, when she came to shop at the market, often bringing him a loaf of bread or dabo kolo snacks. She gave him updates, including the unabated gossip about his supposed conversion to Islam, his living with complete strangers, and his "bad" parents, who were seen as responsible for his conversion and living situation. The latest report was actual news, not gossip. He heard from Saba that Hibist had given birth to her first and only child—a boy—with her second husband.

Desta's rainy season break would have been uneventful except for the talking box a newly hired teacher had brought with him. On bright weekend days, this young man would bring his wooden box, place it on the grass, and let the neighborhood kids listen as it sang music and talked. He called it 'radio,' and it was a total mystery to Desta how such a simple box could do all those things as if it were packed with people. Although Desta had seen a similar box at Masud's store, he had a keener interest in it this time than before. And he spent hours thinking about a mystery he couldn't unravel nor which anyone could adequately explain.

FIFTY-THREE

At the end of the school year in 1962, Desta knew that his pursuit of a modern
education and the Coin of Magic and Fortune would come to a dead end. He
didn't have relatives in Finote Selam or Burie, the two towns that had classes
through the eighth grade. And, as it turned out, he had little hope that Negasu,
his adoptive father, could serve as a bridge to other potential helpers in the two
towns. Negasu was new to the area and had friends in neither town. The only
people he knew were through his work, and didn't know them well enough to
ask any of them for a favor. He said that his hundred-birr monthly salary barely
covered the household expenses and that he couldn't support Desta while he
attended school away from home.

Desta had long given up counting on his own family in this regard. Abraham
had no cash, although he was willing to occasionally support Desta with grains.
The boy was left to pursue his dreams on his own.

Repeating the fourth grade, like many had done, because he had no one who
cared enough to make sacrifices for him seemed a cruel punishment to Desta.
He knew that if Abraham really believed in him, he could sell a cow or one of
his mookit goats and hire a woman to look after Desta in Burie or Finote Selam.
If Negasu had really considered him his son, he could have gone to extra lengths
to make sure he continued his education. Other policemen who earned less
than Negasu sent their children to other towns so they could advance in their
education. But Desta didn't really hold the man responsible for his own hardships; if he hadn't been able to count on his own family, how could he count on a
complete stranger he had barely known for a year?

But Desta also realized that things were not as dismal as they might appear
to be. From living in Dangila, he had discovered that going hungry hadn't killed
him. His body was strong and resilient; he could manage and sustain himself
even in the worst of circumstances.

And he knew there was a powerful essence within him; it could make a cross-eyed boy see straight, cold water warm, a vicious dog suddenly repentant and submissive and a hostile village conciliatory. The coin was his protector and also a device that helped connect him directly and quickly to his power within.

Desta also had learned to have faith in Providence and strangers. People who were not related to him had genuine affection for him, and they wished him well. They treated Desta like a family member, a friend, and a confidante. And from these experiences, he loved the people he had yet to meet.

Armed with these thoughts and feelings, Desta decided to go to Burie on his own in July, deep in the rainy season, to look for strangers who might give him food and shelter while he attended school in exchange for his part-time services. After getting permission from Negasu, he arranged to go to Burie with Debeb, an animal-skins merchant. One weekday morning, Debeb loaded his two mules with cowhides and goat and lamb skins, and they left.

The day was overcast and it appeared as if it might rain even before they left town. But as they went farther west, the rain clouds evaporated into feathery wisps and spreading sheets. By the time the sun touched earth, they had reached Burie.

Cloaked in the pervasive eucalyptus trees, etched with a series of muddy footpaths, and inhabited by a disorderly mixture of huts and corrugated tin-roof houses, the town of Burie didn't exactly fill Desta with excitement. But he was not looking for comfort or convenience. Anything would do so long as he could continue his education.

Debeb led the animals to a warehouse at the center of town where he would sell his skins. After they unloaded the mules, the owner of the warehouse weighed each bale and paid Debeb the price they had agreed upon. Desta spent the night with the relatives of Debeb in town.

THE FOLLOWING DAY, while Debeb went around to the various stores to purchase things he planned to sell at his shop in Yeedib, Desta set off on his own. He spoke with shop merchants and office people in the plaza to see whether they would take a student.

He battled flies, hopped over rain puddles, and skirted mud patches on his way to the center of town. The road he walked on ended at a large open space resembling the market grounds in Dangila and Yeedib, lined with shops all around. Although it was not a market day, there was some sort of celebration going.

A great number of people packed the plaza. Desta navigated through the crowd that included noisy peddlers who hawked merchandise from baskets that hung around their necks and who tried to get the attention of shop owners and others in the plaza.

Desta learned the many different ways people had to say the same thing to him. The simple two-letter word *no* came from people with gruff and curt voices as well as those with kind and promising faces. And it came from merchants who sliced the air backhandedly but at enough of a distance to keep from striking Desta in the face. *No* came from people with intolerant and impatient eyes and from those whose intense, reprimanding gaze stirred the air as they drilled holes in Desta's face. And it came from the mouth of a kind old man who shared his freshly baked loaf and tea with him. Yet Desta was unfazed. He knew it was the kind of thing he must endure.

He left the rows of shops and the musty air and walked to the center of the plaza. He had hoped to run into well-to-do and openhearted people who might need an errand boy in their homes. Instead Desta met passive faces, stoic faces, masks of pride and dignity, polished and radiant ones reflecting contentment from within, and those whose expressions didn't say much one way or the other.

On the fringes of the plaza people perched on rock seats, patches of animal skin or cloth spread before them, begging for their livelihood. Elsewhere people pleaded to be noticed and admired as they walked across the grounds, going from one shop to another: women in their modern floral skirts, their waists fastened with colorful elastic belts and their feet sheathed with leather or plastic Congo shoes; and men in their woolen suits or khaki pants and sweaters, felt hats, and black leather shoes.

He walked through a painter's palette of white, cream, and ivory, with specks of blue, red, and green. It was a scene one always observed in such gatherings. Desta approached everyone without fear or prejudgment, but people here had no patience, interest, or need of what the boy tried to offer. *No* was the word of the day—the two-letter word he had walked all day from Yeedib to Burie to hear. It burned in his head.

Disheartened but not defeated, Desta left the plaza to look for Debeb. He walked past the row of beggars and saw a half-dozen men sitting on a bench getting their shoes shined by poor-looking boys.

Desta studied the boys, wondering whether they were once dreamers like himself—whether they had come from other small towns hoping to find people to live with and go to school. But instead they ended up becoming *listros*—shoeshine boys—abandoning their dreams when they couldn't find someone to take them in. He shuddered with fear.

He left the plaza by a stone walkway along a set of closed buildings, his head down, thinking about all that he had heard and seen. A gentle breeze blew, driving crumpled papers and dead leaves against the direction of his walk, bringing with it the odors of the neighborhood and camphor, in addition to the aroma of roasting meat.

He heard a sharp, squalling cry and looked up. On the opposite side of the street stood a lone shack of grass and sticks. Before it sat a woman with two boys about two and four years of age. The woman held a chicken leg over an open fire with one hand while she cradled the younger boy with the other. Desta walked across the street and stood before them, stunned. The mother had a cross tattooed in the middle of her forehead, and another on her pretty chin. The bottom half of the tattoo's vertical line wrapped under her jutting jaw. Her skin was dry and pale, her hair a storehouse of dust. The woman's lips appeared parched, even desolate, their corners drawn tightly, the deep lines around them making her appear a lot older than she was. Dried tear tracks marked her cheeks, and Desta doubted the tears that had flowed were caused by smoke.

She eyed Desta suspiciously, like a feral cat jealously guarding its kill. Realizing he was not in the class of people who would give alms to someone like her, she retracted her gaze and looked down on the chicken leg. Next to the older boy was a pile of what appeared to be excrement. Flies feasted on the boys' eyes, noses, and mouths, and on the unholy pile next to them. Desta shuddered as he drew with his eyes the line between the flies' love of excrement and the boys' insect-ravaged faces.

Through the open door of the hut, Desta saw straw bedding on the floor and a dirty blanket. He wanted to ask the woman what had happened to the father of the boys or her family, that she and her sons should be living like this. But he realized there was no polite way to ask, and he had nothing to offer her to lighten her load and console her heart. He said nothing.

Passersby from the opposite direction walked briskly past them without even turning their heads, as if the family were made of stone or trash tossed on the side of the street. Others who came by tossed coins and walked on without saying anything to them.

Soon after Desta, too, simply walked away, but wishing he had coins with him to give to this desolate family.

A little while later he came to a small grove of trees a short distance from the
street. What had accumulated in his head that day was just too much to bear. He
hurried to the grove and urinated. As he headed back to the street, he noticed
a tree stump. Desta decided he would sit and think. But instead of thinking, he
found himself starting to weep, slowly at first, but then it poured out of him like
a mighty wave. He cried not so much for his own misfortune but for that of the
woman and her children. He'd give anything for a pair of wings so he could fly
into another world and follow the sun away from this life of misery. Feeling a
little better, he got up and walked back to the street.

THAT NIGHT AS HE CRAWLED TO BED, he told himself he would give his
first month's salary to people like that woman and her two children, and not buy
a sack full of firno as he had promised himself he would do when he lived in
Dangila.

In his sleep Desta had a dream. He was being fitted with a large pair of feath-
ered wings, like those of the man on the wall at his parents' church. Then he
was up in the clouds, flying west, his eyes on the setting sun. He heard a voice,
almost a whisper, similar to the one he had heard when Damtew's goat was
killed, along with the other animals. The voice said, "Be patient with yourself
and the world. Everything about your future was set in place long before you
were born, long before . . . long before . . . long before . . ." The voice seemed to
have difficulty spitting out what it wanted to say. "Let's just say as long ago as
when the mountains facing your country home were created. The same mountains that tell your story."

"What?" Desta asked, steadying his wings and allowing just the drift of the
air current to carry him.

"Yes, certain events are already in motion for your benefit, some at the
expense a very important person. You need to be patient until some of these
events catch up with you. Remember: you still need to go through life like
everyone else to earn the privileges you have been granted."

When Desta awoke, he was still floating in the clouds. He was sad to realize it
was only a dream and mystified by the messages he had received. If this premo-
nition had any validity, it served as a consolation to his otherwise dismal trip.

As Desta and Debeb returned home the next day, the mules loaded with all
kinds of merchandise, Desta thought about his dream and what the voice had
said. He accepted his fate. He would repeat fourth grade like several other
students, his friend Fenta among them.

BY AUGUST THERE WAS STILL NO SIGN that he would be able to attend one of the schools, but Desta got the opportunity to do something for himself. The director of the Yeedib school said he needed a student to help bring a few cartons of the Point Four powdered milk from the Finote Selam school's store-house. Maybe this was the break the voice had told him about. He immediately volunteered to go.

Desta and a hired man drove a mule and donkey team to Finote Selam. They braved rainstorms, muddy roads, and sharp rocks that left their toes bleeding. The road passed through a wooded flatland where hundreds of gray, honeycomb rocks littered the grounds.

In Finote Selam, like he had done in Burie the previous month, Desta spent the day after their arrival asking shopkeepers if they would give him a room and food in exchange for part-time work while he went to school. A couple of the shopkeepers said they might be able to take him but not right away.

Desta and the man loaded the animals with the Point Four milk cartons and returned home. On their way back, the donkey with its six cartons got swept away while crossing a suddenly surging river. The mule crossed the river unharmed. Desta and the man were knocked down and carried away by the rough current, too, but managed to cling to an overhanging tree branch near the embankment, where they got out. The man climbed out under his own power, but Desta had to appeal to the coin image on his chest.

After they got out of the river, they removed their clothes, squeezed and wrung them to remove as much of the water as they could, and put them back on. Wet, hungry, and shivering, they traveled another three hours before they finally reached home.

Tshai made a roaring fire, placed a skin mat near it, and let Desta lie down and get warm. The heat instead seemed to bring out the cold in Desta's body. He shivered wildly for a while before he finally calmed down. He ate his dinner, enough to kill his hunger, and drank a lot of warm tea. In bed that night, Desta wept for his misfortunes that never seemed to end. When done with his crying, he wiped his sniffles and closed his eyes, hoping sleep would take him to anoth-er world where his fortune was better. The next morning he rose feeling well rested and refreshed.

BUT WHEN THE SCHOOL OPENED in September, many of the graduated fourth-graders had either gone back to their villages and become shepherds and farmers, or had gone to the bigger towns to continue their studies. When he learned that Fenta too was going to Finote Selam with his uncle, who got a job there, he became severely depressed. Now, he would not be continuing his schooling *and* he would be losing his best friend and confidante.

Staying in little Yeedib for the next nine months and doing the same things he did the year before sounded to Desta like a punishment he didn't deserve. Yet he felt there was somehow a silver lining to his ordeal: the voice in his dream had told him that he needed to be patient and that everything would work out. Desta thought he might not even have to wait the entire school year. A new opportunity might soon take him to Burie or Finote Selam so he could continue with his twin missions. But nobody came to take him to one of the schools he dreamed of attending. He then thought something would probably break after the Christmas vacation, which was the next time he could transfer. Christmas came and went. Still nothing happened. Desta began to doubt the credibility of the voice in his dream.

FIFTY-FOUR

Desta felt trapped once again. It was not like the physical barriers of the mountains of his childhood that used to make him feel walled in. It was not like the circumstances of his life in Dangila, in which the ubiquitous eucalyptus trees had symbolized his sense of oppression. It was by the absence of a family that cared enough, that understood his dreams enough, that could make sacrifices for him so he could further his education and continue his search for the Coin of Magic and Fortune.

When it became certain that he would repeat the fourth grade again, Desta made up his mind to teach himself how to fly. The idea had first occurred to him when he saw the picture of that man with the beautiful set of wings on the wall of his parents' church. That wistful desire to fly had again come upon him when he first saw the sunrise a year and a half ago. And his most recent flight dream had been very exciting. All these incidents had inspired him to build his own set of wings.

He had never seen people fly under their own power but the idea didn't seem farfetched or impossible. Birds of all sizes flew. Eleni always came flying through the air. For a boy with a magical coin on his chest, the dream might be turned into reality.

The 1963 new year could be the blessing Desta needed to move ahead with his aspirations. As in the first semester, he didn't need to do much schoolwork, just enough to keep his skills and mind sharp.

He realized that the wings were crucial. Although he had never seen airplanes up close, their wings were big, silvery spreads. He didn't know what enabled airplanes to fly. For the birds, feathers were the key to their ability to fly. So first he had to study how wings were made and how they worked, and then he had to collect a lot of feathers.

He chose the chicken as his model. Tshai killed a chicken almost every week-end, so chicken feathers were readily available. And he was the one who cut off the heads of the chickens, a task that at first was very repulsive for Desta. Since only men were supposed to do the job, and often he was he only male in the house, the grim task had been relegated to him.

Amazingly, one Sunday afternoon as he turned the corner near the court-house grounds, he ran into one of his remaining classmates, named Yonas, followed by a man and his son. They stopped. The man was carrying a fettered chicken in his arm.

"What a coincidence!" Yonas said. "We were coming to your house because they were looking for you." He stepped aside so that Desta could have a full view of the boy and the man. The boy looked familiar, but Desta had never seen the man before.

"We have been coming to town and your school for some time hoping to meet you," the man said. His voice was soft and retiring. "Thank God we could finally meet."

When Yonas noticed Desta's apparent loss, he said, "This is the father and son we had told you about; they had come to our school looking for you. . . ."

It dawned on Desta. "Are you Yewegey?" Desta asked, surprised by the even set of eyes that gazed at him. He studied the boy. He wore a cream-color *avooje-day*—cheap fabric—shirt that was sliced halfway on the sides under his arms, the two lengths extending down to his knees. He had draped himself with his gabi and carried a hockey stick. His wooly hair was cut into a *terraye*—a strip of hair, running from front to back, longitudinally, across the boy's otherwise shaved head.

"Awwe," Yewegey replied shyly.

"I want to thank you in person for what you have done for my son. It's a mira-cle. Yewegey could see straight now. And he has been the happiest ever since. . . . As a token of our appreciation, we brought this chicken. You can breed her or have her for a meal with your parents." The man extended the hand that held the chicken. The bird unfurled her wings and quaked, looking at Desta with sad, beady eyes.

"No. I really didn't do much for him. I . . I thank you but . . ."

"This is nothing for us. We have plenty. It's only a small token." He tossed his hand, prompting Desta to take the chicken.

Awkwardly, Desta took the hen and cradled it in his arms. The fowl flapped her wings, wishing to be let go. "I thank you very much . . . . I must admit, on second thought . . ." Desta began to say, looking up at the man and then the boy, "I . . . I can certainly use the feathers." Desta smiled.

"And her meat would be good, too," the man said, cracking his handsome face into a grin. "We could have brought eggs as well, but since we didn't know if we would ever see you, we didn't. . . . Come see us on the weekend when you have free time. . . ." Father and son left. So did Yonas. Desta headed home excited by his windfall.

He couldn't have asked for a better gift for his project. Chicken in hand, he went to the back of the house and placed her on the table. With her legs still tied, he pulled open the wings and studied their structure and design. He ran his hands over the contours of the wings to find out their angles of construction. He parted the feathers and studied their dovetailing patterns. To the boy's surprise the animal lay quietly—as if she were enjoying the attention. From these inspections, Desta learned that wing feathers had barbs that were narrow and tapering on one side of the horned divider, whereas those from the tail were broad and nearly of equal width on either side of the quill.

Finished with his inspection, he brought the chicken inside the house and told Tshai all about receiving the bird as a gift. She agreed to serve chicken for dinner and so the boy proceeded to kill the hen. After he chopped off the head, he plucked all the feathers from the wings and piled them neatly, making sure not to ruffle them or tear their barbs. Then he dropped the chicken's remains into boiling water to help remove the rest of the plumage.

After three months of plucking the chickens Tshai served, Desta had collected what he thought would be sufficient feathers to start building his wings.

He decided what other materials he needed: five 7-foot by three-inch strips of thick fabric, six 4-foot-long wooden strips, twenty 3-and-one-half-foot-long bamboo strips, one 4-foot-long slender bamboo pole, a 7-by-4-foot piece of khaki fabric, and boiled wheat dough for glue. For his work area he chose the long old table behind Negasu and Tshai's house.

The next day after school, Desta started building his wings. He got his sack of feathers from the shed and brought them to the worktable. Because the feathers were naturally bowed, arraying them on his mounting strips, neatly and without gaps, was going to be difficult. He flattened the feathers by carefully spreading them on the table and placing granite slabs on them overnight. Because their shafts were too smooth to adhere to the wheat glue, he cut off a few inches of each quill so that he could glue the feather leaf directly to the fabric and wooden strips.

Over the next several weeks, he worked on his project for an hour every day after school, before he went to fetch the cow. He glued all the chopped feathers onto the 7-foot-long cloth strips, carefully dovetailing them and brushing them down with the pad of his hand so they lay flat as they appeared naturally. He sewed the strips to the sheet of khaki fabric, and the different shades and patterns made his handiwork appear more like a leopard skin than a work created from chicken feathers.

"Are you now planning to become a church school student?" Negasu asked when he saw Desta's wings spread over the table. "Except that they wear pieced sheepskin and not feathers." The Father-of-the-Breast smiled broadly.

"Considering my circumstances, that might not be a farfetched idea, actually," chirped the boy without looking up. He patted down some feathers that were sticking up.

"You have spent several weeks on this. What kind of school project is it?"

"These are a set of wings," Desta said. "I plan to use them to fly."

"I hope you're kidding," Negasu said incredulously.

"You'll have to wait and see to believe me."

The Father-of-the-Breast went inside. Desta rolled up his project, gathered the rest of his things, and put everything into the shed.

He continued working on his design a few days more. On each side of the wings, he placed ten bamboo crosspieces on top of and below the sewn fabric strips, tying them together with string at several discrete points, a task he accomplished by piercing the large khaki drapery with an awl. He tied six vertical wooden strips onto the crosspieces. Finally, he placed the slender bamboo rod vertically between the adjoining edges of the wings as a spar. He attached leather handles underneath the wings on both sides and two belts made from the same material across the spar and fixed to the crosspieces.

He stood the construction on the ground, held out the edges of the wings, and moved them in and out. Desta could see that they would flap easily once he got underneath, put on the belts, and used the leather handles to beat them. He couldn't wait to try them out. For now he needed to go and fetch the cow. He folded the wings and brought the device to the shed along with all his other things.

In his mind he was already flying with his new craft. From the compound, out to the street, and down the hill to the field, he flew, stretching his arms out and flapping them. The neighborhood children and adults watched Desta, wondering whether there might be something wrong with him. He didn't care what they thought.

The next day after school, he immediately went to the shed and brought out his winged craft. He folded it in half and carried it out of the compound under his arm, through the courtyard, and onto the path that went around the stone wall. Once he got to the open space above the plateau, he opened the wings of the craft, stood it up, and secured the two belts around him. He inserted his hands into the looping handles. His heart raced and his stomach gave into the queasy sensation of butterflies. All of a sudden he was paralyzed by fear. Would he be able to come down once he was airborne? What if something went wrong and he crashed? Who would rescue him? The terrain was full of sharp rocks.

He thought it was very foolish to have come here alone. With Fenta gone, he had no close friends he could confide in about his private project. If he failed, he would rather it be his own personal affair.

He was not going to go home now without making at least an attempt. If it felt like he would fly, then he would invite Negasu and other people to watch him. He spread his wings out. He leaned forward and ran to gain air lift. Nothing happened. He felt not even a tiny sensation that he might become airborne. He rubbed his hand over the coin, concentrating his thoughts and seeing himself flying. Then he ran again, leaning hard and with the wings wide open. Still nothing. Mystified and disappointed, he took off the wings and folded them and walked home. As he walked, he rubbed his fingers over the pen in his pocket and bit his lip, lost in thought.

On each of the next several days he came out with his wings and tried again and again. He still did not leave the ground.

At night, before he fell asleep and whenever his mind was not otherwise engaged, he thought about his failed flying efforts. He wondered whether people could really fly on wings. He wondered whether that man on his parents' church wall really flew. Maybe his wings were just for show. He wondered why the coin image on his chest hadn't helped him become airborne. Did this mean it no longer had magical powers or just that magic cannot occur in the presence of danger? When these mental exertions found no answers or plausible explanations, Desta threw up his hands and went on with his normal activities.

FIFTY-FIVE

One day in June, while the school was on its morning break, there came a whining, sputtering, and popping sound from the western sky. The sound was unlike anything Desta had ever heard, and it seemed unlikely anyone on the school grounds had ever heard it either because everyone stopped their activities to listen and watch. The horrific sound traveled through the earth and air, shaking the rocks on the ground and rattling the leaves in the bushes. The sound came from a small, round object in the sky, which was about to crash down on the famed holy church of Gish Abayi.

"*Awroplane*—airplane," everybody shouted. Without even thinking or bothering to ask permission from the teachers, all the students took to their feet.

Desta didn't think it was an airplane. When he was a shepherd, he used to stare up at the sky every time one passed overhead. Those airplanes were silvery, not black like this thing in the western sky appeared to be. Those airplanes hummed and droned as they flew overhead, benign and harmless. This object sounded deafening, devouring, and ready to destroy anyone and anything that came near it.

Yet everyone, including many of the townspeople, ran down the rocky terrain, across the Abayi River, and onto the spring green turf toward the Gishe Abayi Church. Farmers ran, leaving their harnessed animals behind, shepherds left their animals and ran, and women ran out of their homes, no-doubt suspending their activities, to join the throng.

While everyone was scurrying toward the church, Desta watched as the horrific object circled in the air for a bit and finally spiraled down to earth. No one knew whether they were about to witness a disaster or visitation, but no one was going to miss what looked to be a once-in-a-lifetime event. In Desta's mind, if someone had come to visit, he prayed whomever it was would still be there by the time the crowd arrived. It seemed the same question was on everyone's mind—everyone seemed to be running in an effort to beat time.

Sweaty and out of breath, people started arriving. The source of the earsplitting sound, which had shattered the peace and tranquility of life on the plateau, was far less imposing than the power it exuded. It looked like little more than a giant insect, with body, legs, tail, antennae, and all. And it came down from the sky, nullifying Desta's theory that in order for objects to fly, they had to have wings and feathers—or at least wings. The craft had none of these.

Also, the celestial insect was empty. It seemed as if it had flown toward the Gishe Abayi Church and landed on its own, like a bird. But this presumption was short-lived. The three men who had flown in it suddenly appeared. They had gone to visit the famous church and the spring of holy water, the source of the Abayi, the Blue Nile River. They walked a leisurely pace, thoughtfully talking to one another. Every so often they stopped and surveyed their surroundings.

They neared their craft, and the crowd rearranged itself like a wave, surrounding them and the giant insect. One of the men could have passed for any of the people standing around him, both in skin tone, stature, and features, although he shared only his clothes and bearing with the other two.

One of the two foreigners was so tall and rugged that he looked as if he could easily reach up and, in a single motion, yank a steeple off the roof of one of the grass houses. The second was short and thin and looked as if the wind from his aircraft's engines might easily blow him off his feet. But there were three distinct features that these two individuals of contrast shared. Their skin resembled bleached copper, their eyes were the tint of the spring sky, and their straight hair was the beige hue of summer grass.

The crowd was now several layers deep, staring at the oddities that had dropped out of the heavens on such a beautiful, blameless day. The audience took in the insect machine, which seemed to be resting peacefully, like a well-behaved dog. The smaller of the visitors looked nervous and agitated. His tall counterpart paced around but was unfazed by the attention. He looked up occasionally and appraised the crowd. Then the tall one took a few steps and stood before an older man at the outermost circle of the crowd. The third man, who resembled everyone else, matched the tall man's steps as if he were his bodyguard and also stood before the old man.

The tall man turned to his colleague. "Ask him what's the most miraculous thing he has seen at this church."

The old man said, "I saw a woman get cured of her blindness."

Another, younger man volunteered, "I witnessed a crippled man get up and walk after the holy water treatment."

"I heard that a man got cured of his leprosy within days of his arrival at this place," chipped in a third.

The tall man shook his head, though it was hard to tell whether in disbelief or amazement.

"I hope they have not defiled the water," murmured someone in the back of the crowd.

"I don't think so," said a woman who was also deep in the crowd. "The priests won't let them come near it."

The tall man and the translator walked back to the aircraft. The short, thin man opened the door for the two to go in. The short man hopped in like a rabbit and sat in front. He picked up a curved device and placed it across his head so that the circular, cuplike ends hugged his ears.

He reached for something in front of him and the insect came to life. Its antennae slowly began to spin. They picked up speed, going faster and faster, until they ultimately vanished into the air. The machine snapped and sputtered and then screamed and whined, shaking the earth and whipping the grass and the crowd like a field of wheat in a gale. Some people ran for their lives, looking back to see whether the insect was following them. Others screwed up their courage and stood at a safe distance and watched.

Desta was one of those who stood and watched. His heart thumping, his feet shaking over the trembling earth, his inner ears feeling as if they might shatter into pieces, he watched the insect lift into the air, lash its tail, and turn to fly west. The piercing, yammering sound reverberated throughout the plateau long after the helicopter had gone.

As he walked back, Desta realized there was a third way to fly. Besides wings and feathers, a set of blades that spun and whipped the air. The concept and the workings of this method of flying were foreign and looked complicated. He would not consider it as an option for the aircraft he was trying to build. For now he would have to stick with his feathers and wings.

SCHOOL CLOSED AT THE END OF JUNE. Desta's prospect of finding people to live with in either Finote Selam or Burie was still dismal. The likelihood that he will repeat the fourth grade once again when September came around seemed as real as the rain that poured every day on Yeedib. But this time he was not as depressed or desperate as a year ago.

Then one night while lying in bed listening to the putter-putter of the rain on the grass roof, staring at the pitch black darkness and thinking about his future, the wings that didn't work, the magical channel in the coin that failed him and having no clear idea what he could do to build a better flying craft, he heard a thin but crisp voice. It sounded as if it were coming from very far away, like a ray of star light that comes piercing through the night air.

It said, "there are a few reasons why things have not worked out for you lately.

"You have not made strong efforts to learn and practice the legends ascribed to the seven channels on the face and tail of the coin, whose images, along with the picture of the coin box, you diligently copied from the original goatskin onto a parchment and brought it with you when you went to Dangila. It seems that you're rather been negligent of their importance to you. Your relationship has been purely with the magical channel, reaching for it every time you're in a crisis.

The rest of the attributes are just as important. All of them are the reasons you were born and now set on journey to find the other coin and unit it with the one you own. Their union will be good for all humanity. The attributes were selected by King Solomon, your ancestral father who received the blessings of God after he prayed on each set of the seven items for a week. There are three sets of these or a total of twenty-one attributes."

A sudden squall of wind cut off the voice. It continued shortly after the gust subsided.

"For nearly three thousand years they remained hidden because the original plaques that contained the information about them got lost. They were revealed to your grandfather's spirit shortly before you were born in nineteen-forty-nine, so he could share with you these attributes and their meanings because of the journey you have been destined to travel.

So if you wish your luck to improve—both in building a better flying craft and travel to Finote Selam to further your studies, you better start reciting and praying over the rest of the channels in your scroll. They can be your teachers, door openers to many things." Then the voices faded and said no more.

FIFTY-SIX

For all of July and August, Desta rose every morning, washed his hands and face, and went to the back of the house with the parchment. He sat on a stool under the eaves when it was wet outside and on the bench by the long table when it was a clear day. He unrolled the scroll and began reciting the legends by caressing each channel with the tip of his index finger from the center outward; he recited them each seven times, or a total of forty-nine recitals. Once finished he rolled up the parchment and went inside. Since there were three sets of the seven channels, he repeated each set every four days.

On September 14, three days after the New Year's celebration, Tshai sent Desta to town to purchase packets of tea and sugar cubes. Because it was a rainy day, he used an umbrella. But it was also very windy. As he walked, the force of the wind kept threatening to snatch the umbrella out of his hand, lifting him off the ground each time he tried to hold it securely. He barely managed to keep himself sure-footed and the umbrella in his possession.

That night when he went to bed, a light went on in his head. It occurred to him that the best flying craft would probably be one he could build using umbrella fabric and constructed in such a way that air could be suspended inside it.

The following day, he went back to his workbench with a basket of snacks: roasted barley, chickpeas, and peas. He set the basket on the table, went to the shed, and brought out all the things he stored in it. He set the wings across one corner of the table and looked at them, thinking for a long time, his hands making multiple trips to the basket. He realized his wings were too stiff, bulky, and hard to manipulate. The umbrella concept, particularly the fabric, was his only glimmer of hope.

Then out of the blue, as usual, Eleni showed up, swooping down from the sky with her garments billowed, their hems fluttering in the air.

"Having problems?" she asked.

"Yes."

"Your first problem is," said the Wind Woman, holding the boy's gaze, "that you didn't plan well. You didn't think of the potential difficulties ahead of time. Second, you're stuck with your feather and wing thoughts. You didn't realize that there might be other ways to achieve the same goal. The helicopter you saw last June should be a good example. It had no wings or feathers, but it still flew."

"I know, but up until now, all I knew was feathers and wings. I thought that everything that flies had either one or both of them."

"Always allow yourself to think of other possibilities if the familiar doesn't seem to work."

She opened and fanned the top layer of her voluminous skirt, pointing to several fist-sized air bags secured inside the lining of the lustrous garment. "These are the air pockets that allow me to travel through space. I hope this gives you an idea for your craft, including the kind of material you should get."

Desta asked for permission to touch the fabric. He held it between his thumb and index finger, trying to determine the kind of fabric. Sure enough, it felt similar to that used to make umbrellas.

"Got it?" Eleni asked, looking down at the boy.

Desta nodded. "It feels like harr, the kind I once saw in a shop in Dangila."

"Get something that is strong, soft, and smooth, and that has little resistance to the movement of the air."

"I know exactly where I can get some. Thank you," Desta said, letting go of Eleni's clothes.

"Good. Get to work, then," she said, rising into the air. When he looked up, she was gone.

THAT NIGHT DESTA remembered the last place he had seen fabric similar to Eleni's, although hers was much thinner. It was at Masud and Sheik Ibrahim's store in Dangila. The following morning after he recited the legends, he wrote a letter to Masud:

Dear Masud,

How have you been? It's over two and a half years since I left Dangila and since I saw you and your baba. I had hoped to return after I came home for Christmas but, as you know, living with Zewday had been so hard that I decided to stay here and finish my fourth grade in our little Yeedib. Sorry I didn't come back as I had hoped. I miss you and Sheik

Ibrahim and Khadija.

A month ago I learned about a tailor here named Fikru, who goes to Dangila to shop for fabric. I had meant to send you a letter the next time he came there, just to let you know what has been happening with me since I left your town. And as you will see below, I now have an additional purpose in writing.

I finished the fourth grade a year ago last June, but now I am waiting until I get an opportunity to go further with my studies, probably in Burie or Finote Selam. I'll still be in school when it opens in two weeks, though, repeating the fourth grade, unfortunately. But I'm learning as much new stuff as the teachers can find for me. A few months back I was involved in a personal project that I was excited about and which I want to resume as soon as possible.

One of the reasons I am writing you this letter—I feel very awkward about this, but Masud, you're the brother I never had and I hope you will understand—is to ask you a huge favor regarding this project.

Do you remember that smooth, lustrous fabric you showed me when we were trying to choose material for my jacket and shorts, which you said is used to make women's dresses? I think you called it *harr*; I don't mean the linen.

Well, I am in need of that material. Don't worry, I'm not suddenly wanting to dress like a girl . . . tsk, tsk, tsk . . . I've been trying to build a set of wings so that I can fly. I want to follow the sun and see where she goes after she leaves our world—something I can't do by just walking. I know it's a crazy idea, but I have been curious about the sun and where it goes ever since I was little.

I first used ordinary cotton fabric together with feathers, which didn't work. The harr material will. I will be frank and tell you that I have no money to pay you, but I'll make it up to you in the future.

Send me about seven yards of it, more if you can afford it. I know I might be asking you for too much, especially since I am not paying for it now, but I need that material. I cannot count on my family to help me. My father would see it as frivolous. Other relatives would laugh at me. You and your dad have been wonderful to me and know that I'll return the favor one way or another.

Finally, send me that brown powder I once saw you mix with water and use to mount your dad's picture on the back of cardboard. I think you said it was called gum Arabic. I need that badly also.

Thank you so much, Masud. I hope to see you in the not-too-distant future.

With best wishes,

Desta.

P.S. Please give my love to your father and Khadija.

WHILE WAITING FOR A RESPONSE from Masud, Desta asked Yihoon to provide him with seven bamboo strips, nine half-inch whole bamboo rods, and four one-inch bamboo rods, two three-inch wooden rods, fourteen feet of leather straps, and a similar length of jute strings. All the rods and strips were to be six feet long.

Then on paper he drew up many different designs. Initially, he had wanted his craft to be in the shape of an actual set of wings. Then he realized that with his material and tool limitations, that couldn't be easily accomplished. He settled for a simpler model but with a still-effective flight system.

It would be rectangular in shape and taller and wider than his body. The one-inch-diameter solid bamboo pieces would frame the outer borders. The two wooden rods would attach two feet apart from each other half way from the ends under the craft. They are to serve as spars on which Desta's hanging leather straps affix.

The strips would be attached to the fabric with the gum Arabic glue, with seven inches of loose cloth between them. This cloth when filled with air would turn into balloons.

Desta flying in his self-built aircraft

FIFTY-SEVEN

Three days later on a Saturday morning, having returned from Dangila, Fikru sent for Desta and he ran to the tailor's shop.

"What have you done for that merchant?" Fikru asked.

"Nothing. Why?"

"He was so happy when I told him I had a letter from you. And then when I was about to leave, he reminded me several times to make sure I gave you his letter." Fikru pointed to an envelope on the counter.

"No, I have not done anything for him. But he has done a lot for me."

"Here is the roll of cloth you requested. . . . and the letter, of course," Fikru said, handing Desta both shipments. "Come back if you need any help."

Desta stammered, "Thank you. I will." He flew home, anxious to open and explore the contents.

He went to the back of the house, dropped the rolled cloth across the table, and sat down with the letter. He hesitated a little before opening it, trying to catch his breath both from his running and in anticipation of the news from his friend.

Starting from one corner, Desta carefully peeled back the envelope's glued flap. To an onlooker, it might have appeared that the boy was trying to save the envelope. But for Desta, memories of his life in Dangila, both good and bad, had begun to filter in, and he was allowing his thoughts to run their course before engaging in something new and different. By the time he got the envelope open, Desta was back to the present.

He unfolded the letter methodically. He laid it on the table before him. His head tipped down, Desta planted his elbows on the table, framing the letter. His fisted hands probing his cheeks, he went on to read:

Dear Desta,

It was so good to hear from you. Baba and I, and Khadija, too, have wondered why you did not return to Dangila after your Christmas holiday. We hoped and prayed that all was well with you. I know your situation with Zewday and his family had not been the best. I told baba that it was probably why you didn't come back.

Anyway, we're glad to hear you're in school still and have reached the fourth grade. Education is very important. It'll open many doors for you. You can go so much farther in life. The alternative is often limiting. You might remain a farmer the rest of your life, or a merchant like me, to give you another example. Don't ever give up. You're a hardworking and dedicated fellow. I am sure that won't be the case with you. Whatever you do, I know you'll be successful at it.

Regarding the fabric you asked me to send you for your school project, you're a lucky guy. We had a leak in the roof of the shop the last rainy season and water damaged much of our stock. The harr piece I'm sending you is from one of the rolls that was spoiled by the rain. Given what you're using it for, it should be fine. Just don't try to make clothes out of it for yourself. You'll confuse people . . . tsk, tsk, tsk.

What I am sending is more than what you requested. Perhaps you can give the remainder to one of your women relatives to make a dress out of it.

Good luck with your project. Come see us when school closes for Christmas.

Both Baba and Khadija send their *selams.*

Your friend,

Masud

P.S. By the way, one of the merchants you met at our mesgid said that he knows someone in Bahir Dar who may know the woman you are looking for.

"THAT IS JUST LIKE MASUD," Desta said to himself after he read the letter. "He is all kindness." He felt his heart smile. Somebody, once a complete stranger, unrelated to him by blood or religion, was doing all this for him. *How wrong Abraham is about this blood-relation stuff. How wrong Ayénat is for maligning people like Masud.*

That morning, Desta's faith in the kindness of the world was stronger than ever. All he needed was to keep going. He could always find somebody kind and giving like Masud. In his heart he felt certain that he could find someone who would give him shelter and food if he decided to go to Finote Selam or Burie on his own.

He cut the string that bound the fabric and unrolled the limp, flowing cloth. He laid it across the table while it was still in its multiple folds. The morning sunlight tickled out tiny star-like iridescences. He placed his forearms across the drapery, his open hands down with thumbs touching, and thought about what Masud had written, particularly about the importance of education and how it would open doors for him if he went further. He certainly didn't want to become a farmer or a merchant or a clerk in the courthouse or a listro, like those boys he saw in Burie.

What his friend had not mentioned, and it hit Desta strongly as he stared at the fabric, was his freedom: the freedom to be whatever he wanted and the freedom not to be controlled by anyone, anything, or any circumstance.

It had been his belief that he had to have a family member or a relative or an acquaintance to support him. This was why he stayed in Yeedib and kept repeating the fourth grade. His fears, based on his reliance on others, were keeping him from discovering what might be waiting for him at the other end of the journey he might take. As he found out in Dangila, the world could be benevolent. Many people had been so kind to him. Besides the father-son merchants and Khadija, there was the girl, Helen, and her parents, Colonel Asheber and Weizero Tigist, and Almaz the hair braider. None of these people were his family or relatives.

Desta felt like he had just awakened from a long sleep. Why didn't he think about these things before? He shook his head, annoyed for letting this happen to himself and wasting a full school year. He drew back his arms, propped his chin with the palm of his right hand, and drummed the table with the fingers of his left hand, barely audibly. He lifted his face stared at the half-dozen daisies and dandelions that peeked out from between the branches of the thorn bushes.

Bees buzzed over them, as if briefly paying homage before flying over to the more abundant flowers farther to the right, in the corner near the stone wall. Desta's eyes locked on the bees, watching their every move and dance and listening to their hum. Then they flew away, making flying seem as easy as walking was to Desta. He wished he could fly instead of walk because he could cover so much distance in a short time.

The usual metal-on-metal clanging, and feet shuffling and crunching in the jailhouse compound next door—sounds of punishment—brought Desta back to the moment, to the things he must do that day. He opened and spread the fabric lengthwise. He planted the elbow of his right arm at the end of the fabric before him, and then slowly dropped it, stretching his fingers and holding them tight. He placed his left thumb where the middle finger of the other hand terminated, slid the textile down, and planted his right elbow again where he had marked the spot with his finger. In so doing, he measured the full length of the fabric, determining a total of fourteen yards.

Masud had sent him twice the amount of material he had requested. He smiled. Deep rusty rings circled light brown patches, indicating the water damage Masud had mentioned in his letter. It smelled of mildew, signifying that the shopkeepers hadn't unrolled the fabric to air and dry it.

Desta was indeed lucky. It mattered not that the fabric had those water marks. He had got what he wanted without feeling like he had really imposed himself on his friends. It was a sort of throw-away fabric, and they had been glad to give it to someone they knew.

THE WIDTH OF THE FABRIC Masud sent Desta was three feet. For his balloon construction he needed 6-by-21-foot-long fabric. Desta took back the roll to Fikru and asked him to create the desired dimensions by unwinding the drapery, cutting the necessary lengths, and then sewing them together to obtain the six-foot width.

Once this was done, he returned to the backyard and was ready to build his craft. Before he did that he needed the assistance of the coin image on his chest. He closed his eyes and imagined building the most beautiful aircraft, one that can help him fly all over the place. He slipped his right hand under his jacked over his chest and rubbed the coin image over and over again. He immediately felt a sense of ease and clarity. "Thank you," he said and went to work.

He opened the little box and found the honey-colored gum Arabic powder rolled in a cloth and a palm-sized paper containing the instructions for making the glue. He could now build wings with larger pockets.

He measured with his arm and cut nearly twenty-one feet of the fabric. About seven inches from the border he placed the first bamboo strip. With a pencil he marked all around the strip, transferring its image on the fabric. From the side of this image he measured three boy's arms-long or approximately three feet and set down the next strip, marked the inscribed borders with his pencil again and continued. Once finished, the images of the bamboo strips arrayed neatly like marching soldiers across the length of the lustrous fabric, each separated by three feet.

Desta's next round of activity entailed applying the glue in the marked spaces and placing the bamboo strips right afterward. Applying the glue was a tedious and complicated process.

He dipped the tip of a feather brush into the glue. He held the brush up during transit from the cup to the marked area on the fabric. Keeping the applicator within the prescribed space, Desta brushed on the glue in a sweeping unidirectional motion. He made multiple trips to the cup, until he had finally coated the entire narrow rectangular space. He let the glue sit for a few minutes, then tacked on a bamboo strip and pressed on it. He let the strip make a solid contact with the fabric before he continued with the next. The whole activity took five days.

Separately he built the mounting structure, first by creating a rectangular frame using the four two-inch bamboos and tying them securely at the corners. Then within this box he laid the five one-inch bamboo rods, leaving a two-foot gap between them. He tied their ends with the top and bottom edge of the two-inch bamboos. Finally he laid the remaining four one-inch bamboo rods, set at equal distance as cross pieces and tied them to the existing parallel rods.

Now he was ready to mount the glued on strips onto the supporting structure. Starting from one side he paired the strips with the bamboo rods and tied them with a string, each pair at seven discrete points. To ensure fidelity, he fastened the rod-strip pair by passing the strings through the fabric. At the end he wrapped the loosed drapery around the sides of the frames and tied it with a string also. Finally, he attached the wooden rods two feet from either end and tied them with a rope to the bamboo sticks and frames at several places. Ultimately, he attached looping leather straps from the wooden rods for his legs, waist and hands. Now he was ready to try out his new flying craft. This time he felt confident enough to have someone watch him.

The weekend would arrive in two days. Negasu had a little more free time then and Desta thought he would readily come to watch when he made his second attempt to fulfill his dream of flying.

In the evening, Desta shared his thoughts with his Father-of-the-Breast. Negasu thought it was a crazy and dangerous thing to do but said he would come and try to dissuade Desta from killing himself.

The following evening, Negasu asked to see the boy's new construction.

Desta led the way to the back of the house. While Negasu waited at the table, Desta dashed to the shed and returned with his new flying gear. He laid it across the table for Negasu's inspection.

"You did all this by yourself?" Negasu asked. His eyes said more.

"It took many weeks, but yes," Desta replied.

"This looks like excellent, detailed work. If it works like you're saying, we could use something like this for some of our remote area work—flying to places where there are no car roads or the terrain is difficult to walk on."

"Don't be that quick to judgment. I've yet to try this thing and see if it really works," Desta said, smiling.

"I know," Negasu said sheepishly. "What you have done and said convinced me to have those wishful thoughts." He smiled again, a little less awkwardly.

"Don't worry. I think this is going to work," Desta said, trying to get Negasu out of the hole he had unintentionally got himself in.

The next morning after breakfast, father and son went to the shed and brought out Desta's craft. Negasu seemed just as anxious and excited as the boy. They went out of the fortress and to the open space behind the stone wall.

Desta moistened his index finger and stuck it up in the air. "Just what I had hoped," he said. The wind was blowing from the east. He looked around for the highest rock that they could easily walked to. The boy opened the wings, strapped the contraption to his body, and climbed atop the rock. Negasu stood behind the craft and held it in place while Desta inserted his feet in the straps. Nervous and anxious, he reached for the coin image and rubbed his fingers over it, asking, please, for help—this time. He then grabbed the handles under the wings and pitched his body forward.

Desta heard the long tube-like pockets begin to pop, one by one, as they inflated. *So far, so good.* He could feel the lifting pressure on his body. The craft swayed, as if he could be airborne at any moment. Negasu crossed himself. Desta counted to three and then pushed off the ledge of the rock. In an instant he was up in the air, soaring easily and naturally in his craft. The wind was brisk on his face and every fiber in him was smiling with joy. First he flew south, edging a grove of trees, then after gliding for some time, he swung around and headed north. He could see kids at the outskirts of town shouting to one another and pointing at the new bird of a boy in the sky.

As he was flying north, Desta saw a speck of an object out of the corner of his eye over the distant eastern peaks. It glided west on a straight course, almost perpendicular to his line of flight. The boy at first thought it was probably a bird, so he looked directly ahead. He didn't have much tailwind. He floated at a slow pace, which allowed him to study the landscape and a lot of the bigger things on it: checkered farmlands; grass rooftops; and tiny, blurred images of animals and people.

"You finally made it, eh?" shouted a familiar, female voice, startling the boy.

"Oh, it's you, Eleni. . . . I did," he said, looking back with a smile. "I never thought I'd realize this dream in a million years."

"Come follow me. Let's go to your birth valley," Eleni said, tapping on Desta's craft.

He hesitated and then said, "Really?"

"I'll give you a hand if you get in trouble. We won't be gone too long."

It sounded absolutely crazy to go that far on his first flight, but also very appealing.

"I'll have to tell someone on the ground first," he finally said. "Follow me."

When he neared the stone wall, Desta couldn't believe his eyes. There was a large gathering of children and a few women, capping their faces and staring up at him. An excited chatter ensued when he hovered over the crowd. Eleni was invisible to them. Desta dropped his face toward Negasu. "I'm going a short distance. Will be back soon!" he hollered.

"Come down! Don't take too many chances!" Negasu yelled back.

Desta didn't want to come down. He would rather stay up there forever. It felt like the first time he saw the sunset. He didn't want to go home then. And he didn't want to come down to earth now. "Let's go!" Eleni said, tugging at him.

Light-headed from the sheer excitement, he flew like the wind with Eleni. They moved swiftly across the nearly flat farmland and clusters of villages. Then they soared over Mount Wondegez and cut over the wavelike ridges and into Desta's birth valley.

They sailed side by side, Eleni slightly ahead, leading the way. With all her clothes completely inflated, she looked more like an air-filled toy than a human being. That fist-size object behind her neck was now completely invisible. Once they got into the valley, first they flew east, toward the pass that the sun rose through, the U-shaped gap that allegedly contained information about Desta, then north over the Avinvera Church and the Lehwani Mountain. Some of his most thrilling moments were when they flew through the clouds, Desta extending his hands and trying to catch and hold them. He was living his dream of climbing the mountains that circled his valley to touch the sky and gather the clouds.

Just about everything down below was emerald green, with white patches here and there in some of the mature grain fields. Blossoming yellow and white daisies adorned the hills and valleys.

As they headed back to the western foothills, over Desta's family residence, he got nervous. "I don't want to go anywhere near my home!" he shouted.

"You don't want to land and surprise them?" Eleni asked, surprised.

"No! That's the last thing I want to do. My father is probably not at home, my mother would blame the Saytan for my homemade wings, and my brothers wouldn't care." And then there was that nasty rumor still circulating in the valley about his having converted to Islam. "I don't think I would be welcomed by many of the valley people either, so what's the point?"

"I know every nook and cranny of this valley!" Eleni shouted. "I've come to this valley hundreds of times, since before your grandfather came and was murdered." Desta heard only snatches.

All the things he thought about his family and the valley people had damped his excitement a little. He wanted to leave the area immediately. "Let's go back!" he shouted. "Negasu must be wondering where we are."

Just before they got to Yeedib, Eleni said, "I hope you had fun."

Desta told her it had been a dreamlike experience.

"I'll see you next time," she said. She veered north and instantly vanished.

He looked down and his eyes grew in awe. It looked as if the entire town had come out to receive him. Children, men, and women had packed the open ground and pressed up against the stone wall. Policemen stood on top of the wall. Prisoners' faces peered over the stone ledge.

Nervous and anxious, Desta pulled on one set of the strings, to reduce the inflation and his speed. He pulled another set of strings to deflate the air pockets around his feet, allowing him to achieve a nearly vertical position. Negasu and a few other men had their hands in front of them, prepared to catch Desta if it looked like he might crash.

He didn't. Directly above where he took off, he slowly lowered himself and landed with a few hopping forward steps.

Everybody clapped and roared with excitement.

Negasu and a couple of the men helped Desta undo the straps from his aircraft. The crowd converged around them, making Desta feel nervous and uneasy. He had never felt comfortable when there were too many people around him. Negasu collected Desta's wings and motioned that they should go home.

The children yammered with questions; the adults eyed him in wonder. "Sir, can you tell us how this boy managed to fly on his own?" a tall, brown man asked as Negasu signaled to let them pass. He didn't answer.

"Who made the craft for him?" another man shouted over the noise.

Negasu said to Desta, "We didn't invite any of these people. Don't feel obligated to say anything to them."

Desta never wanted this kind of attention. He hadn't done it for the glory. He had done it to find a solution to his problem and to fulfill a dream. This was a personal and private affair.

"Let's go home quickly," Desta whispered to Negasu.

One of the guards who had stood on top of the stone wall and watched with everybody else, hopped down and came to help clear a path so Desta and Negasu could pass.

The clamor continued. A few children continued to follow and ask questions.

Negasu turned and said, "Desta is too tired to answer any questions. You can ask him another time." By the time they reached the gate, their followers were few.

That night, as he lay in bed, Desta felt he had touched the sky. His confidence in his ability to do anything he wanted, including finding someone in Finote Selam to live with and pursue his dreams, had increased greatly. He decided to go there on his own after the Christmas break, the next time he would be allowed to transfer to a new school.

FIFTY-EIGHT

Desta woke the following morning feeling as if he had lost all his senses. Although fully alert and able to recognize his surroundings, inside his head he felt transported to another world.

His profound sensation had seized all his being, leaving him outwardly numb. He tried to understand this sensation—to name and explain this unusual feeling to himself and to anyone who cared to ask, but no precise word or phrase came to him.

This experience was neither like the pleasure of the cool breeze on his face when he was flying nor the ecstatic welling up of joy that registered in his head as he glided effortlessly through the air and clouds. These feelings left him after he landed, giving way to this other, nameless sensation that had put his body into a state of tranquility.

While Desta lay there enjoying the moment, by degrees he began to regain his everyday senses. Once he had fully recovered, he decided to go on a walk where he could be alone and undistracted. He wanted to think about his flight and what his newly-found freedom would mean.

It was Sunday. Negasu and Tshai were still asleep. Desta rose, put on his clothes, and slipped out after quietly unlocking the door and shutting it behind him.

He strode briskly down the stone walkway to the gate. He opened it after struggling with the sticky latch for a few seconds. Exiting, he turned left, walked several paces and then turned left again at the courthouse grounds.

He followed the path to the compound's front entrance and out to the main road, which continued directly to the marketplace. This was one of Desta's favorite spots because, unshielded by the prevalent eucalyptus trees, he could see a greater part of the earth and sky.

In the open space, people buzzed and stray dogs romped about playfully. Near the south end of the market, he stopped and looked at the distant horizon beyond which the town of Finote Selam lay. An image of his flying there someday came to him like a dream. He smiled.

"Now I can do that!" Desta said aloud. "I will join my friend Fenta and continue with my studies through the eighth grade." He couldn't wait until the second semester in January. This time he would be arriving for school before the semester began. Two years before, he had gone to Dangila after the second semester had begun and was nearly refused admittance.

He dropped his eyes to the ground, remembering he still had nobody he could live with if he decided to attend school there. But just as quickly he put that thought out of his mind. He was not going to let doubt sabotage his dream.

That thought put to rest, he looked up once again. This time he turned slightly to the right and gazed at the sun's boundless path, following it to the horizon where it sets. He wondered how far he would have to fly, trailing the sun, to find out where it really goes after it leaves his world. He wondered whether his craft would be sufficiently durable and he strong enough to make the long journey over and back.

If he were to fly in the evening, he wondered whether he would continue to see the many hues of the setting sun—the browns, reds, oranges, and numerous shades of gold. Desta thought this would be a thrill of a lifetime, chasing those amazing gradations of color as far as he could see them no more. Suddenly, he remembered what the Cloud Man, his grandfather's spirit, had told him.

The place past which he could go no more was supposed to be a valley. Next to it lay a vast blue sea. It was supposed to be this sea that swallows the sun— along with its dazzling colors in the sky—after the familiar celestial orb vanishes, leaving a shroud of darkness behind. It was near this sea where the person who holds the Coin of Magic and Fortune lived.

Desta drummed his fingertips on his lips, pondering whether that place would be Bahir Dar. Lake Tana, near the famed town, was supposed to be the largest sea in the whole of Ethiopia. Desta's heart fluttered at this possibility.

There were also other places that had lots of water. His teacher, Betew, in his Dangila school, had mentioned this fact when he was showing them the world map, but Betew never said whether those waters were bigger than Tana. Desta's heart quieted a little at this realization.

He lowered his head toward the earth and decided not to bother about these things for now. He was hungry and wanted to go home.

As he walked back, he came upon the pair of benches he and Tru had sat on after their walks, when he was living with her and his uncle. Desta stopped and lowered himself to the same bench Tru had lingered on, conjuring up her memory for a few minutes.

Desta recalled what he had told her at the end of their visit at this same spot. "I'll tell you what happened to me and my family when I return for school in September," he had said. Unfortunately, that promise was never fulfilled. Desta still couldn't believe it: Both Tru and Mekuria were dead—killed in a bus accident. Tru, one of the few persons in his life who showed him genuine love, was gone. His emotions welled up, choking him.

Desta was just about to rise and go home when he heard footsteps and a rustle of something. He turned around and nearly gasped when he saw Eleni standing behind him like a shadow. The Wind Woman apologized. She said she had intended to pleasantly surprise him.

"Not a surprise to me," Desta replied peevishly.

"I came by to explain things and answer questions, if you have any, and then sing and dance for you in celebration of your successful flight.

Rattled by her unwelcome presence, Desta looked at her, wishing she would go away.

Without any further preamble, Eleni said, "First, let me say that what has been going on with you in the past fifteen or so hours is called 'Bliss.' It's the ultimate level of happiness—surpassing pleasure and joy. After all that has happened to you in the past two years, your flight yesterday and, consequently, your blissful state of mind are your rewards."

When she saw Desta staring at her, Eleni said, "I'll explain all this shortly. Mind if I sit down for a bit? I will take the bench you sat on when you and Tru came here once," she said, smiling.

"Did you enjoy yourself yesterday?" she asked after she sat down.

Desta told her he had had a wonderful time.

"You should take that flight as a metaphor for life. One, it was meant (although you didn't act on my suggestion) to let your mother and the rest of your family know that you have attained your freedom; you now have the ability to fly like a bird.

"Two, it served to show that you do not have to count on relatives or acquaintances as you embark on your journey. You cannot allow yourself to think in those limiting terms.

"Have faith in the power that is within you. Have faith in the world. It's composed of many good people who can be like family to you but without any strings attached. A truly free life is when you have no strings attached—when you don't have to count on someone or something or feel obligated to people and things.

"Wherever it is you want to go, you have to go there and hope for the best. That is the kind of risk you have to learn to take if you wish to achieve your dreams."

Desta looked away thinking about what Eleni just said. It was the truth, but it sounded too lonely and scary.

"Do you follow me?" Eleni asked, eyeing him critically, almost like a mother scolding her child who is afraid to dip his toes into cold water.

"Yes, I do. . . ." Desta replied, shifting his face, his eyes meeting Eleni's. "Especially now since I can fly. That should make things easier."

"That's right. If you can achieve a feat no one in the whole province—or the whole country—can do, you can overcome any challenges. Take advantage of this privilege and keep going."

"Thank you," Desta said, now gaining even more courage to pursue all the things he was dreaming and fantasizing about earlier. Just then he appreciated Eleni more than ever. At that moment he felt as close to her as he ever had to his own family. At least close enough that he wanted to know more about her.

"Can I ask you a question?" he said, glancing at her pensively.

Eleni nodded.

"Where do you really live? Are you always traveling or do you have a home you go to?"

"I might have mentioned this to you before. My home base is called Washaa Umera. It's one of the largest caves in this part of the world."

"Is it far?"

"Why—would you like to visit me there?"

"Maybe, particularly if it's not too far," Desta said. "I've never been in a cave."

"Distance is not something you should worry about in the adventure you're set to pursue," Eleni said, smiling. "To answer your question, though, Washaa Umera is nearly a full day's journey if you fly from here."

Desta was wondering how far that would be in actual distance. It took his father and him a day and half to travel from his home to Dangila on foot. He hadn't the vaguest idea how long would it take to fly to Dangila.

"It's a fascinating place. You will see things there that don't exist in the world you live in," Eleni added, interrupting the boy's thoughts.

Desta looked up, his eyes flaring. "Really—like what?"

"Too many things for me to list. It's better if you find out for yourself when the time comes. In addition, you will get to meet many of my Wind associates and, if you are lucky and the portal to their part of the cave is open, our neighbors, the Zarrhs. . . . They all know about you."

A little let down but excited by the idea of flying to a new place, Desta looked away thinking about Washaa Umera and the things contained in it Eleni wouldn't divulge.

The Wind Woman continued, "Let's keep that as a possible adventure for you, far from this land you have come to live in." Eleni smiled broadly, herself pleased by that possibility. Then she said, "If and when you come, perhaps you will bring your coin. We all want to see it."

Desta looked at her curiously. "The coin is in my father's hands. I've never seen it since it was dug out of the ground."

"You're the owner of it. He is just keeping it for you."

"I thank you for all your advice, but regarding the coin, I cannot show it to you," Desta said firmly.

"Not now. I mean down the road when your father gives it to you. . . . Need to go," the Wind Woman said suddenly. Then almost as an afterthought, she said, "Before I go I want to sing and dance for you as I promised, to celebrate your successful flight."

Eleni rose and stood before Desta. She put her right foot out, raised her right hand, and snapped her fingers. "You're free at last," she serenaded, "from your dire, hurtful past. . . ." In one flowing motion, she twisted her hips, slid her right foot back, and put her left foot out. She dropped one hand and raised the other, snapping her fingers and continuing, ". . . from the family that tried to keep you from your dreams." Then she bent forward slightly and pushed her hip out and continued to do a jig: one foot out, the other in; one arm up, the other down. Spinning on the balls of her feet, her voluminous skirt swooshing and bellowing as she moved, Eleni continued to sing:

Desta, you've been set free at last!

  From your dire, hurtful past

  From the family that

  tried to keep you from your dreams.

  Until your mission's done,

  Keep track of your vision and follow the sun.

  You're headed for adventures unseen!

Your feet will take you far

  From the only world you've known.

  I understand why you feel so alone.

  So let me reassure because soon you'll learn,

  There is no cause for alarm or concern.

The coin you seek is real or just an imaginary pie,

  Like the mountains you once had climbed so high

  To feel the clouds in your hands and touch the sky

  That vanished once you got there before your eyes

  To spend your life seeking with spirit so bold,

  but I hope someday you trust enough to

  show us your piece of gold.

A surprise is around the corner. It's just around the bend.

  A stranger will appear at your door

  to take you to the place of your dreams,

  Followed by a gift of money that'll last you for a while

  That is what I meant when I said have faith in the world.

Young man, you've been set free at last!

  From your dire, hurtful past

  From the family that

  tried to keep you from your dreams.

  Until your mission's done,

  Keep track of your vision and follow the sun.

  You're headed for adventures unseen!

And let me bid you farewell for now

  Till we see each other again when time will allow.

When she finished, although she had no hint of perspiration, she was out of breath. She bowed to her audience of one.

Desta just looked at her, mesmerized by Eleni's novel moves and beautiful singing voice.

"When someone finishes performing for you, you are supposed to applaud," Eleni said, smiling. "Like this," she said, bringing her open hands together and clapping several times.

"Ohh," Desta puffed, a little embarrassed.

"Next time," Eleni said, grinning.

When Desta seemed lost by Eleni's suggestion, she said, "Need to go now." She faced the wind, which was coming from the south. She waited for a few seconds, waved her hand at Desta, and said, "Good luck!" instantly becoming airborne.

Desta stood and watched her until the Wind Woman from Washaa Umera became a vanishing point in the sky. He was not envious this time. He just couldn't wait to do that himself once again.

As he walked home, Desta realized that much of the bliss in him had dissipated. He hoped he would have that experience once more as he flew to Finote Selam, shortly before the second semester began in January. Desta counted the weeks in his head. "Seven!" he exclaimed, pleased that the number of weeks he had left was the same as his lucky number.

FIFTY-NINE

November 1963

On the last Saturday morning in November, Negasu walked in the house looking apprehensive. "Desta, someone is looking for you. Go talk to 'em," he said, and went into his bedroom.

Desta first thought that his mother had come to inquire about what he was doing flying over their house with a Saytan machine. Then he realized it was as yet too early for his mother to be in town. Desta hated surprises like this, people showing up at the gate without warning. Unfortunately, that was how the whole of society seemed to operate.

He went to the door and the chill morning air hit his face like a splash of cold water. He went back inside, put on his gabi, and came out again. The twenty feet of stone walkway from the entrance of the house to the gate felt like a mile. Was it a harbinger of bad news that waited, and if so, what bad news?

"Are you Desta?" asked a tall, fair-skinned young man.

"I am. Is there anything wrong?"

"I'm Mehiret. I go to the secondary school in Debre Marcos. I understand that you have been wanting to go to Finote Selam. Is that right?"

Desta hesitated for a few seconds, wondering who this person represented that cared enough to come and inquire about his dilemma. "Yes, I have."

"Could you be ready to go with me tomorrow morning?"

"Yes, of course . . . but . . . but. . . ." Desta was unsure what he really wanted to say.

"I know. You're probably confounded by the urgent nature of my request and why I'm here on your behalf."

"Yes to both. . . . I was planning to go there after the Christmas break. I suppose an opportunity that comes sooner is better than any that might not come later." Desta was thinking of the promise that the voice made him in his dream while he was in Burie.

"It's a bit complicated to explain everything at the moment. Let me just say that a teacher at my high school who is aware of your situation sent me to accompany you to Finote Selam."

A series of questions popped into Desta's head, but since Mehiret had indicated he was not predisposed to disclose the details of his visit, he simply said, "I am ready to go at any moment, but I need to get permission from my father first."

It turned out Mehiret was the son of a prominent government employee in Yeedib, and Negasu knew the family well. His younger brother was a classmate of Desta's. Going to the town of his dreams with Mehiret wasn't a problem for Desta, and Negasu's only concern was about Desta transferring to another school in the middle of the semester. Desta said that he was not concerned so long as he was at a school where he could learn new things and had the opportunity to advance. Seeing how determined he was, Negasu backed off from dissuading him.

The next questions were who he was going to live with and how he was going to support himself. Desta didn't want to discuss these things because he had no answers, but he was not going to allow himself any thoughts that might sabotage his decision to go, no matter what awaited him in Finote Selam.

For pocket money, he had the two silver dollars he took from under the stone where the farmer woman had hid them. The money still had value on the black market, trading one silver dollar for as much as three paper birr. So for sure he had six birr he could use for food. He had hoped Negasu would give him five or ten birr, but his Father-of-the-Breast said that since it was the end of the month, he had no cash money left and his salary would not be coming for another five days.

So Desta, with his two silver dollars, his notebooks, and the clothes on his back, was ready to go to a town where he knew no one except his friend, Fenta. He was a bit saddened by Negasu's indifference toward his decision to go, and his making no effort to borrow money from his friends to give Desta, as he would have if he were Negasu's real son. Desta swallowed his disappointment and let his dream of living in the new town be the happy beacon that drew him. Desta was still grateful for the stable and peaceful home environment Negasu and Tshai had provided him for nearly two years. He had never gone hungry, however hungry he had been to bond and connect with them.

In the evening, Desta went to Mehiret's house and told him he had permission to go and was ready to leave with him in the morning. "I'll pick you up at daybreak," Mehiret said.

When Desta returned, he went to the shed, collected all the loose things from his first wing-building project as well as from the second one, and put them into a jute sack. He left the floating aircraft from the successful second project sanding in a corner of the shed. He wanted Abraham, when he came to town, to take it and save it for him. He got a match from the house and took the sack to the place behind the fortress where he had launched his flight a week earlier.

It was the time of evening when cicadas in the grass and bushes nearby had just started their ancient rituals of singing, after the shadow of the plateau on the green valley below had died. The prisoners had taken their evening walks and no longer filled the air with the metal-on-metal clanging. Dusk was turning charcoal gray, and the stars were becoming visible to the naked eye. A light breeze from the east had begun to blow when Desta lit his pile of feathers, fabric, sticks, strings, and twigs. A golden flame twice his five-foot height leaped to the heavens and lit up the sky. The smell of burning feathers was intoxicating.

Alone, wrapped in his gabi, clad in the shorts and jacket from three years ago, Desta sat cross-legged in front of the bonfire, now celebrating in his mind his successful flight, now dreaming about his future and wondering who was the benevolent teacher who had sent for him.

Shortly after the fire went out, he rose and went home. He packed his books and writing things in his bursa. He wrote a letter to his father telling him about his decision to go to Finote Selam on his own. In this letter, he also told Abraham about an important flight craft he had built, which he left in Negasu's shed. He indicated that he wanted Abraham to bring it home and save it for him until his living situation in the new town was properly established. Then he ate an early dinner and washed his feet outside. He needed to be able to rely on them for the long and arduous journey.

THE NEXT MORNING, he rose early, ate his breakfast, and waited for Mehiret on the bench outside. When he saw him turn the corner near the fence, he went inside and said good-bye to Tshai and Negasu, thanking them for the good, comfortable two years he spent with them. Before he parted, he gave his father's letter to Negasu, asking him to pass it on to him when Abraham was in town again. He also told his Father-of-the-Breast to save his flying craft for him as Abraham would be coming to collect it. That was the only belonging he left at Negasu's house.

"Glad to see you're out and ready to hit the road," Mehiret said, smiling.

"Of course," Desta replied, picking up his bag. "I've long been waiting for a day like this!"

"*Beselam gibu*—may you arrive in peace," Negasu said, waving his hand.

Mehiret thanked Negasu for his good wishes and they left. It was an all-day journey and they needed to get going right away to arrive in Finote Selam before nightfall.

They went on the same route Desta traveled when he went looking for the woman with the coin— past the giant warka tree, down the side of the plateau, and into the flat, green valley of Lake Gudera. At the bottom of the hill they took the path that went straight to the lake. He was happy to see the lake again, but his attention was focused on how to find people who would give him shelter and food and still give him an opportunity to go to school. The more his mind dwelt on this, the more nervous he became. For a time as they walked, his only hope was Fenta and the family he lived with, or the mysterious teacher who sent for him.

Although Desta had been curious about this person since Mehiret mentioned him the day before, the boy had kept his questions close to his chest until the moment was right.

After they passed Lake Gudera and just before they began walking through the wooded area of blue-gray stones, Desta asked, "Mehiret, who is the kind teacher who troubled you to come from so far away in the middle of your semester?"

"Did you hear about the death of President Kennedy?"

Desta said he didn't know who this man was or about his death.

Mehiret explained who President Kennedy was, and about the Peace Corps teachers. "President Kennedy was the leader of America, like our King Haile Selassie is the leader of our country. When Kennedy died, the director of our school gave the American Peace Corps teachers a day off to mourn the loss of their leader. One of them, who somehow found out where I come from, asked me to bring you to Finote Selam. He said he was planning to send for you during the Christmas break, but because all of us who have Peace Corps teachers had a day off, he asked if I would mind coming home for the weekend. He paid my bus trip. I was happy to do it for him and the trip gave me an opportunity to see my family."

Desta was stunned and mystified. "Is this man like a Ferenge then?"

"Yes, a *netchi*—white person."

"Do you know anything about him or how he knew about my desire to go to Finote Selam?"

"He is just one of my teachers. I don't know anything about him beyond that or how he knew about your situation."

Desta thought for a long time about what Mehiret said. "Hmm, the king of Amarika had to die for my long, luckless spell to break?"

Mehiret smiled. "In America they call their leaders 'president.' As to the other stuff, I think it's quite a stretch for you to connect your luck to the death of the leader and a nation so far away. You better not tell other people that, lest they call you a lunatic. I think it's just a coincidence."

Desta remembered what his father often said about coincidences: "people call predetermined events coincidence when they happen." He had more question to ask about the teacher but Mehiret had little more to say about him.

BY THE TIME THEY REACHED FINOTE SELAM, the sunset colors atop the famed town's low plateau had turned beyond red to burnt sienna. Just as the boys began descending the low, shallow slope, loud strident horns rent the air. "Stop!" Mehiret said, throwing his right hand over his heart. Desta stopped and mirrored his companion. He looked to their right where the sound had come from. Between two rectangular buildings with pitched roofs stood two men, one lowering a flag from a pole, the other blowing a horn.

Desta stared at the straight road before him that seemed to split the town in half, beginning from the foot of the plateau where they stood and traveling in the direction of the setting sun, to vanish into the forest far away. Desta loved looking at this road. He hoped it was a symbol for his own life path—straight, flawless, and continuous. And he loved the air about the town.

"That was a Somali man playing our national anthem," Mehiret said. Desta wondered how the Somali man came to live from far away. The only thing he knew about Somalis was they live in a desert country in the East and they were always at war with Ethiopia.

They entered the town. Mehiret stopped at the proximity of the house where

Fenta now lived with his uncle. He reached into his pocket, brought out five rectangular red bills, counted them, and handed them to Desta, saying, "This fifty birr is from the teacher who sent me to bring you here." Desta's eyes instantly grew large.

"You still won't tell me who this man really is?"

"I'm as mystified as you are. I thought you two somehow knew each other," he said thoughtfully.

"I wish I could personally thank him." He looked at the money and then at Mehiret. "I'm at a loss for words. You have no idea how grateful I am for this kindness."

"You may have a chance to express your appreciation. Here's his card."

Desta took the stiff piece of paper and looked at it. "What does it say?" he asked, handing it back.

It says, "'David Hartman. Graduate Student. University of Chicago, Department of Egyptology and Middle Eastern Studies, 773-702-0000. By the way, he said he will come to meet with you during the Christmas break. So do not plan to leave town. I will give him Fenta's address since you don't have your own yet."

Desta and Mehiret shook hands and parted. Desta walked to his friend's home dizzy with thoughts.

SIXTY

The house Fenta and the relatives supposedly lived in was set far off the road in a grove of trees. That Mehiret hadn't said with certainty who it belonged to had caused Desta to feel wary. He took measured steps. What if the family was gone for the weekend, or worse, what if they didn't actually live there? And he knew no one else in town. Further unnerving him was the idea that there might be dogs. They could sink their sharp teeth into the leg of anyone who ventured near. Rushing back to him was the memory of those ferocious canines near the villages by the lake, when he went looking for the woman with the coin.

Twilight was quickly giving way to the gray hours of the evening. Mehiret had vanished and Desta looked around for a stick he could use as a protection. There was none. As a last resort, he could have always relied on the coin image on his chest.

His concern about the dogs evaporated when he finally reached the entrance. There was no sign of any. He walked into the courtyard and his anxiety about the home and its owners dissipated also. He saw his friend Fenta sitting by the door fixing something, or so it seemed. Desta continued to walk cautiously, as if he were going to the edge of the earth. He had come to this place impulsively, heeding the call of a Ferenge man who didn't even live in the same town.

Fenta's back was to Desta. In an attempt to get Fenta's attention without startling him, Desta cleared his throat. Fenta looked up. He was refilling a small kerosene lamp.

"Era!" Fenta exclaimed, rising. "Is that really you, Desta?" he asked, as if the verbal query was necessary confirmation to what his eyes already knew.

Desta said he was, smiling. He stepped across the blurred shadows of the eucalyptus trees, effects of the rapidly waning dusk. The two boys shook hands and exchanged the customary three kisses on the cheeks.

"*Dena neh?*" Fenta asked, letting go of the visitor's hand. "I never thought I'd see you again—not in the middle of the semester anyway."

"I know," Desta replied, and asked, *"Ante dena neh*—you're well?"

"I'm well," Fenta said. "Good to see you. I often wondered why you didn't come as you said you might, after we all left Yeedib to live here a year ago. And then when you didn't come this past September, I thought you might have either gone to Burie or given up on school altogether and gone back to your valley to become a farmer."

Desta smiled at the very suggestion of his returning to the valley to become a farmer. "No," he said, after pausing a little. "Things had just not worked out for me to come here any sooner."

Fenta's face lit up. "You're here to register at our school then?"

"If they will let me," Desta said, his voice trailing. "I know I am coming in the middle of the semester."

"They will. . . ." Fenta was saying when his uncle's wife, Senayit, came out of the house.

"Is that Smiley?" Senayit asked, squinting a little. That was her name for Desta because he often smiled at everybody.

Fenta told her he was, and the guest and Senayit kissed and chatted for a bit. Shortly thereafter, all of them went inside the house.

Aba Bizuneh, Fenta's uncle, sat at the table in the middle of the rectangular living room, poring over some documents before him. A corpulent man with chubby cheeks, Bizuneh was a court clerk and record keeper. He looked up at the three people as they filed in. He tilted his head slightly to get a better look at the guest. Then he sat back with a noncommittal face, watching Desta come to greet him. Desta kissed Bizuneh's knee first, and then the man planted three of his own on the boy's cheeks, completing the ritual.

Desta and Bizuneh chatted for a bit, the boy ultimately telling him the reason he had come to town.

"I'll take you," Aba Bizuneh said, once he found out that Desta had come alone and had nobody in town who could take him to register at the school.

When darkness seemed about to take over the room, Fenta went outside and brought the kerosene lamp and lit it.

An hour later, dinner was served. Senayit and Bizuneh ate at the table and the two boys at a mosseb in the corner of the living room. While they ate, Fenta, finishing his earlier thought, told Desta that the school would probably accept him not for the fifth grade, as he was hoping, but for the fourth. Even if they had repeated the fourth grade and knew their lessons well, almost all the students who came to Finote Selam from rural schools had to repeat the grade they last completed.

"Repeating the fourth grade is not really my primary concern," Desta said. "Finding someone to live with is."

Fenta in turn told Desta that he would probably have no difficulty finding someone to live with. There were always families in need of a boy who could do part-time work in exchange for room and board.

Once they all finished eating and washed their hands, Bizuneh and Senayit went to bed. Fenta, with the kerosene lamp in hand, suggested to Desta that they go to the kitchen house in the back to sleep. This grass-roofed structure was located about a dozen steps from the main house, a rectangular building topped with corrugated tin.

In the kitchen, there was the fireplace at the center of the living room and miscellaneous cookware and sacks of things at the far corner. Two alcoves along the left wall were separated by a bamboo parapet. Each alcove had a mattress, two bed sheets, and a blanket. Fenta said that his cousin Sayfu used to sleep in one of the alcoves until last September, when he left for the province's capital to train as a policeman.

Desta was to sleep in one and Fenta in the other, their heads on the leather pillows butting against the partition. After they undressed and got under the covers, Fenta blew out the lamp and darkness closed in on them.

Desta closed his eyes for a few seconds and then opened them.

For what seemed like an hour, the two boys talked about many things, but the lion's share of their conversation had to do with the school, Haile Selassie First Elementary School, which offered grades one through eight. Fenta said it was probably the most beautiful school in the whole province. The buildings were made of stone—not sticks and mud—like their school in Yeedib. The floors were so shiny you could see yourself. Each classroom desk sat three students comfortably. Near the edge of the desk were grooves for pens and pencils. There was a hole in the middle for an inkwell and a pocket underneath for notebooks. What's more, the school had different teachers for different subjects. The campus was enormous, encircled by a wire fence all around, and there was even a beautiful soccer field.

To Desta his potential school sounded like a dream. The more Fenta told him about it, the more nervous and anxious he got. "Are you sure the director would still accept me even though I'm coming in the middle of the semester?" he asked guardedly.

"I can't be absolutely sure, of course, but tell him you finished at the top of the fourth-graders and you already repeated it once before because you had nobody to support you. You came here hoping to find someone to live with and pursue your schooling."

Desta sighed.

"Don't stress yourself over nothing. Let's go to sleep for now. I am sure you must be exhausted after the long journey," Fenta said.

"Okay, thanks. . . . Good night," Desta said, welcoming the suggestion, not really out of the need to go to sleep. However, he was grateful for a quiet moment to think about the anxiety that had been building inside him.

He lay straight on his back, resting his hands on his sides, his eyes closed in thought. He knew one of the things he must do is go with Aba Bizuneh to register at the school in the morning. If they were to accept him, he would stay in class until the noon lunch break. Then after he ate something with the money he had, he would go look for people who could use a student for part-time work in exchange for room and board. Where he might go and whom he would ask he had no idea, but he thought the merchants would be a good place to start— Muslim merchants, if there were any.

"Muslim merchants?" Desta asked himself, his past suddenly coming back to haunt him. For having associated with Muslims and eaten their meat and attended their mesgid, Zewday had made him feel like he had committed a terrible sin, his mother like he was the dirtiest person in the world—not to be touched or allowed to come into her home or drink from her cup. In this moment Desta remembered what his grandfather's spirit had told him: before he could let new people and new experiences into his life, he must first rid himself of the bad. Desta had had quite a few of them in his young life.

He remembered when he started modern school four years before—he had to purge the memories of some of his cruel relatives and their spiteful deeds before he could find peace and freedom within himself and happier relationships with others.

That is what I must do this time, too, Desta thought. He realized that parting with people who had done him wrong meant forgiving them. He would've preferred to avoid these bad memories, but he knew that he had to relive them in order to unburden himself.

He clasped his forehead between his thumb and index finger, closed his eyes, and tried to go deep within his mind. His chest heaved. His throat burned. He thought he would get the worst memories out of the way first: his experience in Dangila with Zewday's family. He heaved again, feeling the air exit his nostrils with a hiss.

"Mebet," he said, "You caused my body to reduce to near skin and bones. You put me through such desperation—I'll admit it now—that I stole those bread crumbs out of the neighbor's basket when the opportunity presented itself. . . ."

Desta's eyes brimmed with tears.

He continued with the unburdening. "Some nights my hunger became so intense that I rose and went out with a flashlight to search and pick stray peas and grains from out of the dirt around the grinding stone. . . ."

The tears overflowed, trickling down the sides of his face, wetting the sheets on one and collecting in the shell of his ear on the other.

"You tried to undermine Lesim's trust in me when you counted the injera that same night you refused to let me have dinner. And you destroyed the faith I had in myself when I was forced to hoard the coffee beans and sell them to Almaz. I had to find some way to supplement what little food I would be getting during the rainy season—because you decided to store my father's supplies for your own security, among other reasons."

He wiped his tears and placed both hands over his mouth. He thought hard and continued his tirade. He raged about the livestock-quality dagussa Mebet gave him, which mocked and tested the limitations of his body as it pushed his brain's ability to endure.

"The irony, Mebet," Desta said, removing his hands, "was that the rest of you looked well, at least not as emaciated as I was." Desta paused, struggling with his feelings, and then continued, "No matter, for all the things you have done to me, I will forgive you. In so doing we all may heal and find peace."

He followed this with pardoning Zewday for his beatings and breaking his tooth and for the many nights he stayed up hungry because Zewday's drinking habits took precedence over his family's dinnertime.

Desta forgave his seatmates for shaming him in front of the class by abandoning him and the unidentified boy for kicking him on his way to lunch that one day.

He pardoned his mother, Ayénat, for her stubborn ways—specifically, for refusing to give him food and water when he arrived home for Christmas after his ten-hour journey. And he forgave himself for disowning her. He also forgave Tshai for declining to be his Mother-of-the-Breast.

Tears had streamed quietly the whole time. At the end he felt cleansed, freed, and happy. He wiped his eyes and sniffles with his fingers and the sides of his face with the pads of his hands. He sat up. He dried the remaining tears with one corner of his gabi. Finally, he cupped one hand, imagining it was filled with the bad people and hurt that had accumulated in his heart and head, and then he made a quick motion, as if flinging them over his shoulder. Desta immediately felt added ease and comfort.

With this done he crossed his forearms over his bent knees and expressed gratitude to all those who were kind to him: to Masud for his brotherly generosity and unconditional support; to Almaz, the hair braider, for making the mutually beneficial arrangement with Khadija so Desta could have his supplemental meals; to Helen and her parents for the opportunity they gave him to travel to Bahir Dar to look for the bearer of the second Coin of Magic and Fortune; and to his generous sister Saba for her advice, support, and truly unconditional love.

Finally, he recited each of the twenty-one legends from memory.

With these things in order, Desta spread his gabi over the bottom sheet to protect his skin from the tear-stained fabric and laid down again on his back. He pulled the covers over his face and crossed his right hand over his heart. He sighed heavily. He closed his eyes and kept quiet, listening to nothing but the thumping of his heart and gentle breathing of Fenta on the other side of the parapet. In his mind he saw the kind faces of the families in town and the friendly students and teachers at the school. He imagined flying in his new craft to Washaa Umera to visit Eleni and meet her Wind friends, and tour their cave, which supposedly had amazing things in it that the Wind Woman wouldn't reveal.

He had a tingling sensation in his fingers and on his palms and a gentle rocking movement to his body. He held his breath, waiting for sleep to come and take him across the night to the morning so he could go register and begin to attend the beautiful school. He didn't have to wait long. Almost immediately, he vanished to himself and the world.

Acknowledgments

My wonderful wife, Rosario, has been my greatest ally and the most ardent of Desta fans. She has unwaveringly supported and encouraged me to continue with the series, even as I embarked on the second volume. They say writing is a lonely experience, and Rosario allowed me the quiet and secluded space I needed to write this volume. I am grateful for this and her limitless grace and patience with all my efforts.

I am grateful to my father, whose many wonderful personal traits continue, in this second volume, to infuse the character of Abraham. I am grateful to my mother, who carried me in her womb for nine months and has helped make me, more than she'll ever know, the person I am today.

I am thankful to Merrill Gillaspy and Joel Palmer, who edited the original manuscript, and to Vinny Cusenza who proofed the final copy and turned it into what it currently is. Their professional and timely work is greatly appreciated. I appreciate David Klein's help with the poems.

I owe many thanks to Phil Howe for his great work on the cover of the book and for his patience and understanding of my need to make the details in it as authentic as possible. I am also thankful to Dr. Alula Wasse, Dr. Worku Negashi, and Getachew Admassu for their enthusiasm, support, and encouragement for the Desta series. They and my nephew Tadesse Alemayehu in Ethiopia have been great sources for some of the cultural details that appear in the book.

I extend my thanks to my friends from Writers Unlimited—Monika Rose, Dave Self, Antoinette May, Glenn Wasson, Joy Roberts, Linda Field, Stephen Holmes, and Ted Laskin.

Lastly, I am grateful to the Creator, who gave me healthy faculties so I could record what I saw, read, heard, and experienced to use as material for this novel.

DESTA's Characters

Humans

Abraham – Desta's father

Aba Yacob – The head priest at Desta's parents church

Abdullah – Muslim merchant

Aberra – Fence builder

Almaw – Aunt Zere's youngest son

Almaz Beyene – the hair braider, Desta's lifesaver

Amelwork – Desta's ancestral relative

Ashager --- farmer coffee picker, Mebet's relative

Ashber, Colonel – Dangila's chief of Police

Asqual – a single woman in Yeedib

Asse'ged – Desta's second oldest brother

Astair – Desta's niece, Yihoon and Saba's older daughter

Awoke – Desta's second-generation cousin, Yisehak and Maray's son

Ayènat –Desta's mother

Belie, Grazmach – the district governor of Sekela. Girazmach is his title

Beshaw, Abraham – Father

Bizuneh – Desta's friend, Fenta's uncle

Brook – Teacher in the Yeedib school

Damtew – Desta's fourth oldest brother

Daud – Fence material supplier

Debeb – the skin merchant

Deb'tera Tayè – The sorcerer

Destaye – Saba and Yihoon's son, named after Desta

Dinku – Fence builder

Eleni – from the land of Nogero, member of the International Order of Zarrhs and Winds

Helen – Desta's school friend, daughter of Colonel Ashber and Weizero Nigist

Enat – Desta's older sibling (the fifth youngest)

Fenta – Desta's friend in the Yeedib school

Haile Selassie – the last emperor of Ethiopia

Hibist – Desta's favorite, immediate older sister from same mother and father

Ibrahim, Sheik – a shop owner in Dangila, father of Masud

Imam Mohammed – the head of the Dangila mosque

Khadija Lugman– Muslim restaurant owner in Dangila

Laqechi – Teferra's wife

Lecho, Negasu – Desta's Father-of-the-Breast, head of police at Yeedib

Lesim – daughter of Zewday

Marka – short for Marva and Kamala

Marva and Kamala – the supposed hermaphrodite bearer of the second Coin of Magic and Fortune

Masud – Muslim merchant in Dangila who became Desta's good friend

Mebet – Zewday's wife

Mebrat – a neighbor's housekeeper

Mehiret – the boy who took Desta to Finote Selam, sent by a Peace Corps teacher

Mekibeb – the hired shepherd in Desta's parents home

Melkam – Damtew's wife

Mekonen – Abraham's grandfather

Mulu – Asse'ged's wife

Negasu – (see Lecho)

Saba – Abraham's daughter from his first marriage

Saleem Nuru – a precocious Muslim boy in Begeimider province

Sayfu – one of Desta's Yeedib school mates

Senayit – Bizuneh's wife, the family Desta's friend, Fenta lives with

Tamirat – Desta's third oldest brother who abandoned his priesthood

Tashere – The pharaoh princes, King Solomon's first wife

Taye, the Debtra – The middle-aged witchdoctor who invoked the Cloud Man

Tedla – Director of the Dangila school

Teferra – The oldest son

Tenaw – Husband to Enat (one of Desta's older sisters)

Tesfa – Zewday and Mebet's son

Tessema – See Zewday

Tigist –Colonel Ashber's wife, Helen's mother

Tru – Mekuria's wife

Yengus – a single woman in Yeedib, girlfriend to Desta's brother, Teferra

Yihoon – Saba's spouse

Yisehak – Abraham's uncle who lived across the river

Yitbarek – The head teacher and administrator at the elementary school where Desta is registered

Zena – Desta's niece, Yihoon and Saba's daughter

Zere – Abraham's oldest sister

Zewday Tessema – Desta's relative in Dangila (wife: Mebet; daughter: Lesim; son: Tesfa)

Animals

Dama – Abraham's beloved horse

Kooli – Desta's beloved dog and best friend

Vervet Monkeys – The silver-haired, notorious crop raiders, Desta's friends

Spirits

The Cloud Man – the ghost-like creature invoked by Deb'tra Tayé and revealed to Desta

Saytan – Satan

The Winds – a world-wide order of spirits who function as balancers of good; they represent the negative aspect of things.

Zarrhs – a world-wide order of spirits whose function as balancers of evil; they represent all the positive aspect of things.

Cultural Terms and their definitions

Aba – father, a honorific term applied to most elderly men.

Abo – a luxuriant plant with large and shiny leaves that are often used to wrap dough and bake in a fire pit.

Abol – first brew of coffee

Akrimas – plain basket weaving strands

Alelas – the colored basket weaving strands

Allahu akbar – God is great

Amarika – America

Amesegnalhu – thank you

Antennae – you and me

Areqey – a double or single distilled home-made whiskey.

Ashkers – houseboys (ashker, singular)

Asquala Temareebet – modern school. "Asquala" is derived from the Italian or Spanish word with similar name "esquela". Temareebet literally means house of learning

Ater – munchkin

Ato – the Amharic equivalent of Mister

Atasbee – don't worry, when addressing a female, Atasb, when addressing a male

Awazay – red-pepper paste

Awwe – yes, less formal than (see Ishee)

Badima – old homestead

Bahir – sea

Bandira –flag

Bereka – weaker, the third brew of coffee

Berrari mekeena – shuttle bus

Besmam wold woaman fis kidus – a prayer- or blessing- opening phrase involving the Trinity

Betchristian – church, literally: bet = house of Christian

Bet serategna – women servants

Birlay – a round, narrow-necked drinking glass

Biyee – marbles

Braana – parchment paper

Buena bet – literally café but they also serve alcoholic beverages and food

Cantim – a cent.

Chenger – stripped twig, used as a whip

Dabo Kollo – in the countryside, this is an apricot-size dried bread travelers bring with them as a snack. In cities, dab kilo comes in different sizes and is served as a snack anytime.

Dabo – loaf

Dagussa – low grade grain used by poor people and to feed animals, sometimes also used to make **Areqey**, the home-made whiskey

Dawit – a book containing the gospel in the Bible

Deb'tera – shaman, sorcerer

Debters – notebooks

Dehina – well

Demoz – salary

Doro wat – stew with chicken or hard boiled eggs

Duba – pumpkin

Enkutatashi – a greeting term used at the new year

Era – an expression of surprise, not really a word

Fasika – Easter

Ferenge –a term used to refer to all white people, similar to the Mexican's Gabacho or Gringo

Fidel – the Ethiopian alphabet

Firfir – minced injera or loaf

Firdbet – courthouse

Fukera – a skit of bravery

Gabi – a double-ply heavy cotton cloth, roughly 7 feet by 6 feet, worn for warmth over the shoulders like a blanket.

Gashé – honorific—a term of respect used to address an older male, usually as prefix to the first name. Example: Gashé John, Gashé George, Gahé Tom.

Gebeta – a board game played with pebbles or beads on twelve dug out holes in a wooden board or stone slab

Gedel – hole

Genna – hockey game, also Christmas

Gibena – usually a kettle made from clay for brewing coffee

Godana -- road

Gottem – a round tree whose branches grow packed together with small dark green shiny leaves.

Grammitas – see akrimas above. In the province of Gojjam, where the story of Desta is set, the same basket-weaving straw is called grammita (singular). Elsewhere it's referred to as akrima.

Gulels – mounds

Gulichas – cooking stones

Haimanote – religion

Hallelujah – praise God

Harr – silk

Hyke – lake

Indalh – whatever you say

Injera – a spongy flat bread made from fermented dough of teff, barely or wheat

Irsas – pencil

Ishee – yes, a formal form of (see awwe)

Islam -- Muslim

Jebena – kettle

Kat – a leafy narcotic

Kettema – a tall pulpy grass, often sprinkled on the living room floor during a holiday.

Kiremt – rainy season

Kitibat – vaccination

Kitigne – syphilis

Konjo – beautiful

Kooris – snack

Kubet – dried cow dung

Lidet – Christmas/birth

Liqmoshi – usually a pebble game where the players scatter a bunch of pebbles on the floor, picks up one pebble, toss it up in the air and to try to collect those on the floor with a sweeping motion of the tossing hand and then catch pebble while still in the air.

Listro – a shoe shine boy

Lule -- prince

Madd-bet -- kitchen

Maskel/Meskel – the finding of the True Cross, celebrated in Ethiopia on the 27th or 28th of September (depending whether it's leap year or not)

Masinko – a single string instrument played with a bow

Masmeria – ruler

Mateb – a cord worn around the neck, a symbol of ones Christian-ness

Medehaneet – medicine

Mekleft – the bread (injera) the church goers break their fast with

Melaga – lazy

Mergeta – teacher

Mesgid – mosque

Mestawit – mirror

Mitsion – missionary

Mookit – applies generally to a male goat or bull whose testicles have been pounded to a pulp of tissue so that it won't waste its energy chasing she-goats or cows. This goat or bull becomes fat and big, fetching top price when taken to the market.

Mosseb – an often colorful basket with a round skirt-shape bottom and a lipped circular top used to serve food. It comes with a cone-shaped and colorful top.

Negus – king

Netela – a single-ply fabric, worn mostly by women as a shawl or to drape the shoulders with.

Qur'an – the Koran

Ra'ka -- the Muslim prayer cycle

Saytan – spirit/devil

Shahee – tea

Shahs – a lighter, often white turban (see timtim)

Shemma – cotton fabric

Sherra chamma – tennis shoes

Set'eyo – lady

Shint bet – toilet

Shiro wat – pea sauce

Sholla – related to the warka tree but less rugged. It produces a great number of green figs which turn edible and fire red upon ripening.

Tabot – a square wooden plaque upon which the Ten Commandments are inscribed. It is kept in the inner sanctuary of the church, wrapped in a colorful cloth. On church holidays, the Tabot is carried by a selected priest and taken on a procession out of doors accompanied by dancing and harmonizing priests

Teff – the smallest grain in the world which comes as either brown or white variety, and is the staple food of Ethiopians.

Tej—honey Wine

Tella – a black or brown home-made beer made from hops and barley.

Timatim – tomato

Timtim – a white, heavier turban worn mostly by priests.

Warka – a spreading, large-trunked tree with broad, thick, leathery leaves and long, hefty branches. Perhaps related to the sycamore tree.

Wallahi – I swear to Allah

Washaa – cave

Weizero – Mistress (Mrs.)

Wetetay – smallpox

Weeyee – a form of surprise, equivalent to "Oh may!"

Wudu – Muslim ritualized cleansing

Yalem karta – world map

Ye kettema noore – a town's life

Zebegna – custodian, guard

Zema – a musical note

About the Author

Getty Ambau is a graduate of Yale University. Although educated both in the natural and social sciences and has run his own businesses over the years, writing has always been his inner calling. He has written books on health and nutrition which have sold internationally. *Desta and the Winds of Washaa Umera* is his second in a series of novels. He lives in the San Francisco Bay Area with his wife, Rosario and a devoted terrier called Scruffy—perhaps not as devoted or self-sacrificing as Desta's pet and friend, Kooli.